THE SCARLET SEAL

The Continuing Story of Bron
Part IV

Iris Lloyd

Pen Press

© Iris Lloyd 2011

All rights reserved

No part of this publication may be reproduced, stored in a retrieval system, or transmitted in any form or by any means, without the prior permission in writing of the publisher, nor be otherwise circulated in any form of binding or cover other than that in which it is published and without a similar condition including this condition being imposed on the subsequent purchaser.

First published in Great Britain by Pen Press

All paper used in the printing of this book has been made from wood grown in managed, sustainable forests.

ISBN 978-1-907499-89-0

Printed and bound in the UK
Pen Press is an imprint of
Indepenpress Publishing Limited
25 Eastern Place
Brighton
BN2 1GJ

A catalogue record of this book is available from
the British Library

Cover design by Jacqueline Abromeit
Photograph by Sarah Cook

PRAISE FOR BRON

Parts I and II:

The book makes for a most entertaining read.
Daily Mail

This is a brilliantly written book, even more enthralling than her first novel—the crafting is precise and there is a sense of destiny in the writing.
Diane Morgan, Newbury Weekly News

A series of wonderfully accomplished historical novels. Gripping, insightful, funny and inspiring – unreservedly recommended.
Doug Watts, Jacqui Bennett Writers' Bureau

Readers:

A reader on holiday in Crete: *I could not put the book down. In fact, the sites of Crete were put second best to reading the book.*

Quite simply, a superb read. The story was a real page turner...

Thank you for a brilliant book.

I haven't enjoyed a book so much in a long time. I was completely spellbound. Thank you for giving me such enjoyable reading time.

Part III:

I have just finished your third book and can't wait to find out what happens next. Each book got better as I got involved in Bron's life...

ACKNOWLEDGEMENTS

My thanks to…

All the readers who have bought or borrowed the books in the series, have told me how much they enjoy reading about Bron's adventures, and have encouraged me in this project.

Also, to Jacqueline Abromeit for the stunning covers.

DEDICATION

to Don
who came with me to explore
the Circus on the Appian Way
on a sunny Friday afternoon
in February 2003

and

to our Roman invaders,
who left such an indelible mark on our nation

Greece and Rome, the Birth of Western Civilisation,
R.A.G. Carson, 1986, writing of the end of the Roman Empire:

"—the irresistible tide of internal change, and invasion from without, submerged all.
"But the idea of Empire lived on. Men still travelled along the countless roads that led to Rome, as they have done ever since, spellbound by magnetic memories of its mighty past."

CONTENTS

The Story So Far...

Section I
THE LORICATUS HOUSEHOLD
AD 408, May – July
Chapters 1 – 23 1

Section II
THE ICONICUS HOUSEHOLD
AD 408, August – September
Chapters 24 – 48 113

Section III
HONORIUS, EMPEROR OF THE WESTERN EMPIRE
AD 408, October
Chapters 49 – End 243

Bron's Family Tree 311

Reminder List of Characters 313

Glossary of Terms 315

Author's Note 316

Author Biography 317

THE STORY SO FAR...

The first two books in the series, **Part I – Bron, Daughter of Prophecy** and **Part II – Flames of Prophecy**, are set on an archaeological site I help excavate at Beedon, north of Newbury, on top of the Berkshire Downs. I have worked some of the finds into the narrative.

The year is AD 385. Bron, a pagan of the Atrebate tribe, is born in the settlement of Byden, southern Britannia, during the late Roman occupation. Her growing-up years are intertwined with the lives and traumas of her family, friends and enemies, of whom High Priest Vortin is the most dangerous. He had hoped to make Bron his High Priestess and had raped her when she was only eleven years old, so breaking Temple law.

When it is discovered that she is pregnant, to hide his guilt, he forces her into a marriage with her childhood friend, Soranus. Bron smothers her baby son to save him from being taken into the Temple at three years old and corrupted by his father.

Later, she gives birth to a daughter, Layla, and son, Alon. However, she is not sure whether her last born, Darius, is the son of her husband or a young Roman officer, Aurelius Catus, with whom she has fallen in love. She and Soranus later adopt a motherless baby girl from a brothel, whom they name Gift.

Rebelling against corruption, the people banish the Temple hierarchy from the settlement. When Vortin and his mercenaries attack the village, in an attempt to abduct Bron, Soranus releases her from her marriage vows and she escapes, accompanied by her friend, Veneta (one-time priestess and now a Christian), her four children and her widowed brother's young daughter.

They are discovered hiding in Byden wood by one of the mercenaries, a deserter from the Roman army, and Bron secures their escape by bribing him with her amber and pearl necklace. This had been a gift from her Roman father to her mother, his slave, when she fell pregnant with Bron.

Part III – The Girl with the Golden Ankle. Bron's party sails to Italia aboard the *Juniper*, in the wake of the troop ship taking Aurelius Catus and his legion back to Rome.

The *Juniper* is attacked by pirates in the Mare Nostrum (Mediterranean) and, being weakened, is wrecked in a storm. The survivors spend several months on an uninhabited island north of Corsica, during which time Bron has a secret, shameful affair with the bo'sun, a man of changeable, dangerous moods.

They are rescued and eventually arrive in Ostia, where Bron learns that Aurelius's legion has moved out; obviously, he had concluded that their ship and all on board had been lost at sea.

Bron discovers she is pregnant and, ashamed, flees to Rome, leaving the five children with Veneta and Declan, a young sailor off the ship, who is in love with Veneta.

Her hiding place is a brothel, where she works as their enticer. Round one ankle, she wears a small golden torque with hollow finials, each containing a golden nugget that rattles as she walks. So she becomes known as 'the girl with the golden ankle'.

Her son is born and named Honorius (Rius), after the emperor. To avoid kidnap by his father, the bo'sun, who has tracked them down, she agrees to Rius being adopted by a childless couple, Senator Loricatus and his wife, who live on exclusive Palatine Hill. Bron will be allowed to accompany Rius as wet nurse as long as she does not divulge their relationship.

Part III ends as Bron, with Rius in her arms, knocks at the door of the Loricatus house.

Now read on...

SECTION I

AD 408

May – July

THE LORICATUS HOUSEHOLD

CHAPTER 1

Gravel crunched beneath Bron's sandals as she walked resolutely along the drive towards the house, holding on to her courage as tightly as she was holding on to her son.

"Darling Rius, Rome may be where you were born and your home for now," she whispered to him, "but one day I shall take you away to *my* home in Britannia, where your father will never find us. But we mustn't tell anyone about that, it's *our* secret."

She mounted the steps to the portico and front door, and taking hold of the iron ring gripped in the mouth of a lion's head, rapped sharply, twice.

Behind the door, she heard the approach of shuffling feet and slowly it opened a few inches. A face peered through the chink.

"Please tell your mistress that her son and his nurse have arrived."

"I know who you are," muttered the face, "and about time."

The door opened wider to reveal the face's mass of wayward hair and whiskers, as white as the tunic hanging loosely on the thin body.

"Follow me."

Bron followed as he shuffled across the black-and-white-patterned mosaics, Rius still clutched tightly in her arms. They passed wide-open double doors that led to an inner courtyard, and she caught the perfume of roses and heard women's chatter and light laughter.

The old man led her into a room off the hallway then turned and looked at them both. Although his eyes were weak, a watery blue, Bron felt they missed nothing.

She knew he could find no fault in her appearance. Her new employer, Fausta Loricata, had provided this pretty yellow undershift and tunic. She had also sent a beautician to the inn to make up Bron's face and dress her hair, both tasks having been accomplished most skilfully. Final touches had been added with a necklace and bracelet of green and yellow glass beads, though she wasn't able to wear the matching earrings because she had never had her ears pierced.

The old steward appeared satisfied, so his question surprised her.

"Will you be staying long? They never do."

The truthful answer was, *no*.

"Yes, of course," she stammered, "until Rius – I mean, Honorius – grows up, at least till then, perhaps longer. A baby needs his m – his nurse – when his mother is busy in public life."

She scolded herself for being so careless. She had been in the house no time at all and had already almost blurted out things she had promised not to mention.

The old man glanced out of the large window. "Not that you will have any say in the matter," he continued. "If the mistress wants you to go, you'll go."

"I'll give her no cause—"

His attention snapped back. "Cause? From what I've seen, one nurse is no better than another. If the boy dies, you'll be out of a job, anyway."

Bron was appalled. "But he's not going to die."

"Neither were the other two, everyone was very upset about it, but they did. I hope for my mistress's sake that this one lives. It's your responsibility to make sure that he does – whatever else is taking your mind off the job."

Her face expressed her bewilderment.

"Proprieties disregarded and rules flouted." The steward's comment was a criticism of something or someone. "None of my business, of course."

His explanation had not enlightened her and she was annoyed by his interrogation.

"Be assured that I will take my duties very seriously," she responded coldly.

Her words seemed to mollify him, at least for the time being.

"I'll tell my mistress you've arrived."

She had the feeling that the enigmatic conversation had not finished and they would be returning to the old man's concerns, whatever they were, real or imagined.

He had left her standing in the centre of a small room. She buried her face in the white woollen folds of her son's expensive shawl.

"I must get it into my head that I am not your mother. I must remember that I am no longer your mother. Senator Loricatus and his wife have adopted you and she is now your mother and I am your wet nurse. How ridiculous is that, Rius? Of course I'm your mother. But no one must know it. You can't tell, and I must be careful not to."

Looking about her, she saw she was standing on a colourful mosaic of gods and goddesses disporting themselves in water gardens, and above her head, the same deities floated among painted clouds and garlands of stars. More of their exploits, some very explicit, were embroidered on heavy tapestries hanging on the walls.

She crossed to the glazed window. On the other side of the pumice-shaved lawns and flower beds, disciplined by low hedges of yew, lay the large cobbles of Palatine Hill, and below, the city stretched out in all its magnificence and majesty, dissected by curves of the great River Tiber in the middle distance.

"Rome is certainly a beautiful city," she said to her son, "but we don't belong here."

Her confidences were interrupted by the arrival of two women who entered the room with much hilarity. The first was flushed and highly excited and Bron guessed that this was her employer, Fausta Loricata, the woman who had adopted Rius and employed her as his wet nurse.

She was shorter than Bron, her hair an indeterminate brown, with a not unpleasing face, though her features were somewhat clumsy.

She held out her hands towards Bron, who went forward in anticipation of a welcome of some sort, but instead, Rius was whisked from her arms and carried back to the window. Bron's instinctive protest at the rough handling of her son was cut short when she was jostled aside as the other woman followed.

"Oh, Fausta, he's adorable," she cooed, "and as handsome as his father, don't you think?"

"Yes, Julia, I suppose he does favour Laenus."

"So he's sure to be breaking hearts one day – all the young daughters of the Senate! Though," she added with less conviction, "he has your chin."

She was leaning over the baby, seemingly entranced. "Just look at his hands, so strong, and those tiny fingernails. Fausta, he's perfect! But, of course, he would be, wouldn't he, with Laenus as his father?" She paused, just long enough for her words to take effect, then added quickly, "And, of course, with you as his mother. May I hold him, this very special baby?"

Wearing a tunic with low-cut neckline, girdle tied tightly below her conspicuously shapely bust, and her dark brown hair piled on top of her head in an elaborate coiffeur, this young woman was all that Bron's employer was not.

Fausta handed Rius over as if he had been a parcel. Bron, hovering near, longed to take him from them.

Julia moved away from the window and elegantly lowered herself onto a couch, then proceeded to bounce him up and down on her lap. It was not long before he was sick, as Bron guessed he would be, all down the front of her tunic, which had been a beautiful sea green.

Furious and protesting loudly, she jumped to her feet, holding him out at arms' length, his little head unsupported so that it wobbled about alarmingly.

With consternation, Bron took a step towards her, apologising profusely. However, she was prevented from rescuing him by her employer, who pushed past, uncaringly treading on her toe. Bron's exclamation of pain went unheeded. She wondered whether she had suddenly become invisible.

"Julia, you shouldn't be bouncing a young baby about like that. I think I'd better take him." Fausta extricated Rius from her friend but was holding him very awkwardly.

Bron took another involuntary step forward, which brought her into Fausta's line of vision.

"We seem to be making Nurse somewhat nervous."

Julia turned her head as if noticing Bron for the first time then dropped onto the couch again and began dabbing at the wet patch on her tunic with a kerchief, making matters worse.

"What have you and Laenus called him?" she enquired as she rubbed.

"Honorius, after the young emperor," Fausta replied. "We decided it was appropriate, with Laenus having been called to the Senate."

"*You* decided!" thought Bron indignantly.

"A noble name," approved Julia.

Fausta looked at her friend, irritatingly smug. "Did I tell you that he received Constantine's casting vote in the ballot?"

"So the Senate allowed the usurper to vote?"

Fausta rushed to the defence of her kinsman, the Roman soldier who had been elected Emperor Constantine III by the Britons and sent over to oust Honorius.

"We need an imperial presence here in the city while Emperor Honorius and his court are holidaying in Ravenna."

"'Holidaying', you call it?" sneered Julia. "My husband says he's run away from the barbarian threat and is as helpless and useless as a kitten up a tree!"

Fausta looked confused, as if not knowing whether her loyalty lay with the hereditary emperor in Ravenna or her kinsman, the would-be emperor in Rome.

"Of course, we all know you are distantly related to the Constantines, don't we?" Julia continued with more than a hint of sarcasm, which Fausta didn't notice or ignored. "Let me think, now." Her mock concentration was laboured. "Yes, I do seem to remember your saying something about Constantine's casting vote – several times, in fact." She paused then added sweetly, "It's surprising, in the circumstances, that you didn't name your son Constantine." She hadn't quite finished. "But, of course, Laenus richly deserves the honour of becoming Senator – no one would disagree with that."

Fausta didn't respond to any of these barbs. She was wrinkling up her nose, distracted by the smell of rancid milk.

"Take him, Nurse." She unceremoniously handed the baby over, and rang a bell that was standing on a table by the window. "We must get you cleaned up, Julia. Nurse, your place is in the nursery. Julius will show you the way. He's waiting outside the door. I'll come over later."

"Yes, madam," replied Bron, glad to escape, and felt she needed to drop a small curtsey.

"At least she hasn't changed our names, Rius," she whispered as she followed the old man through the double doors and into the open courtyard.

They skirted the colourful beds of autumn damask roses, their perfume heavier now that she was among them, passed marble statues and benches, and fountains whose water droplets shed rainbows, then walked along a covered walkway on the opposite side of the house.

Hoping to lessen the antagonism Julius obviously felt towards her, for a reason she could not fathom, Bron introduced herself.

When he didn't reply, she asked, "Have you been here a long time?"

"Served the master twenty-four years, since he was a lad of twenty, *and* his father before him."

"What's he like, your master – did I hear his name was *Laenus Loricatus*?"

"*Senator* Laenus Loricatus to you. He's his own man with his own ways. You'll find out. We're here – that's the nursery. Ring the bell if you want a slave to attend you."

And with that, he left.

CHAPTER 2

Bron was glad when she was alone with her son. Now, no one could see her shoulders droop beneath the weight of her predicament, which threatened to crush all her determination and optimism.

"Oh, Rius, what have I done?" she anguished and began to cry. "I don't know whether I can keep up this ridiculous pretence."

Rius started crying, too. Bron dried her eyes on her sleeve.

"Oh dear, you don't have to blabber because your pitiful mother is feeling so sorry for the pair of us. Though you must be hungry, having puked up most of your last feed. That stupid Julia! Come on, then. This will do us both good."

She made herself comfortable in a basket-weave chair then unclasped the chained brooches on her shoulders, pulled her tunic and undershift down to her waist, removed the stained linen band from around her breasts, and let Rius find her nipple. He began to suck vigorously.

"That's a relief! So how can I be unhappy when I have you with me? And your father will never think of looking for us up here – he'll be searching in all the back streets and alleyways down there."

She gently stroked the soft golden down on top of her baby's head.

"In the meantime, we've got to pretend that you belong to *them*, but we can do that for a while, can't we, until I've saved enough for us to get back to Ostia, then home to Britannia?"

Her eyes fixed on the antics of a spider in her web in the corner of the room, but Bron's thoughts were far away, on the gently rolling hills around the settlement of Byden. An over-enthusiastic tug at her nipple brought her sharply back to the present.

"Oh, that hurt! More gently, Rius, if you please."

He obliged and she smiled, again taking him into her confidence.

"But we both know there's someone I must find first and plead forgiveness for what I did – though I can't be sorry for it because your father and I made you. Do you think I will find Aurelius? I love him so much, I've *got* to find him, no matter where he's stationed, and beg him to come back with us to Britannia! That's enough for one side. Try the other – and don't fall asleep or you'll leave me talking to myself!"

Rius did fall asleep and she laid him gently in the rocking crib made ready for him.

Next to it stood a wooden chest, and on lifting the lid, she found inside all the clothes and utensils he would need up to the age of about one year old.

A doorway led into her room, where she discovered a similar chest containing clothes for herself. Like the cotton undershift and tunic she had been given to wear today, every item was more expensive than anything she had ever owned, and she couldn't wait to try them all on.

A bowl sat in an iron tripod and beside it stood a ewer of cold water. A dish of olive oil and a couple of rough-weave towels, neatly folded, had been placed on a small table. Gratefully, she washed her face and hands.

Having bounced on the bed and found it to her liking, she was unpacking her few possessions and putting them away in the chest when Fausta Loricata walked into the room. Bron only just stopped herself from asking if she wouldn't mind knocking in future.

"Ah, Bron, I hope you're settling in. Where's my son?"

Again she had to bite her lower lip to avoid a retort she would regret. "He's asleep in his crib, madam. I've fed him to replace the milk he sicked up over your friend. I'm sorry about that."

Bron was surprised when Fausta grinned. "I'm not. It was her own silly fault. She's gone home smelling a lot less alluring than when she arrived!"

She flopped down into a chair, leaving Bron standing, unsure whether or not to sit. She decided against it.

"Now, to business. There are ground rules to be laid down that I trust I won't need to refer to again."

"Yes, of course."

"Madam," Fausta corrected her.

"Madam," Bron added.

"Very well. You will be responsible for my son—"

She means to rub it in, thought Bron.

"—and all his needs from morning to night and during the night. You will be available at any time, bringing Honorius to us whenever required. I want him looking a credit to his father and me at all times. We conduct a very busy political and social life and he will often be on display. You've found his clothes and things?"

Bron nodded.

"So he must look clean and smell sweet whenever I send for him. That is the last time I expect him to be sick, and I don't want him crying. My husband won't tolerate a crying baby."

"But all babies cry sometimes, madam," Bron protested.

"Maybe, but in the nursery only and not anywhere where he can be heard in the rest of the house. And don't interrupt."

Bron was appalled at the manner in which she was being addressed but managed to say between gritted teeth, "I'm sorry, madam." If her employer noticed the reluctance of the apology, she ignored it.

"Of course, it goes without saying that you will also look a model nurse with not a hair out of place. There are other nurses in the neighbourhood and I want you to look the best, without drawing attention to yourself at any time, of course, and certainly not flaunting—never mind. Do you understand?"

"Yes, madam."

"And you will speak only when spoken to, is that understood?"

"Yes, madam."

"Provided you give satisfaction *in every way*, at the end of each month, you will be paid the sum previously discussed. If I am not satisfied with you at any time, for whatever reason, you will be dismissed on the spot. Is that understood?"

"Yes, madam."

"If the baby gets sick—"

"He won't, madam."

"Good. We paid your agent a not inconsiderable sum for him and don't want our investment wasted again. Third time lucky, eh? I'm sure you will do your best."

"Of course, madam."

"Then there remains only one last matter. Our stories should agree. You should know that we moved here when my husband was called to the Senate, three months ago. Prior to that, we were living in the country. As soon as this house was furnished and decorated to our liking, we sent for you and our son. How old is he?"

"He was born in November."

"Six months, then. Don't let me forget his birthday when it comes round."

The stern expression on Fausta's face softened a little. "I'm sure we will get along very well – as long as you do *everything* I tell you *when* I tell you."

She waited for an answer but Bron remained silent. Fausta stood.

"Good. You both may take the rest of the afternoon off. All your meals will be served in here. I will send for you when my husband comes home from the Senate."

"When will that be, madam?"

"There's no telling. He's often very late. Julius will fetch you when it's time."

She nodded briefly and left the room.

Bron groaned then raised the lid of the chest and banged it down three times in quick succession to release her anger and frustration.

"Your *father*! Your *father* indeed! Your *father* is down there somewhere, in the city, looking for us. That's why we're up here. That's why it's 'Yes, madam', and 'No, madam', and 'Kiss your—'"

She went through to the nursery, to check whether she had woken Rius.

"*Madam* wasn't even interested enough to come through and have a peek at you. But we won't be staying long. I promise you, my son, we won't be staying long!"

She had eaten her supper of cold chicken and salad, listening meanwhile to the contented cooing of pigeons as they returned to their lofts, when the summons came to take the baby to see his father.

She checked her reflection in a polished silver hand mirror then reluctantly lifted Rius out of his crib, grateful that he didn't wake.

The bracelet was catching in the baby's shawl so she took it off, but the necklace was still in place. She decided to find a jeweller who would pierce her ears so that she could wear the pendant earrings.

Her employers were in the triclinium, reclining on one of the sloping couches round the table, finishing their evening meal, when Bron was ushered in by Julius. For a moment, she stood uncertainly just inside the doorway then moved forward, her sandals crushing the dried flowers sprinkled there, which sent up waves of lavender perfume.

The couple had their heads close together and were laughing over some shared confidence. Fausta turned on hearing Bron approaching. Her husband was more interested in proffering a glass goblet to a young male slave, who was pouring wine from a silver flagon.

"Ah, Bron, come and meet Senator Loricatus."

The senator held up his goblet towards the lights of a candelabra to inspect the sparkling red glints, sniffed it appreciatively, then took a sip and rolled the liquid around in his mouth before swallowing and grunting his approval. With a curt nod, he allowed the slave to fill the goblet to the brim, then dismissed him.

"Laenus, our son is here."

"Mmmm." He helped himself to a slice of blue-veined cheese and a handful of black grapes.

"Bron, give him to me," Fausta said.

"Madam, he's fast asleep. I don't want to risk waking him as I might not get him off again for hours."

At the sound of Bron's voice, the senator turned, leaning back on a cushion for support. His concentrated stare embarrassed her into lowering her eyes. She wondered whether she had been too argumentative in what she had just said.

Fausta knelt up on the couch. "I asked you to give him to me."

Obviously, she had.

The senator put the grapes to his lips and with even, white teeth slowly pulled one, then a second, then a third from the stem, all the while looking intently at Bron from beneath heavy dark eyebrows. She had to admit that Julia was right. With his sensual, Roman features, his skin unblemished and tanned by the sun, he was certainly a very handsome man – and he knew it.

"There's no—no need to wake him up, sweetheart. Tomorrow will do." There was a slight, wine-induced hesitancy in his words as he chewed the grapes.

"She can bring him over here, though, so I can get a look—get a look at him—and her. It would be embarra—embarrassing not to recognise them if I passed them in the street. Come here, girl."

Obediently, Bron walked across and stood by the couch. He made no effort to move towards her. "You'll have to bend over so I can see him. Don't be nervous. What's your name?"

"Bron, sir."

"Well, Bron, he's a fine-looking boy. I reckon he'll do."

But he had only glanced briefly at Rius. His attention was fixed on the necklace glittering at the base of her neck and she felt extremely uncomfortable when his eyes dropped even lower. Conscious that his wife was watching, Bron straightened up.

"Will you join us for a goblet of wine, Bron?"

"No, thank you, sir, not while I have charge of your—your son."

"Very commendable," he nodded.

"Laenus!" his wife reprimanded him.

"I was testing her, darling, and she gave the right answer, didn't she?" He turned back to Bron. "Oh well, perhaps some other time, when you're—when you're off duty."

"She's never off duty, dear. Bron, take Honorius back to the nursery now. I'll see you in the morning."

"Yes, madam."

As she crossed the room, she heard the senator ask, "Is this one going to live, do you think? These babies—these babies are costing us a lot of money and there's nothing to show for it. This one's the prettiest, though."

"You can't call a boy 'pretty', Laenus," his wife protested.

"I wasn't referring to the baby," he said.

CHAPTER 3

Bron woke next morning to the sound of delivery carts trundling along the service road behind the villa and wondered for a moment where she was. Then she heard the cooing pigeons, and remembered.

Jumping out of bed, she prepared her son and herself for whatever the day might hold, then rang the bell. Her call was answered by a young slave, not more than thirteen years old, who nervously introduced herself as Izmira. The girl returned a little later with a simple breakfast, "with Cook's compliments".

She was tall and thin with a figure that would benefit from rounding out once she reached puberty, which couldn't be far ahead. Her skin was a shade darker than was usual in the city and her face, with its broad features, was framed by unruly black hair tied back in a bunch at the nape of her neck.

"Cook says, don't be afraid to ask for anything you need for the little one," the girl said, "and she says, when you've settled in, perhaps you'll come along to the kitchen and make her 'quaintance."

The words had come out in a rush, without expression, and were followed by a deep breath, as if she had repeated the message word for word, and was relieved to have remembered it. Bron smiled and sent back her thanks.

When the girl had left, with time on her hands, she could not resist trying on the new clothes in the chest, styled in Rome's latest fashions and colours, and was pleased with the image that gazed back at her from the long mirror in its wooden frame.

She had already chosen a tunic in pale green for her first day at work and had dressed Rius in blue. Bundling up the clothes they had worn yesterday, she dropped them into a basket. What luxury not to have to do their laundry herself!

About mid-morning, Julius came to the door, requesting her presence with Rius in the triclinium, "immediately".

Fausta Loricata was standing by the window, looking out over the city skyline. The fragrance of lavender lingered in the air, although the floor had been swept. All signs of the previous evening's meal had been cleared from the table and replaced with a bowl piled high with peaches and another with white oleander flower heads floating in water. A wax tablet lay between them.

"Good morning, Bron," her employer said, coming towards her and looking closely at Rius. "I hope you both slept well."

"Very well, thank you, madam."

"Good. I have scratched your daily routine on this tablet for you to memorise. You do read Latin, don't you?" Bron nodded. "The routine will soon become second nature. In the mornings, my husband conducts his business affairs, usually from his study but sometimes he likes to walk in the gardens. I breakfast in bed then reply to my correspondence, receive guests or go visiting.

"After our midday meal, while he is away attending to affairs of state, I take a rest, which gives you opportunity to walk out with Rius. Stay on the Hill – there are plenty of parks and open spaces. You'll meet other nurses with their charges. Don't become too familiar with any of them, just remain polite and sociable. It goes without saying that you will not gossip about anything that goes on in this household."

"Of course not, madam," agreed Bron, offended that her mistress could suggest she was loose tongued.

"I don't need you this morning, so you can amuse yourselves in the gardens. If my husband puts in an appearance, you should withdraw."

"Yes, madam."

"You may go now."

Bron curtsied and took Rius back to the nursery to retrieve toys and a pile of blankets to take into the courtyard. It was very hot, even in the shade of an orange tree, and she was glad to drink the cool water pouring from a marble fish's mouth and to dip a cloth into the basin to wipe the face and neck of her son.

She had been singing to him and they had been playing together for about an hour when the senator wandered out. Immediately, she began packing up the toys and blankets and would have withdrawn, but he stopped her.

"Don't go," he said, sitting near them on a bench. "I'm sorry, there's a lot that I *do* remember about you from yesterday evening – especially that fetching necklace – but I'm not very good at names. You'll have to remind me."

He smiled and Bron knew she was blushing. "Bron, sir."

"Well, Bron, you seem to me to be an intelligent girl with a mind of your own. Have you any understanding of politics?"

"No, sir."

"Never mind," he continued. "Tell me this, anyway. If you had uncivilised pagans baying outside the walls of your home – where is that, by the way?"

"Southern Britannia."

"Would you defend your town or make peace with them?"

Bron thought for a moment about the attack on Byden, her village, by High Priest Vortin and his mercenaries, and the battle that had precipitated her flight.

"I suppose it depends how strong they are," she replied. "We would definitely fight off any attackers – in fact, that is exactly what we did – but if I was the emperor and they greatly outnumbered my army, I would negotiate peace terms at first, promise them anything they wanted to go away."

"Then what?"

"I've heard it said, 'Never trust the untrustworthy'. Peace talks would give me breathing space in which to gather my forces together and prepare for battle."

"Then who would be 'the untrustwothy', the emperor or the pagans?" he mused. After a moment's silence, he added, "That's just what I was thinking. Now, what was that phrase you used? 'Never trust the untrustworthy'? That's good. Where did you hear it?"

"I can't remember."

"Do you mind if I quote it?"

"Quote it, sir? Where?"

"During my speech in the Senate, this afternoon."

"Before the emperor?"

"Depends which emperor you're talking about."

"I was meaning Honorius."

"Huh." Bron heard the contempt in his voice. "Honorius is sitting out the emergency, skulking in the marshes of Ravenna, and seldom comes near Rome." He brightened. "But Constantine has now been declared emperor in his place and, yes, he'll be in the Senate this afternoon, and I hope to impress him. You see, Bron, until now he has known me only as the husband of his kinswoman. So my feet are on the first rung of his political ladder. Now I want him to notice me as someone who could be useful to him."

He began to pace along the paths, backwards and forwards among the large plant containers and statues. Then he stopped and came across to her.

"That just about finishes my speech. Will you listen to it? I would appreciate your telling me what you think."

She nodded nervously.

He backed away a few paces, stood tall and addressed the air above her head.

"Most august Constantine III, mighty emperor of Rome's Western Empire—"

He stopped mid-sentence and grinned at her. "Do you think that's over-egging it somewhat?"

She shook her head. "I don't know, but better too much than too little, perhaps?"

"My sentiments exactly!" He straightened his back, lifted his chin and continued.

"—and brother Senators, we have gathered here this afternoon to debate resistance or conciliation, war or peace with our long-term enemy, Alaric the heretic, and his hordes of Visigoths and their allies. You have heard many words this afternoon promoting first one course of action and then another.

"Beware! Because Rome has not been invaded for eight centuries does not guarantee that she will not be invaded now.

"So I say, let us prepare for battle, but gain time for preparation. Let us negotiate with the enemy, prevaricate and procrastinate until ready to come to an agreement – no matter what agreement – any agreement that will act as a smokescreen, concealing our real intentions. However, we should be wary of their double cross. As has been said by one of our great generals, 'Never trust the untrustworthy'.

"There, Bron, how does that sound?"

"I would say it's a fine speech."

"And no one will know that splendid quote wasn't uttered by one of our great generals."

"Well, sir, you could hardly say that you borrowed it from your son's nurse."

He laughed with her.

"Will it do the trick, though?" he asked. "I despair of some of our old men. They should be pottering around their country estates and not sitting in the Senate. Like Honorius, they seem to think that Rome is impregnable, and by sitting it out, doing nothing, Alaric will grow weary and go away, but don't you believe it!"

He regarded Bron closely as she nodded in understanding.

"I intend to climb that ladder, Bron. I will present myself to Constantine as a man of loyalty and integrity, a man who lives up to his fine Christian principles. My life will be an open book—" he paused and grinned mischievously at her, "—at least, as far as he is concerned. So, young lady, may I let you know how it goes this afternoon? My wife has no interest in my speeches and I should like to confide in someone, win or lose."

"I would be honoured—"

"Then I will seek you out this evening."

An alarm bell rang somewhere in Bron's head, but she felt ashamed of her unease and muffled it.

"Does the safety of the citizens depend on how the voting goes?"

"If the worst came to the worst and Alaric's forces overran the city, he would need some of us to enforce his rule. There's no cause for anxiety. I would make sure that this household was kept safe."

Having given her this reassurance, he turned and left the courtyard.

CHAPTER 4

At about the time the senator rose to deliver his speech, Bron left the house with Rius in a little push-cart Julius had unearthed for him. Fausta Loricata had gone to lie down, leaving Bron free for the whole afternoon.

Once outside the iron gate, she turned left and descended the hill, again admiring the homes they had passed on their arrival yesterday.

Between them and a block of luxury apartments at the bottom of the incline was a rough path leading away from the road, which she followed, out of curiosity. It ran round the side of the hill overlooking the city. The path was too rough to follow any further with the push-cart but she read the notice that stated it led to the sacred cave where the she-wolf had suckled Romulus and Remus, the legendary founders of Rome.

She retraced her steps and climbed back up the hill. The homes became larger and more elegant. Pristine in appearance, with gardens immaculately designed and maintained, many of their gates were chained and padlocked, and fierce dogs roamed the lawns, barking at strangers.

The noise frightened Rius as he sat propped up on his pillows, taking an interest in everything around him, so that he cried loudly until his mother stopped the push-cart to comfort him.

Their attention was distracted by the ring of iron shoes and iron-rimmed wheels across cobbles and the pungent whiff of horses. Bron turned and saw a black carriage approaching. It was pulled by four black geldings, who were panting with the exertion of pulling the heavy carriage up the hill.

They stopped a little way in front of her and the young coachman secured the reins then jumped from his seat, followed by his co-driver.

Bron would have continued her walk, but the second man planted himself in the way, his back to her, legs apart, preventing her from moving forward. She tried to peer round him to see who was emerging from the carriage – obviously someone of importance.

There was a better view when he was obliged to move away to quieten one of the horses, nervous of a large mongrel dog across the road. The animal was doing his job, barking and growling and flinging himself against the iron gates of his master's property. Rius started to whimper.

The coachman opened the door and placed a wooden step in the road for the convenience of the occupants of the carriage. Bron noticed the gold crest painted on the door that now faced her, but didn't recognise it.

First to emerge were two young maidservants, who jumped down without difficulty, then turned to help the third occupant, though they seemed far more interested in the coachman than in their responsibilities.

Next to emerge was an old lady, a very old lady. Her haughty face was creased and wrinkled, the folds of skin under her eyelids drooped, and the flesh under her chin was loose and floppy, though her hair was incongruously dark – obviously a wig. The long sleeves of her undershift were cream and her tunic purple. *Someone imperial?* Bron wondered.

One misshapen foot with swollen joints, its nails painted bright pink, in an elegant pink leather sandal, was placed on the step. Its owner had to bend forward to leave the carriage, leaning heavily on the arm of the coachman and stretching her other hand towards one of the girls.

Then Bron gasped, and unconsciously reached out, impelled to touch the necklace lying on the folds of skin beneath the stranger's neck. At the same moment, the old lady stumbled and was propelled forward off balance.

Misunderstanding Bron's intention, she grabbed hold of her outstretched arm and held on to it tightly while steadying herself, then soundly berated her maidservants for their neglect, inventing such punishments that even Bron paled beneath her threats.

Eventually, she released Bron's arm and planted both feet firmly on the roadway.

"Thank you," she said and smiled warmly. "Not so steady on my feet these days. I could have broken or twisted my ankle if it hadn't been for your quick action. I'm very grateful to you."

Bron was relieved about the misunderstanding. If she had touched the old lady's neck, she could have been arrested for assault or theft.

The driver opened gates, shaded by a large fig tree, to allow the maidservants to escort their mistress along the path to the house, a small white-and-pastel-yellow palace gleaming in the sunshine.

The co-driver had pacified the horse and came back to close the door of the carriage.

"Who is she?" asked Bron, overawed.

"That's Aelia Flavia Claudia Antonia, to give her full title, grandmother of Emperor Honorius. She visits friends here," he said as he clambered back onto the driving seat and urged the horses further up the hill. Turning them where the roadway was wider, he returned to pick up the coachman, passing Bron and Rius on the way.

They left her with a mind in turmoil as she walked, unseeing, her thoughts concentrated on that beautiful necklace, not interested now in the luxurious properties around her.

It had been hers – precious stones of amber and pearl – 'the gold of the north and the silver of the south' – passion and tears.

Her Roman father had given it to her mother, his slave, when she fell pregnant with Bron. They had been very much in love but he was already married with a family – the passion and the tears.

While escaping from their burning village with her children and friend, Veneta, their hiding place had been discovered by one of the attacking mercenaries. He had left them unharmed on being bribed with the necklace, and that was the last she had seen of it, its shining stones clutched in the hands of that dirty, sweating, swearing legionary in a wood in south Britannia.

Then how was it now clasped round the neck of the emperor's grandmother? It didn't make sense. It must be a similar necklace, it couldn't be the same, she decided. But it was of a distinctive arrangement, the amber beads heart-shaped and each pair separated by one lustrous pearl. Her father had commissioned it especially for her mother, to his own design.

It was a mystery she was unlikely to solve. It hurt her very much to see its beauty adorning the neck of another woman, and such an unattractive woman, but there was nothing she could do about it.

CHAPTER 5

She took Rius back to the Loricatus house with tears in her eyes, acutely missing her mother and the rest of her family and friends in Byden.

Even more, she missed her own dear children, whom she had abandoned in Ostia ten months ago, leaving them in Veneta's care. Would they ever forgive her? How much had they grown? Was Veneta coping without her? Once again, she vowed she would take them all home to Britannia as soon as she could.

But first she must find Aurelius. Aurelius, whose love she had totally betrayed. But when she found him, and she had no doubt of her success in this, would he forgive her? How could she put all the blame on the bo'sun, whom she had allowed to indulge himself exploring the depths of her passions? Or Aurelius, who had aroused them in the first place? No, the blame was firmly on her shoulders, not theirs.

Now, she wondered how she could find out about the old lady. Who could she ask who would be likely to tell her? Certainly not her employers, nor Julius, who was so antagonistic towards her whenever they met, and as yet she didn't know anyone among the servants and slaves whom she could trust with her questions. Except—yes, there was one person who had been kind to her from a distance.

On the pretext that she needed a bottle of fennel water to cure his suspected stomach ache, she took Rius along to the kitchen at a time when she thought Cook would not yet have started preparing the evening meal. Senator Laenus Loricatus had told her this morning that he expected the Senate to be debating the 'attack or reconciliation' issue until early evening and she guessed correctly that he was not yet home.

Cook welcomed them warmly into her large and bustling domain and invited her to sit at the long wooden table and chat to her while she supervised the work of Izmira and three other young slave girls.

She looked twice Bron's age, with a smiling face and personality to match, and a plumpness that betrayed she enjoyed her own cooking. She confessed that there was not much that put her out of sorts, except when the slave girls hung her pans on the wrong hooks or returned cutlery to the wrong compartments in the drawers. The girls were giggling together and Bron guessed that this didn't always happen by accident and that the kindly woman was probably fully aware of it.

She sat relaxed among the homely kitchen smells of herbs and vegetables and salads being prepared in an atmosphere of calm efficiency. They chatted about babies and children, Rius in particular but also Cook's grandchildren, the routines in the Loricatus household, and the neighbours' scandalous 'goings-on'.

She wanted to tell Cook about her other children, her own four and her young niece, but decided against it. She was deeply ashamed at having left them behind in Ostia and the reason for her flight, of which they had been unaware – her pregnancy and the baby she now held in her arms.

Propping Rius up in a chair that was deep enough to take Cook's rear end, she offered to help. While slicing courgettes, she asked if her new friend could tell her anything about the grandmother of Emperor Honorius. Cook looked surprised.

"I helped her out of her carriage this afternoon on the Palatine," Bron explained. "She seems quite a character."

"So what is it you wants to know?"

"Anything interesting."

"Raised in Roman Spain, I've heard, and mother of the emperor's mother," said Cook. "Her daughter was the first wife of Emperor Theodosius and bore him Honorius and his brother, Arcadius. Unfortunately, she died in 385—"

"That was the year I was born," said Bron.

"The grandmother was pensioned off when her daughter died, but the old dear hung around, getting in everyone's way, interfering too much in politics, until Theodosius married again two years later. But she won't die and won't go away! She's fairly harmless these days, I hear, and they allows her plenty of freedom to roam around the city, as long as she gives no trouble to nobody."

"She's very flamboyantly dressed," ventured Bron, watching Cook mixing the pounded fennel in water, straining it and pouring the liquid into a small bottle.

"If you means 'loud and peculiar' by what you said, you're right enough there!"

"And she was wearing a most beautiful necklace of amber and pearl."

"Both her grandsons, emperors of West and East, lavish on her all the little luxuries of life, to keep her quiet, I expects, and they do say her wardrobe and jewellery come from all over the empire."

"Does she travel, then?" asked Bron.

"No need," replied Cook, handing Bron the small bottle of gripe water, "when everything she could possibly ask for is brought to her feet."

Bron thanked her and took Rius back to the nursery, wondering how she could find out more.

Now it was late evening, and all the candles had been lit. Rius was fast asleep and Bron was thinking of going to bed when there was a light tap at her bedroom door. With some trepidation, she answered it, and found her master standing there, looking somewhat flushed and holding a silver flagon and two glasses.

He greeted her happily. "Good evening, Bron."

"Good evening, sir," she replied cautiously.

"I promised to let you know how the vote went this afternoon, so here I am. I'm sorry it's late but I brought some friends home and we sat a long time over our meal and my best red wine. They've gone home to their wives now and Fausta has gone to bed with a headache, so I thought I'd come over. Well, aren't you going to ask me in?"

"Sir, I was just going to bed myself."

"Not until you've had a glass of wine with me," he insisted. "You refused me last night and you're not going to refuse me again, are you? Honorius is asleep, I dare say, and doesn't need you at the moment. One glass isn't going to make you neglect your duties, now is it?"

When she still hesitated, he pushed the door open with his foot and stepped across the threshold. Against her better judgement, Bron stood back to let him in. Once inside, he looked round appreciatively.

"How unusually tidy you keep it," he commented, sounding surprised. "Quite a home from home."

"It *is* our home," said Bron, just in time stopping herself from adding, *for the time being, at least.*

He put the two glasses on a small table and proceeded to fill them with the rich, dark-red liquid, then handed her one and took the other.

"A toast," he said, raising his glass.

"You won the vote then, sir?" she asked.

"Indeed we did! Come, Bron, raise your glass and drink with me."

She felt she had no option but to do as he asked. He chinked their glasses together and waited for her to take a sip before doing so himself.

"And I give you permission to call me Laenus when we're alone."

Bron was feeling very uncomfortable. "I can't do that, sir," she replied.

"You will," he said confidently. "Now, sit down and I'll tell you what happened this afternoon."

He sat facing her, the table between them. As she sipped her wine, which was smooth and flavoursome and the best she had ever tasted, he regaled her with a blow-by-blow account of the speeches and debate that had taken place in the Senate, with the mood shifting first towards full attack and then towards appeasement. He was a clever mimic and Bron could not help but laugh at the speech idiosyncrasies and mannerisms of the senators he portrayed.

To her surprise, she found twice that she had emptied her glass and it had been refilled, without her noticing. She began to feel slightly light-headed and determined not to drink any more. If Rius needed her during the night, she wanted to be in full command of her senses, and she didn't know if alcohol would contaminate her milk.

"I stood twice to speak," Laenus Loricatus was relating with enthusiasm, "and it was your phrase that won the day – indeed, I had my supporters chanting it over and over again – 'Never trust the untrustworthy' – meaning Alaric, who at first fought side by side with our great general Stilicho then did a complete turnaround and fought against him – 'Never trust the untrustworthy!' – and we won the vote! What a day it has been! Drink up, Bron!"

"I am so pleased for you, sir. Will it help your career?"

"It won't do it any harm, certainly. Constantine was following the debate with great concentration."

"Sir, Rius wakes me early, and I really should be going to bed," Bron said hesitantly.

"May 'Sir' not stay a little longer? We haven't emptied the flagon and you still have a full glass."

Bron wasn't sure how to handle this situation and was beginning to feel somewhat nonplussed. He was in no mood to leave and she couldn't forcibly eject him.

They were interrupted by a knock at her door and she jumped guiltily. When she opened it, she found Julius standing there.

"Is the master here?" he asked, trying to peer round her into the room.

"Yes, I'm here, Julius," the senator called out cheerfully. "Is there an emergency?"

"The mistress has sent me to find you, sir. I said I thought you were in your study."

"Then that's where I am," he replied obligingly. "I'm coming now. Take the flagon and my glass back to the kitchen, will you? Leave the young lady's. Good night to you, Bron. Thank you for your company. Lead the way, Julius," and with that command, they had gone, the door closing behind them.

Bron breathed a sigh of relief at her rescue from what could have been a difficult situation. There was no reason for her to feel guilty, but she did. What if Fausta Loricata found out that her husband had been in Bron's room, laughing and drinking and not wanting to leave? Nothing must endanger her position here! She would have to discourage any further intimacy, but guessed that was going to be difficult. He was very determined. Secretly, she wished he wasn't so handsome.

Her immediate problem was what she was going to do with the wine in her glass, which she had no intention of drinking. Seeing a crack between the floorboards, she tipped it through, then went to check Rius before shutting their communicating door and beginning to undress.

She was sitting on her bed in her undershift, removing her stockings, when the door flew open and Laenus Loricatus strode back into the room. Dumbfounded by the intrusion, she just sat there, staring at him.

"Came back for your glass," he said. "We don't want the slaves gossiping, do we?"

His eyes were all over her and her cheeks burned.

"It goes without saying that there's no need to mention to my dear wife anything about my visit. I don't think she would understand that I only came to tell you about my success in the Senate this afternoon. I'd like to stay but I'd better not."

He seemed to make a supreme effort and dragged his gaze away from her, then headed for the door, but paused and turned back.

"By the way, I notice you've never had your ears pierced. I hope you'll allow me to arrange that for you. I'll send my jeweller to see you one afternoon. He'll show you some earrings so you can choose a pair – a gift from me – for helping to write my speech." The door closed behind him.

Her empty glass was still standing on the table.

CHAPTER 6

The jeweller arrived three afternoons later. Bron guessed that the senator had chosen a time when he knew his wife would be resting and unlikely to meet the visitor. She had had a taxing morning. Fausta Loricata had visited a friend, taking Rius and Bron with her. Bron had been directed to sit in a corner, while the family passed Rius around from lap to lap, extolling his virtues and complimenting Fausta on the baby she had produced with such heroically-borne pain and effort, or so she said.

There were two young children in the family and they succeeded in making Rius cry by being too boisterous in their play. Bron rushed forward to rescue him from their game and had been reprimanded sharply by her employer, who told her to leave him where he was. Bron retired to her chair, tears not far away as she saw the rough way her son was being handled.

Fausta gave her a dressing down on the way home in the carriage and it was all Bron could do not to answer back that the woman knew nothing about babies, having had none of her own, and that this was Bron's sixth and she knew what she was doing. She wanted to say that the children had been unnecessarily rough with Rius, quite spiteful, and should have been restrained by their mother or Fausta, and she couldn't be expected to sit there, saying and doing nothing. However, with great control, she managed to hold her tongue.

Now she was sitting in the nursery rocking chair with Rius on her lap, dozing after her midday meal and his feed, when there was a knock on the door, and there stood the jeweller.

The Scarlet Seal

He was a rotund little man, balding, with a quick and fussy manner that suggested he was just about to leave for another, more important appointment. However, Bron guessed that this was probably his most important appointment of the day.

He introduced himself then set his black case on the table and threw back the lid with a flourish. Bron gasped at the display that met her eyes.

"Choose!" he commanded her.

"Which ones?" asked Bron, mesmerised.

"Any of them!"

When she didn't move, he held up a pair of diamond studs. "How about these? Or perhaps you prefer pendants? Sapphires, maybe? The choice is yours."

"I don't know where to begin," she confessed in bewilderment.

"Take your time." His words belied the nervous drumming of his fingers on the table top.

Her confusion was caused not only by her inability to choose from the expensive array in front of her. When the senator said he would buy her earrings, she had assumed they would be of good quality but suitable for her position, and not the glittering, ornate creations being shown to her. A gift of these was quite inappropriate and she felt compromised and apprehensive.

The jeweller unclipped a silver hand mirror, with ornately-decorated back and handle, from the underside of the lid.

"First you need to decide whether you want colour, and if so, which colour, or whether you prefer diamonds or pure gold. Then you should decide on the style."

"I can't accept this gift," Bron told him.

The jeweller looked put out and scratched the top of his head, reddened by the sun.

"The senator wishes you to have them."

"It's too much."

"Perhaps to you, but the cost is negligible to him."

"I won't be bought in this way."

The jeweller looked at her with understanding. "He told me you had helped him write a speech for the Senate, which carried the day, and it will give the emperor – whichever one you consider to be emperor – time to reinforce his defences, and that is worth a cartload of these trinkets. So it seems that all Rome is in your debt if what he says is true, and who am I to doubt him when he will be paying me a not inconsiderable sum of money? If you don't accept his gift, he will be very angry, with me as well as you, and I will not have made a sale. I would consider it a great favour to me personally if you would choose a pair."

Bron sighed. "You are very persuasive. Then I will accept his gift, for you and for Rome."

She tried several against her ear lobes, and with the help of the jeweller and the evidence in the mirror, finally made her choice – a pair of deep red garnet studs with another two hanging from each of them on delicate gold links.

The jeweller smiled happily and nodded his approval, then deftly pierced her ears with a sharp metal instrument, wiped away the few drops of blood, and inserted the earrings.

"By the way, the senator wishes you to wear them this evening," he mentioned casually as he closed his case.

She knew her face must be displaying her disquiet.

"For Rome!" the jeweller reminded her, and hurried out.

CHAPTER 7

Rius began crying later in the afternoon, after Bron had brought him back from their walk, and would not stop. She left him for a while, hoping he would cry himself to sleep, but he didn't.

Pulling her chair up to his crib, with one foot, she began to rock him gently backwards and forwards, meantime sewing on a tassel he had sucked off the corner of a cushion. When the rocking made no difference, she removed her thimble with a sigh and lay the cushion on the table.

"What's wrong, Rius?" she asked, lifting him from his crib. "It's not time for your next feed."

She walked him round the room, rubbing his back and trying to soothe him with shushing sounds whispered in his ear, all to no avail. She gave him his comforter to suck, a piece of many-times-washed lamb's wool, but he resolutely pushed it away.

There was a knock at the door and Julius came into the nursery.

"The mistress wants to know what's wrong with Honorius. She's *trying* to take her afternoon rest and the master is in his study, *trying* to work."

"Please apologise to them, Julius. I don't know what's wrong with him. I'm doing all I can to quieten him."

"Then it's obviously not enough," commented the old man acidly and left the room. Rius was still screaming.

"Do hush, son," pleaded Bron. "You'll get us both into trouble."

When laying him down on his side then on his stomach made no difference, she tried to feed him, but he would not suck and drew both knees up to his chest. Bron was beginning to feel desperate.

It was not long before Julius was back with another reprimand.

"His screaming is upsetting the whole household. The other two babies never made this noise."

"The other two were probably sick!" Bron retorted.

"And he isn't?" asked Julius sarcastically.

"No, he's not! He's a normal, healthy baby. It's probably just a pain in his gut."

"Then do something about it. You're his nurse. You're supposed to know what to do. Have you asked Cook for poppy seeds to mix in your milk?"

Bron could not believe what she was hearing. "No, of course not."

Julius grunted. "The other nurses used poppy seeds all the time. Worked a treat. Never got a peep out of either of those two little boys."

"I'm not drugging him just so the mistress can have her afternoon nap!"

"On your head be it. She says her nerves are on a knife edge, and is proving it by screeching at all of us."

"Please tell her that he can't cry for much longer, he's exhausted now. And please say that I apologise yet again."

When Julius had gone, she changed the baby's nappy once more, which was hardly necessary. Far from becoming exhausted, he was working himself up into more and more of a frenzy and she could feel how hot he was.

Cook sent over a bottle of fennel water, and when that had no effect, Bron tried laying on her bed with her fingers in her ears, but could not block out her son's insistent screams.

By now, he had been crying for three hours. Perhaps he *was* sick. Perhaps she was wasting time waiting for him to calm down and she should be sending for the doctor – anything to relieve her baby's distress and her own desperation.

She scrambled off her bed when there was yet another knock at the nursery door, picking Rius up on her way to open it. She made up her mind to tell Julius and his mistress to come and deal with the situation themselves, if they thought they could do any better!

She flung the door open and shoved the baby at the man standing there. His arms came up automatically to hold the noisy, wriggling bundle and he stared back at her with as much astonishment as she stared at him.

"And what do you expect me to do with him?" asked the senator.

"Oh, sir, I'm so sorry," gasped Bron in embarrassment, taking the baby from him. The sudden movements quietened Rius for a few moments, but not for long. "I thought you were Julius back to complain."

"And what was he supposed to do with him?" asked the senator.

"I don't know," mumbled Bron shamefacedly. "I'm at my wits' end."

"We all are," Laenus Loricatus said. "May I come in?"

Bron stood back to let him pass her.

Rius was still crying, though with a little less volume, Bron thought, but that may have been wishful thinking.

"I can only apologise again, sir, for the noise he's making. Did my mistress send you? I'm sorry he's disturbed her rest. He's not usually a baby who cries overly much, and I don't know what to do. I've tried everything I can think of, except poppy seeds. I won't drug him. He'll quieten in time – he's got to – he can't keep this up all night."

"Hush, Bron. I'm sure you're doing your best. No, Fausta didn't send me. I came of my own volition. She was in such a state, with her nerves causing her and all of us such grief, that I've sent her off to her mother's for the evening. She won't disturb us – you – for a few hours."

"Then why?"

"Thought I might be able to help. May I stay?"

Bron was nonplussed but he was her master, after all, so she nodded.

"Do you know about baby massage?"

She shook her head.

"Would you like me to show you? Massage can work wonders – in lots of ways." He was smiling at her. She nodded, feeling incompetent and foolish.

"Then let's take him through to your bedroom. Is there water in the bowl in there?"

Bron nodded again, anxious about this strange situation. He had banished any formality between them, and she was wary, though grateful to have help, no matter how bizarre.

She carried Rius through to her room and laid him on the bed with a blanket under him, then undressed him and gently wiped his hot little body with a cloth dipped in the water. The senator was rummaging in the bedside cabinet.

"It was here – ah, yes."

He had found a bottle of olive oil and poured some into the palms of his hands, then massaged them together.

"Watch me, then you'll know what to do in future."

Bron was amazed at his gentleness and skill as he gently smoothed the oil into the muscles of the gradually relaxing body of Rius – from shoulders down to feet, up again over his chest and shoulders then down his arms, and finally in a circulatory movement over his stomach, repeating each exercise several times. Gradually, Rius stopped crying. Bron went limp with relief.

"He should sleep through the night now," said the senator cheerfully as he wiped his hands on a towel.

"Who taught you about massage?" Bron asked as she dressed Rius in his night clothes again and put him back in his crib.

"I learned it from experts," he told her. "There are plenty of them in Rome – nothing to do with babies, of course."

She thought it prudent not to pursue the matter. "I am *so* grateful to you, sir."

"Not 'sir' – my name is Laenus – not in front of my wife or the slaves but when we are alone together." He looked down meaningfully at her bed.

Bron groaned inwardly. *Don't spoil it,* she thought. She was feeling very warmly towards him at the moment, but not that warmly. She had learned a lesson the hard way on board ship and was not about to repeat her mistake, even though her adored Rius had been the result. But this man was her employer, and her job and the safety of both herself and her baby was in jeopardy.

He took a step towards her and reached out and flicked an earring.

"I haven't yet thanked you for them," Bron said. "They're beautiful."

The senator smiled. "And only modestly expensive. You could have been more adventurous, you know, and chosen diamonds. But I like garnets, too. Not so blatant. Their fires blaze deep inside the stone. Your ears didn't bleed after the piercing?"

"Not unduly, thank you, sir."

"Laenus," he corrected her.

"I can't call you by your name, sir, when you are my employer."

"Pity," he said, kicking off his sandals and climbing onto her bed. Then he lay back, hands clasped beneath his head. "Don't I please you, Bron?"

"Sir, you are a kind master, I have no complaints."

"I could be even kinder. Are my features not to your liking?"

Bron thought that she had no complaints in that area, either. He was probably the handsomest man she had ever met.

"Sir—"

"Laenus—"

"Sir, you *must* know that everyone thinks you are one of the most—" she stopped, not knowing how to continue.

"Then what is your difficulty? *You* must know that I think you are also one of the most—" He didn't finish his sentence, either.

When she said nothing, he continued, smiling at her, "You intrigue me, Bron – but you know that. I have detected those garnet fires smouldering deep inside you. Are they as difficult to reach as you would have me believe? Of course, we cannot dismiss the little fellow asleep next door, so someone must have found and fuelled them. Who was he, Bron? Who was the father of Rius, lucky man?"

The guilt she felt whenever she thought of Brunus brought heat and colour rushing to her cheeks and neck. He could not help but notice and now the huskiness of his voice betrayed the intensity of his desire. He said quietly, "Yet you radiate such unconscious innocence, you are so like a child, I find you irresistible, utterly irresistible. I imagine most men do."

He seemed encouraged by her silence.

"But I have a problem. My hands are still covered in oil." He sat up and rubbed them together, all the while looking at her as she stood at the end of the bed. "What do you suggest I do with it?"

She picked up the towel and came across to him.

"Of course, you're worried that my wife might find out and you'd lose your job. I am always very discreet. The slaves won't tell, even if they suspect anything. Julius knows everything that goes on in the household, but he won't talk. He's very loyal to me and very protective towards his mistress, and anyway, he wouldn't get a job anywhere else if he tittle-tattled, *and* he's too old. So, you see, we're quite safe from busybodies running with tales to Fausta."

Bron held out the towel towards him.

"I know the bed's comfortable," he wheedled. "I've sampled it many times in the past. And I promise to use plenty of oil to protect you from any unwanted consequences."

Bron thought of Aurelius and all she had to lose if she took up this offer, and all she might lose if she didn't. She would have to take that chance. Of one thing she was certain, if she was made to leave, Rius would be going with her.

She laid the towel on the bed and walked back into the nursery. After a few moments, Laenus Loricatus was by her side, his sandals replaced. He looked flushed and annoyed.

"All right, I can wait," he said. "You'll come round – they always do."

Yes, I expect they do, Bron thought after he had gone and she was getting into bed, *but not this one, not this time.*

CHAPTER 8

She was much too sleepy to answer the light tap at her door, and was irritated when it was repeated, a little louder.

"Who is it?" she called, dragging herself half awake and sitting up in bed.

"It's me, Izmira."

"Come in!"

A scuffling at the door reminded Bron of the chair she had wedged under the door handle.

"Wait a moment, I'm coming," she called, climbing out of bed and wondering what problem couldn't wait till morning.

The girl stood at the door, dishevelled, her dark hair falling untidily about her shoulders.

"Well, Izmira, what is it? I was almost asleep."

"I'm sorry, miss, but you're wanted in the triclinium."

"Wanted? Who wants me?"

"The master. He says you are to dress and go to him there, and dress Rius and take him with you."

"Are you sure you've got the message right?"

"Oh yes, miss. He made me repeat it back to him."

"But what is so urgent that he needs to see us now?"

"I don't know, miss, but Julius was sent to wake me up especially."

Her eyes were half closing as she spoke.

"I'll have to do as he says," Bron conceded, "but there's no need for you to stay up any longer. Off you go back to bed before you fall asleep standing up."

"Yes, miss. Thank you, miss."

Bron was bewildered by this summons. He had made such an effort to get Rius to sleep. What was he playing at? Then her mind cleared of sleep and she understood. She had refused his advances and this was his way of getting back at her. How mean and spiteful! He knew it would distress her if Rius woke up and started crying all over again. She considered not answering the summons, or going on her own, but knew that spelt trouble and it would be much better to do as he asked.

Angry now, she threw on some clothes and tidied her hair, then went into the nursery. Hopefully, she could dress her son without waking him. He stirred a little while she was doing this, which caused her to pause, but returned to his deep sleep. Thankfully, she wrapped him in a blanket and left the room, crossing the courtyard and entering the triclinium.

The senator was lounging on a couch, a slave hovering round him and keeping his glass filled.

"Ah, Bron, there you are," he said as she came in.

"You sent for me, sir," she stated flatly. "Is there something I can do for you?"

"Yes, there is something you could do for me, and you know what it is, but in view of your reluctance, you can sit down and keep me company. My wife has sent word that she is staying at her mother's for the night, and I'm feeling lonely. So sit down and talk to me."

Dutifully, Bron sat on the couch, as far away from him as she could get, still cuddling Rius.

"Sir, what do you want me to talk to you about?"

"Anything to put 'Sir' in a frame of mind to go to bed *on my own* and go to sleep *on my own*. Politics, religion, my work, the theatre, the weather – anything. More wine, boy!"

Bron began to tell him about her day. She saw one route to finishing this charade, and made sure her conversation was as boring as possible. When the senator's head lolled forward for a moment, she smiled at the slave and indicated that he should keep his glass filled.

There was one question she could ask, the answer to which might prove fruitful, and that was about the grandmother of Emperor Honorius. When the senator's head shot up again, she broached the subject carefully.

"Senator, do you know anything about the emperor's grandmother, Aelia Flavia Claudia Antonia? I met her while out walking."

"She's old, very old," he said, "and an interfering busybody from all accounts. You met her, you say?"

"Yes, she stumbled getting out of her carriage, and I gave her my arm for support."

Bron didn't know how to find out the information she needed so asked, "Does she travel much?"

"How should I know? I'm not privy to her diary. You'll have to ask *her*."

"Has she anything to do with the military?"

"I believe Honorius made her commander-in-chief of one of the legions – to give her something to do and keep her out of his hair, I suspect."

Bron concentrated on keeping the excitement out of her voice and asked as casually as she could, "Do you know which one?"

"No, I don't – it may have been one of the British legions. Enough! I didn't bring you over here to interrogate me. Boy, more wine! And bring a glass for the lady. Drink, Bron!"

"I had rather not."

"Drink, blast you, and keep me company!"

The boy brought her a glass but only half filled it when she shook her head at him. She took a sip and put the glass on the table beside her.

"Why all these damn fool questions?"

"She intrigues me, sir."

He moved closer to her and tried to take hold of her hand, but fumbled the attempt and gave up.

"And you intrigue me, Bron, as I seem to remember telling you. You're an intrig—intrig—intriguing young woman. Why won't you come to bed with me? Fausta won't come to bed with me and you won't come – I didn't think I was that repulsive."

His words were slurred and his speech was slowing. Finally, he leant towards her as if to put his head on her shoulder, but she moved away and he toppled into the space between them.

"Go and fetch Julius," she instructed the slave, "then help get him to bed. Please take away my glass – and I'd rather you didn't tell Julius that I was here."

The lad nodded and Bron stood, but her request was in vain because Julius was already in the room, making his way across to the couch. *That man is everywhere*, Bron thought with annoyance, and wondered how much of their conversation he had overheard.

"You can go now, miss," Julius told her. "Take the little lad back to the nursery – I can manage the master. He'll sleep till morning. I'm sorry you were disturbed."

Bron, surprised at the strength in the old man's wiry body, watched as he tugged the protesting senator into a sitting position then, with the help of the slave boy, heaved him to his feet. As all three began to make stumbling progress towards the door, she took Rius back to bed.

As she was falling asleep, she realised once again that she would have to tread very warily where Laenus Loricatus and his wife were concerned if she was to keep her job.

She also realised with surprise that Julius had been civil to her for the first time since she arrived.

CHAPTER 9

"You shouldn't be here with us," said Cook next morning as she prepared lunch.

"Rius and I like it here," Bron told her. "No one knows where we are."

"By 'no one', I 'spects you mean the master," Cook replied shrewdly. When Bron didn't answer, she continued. "Stands to reason he can't keep his hands off a girl pretty as you. So, what's he been up to now?"

"Please, Cook, don't say any more – nothing's happened, really it hasn't."

Cook regarded her closely. "I believe you, though there's many as wouldn't, knowing him as we all do. It's only a matter of time, though – he's powerful determined, 'specially when he can't get his own way."

"I would hate the mistress to hear anything that wasn't true," Bron pleaded.

"Then there's not much that wouldn't be said."

Bron remained silent for a moment then simply murmured, "Rius."

"Ah. Frightened of dismissal, are you? No need to worry there – you'd get a job anywhere on the Hill."

"But I don't want another job!"

"It's the boy, isn't it? Seems to me you're closer to him than his own mother. None of my business, of course, but it seems to me—"

"It seems to me that I'd best be getting back to the nursery," Bron interrupted hurriedly. She gulped down the remainder of the water in her beaker. "Thanks for breakfast, Cook, and please keep your observations to yourself. There's so much at stake."

"Don't worry on that account. If I gossiped about what I knows, or even what I thought I knows, I'd never—"

Bron made her escape and had to guess what Cook would never do.

One morning several weeks later, Fausta Loricata demanded, "How soon before you can wean him off your milk?"

"It's not time yet, madam!" Bron protested. She had been dreading this moment.

"How soon?" persisted her employer.

Bron knew that Fausta desired more control over Rius, but also knew that her own security would be threatened once he was independent of her milk. Besides, she enjoyed feeding him and wasn't ready to give up this treasured intimacy. Onset of weaning must be delayed for as long as possible.

"He's thrived on my milk, madam, and we don't want his health to suffer," she ventured.

"Very well, but I want you to start weaning him off you as soon as possible. Speak to Cook about baby food."

"Yes, madam."

"We have guests this evening and you will be required to bring him in to see them after our meal, so make sure he has a good sleep this afternoon."

Bron stifled a protest. When his sleeping pattern was disturbed, it was she who was kept awake most of the night, not them.

It had been made plain to her more than once that her employers should on no account be inconvenienced, especially the senator, who always had burdens of state to bear, though what they were, Bron was never quite sure.

However, these great responsibilities had kept him out of her way for the past couple of weeks and on the few occasions they had passed each other around the villa, he had ignored her. She hoped his attention had been distracted elsewhere but thought it more likely that he was planning something devious, though what it was she couldn't imagine.

To take her mind off these worries and to escape from the house for an hour, she decided to take Rius for a walk in his push-cart. Rather than go down the hill towards the city, she turned right, intending to make for one of the open spaces.

Most of those she had discovered were kept tidied and weeded, with the grass cut, but she was happiest in an area where wild flowers grew in profusion. The air there was clean and fresh and perfumed and she would leave the push-cart in a hedge or under a tree and take Rius into the long grasses, where they could roll and play and generally enjoy themselves. She laughed to see him reach for the butterflies or clap his hands to make the birds fly away. Once, they even surprised a young deer that was hiding in the grass. Delightedly, they watched as with three bounds, the beautiful creature was out of sight.

The parks were also places where she could meet other nurses who worked on the Hill, with their charges. She was always careful not to gossip about the Loricatus household, though none of the others felt any compunction about giggling over the weaknesses and vices of their families. In this way, Bron soon learned the purpose of the block of apartments at the bottom of the hill.

She was climbing the Palatine and chatting amiably to her son when someone called her. They were passing the house where Bron had made the acquaintance of the old lady in the carriage and there was a young woman coming out of the gate.

"Do you want me?" Bron asked her.

"Yes. My mistress saw you passing the villa and sent me out to speak to you." Bron was perplexed. "She said you helped her last time she was here, when she almost fell and you gave her your arm for support."

"Is your mistress the emperor's grandmother?"

"I have that honour and I have a message for you. She invites you to visit her at her villa in the country. Would you give her that pleasure? She would come out to speak to you herself but is having difficulty walking and is resting inside to relieve the pains in her legs."

Bron was astounded by the invitation. "I would love to visit her. It is an undeserved honour. Would you thank her for me?"

"She asks that you don't bring the baby, as she is old now and finds children a disturbance."

"Of course. But I will have to ask the permission of my mistress, though I can't think that she would refuse."

"Her steward will make sure your employers know that the invitation is genuine and will arrange a convenient day and give directions to the villa. It's on the Appian Way."

Bron thanked her again and reiterated how pleased and surprised she was to receive the invitation. She guessed that Fausta Loricata would also be delighted that her nurse had attracted the attention of such a noble and high-born lady, and would soon be spreading the news around and basking in reflected glory.

As she continued up the hill, however, she realised that she had not been asked her name or where she lived. She stopped and turned round, but the girl must have gone back inside the house as there was no sign of her.

CHAPTER 10

She was too excited to linger in the park and decided to return home almost immediately. Her mistress was in the courtyard, sitting on a bench with her feet up, being fanned languorously by one of the slave girls. Bron blurted out her news.

Fausta clapped her hands together and laughed.

"How exciting! You've done well, girl! Make sure you let all the other nurses know about the invitation when you next meet them, and you have my permission to speak up this evening when our guests question you, as they certainly will after I've thrown out a few hints. And don't be afraid to embroider the facts a little for the benefit of Julia! Rest assured, I'll back up anything you say."

She waved away the girl with the fan. "I'll inform the senator when he comes in later. Now I'm off to my room for my nap. We've a busy evening ahead and I need to keep alert."

Bron could think of nothing but her visit as she busied herself undressing Rius then wrapping him in a soft woollen blanket. She had been handed an unexpected opportunity to find out about that necklace but knew it would take all her ingenuity to put the questions she needed to ask.

Moments later they were on their way towards the bath house. Rius always thoroughly enjoyed the fun he had in his mother's arms as they played and splashed in the water, and her enjoyment was no less.

The bath complex was past the nursery, at the far end of the covered walkway, in a separate annexe. An ornamental arch led to a corridor decorated pale blue.

The women's changing room was coloured the same watery blue with paintings across walls and ceiling of fish, lobsters, turtles and many more sea creatures, some the creation of an imaginative artist, swimming among the corals or crawling along the sea bed.

Bron undressed completely and left her clothes on the bench that ran along the walls and her sandals in a locker beneath. She guessed they would have the pool to themselves for the next hour and they could be back in the nursery before the senator came home.

The large, warm pool room was designed for relaxation and enjoyment. Here the décor varied through all shades of blue and green, mixing and merging, with painted yellow sunrays lighting the tops of rippling waves. On rocks emerging from the waves sat the sirens, naked girls half human and half fish. Light through windows high in the ceiling played on the surface of the pool, which reflected it back around the walls, giving the whole room an ethereal, watery, dreamlike quality.

Bron approached the edge of the marble tiles and jumped into the warm water, with Rius in her arms. They went under and came up laughing and spluttering.

It was then that Bron noticed they were not alone in the pool. At the far end, a young, naked girl was watching them. Bron waded over to exchange introductions, but when several feet away, gasped, recognising the beautiful, oval face, and eyes the shape and colour of almonds.

"Adama!"

"Bron!"

"What are you doing here?" Bron asked her.

"What are *you* doing here? And our darling Rius. May I hold him?" Bron handed her son over. "He's grown so in the few months since you left the brothel."

"He's sitting up now," Bron told her proudly. "I work here. The senator and his wife have adopted Rius and they employ me as his wet nurse. But you?"

"I'm working here, too."

"The senator?" Bron asked. Adama nodded.

"I'm so pleased to see you!" Bron put her arms around the girl, who was still holding Rius, and kissed her on the cheek. "We've so much to talk about. Why don't we go back to the nursery? I'll send for some wine and something to eat."

"I'd love to, Bron, but I have to wait here for Laenus. He'll be along soon. We don't have much time, just while his wife is taking her afternoon rest."

"If he's coming, I'm going!" Bron exclaimed, taking Rius from her and climbing up the steps out of the water. "Come into the cold plunge with us."

The girl shook her head, disturbing her long hair, which spread around her on the surface of the water like a black cloak.

"He wants me warm when he arrives."

"Are you still at the brothel?"

"No, I'm in the insula down the hill. I have an apartment of my own now."

Bron smiled. "So you finally let your old admirer have his way?"

"Why not? My looks and shape won't last for ever and his offer was the best around."

"Are you happy there?"

"I'm well content. He's such a darling, and worships me, and he gives me my freedom, as long as I'm there when he wants me, and he always gives me plenty of notice. I'm a big part of his life, I think the happiest part, but he has to fit me in with his wife and family and business interests and community service." She smiled as she confided to her friend, "His passions run deep, like a river, without frenzy, no uncontrollable urges."

"Not like the senator?"

"You too, Bron?"

"No, but only because I won't. But I really must disappear now. May we come and see you one afternoon?"

"You shouldn't be seen around the apartments, it wouldn't be fitting."

"Where, then?"

A door slammed beyond the changing rooms.

Bron panicked. "I must go, Adama."

"I think I'll be around for some time, Bron. I'm sure we'll see each other again."

"Do you know the wild park further up the hill?" Adama nodded. "I'll see you there this day next week, early afternoon."

"I'll try, but if I'm not, you'll know why."

Bron was entering the cold plunge room at the further end of the pool room as the senator emerged from the men's changing room. She glimpsed his lean, naked figure making a running leap into the pool and heard Adama's well-practised squeal of delight amongst a lot of splashing, before closing the door.

Later, having settled Rius down to sleep, she changed and occupied herself with some mending, waiting for the summons from Fausta Loricata at the end of their evening meal.

It came at last in the person of Julius. Reluctantly, Bron lifted Rius, already dressed in a white tunic, from his crib, trying not to wake him, and walked across the courtyard and so into the triclinium, perfumed again with lavender.

There were about twenty guests round the three-sided table, lolling on the couches in various positions of indolence, obviously well sated. Slaves were still serving wine, and some of those assembled were still picking at the remains of the food littering the board. One couple were feeding each other with pieces of fruit, another had their arms locked as they drank from each other's goblet, and yet another pair were curled up together and Bron could only guess from their giggles what they were getting up to. She felt it wasn't a situation into which to bring her son and decided to escape as soon as she could.

"Ah, Bron, bring Honorius over here. My guests want to see our son. Give him to me."

Fausta smiled all round the table and, reluctantly, Bron handed him over.

"Friends, I want you to meet our boy, our son, Honorius."

She held him high, for all to see, and her guests made suitable comments and noises of approval. One or two of the women seemed genuinely interested and asked to hold him, but the rest seemed more interested in their wine or their companions.

The senator looked up. "And this is Bron, his nurse. Come over here, girl. My gentlemen friends want to meet you."

Bron hesitated, humiliated and unsure whether to obey him. Slaves and servants usually passed unnoticed and unheeded. Fortunately, Fausta came to her rescue.

"Laenus, you've drunk too much. Of course no one wants to meet Nurse. However, my dears, you should know that she has received an invitation to attend on her grace, Aelia Flavia Claudia Antonia, grandmother to Emperor Honorius!"

There was a ripple of interest round the table.

"Tell them, Nurse, how it came about," Fausta urged her.

"I—I met her a few days ago, getting out of her carriage on the Palatine—" Bron stammered nervously. "The old lady, I mean her grace, stumbled and was only kept from falling because I happened to be near enough for her to hold on to my arm. As a 'thank you', she has invited me to her country villa on the Appian Way – for the day – next week."

"Of course," interrupted Fausta, "it will only be a matter of time before we entertain her here, to return the invitation. As you may be aware, I am related to the Constantine family, but it will be such an honour to welcome the grandmother of Honorius here. After all, he is still the rightful emperor. Don't you think so, Julia? Julia?"

Bron noticed that her employer's best friend was seated on the other side of the senator, looking very flushed. Bron presumed that she had drunk plenty of wine, until she noticed that the senator's hands were hidden from view beneath the table cloth. His wife noticed it too, because she pushed Rius towards him.

"Hold him, dear."

His hands came up to do as he was bidden and the colour heightened in Julia's face. As before, Bron was upset to see her son treated like the prize in a pass-the-parcel game and took a few steps towards the senator.

This brought her into a pool of light spread by a candelabra on the table and she became aware that one of the men was staring at her. Strangely, he was not unfamiliar, but she couldn't think where she had seen him before, though she could guess.

The senator noticed his friend's stare. He smiled and leaned across the table towards him, almost squashing Rius.

"Your inclination is written all over your face," he teased in a low voice. The general hubbub had resumed and only a few in the near vicinity heard his words. "But I regret she's not the last course on the menu."

"Oh, but she was, once," the man replied. "We've met before, young woman."

"I'm sorry, sir, but I don't think that can be," Bron said, panicking.

The senator passed Rius over to Julia, who took him with reluctance. "Where was that, Marcellus?" he asked. Now it was the turn of the man addressed as Marcellus to look apprehensive. "Or can't you tell us with your wife present?" The men around them laughed at the shared joke.

"I have no secrets from my wife!" protested Marcellus, looking uneasily at the woman seated next to him.

"I'm glad to hear it," approved the senator, gazing all round at the assembled company. "Neither have I and neither has any man present." There was a great deal more laughter, louder this time.

The senator climbed off the couch and stood behind it, inviting the other men to do likewise.

"It is time for the ladies to retire," he said, taking Rius from Julia and handing him back to his wife.

"Come along, ladies," Fausta agreed. "Let's leave the men to their politics."

She led the way out of the room. Bron waited until the last woman had left and was about to follow when her arm was grabbed. She turned to find Marcellus, who had walked round from the other side of the table, leering at her.

"You were the girl with the golden ankle," he accused her. "You can't deny it!"

Bron had been dreading such a confrontation.

"The what?" demanded the senator.

"She knows," his friend said.

"I don't think she does. Do you, Bron?"

"No, sir," she lied, grateful for the senator's intervention.

"Marcellus, take your hand off her arm. She comes from Britannia and you are very unlikely to have met her before. Bron, follow the ladies."

"Yes, sir."

As she left the room, she heard the senator ask, "Now what's all this nonsense about a golden ankle?"

CHAPTER 11

Fausta Loricata insisted on helping Bron choose her tunic and accessories for her meeting with Aelia Flavia Claudia Antonia.

"It will reflect well on all of us if you impress the old lady," she commented as she selected and discarded several before holding up a dark red tunic.

"This one," she decided. "You'll need the gold brooches and chain I gave you, to pin on the shoulders, and there were some gold sandals."

She rummaged in the chest and found them.

"Now, jewellery. What about those garnet pendants? They'll go well with the tunic."

Fausta had noticed them a few days previously. Bron wore them one afternoon at the request of the senator. He was entertaining a friend and after their midday meal, had brought him into the courtyard to show off his son – though Bron felt that it was she who was on display. Fausta was with them and had stopped Bron to have a closer look.

"They're very pretty in a baubly sort of way," she said. "I don't remember putting those in your chest. You haven't worn them before."

"That's because I've not long had my ears pierced, madam."

"Your memory is getting so bad these days," the senator joked, kissing his wife on the cheek. "You'd forget your head if it wasn't sewn on. She's right, though, young lady, they are very pretty *baubles*."

His emphasis on the last word made Bron blush and his friend guffawed and winked knowingly at her. It was obvious that he was in on the deception.

"If Fausta bought them for you, she has very good taste," her husband remarked.

Bron had been put into this deceitful situation without her consent. Obviously, it had been naïve of her to suppose that he had told his wife about the gift.

On the morning of her appointment on the Appian Way, the senator appeared in buoyant mood. He was off on a business trip somewhere. His wife was spending the day in the city with friends, taking in a theatrical performance in the evening, and spending the night with one of them.

Fausta had asked Cook to look after Rius and had given Bron the whole day off. Cook was delighted and planned to take him to her friend's for the afternoon. Rius liked Cook. She had several children of her own of various ages, was now a grandmother, and always knew what to do in every circumstance to keep a baby employed and happy.

"I'm leaving now," the senator announced. "Fausta, give my best wishes to Julia and your friends and wish them a pleasant day. Bron, please extend our kindest regards to the old lady. Tell her we still revere the memory of Theodosius, her husband, and his dedicated service to the empire."

"Yes, do commend us to her, Bron," Fausta enthused. "I can't imagine why she is taking such an interest in you, as you must be the lowest of the low in her estimation, but we all know how eccentric she is, how odd, and of course you can't disobey a direct invitation. But do mention our names to her, as often as you can, and make sure she knows who we are, and is aware of the loyal and sacrificial service Laenus has given to her grandson, also the community work I organise, and say we would be proud and honoured if she would share a meal with us some time. Be sure to tell her, Bron. Don't you think so, Laenus?"

"Indeed. Tell her all that, Bron, if you have opportunity. By the way, I'm making a litter available for your use so there's no need to hire a public conveyance."

"Thank you, sir."

"Not at all. I hope you have as pleasant a day as I intend to. Goodbye, my dear, I'll see you tomorrow." He kissed his wife lightly on the cheek and left.

Shortly afterwards, Bron was informed that a litter awaited her.

CHAPTER 12

It did not take the eight bearers long to reach the gates at the city limits. Then they were out into the countryside.

When it began to rain, Bron pulled the curtains round her. It was a heavy shower, though not prolonged, but while it lasted it sounded like a drum solo on the wooden canopy above her head. She would have instructed the bearers to take shelter but they needed to keep up a good pace or she wouldn't be in time for her appointment, and she knew she mustn't keep that grand old lady waiting.

The clamour of crowds around them increased the further away from the city they travelled. She pulled aside the curtains and addressed the slave nearest to her, a well-built man in his middle years.

"Where are we?"

"On the Appian Way, just passing the entrance to the catacombs."

"Why the crowd?" she asked him.

"They're going to the chariot races."

"Where?"

"The arena is further along. People steal time off work to go, though most businesses close, especially today."

"Why especially today?" She waited while he regained his breath.

"They come to watch champion charioteers from all over Italia. They're competing for the Champion of Champions. Very important programme. Very important award."

Bron closed the curtains again. She lay back against the cushions and thought about her forthcoming meeting.

How could she raise the subject of the necklace that she had seen round the old lady's neck, which should be around her own? But should it? What the army deserter did with it was his choice. He could have given it to some girl, or traded it for drink or, if he had been sensible, for a passage to wherever his home was, avoiding the troop ships.

For the hundredth time, she wondered what sequence of honest or dishonest dealings had brought it into the possession of a member of the imperial family. She would not be believed if she said the necklace had been hers – what proof was there? Proof in Britannia, yes, but not in Rome. She would be regarded as a conniving, scheming, lying nobody worming her way into the old lady's acquaintance, if not affections, then laying claim to her priceless jewellery.

The slave's voice broke into her reverie.

"Miss, we're outside the arena now, if you want to have a look. On your left."

Bron peeped through the curtains. She could see very little beyond the people crowding along the cobbled roadway and thronging the entrances built into the high, circular, red brick wall: men, women and children, all dressed in their summer best. The excitement was palpable.

Once they had passed the arena, they were moving against the jostling crowd. Bron was beginning to feel slightly queasy with the rocking, swaying and jerking of the litter, and hoped they would be at their destination soon. She let the curtains drop back in place and fanned herself vigorously.

The instructions conveyed to the senator were that there was a very small village along the road, and beyond that, country mansions. That owned by Aelia Flavia was fifth on the right, with a stone eagle in flight on each of the gate posts.

The litter bearers said they knew it very well but had seemed surprised when she said she was meeting the emperor's grandmother there. Now she came to think about it, they had avoided looking at her directly as they helped her climb into the litter, but had been exchanging glances with each other. Perhaps they were impressed that she knew the old lady on such intimate terms.

The litter slowed and came to a halt.

"Miss, we're here."

Bron pulled aside the curtains on her right and inspected the villa the man was indicating. She was slightly disappointed. Neither the house nor the plot on which it stood nor the entrance gates with their stone eagles were as large or imposing as she had expected.

The litter was lowered a little and a box set in place. She took the bearer's hand and stepped down.

"You're sure this is the right villa?" she asked.

"Quite sure, miss. We'll wait until you're ready to return to the Palatine."

There was a distant roll of thunder and Bron looked up at the sky.

"I think it's going to rain again."

"If it does, there's shelter for us further along the Way," the man reassured her.

He opened one of the iron gates for her to pass through and closed it behind her. She looked around. There was gravel instead of lawns, and in the centre, an ornamental fish pond with a marble statue of a naked, curly-headed boy riding a dolphin – Bron recognised the creature, having seen so many of them during her voyage to Ostia.

A stepping-stone path across the gravel led to five wide steps and a covered walkway. On this stood a long, cushioned seat with wickerwork arms and back, suspended from an iron frame. Bron could just imagine the old lady sitting out here on fine days, watching the traffic passing along the busy Appian Way.

Rather nervously, she took hold of a bell rope and tugged it.

The door was opened by a young man.

She announced herself. "I believe her grace is expecting me."

He grinned widely then stood back so she could enter, and indicated an upholstered armchair standing on the black-and-white patterned tiles of the hallway. Bron sat.

"I'll tell *her grace* you're here."

He was still grinning from ear to ear, which she thought very strange, but perhaps the old lady employed eccentric staff, or perhaps they became eccentric after working for her for some time.

She looked around and was surprised at the sparse furniture – matching wood-and-leather armchairs on each side of a long, narrow table against the wall, and a low wooden, carved chest –

and how minimal the painted decorations on walls and ceiling. It was not at all like the opulence she had expected.

The young man was back. "Follow me," he invited and led her along the hallway, round a corner and into a room. "Please sit. You won't have to wait long." He was grinning yet again. "May I offer you a glass of wine?"

"Not now," she said. "Perhaps when her grace arrives."

"A long wait," he said enigmatically and left the room, closing the door, which clicked noisily.

This room was more inviting, with comfortable chairs and couches, on one of which she sat, several small tables and a stone sideboard. Sheepskin rugs hid the floor mosaics and heavy curtains framed tall glazed windows with views of the Appian Way.

There were two doors in the room. Both were closed.

She was feeling a little apprehensive and wishing she had taken the offered glass of wine, when the door at the far end of the room began to open. She stood with a smile of anticipation that vanished abruptly when she saw the tall figure walking towards her, arms outstretched in welcome.

CHAPTER 13

"Bron, my dear. Welcome to my little hideaway."

"Senator!"

He came up to her, put his arms round her and kissed her fully on the lips. She was speechless. Then he pressed his hands on her shoulders so that she was forced to sit down again.

"Surprised? I hoped you might guess and had come anyway."

Bron began choking with rage and not a little fear. She jumped up, managing to spit out, "I hadn't guessed and I'm leaving right now!"

"Calm down, Bron, calm down. I'm not going to hurt you. I just wanted to spend the day with you without your and my encumbrances." He smiled indulgently. "And as for leaving, you can't. The door you came in by is locked and the boy has left the villa. This other door leads only to my bedroom, and the door to the hall out of that is also locked. So you see, you have no choice. Come, sit beside me."

He sat down on the couch and patted the cushions. Bron sat because she didn't know what else to do.

"That's a good girl. We're friends, aren't we?" He took hold of her hand but she pulled it away. "Don't make it difficult, Bron. You'll come round to my way eventually."

"How did you engineer this?" she asked, curious in spite of her predicament.

"It was easy because you wanted so much to talk to the old lady. Fausta mentioned that you took Honorius out for a walk every afternoon while she was resting, and after a little spying, I discovered which way you usually went. My girl – she's one of the prostitutes from the insula further down the hill, by the way –

only had to hang around that gate for a couple of days, waiting for you to pass, and there you were, hooked with wishful thinking."

Bron could kick herself for being so gullible. It was true, she had been obsessed with speaking again to the old lady, and hadn't questioned the bogus invitation.

"I thought you would enjoy a day off. My wife works you too long and too hard. She knows nothing about this hideaway, of course. She thinks I spend much more time at the Senate than I actually do, poor dear.

"But I haven't brought you here to talk about Fausta. It was the only way I could get you on my own, so you only have yourself to blame. If you'd been more amenable, I wouldn't have had cause for this little deception." He chuckled. "I didn't need to bring the other nurses here. Decidedly not. But you're made of different stuff, Bron."

He moved closer and she edged away until her back was jammed hard against the arm of the couch. "How different I intend to find out, which will be fun – for both of us, I'm sure. And if the difference is exciting enough, we won't go home till tomorrow morning. Fausta is away for the night and I know you've left plenty of your milk for Honorius, so he won't starve. Your milk. Hmm, now that's an alluring thought."

Bron felt desperate, not knowing how to extricate herself. It was unlikely that he would allow her to get him so drunk that he wouldn't know what he was doing. Both doors were locked. That young man had taken the key of one of them, and there was no telling where the other key was.

"Are you hungry? There's food here."

He crossed to the sideboard and brought her back a sprig of grapes. "One for you and one for me – I was eating grapes the first time we met, do you remember? But of course you do. You were wearing that necklace. Fausta gave me a right dressing down, I can tell you. In fact, she went off to the spare bedroom to sleep. Just because I was gazing down your cleavage. I wonder what she would do if she could see us now."

His hand was straying onto her lap.

"She won't let me make love to her. Did you know that? Won't let me touch her, not anywhere. Not that it makes any difference. I tried once, on our wedding night. It was like trying to rouse a corpse. After that, she told me to keep my distance. It's no mystery that there are no babies. So, I play elsewhere."

"I don't want to hear all this," Bron told him, pushing his hand away. "I want to go home. You can't make me stay. I'm your employed nurse and not your whore."

He brought his face close to hers. "You needn't play that little-girl innocence any longer. Marcellus told me all about the girl with the golden ankle. In truth, I had heard her talked about long before you came to work for us, and Marcellus just put two and two together for me."

"And made five!" Bron snapped back, drawing away again. "Yes, I worked as a decoy for the girls, but that was all. It went no further than that!"

"You'll be telling me next that Honorius arrived by spontaneous conception!"

Bron was ousted and knew it.

"So, Miss Don't-Lay-a-Finger-on-Me-Innocent, just remember you're the mother of that child and watch what you're saying! I could devastate your life if I chose."

"You wouldn't!"

"Try me!"

"Not even you—"

"Oh, Bron, Bron!" he appealed to her. "Just be nice to me, just this once. I won't make you do anything you don't want to, honestly."

His hands had begun to stray again, caressing the tunic over her thighs and wandering across her lap, and she fought to intercept them. She guessed he was conceited enough to believe that, once she had given way to him, she would want him time and time again. This was no doubt true for other women he seduced, but she wasn't prepared to slither down that route, there was too much at stake.

"Sir."

"Laenus," he said.

"Laenus," she capitulated, holding his hands firmly and playing for time.

Could she throw a chair through the window glass? It was of the best quality, hopefully thin enough, but she baulked at the thought of clambering through broken and splintered glass. Start a fire? Where and what with? Feeling panic rising, she knew she was trapped and utterly helpless.

Then, suddenly, the front door bell clanged. The senator looked startled. It clanged again.

"Shouldn't you answer that?" Bron asked, utterly relieved.

"I'm not expecting anyone," he said. "Let it ring."

If she could persuade him to open the front door to whoever was standing there, she might be able to make a run for it.

"Laenus!" It was a woman's voice. She had heard it before but couldn't place it. "Laenus, are you there?"

"Oh no, not now!" he groaned and stood up. Bron went over to the window and looked out but couldn't see the front door from there.

"Bron, come away from the window!"

She stood her ground. He came over to her, wrapped his arms round her, lifted her off her feet and took her into the bedroom, laying her down on the bed.

The insistent clanging quickened pace.

"I know you're in there, Laenus! I've seen your litter bearers outside! Darling, open the door! I won't go away!"

"You'll have to go and talk to her," said Bron, "or she'll be there all afternoon. Get rid of her. Then come back."

"Stay just where you are." His voice was thick with anticipation. "I'll get rid of her as quick as I can then we'll finish what we've started."

Finding a bunch of keys in the drawer of a little cabinet at the side of the bed, he let himself out into the hall, locking the door behind him. Bron was no better off. She could have screamed with frustration.

She heard low voices – a woman's, urgent, and the senator's, calm and reassuring, trying to quieten her, whoever she was. Then there was a click and the door to the other room opened. Bron stayed quite still, lying on the bed where he had left her. There were footsteps across the floor of the adjoining room and the communicating door was closed.

She got off the bed and listened, her ear to the door.

"I took a chance that this is where you were," the woman was saying. "I knew Fausta was in the city, so I called at the house and was told you were out for the day. So, what are you doing here all by yourself? You are by yourself, aren't you? You haven't got some girl in bed in there?"

"Of course not." He sounded hurt and reproachful. "Who else would be here? I came because I had work to do and it's so much quieter than on the Palatine."

What a consummate liar he is, Bron thought – *probably born of long practice*. She felt quite sorry for the woman, whoever she was.

"Aren't you going to offer me a drink?"

"Gladly. What shall it be?"

"You know I prefer red."

Bron could hear the wine being poured then the chinking of glasses.

"To us, Laenus."

"To us, darling."

There was silence then for several minutes and Bron could only guess what was happening.

"Take me through to your bed, Laenus."

"Sweetheart, I told you that I have work to do, and I meant it. If I take you through there, it will never get done. You know I can't concentrate on anything else when you're around. Now stop that! You'll have to go."

"Don't send me away!" the woman pleaded in a 'little girl' voice that Bron found highly embarrassing.

"Where's your husband?"

"Away on business. He'll be gone for days."

"If you go home now, I promise I'll come round later. Fausta won't be back till morning so we'll have all night."

"Promise?"

"Cross my heart—"

"I'll have a meal waiting for you, and wine, and our special mushrooms, and—" she dropped her voice to a conspiratorial whisper "—all the toys we like to use."

"I'll count the moments. Now off you go, you baggage!"

Bron heard what sounded like a slap, and a giggle, then their voices receded along the hall. She was into the next room and out of the door in no time. But how to escape from the house? There was no chance while he was at the front door. He would be back at any moment and discover her.

Then she remembered the chest in the hall. She didn't know whether it was full or empty but had to take a chance. While the senator and his visitor were saying, from the sound of it, a very affectionate goodbye on the other side of the front door, she quietly opened the lid of the chest and climbed inside, pulling it down on top of her, hoping fervently it would not be too heavy to push up again. Fortunately, there was room for her to lie on top of the assortment of sandals, bags, belts, walking sticks, and other paraphernalia piled inside.

She heard the senator come back into the hall and close the front door. As soon as his footsteps passed and turned the corner, she was out of the chest, leaving the lid up, had the front door open, and was fleeing down the path.

As they had promised, the litter bearers were still there, lolling about on the grass at the side of the road. They looked surprised when they saw her and immediately stood up.

A woman was walking away from the villa, towards the shelter where bearers of the public conveyances were gossiping together. Her back was towards Bron, but there was no mistaking the owner of those provocatively swaying hips that turned all the men's heads.

CHAPTER 14

Bron had not been imprisoned in the villa for very long, although her ordeal had seemed to stretch throughout the afternoon.

When her litter started out on the return journey, the road was still thronged with people eagerly making their way towards the arena, mostly on foot but also travelling on horseback and by conveyance. Their anticipation of an exhilarating day's chariot racing was infectious and the din of excited voices coupled with iron wheels and iron horseshoes over cobbles was deafening.

It was also very hot and the sun directly above threw out all the heat it could muster. It bounced back off the roadway and the smooth grey stone of the mausoleums and memorials that hemmed them in on each side.

Behind the curtains of the litter, Bron licked her dry lips and pulled the neckline of her shift as low as modesty allowed, vigorously fanning a breeze round her face and neck, attempting to calm herself and counteract the smell of sweating crowd and horse dung.

She was not a heavy burden and her bearers were trying their best but the leather soles of their sandals were slippery after walking over grass and quite unable to grip the surface of the large wet cobbles.

Bron could hear them cursing and swearing as two of them slipped yet again, this time into the storm water channel at the side of the road, and the litter tipped precariously as the remaining six struggled to balance it between them.

Clinging to the wooden framework, Bron felt sorry for them and pulled the curtains aside and leaned out.

The Scarlet Seal

"I'm not in a hurry," she said. "You can slow down. It doesn't matter what time we arrive home as I've been given the whole day off."

The pace slackened and she was glad of the relief of a smoother ride.

Behind her, she suspected, and certainly around and ahead of her, other slaves were experiencing just as much difficulty in keeping their litters and carrying-chairs under control.

One such was an enclosed chair that lurched past her own litter. A woman's shrill and angry voice projected from inside, berating her slaves for their clumsy efforts and lack of speed.

It's hardly their fault, thought Bron, sympathising with the young men at each end of the two carrying shafts, who were stripped to the waist and sweating and panting in the heat. Bron guessed that their passenger was no light weight.

The chair drew ahead and was lost in the press of the crowd. Bron decided she would be very glad when they had left the throng behind and could make more pleasant progress towards the city.

Suddenly, there was a great commotion in front of them and everyone was brought to a standstill. *What now?* she wondered and sighed with exasperation, thinking it would be quicker to walk.

"Young man!" she called to a lad of about sixteen years who was standing a few feet away. "Come here!"

The boy came across to her. She reached into the embroidered bag hanging from her girdle and gave him a coin.

"Find out what's happening ahead and come and tell me."

He was soon back, chuckling.

"They've tipped an old lady out of her chair," he informed Bron.

"Is she hurt?"

"Not enough to quieten her tongue, but her nose is bleeding and they've broken one of the shafts!"

The throng began to move forward again, Bron's litter with it. Eventually, they drew abreast of the accident. The 'old lady' looked little more than forty. She was well fleshed out, and obviously of high station, judging by her fine embroidered tunic and jewellery. Sitting where she had fallen, she was ungraciously refusing all assistance, and was screaming at her slaves, who were trying to right the boxed-in chair. It now had only one usable shaft, the other having snapped in two.

"What do you expect me to do now? Walk? You'll get me to the circus if you have to carry me the rest of the way! And don't expect any leniency! You're in for a good whipping when I arrive home, then you'll be sold at auction in the Forum next week to pay for the damage!"

The four frightened men righted the chair with difficulty, helped by two or three bystanders, then pushed their way through the throng, carrying the damaged chair as best they could.

Their mistress was still sitting in the roadway.

"Just look at my tunic, there's blood everywhere!" she was wailing as she gesticulated vigorously with one hand to those about her and held a scarf to her nose with the other, trying to staunch the blood.

Bron ordered her slaves to stop and lower the litter. She swung her legs round and stepped down without waiting for them to place the box in position. With genuine concern, she approached the woman.

"Please let me help you," she offered and received a resigned nod. Bron appealed to two matronly onlookers and together they raised her, dusted her down, then retrieved a sandal and her other possessions that lay scattered around. The woman grunted her thanks. The two helpers disappeared back into the crowd, which was moving on again, the spectacle over.

"Are you all right?" Bron asked. They were being jostled on all sides.

"Peasants!" the woman shouted at the crowd in general.

"Are you heading for the chariot races?" Bron asked her.

"Yes, and if I'm not in our box for the start, my husband will never let me hear the last of it!"

"Why don't you take my litter?" Bron offered. "My slaves are most careful. They'll give you a comfortable ride, or as comfortable as possible in this crush."

The woman looked hopeful, then doubtfully at the conveyance. "There's only room for one," she pointed out, "especially one my size."

"That's all right," said Bron, "I can walk alongside. We can take you as far as the entrance. I'm on my way back to the city."

"That is so kind of you. I do appreciate it."

As several attempts to get her onto the litter were unsuccessful, and she was becoming increasingly embarrassed and irate, Bron told the slaves to set it down on the cobbles. Climbing on was therefore easier, though raising the burden proved a problem. Bron was glad there were eight of them. At last, this feat accomplished, pausing only to flex their muscles and take deep breaths, they moved forward.

Bron chatted to her guest as she walked along by her side, watching where she placed her feet but keeping up without difficulty as the pace was slow.

The bleeding having stopped, the woman fanned herself vigorously, using her own ivory fan as well as the feathered one Bron offered her. When she had cooled down a little and recovered her breath and composure, she launched into a diatribe against her slaves and described such punishments that lay in wait for them that the litter bearers began to look alarmed in case they too accidentally tipped her into the road. However, when they passed another, similar accident along the way, the woman calmed down and was slightly less aggressive.

They reached the circus and the bearers would have continued towards one of the entrances but the woman directed them to the right, skirting the back of a triumphal arch of massive construction. Bron was surprised and must have looked it.

"You don't know who I am, do you?" asked the stranger in amusement.

"No, I apologise – perhaps I should, but I haven't been in Rome very long."

"So you've never been to our chariot races?"

Bron shook her head.

"Then you are in for a treat today."

"Oh, but—" Bron objected, "I wasn't heading for the circus, I was on my way back to my employers' house in the city. It just so happened that I was stupidly on the Appian Way at this time."

"What's your employment?"

"I'm a nurse."

"Where in the city?"

"Palatine Hill. My master is a senator."

"His name?"

Bron gave it, not without feeling a chill.

"Hmmm. I know him – or perhaps I should say know of him. He has quite a reputation – for the ladies, I mean."

Bron felt uncomfortable and said nothing. The woman looked at her shrewdly for a moment, then said, "Hmmm," again and also fell silent, but not for long. A crowd of young lads were larking about in front of the litter, impeding progress, and she was soon ordering them out of the way and threatening dire consequences if they disobeyed.

Bron looked sideways at her and was intrigued. Obviously well fed, well dressed, imperious, confident.

"You haven't told me who you are," she reminded her.

"Nadica Calidonia," the woman said, "wife of Cato Calidonius. He's the president of the races."

Bron wondered if the president of the races was more important than a senator.

"And what's your name and where are you from?" asked the woman.

"I'm Bron, nurse to Honorius, the senator's son. I come from Britannia."

"Then that accounts for your accent. So, Bron, would you like to see the races? When are you expected back?"

"I've been given the rest of the day off."

"Then come and keep us company for a couple of hours – you'll enjoy it, I'm sure. We have our own box, of course, opposite the finishing line."

"Won't your husband mind?"

"Oh, he'll not object to a pretty girl in his party."

"Thank you, it will be a new experience for me."

By now, they were approaching a wide entrance, more ornate than those she had glimpsed along the Appian Way. They passed beneath the marble archway and into an inner passageway that followed the circumference of the stadium wall. It was cool there and dark, but that may have been because her eyes had not yet become accustomed to the gloom after the strong sunshine outside.

Nadica Calidonia gestured to the slaves and they held the litter close to the ground, allowing her to step off.

"Wait here till you are needed again," she instructed them. "Come, Bron, follow me."

She ascended a wooden stairway, with Bron in tow. At the top of the stairs, they emerged into the sunlight again and descended towards a boxed-in area. Nadica led the way through the back door.

The stone tiered seating in there was covered in long, thick, padded cushions, woven in bright colours – the colours of the racing teams as Bron later discovered – and embroidered with likenesses of horses, chariots and charioteers.

Several men and women already occupied some of the seats. Nadica greeted them all personally, introduced Bron as a friend, then made her way down to the front row where two men were haggling good naturedly, and Bron saw money changing hands. One of them left hurriedly and the other turned when Nadica called him. His toga could not hide a figure as corpulent as his wife's.

"You're late," he observed as she kissed him on the bald patch on top of his head.

"It's a long story," she said. "I'd like you to meet Bron. She's part of the story – I'll tell you later."

The man smiled genially at their young guest.

"Bron, this is my husband, Cato Calidonius." Bron dropped a curtsey and said she was pleased to meet him. He studied her and his smile widened.

"My wife's long stories don't usually have such beautiful endings," he said.

CHAPTER 15

"There, I told you he wouldn't mind having you here," Nadica smiled. "Come and sit with me. What's happening, Cato? Isn't it time to start?"

"The emperor hasn't arrived yet," her husband observed gloomily.

Nadica smiled sympathetically and patted his knee. "You can't expect him to be exactly on time after travelling for several days through the mountains. He'll be here."

"Is Emperor Honorius coming?" asked Bron excitedly. "I thought he never left Ravenna."

"He doesn't usually but he sent word that he intends to be here today. These are special races, you see," explained Nadica, "to discover the champion of champions, and he's going to present the award personally." She lowered her voice to a conspiratorial whisper. "But if you ask me—"

"Which no one is," interrupted her husband, trying to hush her. She ignored him.

"—if you ask me, he's also trying to take everyone's mind off what's happening on our borders."

"The threatened invasion?" Bron asked, remembering the speech Senator Loricatus had prepared for the Senate.

Nadica nodded. "Exactly. People are less likely to worry if they see their entertainment carrying on as normal and their Emperor present."

"You're being fanciful, wife. The pagans will never get in. Rome is strong enough to repel any marauding band of barbarians, however many of them there are and no matter how brilliant their leaders. You're talking treason. Be careful no one hears you or we could be in trouble. Bron, forget the silly woman said that."

"Said what?" asked Bron, and he smiled.

"Whatever the emperor's reasons," persisted Nadica, "there are not many people who know he's coming. Security has been very tight all along his route."

She directed Bron's attention to another box, more ornate, along to their right. It was decked in brightly-coloured swathes of material, again the colours of the teams, and a large, gilded Roman eagle guarded the roof above the viewing platform, its wings outstretched and an imperial crown on its head.

"That's the royal box," she said.

Bron leaned forward, resting her forearms on the wooden rail, to give herself a better view.

Around them, people were streaming in through all the entrances from the Appian Way, either choosing to sit at the same level as the track or climbing up into the tiers of stone benches. They had come in from city and countryside, their colourful tunics or white togas revealing their business, profession or craft – men, women and children jostling each other in noisy, good-natured anticipation of a day's enjoyment.

To her left, at the rounded end of the circuit, stood the ornate triumphal arch, a brick structure, its entrance secured by an iron gate, a balcony above it. She guessed it was reserved for Rome's elite.

At the other end of the arena was the starting gate. She counted twelve stalls, all wide enough to take competing chariots and horses.

Running almost the whole length of the arena was a central sandy barrier, several feet in width. At either end stood a tall pillar, and between the two, large statues of the Roman gods, Jupiter, Juno and Fortuna. Halfway along this spine was a wooden frame containing large circular holes, and into these, two stewards on the top of ladders were dropping large, white, wooden egg shapes.

"They remove an egg each time a lap is completed," Nadica said in answer to Bron's question.

There was commotion on the far side as into the arena ran a gaggle of clowns, chasing each other across the sand and up the stairways, playfully threatening the crowd with buckets of water, brushes, mops and paint. After a while, they were followed by troupes of somersaulting acrobats, then jugglers, and stilt walkers with long tunics down to their shoes, who threw brightly-coloured streamers at spectators in the higher seating.

Bron jumped as a fanfare of trumpets blared from the balcony of the triumphal arch, its iron gate now open, and there he was, Emperor Honorius, followed by an assortment of illustrious guests.

She gaped at the display of brilliantly-coloured apparel, the women's fantastic hair extensions above sparkling tiaras, and jewellery that flashed rainbow colours from ears, necks, arms and fingers of every member of the group, not least the young man leading them.

It took a moment for the impatient crowd to realise what was happening but their greetings were soon roaring round the blocks of seating.

"Hail Augustus!" "God bless Honorius!" "Long live the Emperor!"

He was smiling broadly and with large gestures was flamboyantly waving to all parts of the arena, then to Cato, standing at the rail. Cato bowed and called out a welcome, though his greeting was lost in the general hubbub.

Bron added her voice to the crowd's adulation and cheered as loudly as everyone else. However, she was slightly disappointed. At twenty-four, less than a year older than she was, she had expected someone taller, broader and altogether more imposing. His curls were tawny brown beneath a laurel wreath and his features soft in outline, apart from a prominent nose. In fact, his jewellery was more impressive than he was.

"Who's that behind him?" asked Bron, wondering about a diminutive woman, nondescript in brown, who was practically running in an effort to keep up with him.

"That's Thermantia, the Empress."

Bron then felt sorry for the emperor, obliged to make this political replacement for his dead wife, when every beautiful young girl in Rome must have been available to him. If his first wife had been as plain and unappealing as her younger sister, no wonder people were gossiping about the absence of an heir.

"And behind her is Galla Placidia, the emperor's younger half-sister," Nadica added.

Now she *was* impressive, tall and slim in a white, sleeveless tunic. Her hair, blue-black, against all fashion dictates, was cascading naturally to her waist in a mass of free-flowing waves.

The party mounted the steps and entered the royal box. Bron strained to glimpse them through the trellis-work of the wooden sides.

The crowd remained on its feet until the imperial party was seated. After an interval during which they unhurriedly fidgeted and settled themselves, the emperor walked to the front of his box and signalled to Cato, who in turn signalled to the far end of the arena, and there was another trumpet fanfare as eight horses led their golden chariots into the starting stalls.

"Only four teams in this race," Nadica commented. "Which do you favour, Bron?"

Though a distance away, Bron could see that coloured favours were flying from the handrails of the chariots, were tied to the men's belts and attached to all eight sets of harness.

"I know nothing about them, but I like the look of the green team."

The chariots were now under starter's orders. His green flag swished downwards, and the horses leapt from the stalls like eight hares released from poachers' traps.

The races were run in the opposite direction to the movement of a sundial and the carriageway on the competitors' left was wider than that on the right, to allow space for all the horses galloping neck-and-neck at the start. As they raced past, the red team slightly ahead, Bron drew back to avoid pelts of flying sand.

Having been drawn for the outside of the track, the red team lost ground as they swept round the wide curves, and was soon running last. They raced back to the starting gates and she noticed the stewards taking one egg out of the frame in the centre spine.

The chariots thundered past again. Now they were spread out slightly, green team leading, red team still bringing up the rear. The horses, glistening brown and black, were a joy to watch as each worked with its partner, sensing the other's thoughts and idiosyncrasies, obeying the commands of reins and whip. Another egg was removed.

Bron turned her attention to the charioteers in their short, white tunics. Behind the curved frames of their chariots, fully alert, with knees flexed and reins wound tightly round their arms, they stood firm in spite of the lurching and swaying of their vehicles, heads thrown back, yelling defiance, their expressions determined or exultant as first one then another drew ahead.

Since the monk Telemachus had been stoned by the populace and torn to pieces by wild animals in the Colosseum four years ago, while trying to stop the vicious killing, and since Emperor Honorius had publicly embraced Christianity, he had banned all combat fought to the death. Gladiators were no longer trained to take life in the arena and the celebrated heroes of the past who had survived were ageing, so it was no wonder that the young, handsome and brave charioteers were now the darlings of the populace.

Bron's excitement mounted as the teams raced by yet again. She looked across to Nadica, who was standing and waving a blue scarf, shouting encouragement to the team she favoured. Another egg was removed and then another. They were halfway through the race and Bron thought that the pace was slowing somewhat. The clamour of the crowd was increasing in volume, though.

During the fifth lap, the yellow and blue chariots collided on the bend in front of the triumphal arch.

With effort and admirable skill, the driver sporting the yellow emblem steadied his horses and stayed upright but the other, the blue team, keeled over. The charioteer was thrown backwards out of the damaged chariot but also out of the way of the horses' flailing legs. He rose gingerly to his feet, staggered a little, then raised his left arm in salute. As one, the crowd raised their left arms in acknowledgement and loudly applauded his courage, Nadica among them.

He limped to the nearest exit, stewards appearing from nowhere to release the horses from the traces and lead them out, while others dragged the chariot away and raked the sand where it had been gouged into ruts or flung into heaps.

This was accomplished only just in time as the remaining three teams were bearing down upon the collision area, the green team leading, the red team some way behind and the yellow team bringing up the rear.

Only two eggs remained and the crowd was growing delirious with excitement. Bron understood that an accident in a race added a thrill to the proceedings and satisfied the blood lust of the spectators. Uneventful races would cease to draw the crowds in such numbers – there must have been ten thousand people present.

She had grown hoarse, urging on the team she had chosen, but the outcome of the race was hardly in doubt and their positions had not changed when green team was first to cross the finishing line opposite Cato's box.

"Congratulations, Bron, you chose well," he proclaimed, "but regretfully no luck for me with my wager!"

"What happens now?" Bron enquired.

"As the emperor is present, he will award the winning team," Nadica told her, "with a rosette to fix to the chariot, one for each of the horses, and a laurel wreath for the charioteer."

"No money prize?"

"Only for the champion of champions in the last race. The rest compete solely for the honour."

Bron watched as the winning driver strode to the emperor's box to receive his laurels. With the wreath firmly planted on his head, after a right-handed salute to the emperor, and fixing the rosettes in place, he mounted the chariot again for his lap of honour and exit from the arena to the cheers of the crowd.

A steward entered their box, closely followed by the betting agent Bron had noticed before the race, and spoke to her host.

"Inform the emperor that I recommend the purple team," he said. "They have a good record here when the track is slightly wet."

While Cato and his agent discussed the merits of the teams in the forthcoming race and another wager was placed, Bron wondered how everyone knew who was taking part and for the first time noticed wooden boards placed at intervals along the top tier of seating, on which stewards were changing names and coloured emblems.

When the second set of competitors was finally lined up at the starting stalls, eight chariots this time, and the emperor was ready, he signalled to Cato, who in turn signalled to the starter, who dropped his flag, and the next race began.

The excitement continued throughout the morning. During the intermission, entertainers once again tumbled into the arena to amuse the crowd. When Nadica decided it was time to eat, they shared their lunch with Bron – a feast of cold meats, cheese and crusty bread, salad and fruit, all washed down with wine and beer.

Then the afternoon's programme commenced.

CHAPTER 16

No matter how many teams were competing in each race, it was obvious that the individual ability of men and horses was increasing and the pace of the laps was quickening. The spills became more frequent and injuries to men and horses more serious. One badly injured horse had to be stunned before its throat was cut in front of the spectators.

Bron had never understood the bloodlust of the Romans, and adding to her distress on witnessing this butchery, was a heated argument between Nadica and her husband about the amount of money he had been losing.

"You haven't won a single wager, not one," she accused him, "yet the money you are betting is increasing! That agent is growing fat on your bad judgement!"

Bron began to feel that she had had enough for one day and wished she could leave quietly.

"There's only one more race," Calidonius told her, perhaps sensing her unease, "the climax of the day, ten laps. There are eight teams competing, national champions all, each out for the others' blood and no holds barred because of the considerable prize money. A lucky wager could make a killing!"

Nadica snorted her disapproval at the same time as her husband's betting agent entered their box. Cato turned to his wife.

"All right, my dear," he consoled her, "I'll let Bron choose the winning team this time. We'll see if she has any better luck than I've had."

Bron was nonplussed. She had no idea who was racing nor of the likelihood of their crossing the line first. It had been fun to choose the winning team of the first race, but now she was anxious, knowing that he would be backing her guess with his hard cash. Nadica saw her confusion and came to the rescue.

"Just choose a colour, Bron, any of the colours you see displayed on the chariots. You can't do any worse than he's done, and he won't hold it against you if you put him further into that man's debt."

"Of course not," her husband agreed. "Well, what's it to be?"

Bron hesitated a moment more then decided, on a whim, "The scarlet team."

"Then the scarlet team it is," Cato told his agent, who happily took the wager and left the box.

The chariots began to move forward.

"They begin with a parade," Nadica explained, "a lap of honour before the race, because they'll likely not be in a fit state afterwards."

The mutual taunts of the parading teams began as soon as they left the starting stalls but ceased abruptly when they drew level with the emperor's box. There, they lined up their chariots and horses in splendid formation and saluted, right arms held high before them, fists clenched. They awaited the emperor's acknowledging salute before continuing.

When they drew level with the overseer's box, each turned his head towards Cato Calidonius. Bron delightedly received their smiles and nods of appreciation when she was noticed at the rail.

She admired these tall, fit young champions, beautiful in their youth and vitality, as they laughed and waved their coloured emblems and blew kisses to the adoring women and girls in the crowd.

As they passed each section, their supporters became increasingly noisy, shouting and cheering and stamping their feet, chanting choruses of courage and honour that degenerated into bawdy ribaldry when the parade reached the areas of cheap seating.

The charioteers' previously good-natured jibes were now escalating into shouted insults that culminated in an argument. Bron guessed the row was about who was most skilled, most devious, most likely to walk away with the coveted laurel wreath and pouch of gold coins – the Champion of Champions! By the time they had completed the lap, they were gesticulating, shouting obscenities, raising clenched fists and generally needling each other into a state of tension.

"It's all part of the foreplay," Nadica explained and looked affectionately across to her husband, who grinned in response.

The teams returned to the starting stalls and lined up ready, now in silent concentration, and the whole stadium quietened. After the raucous adulation, the hush was eerie, ominous, and Bron shivered in anticipation.

The starter raised his flag, his arm fell, the race began and the crowd resumed its enthusiastic cacophony.

There followed the fiercest and most frenzied, bad-tempered and vicious spectacle of the day. Each man was out to win, no matter at what cost to his fellow competitors. The final result was in doubt as first one team and then another took the leading position and was jostled or slammed out of the way. At these times, it was purely the skill of the charioteers that kept the horses on their feet and their chariots upright even when bouncing along on two wheels.

As the race progressed, the horses began to tire and the men seemed more vulnerable to misjudgement. At the start of the final lap, the crowd was emotionally drained and their shouts died away. All that could be heard above the cries of damaged men and squeals of injured horses were the vitriolic curses of the remaining drivers, the crash of the colliding chariots and the pounding hooves of horses still in the race.

The scarlet team won. For a few moments there was no recognition from the silent spectators, then a few people started clapping and soon the whole stadium was on its feet, stamping and applauding.

Cato Calidonius was laughing and telling Bron what a clever girl she was to have cleared the debt with his betting agent, and was pumping her hand up and down, at the same time enthusiastically banging her on the back.

She watched the winning charioteer swagger across to the royal box, waving his scarlet scarf above his head. He arrogantly proffered it to the emperor, who accepted it and draped it round his own neck. Four other competitors followed. A sixth was on his knees, trying to rise.

Along the track, another lay quite still where his horses had dragged him, the skin down his back and legs scraped off, red raw and bleeding. The eighth lay under his horses, screaming in agony as stewards tried to move the kicking animals off him.

The emperor held high the laurel wreath, placed it on the brow of the winner, and handed him a leather pouch. The young man turned, arms raised in triumph, acknowledging the acclamation of the crowd.

Stewards were running all over the arena. Those horses lucky enough to have survived uninjured were led away. Overturned chariots were being righted and all of them pulled, pushed or dragged across the sand to the starting gate, their emblems still flying defiantly.

Bron continued to watch as veterinary surgeons, long sharp knives raised high, slashed and slashed at the throats and necks of injured horses writhing on the sand, silencing their screams of anguish. Fountains of blood stained everything scarlet.

Bron involuntarily shook her head. Strangely, a mist in her eyes was filtering out every colour but red. She blinked, rubbed her eyes and blinked again, but could not shift the red haze through which she was peering at the scene in the stadium.

Except that it wasn't the stadium she was seeing. It was her home settlement, Byden. Byden under attack. Byden in flames. She saw them ascending, red and angry; heard the roar as the wind whipped them into greater fury; smelt and tasted again the billowing, acrid smoke as her neighbours' homes burnt to the ground; and heard their screams as they fought off their attackers and paid with their lives.

She had escaped then and knew she must escape now. Panic stricken, hardly aware of what she was doing and not heeding the rising crescendo of Nadica's voice behind her, she ran down the steps and out into the arena.

Instinct drew her to the exit at the far end of the stadium and she ran towards it, seeing nothing else, until intercepted by two burly bodyguards. They caught hold of her in mid flight, dragged her to her knees in the sand, and pinioned her arms behind her back.

The rough treatment, her involuntary cry of protest and sudden pain in her shoulders cleared the red mist from her eyes. All around were clustered faces of stewards and charioteers, staring at her, alarmed or amazed. A stentorian voice from above drew her attention upwards and she raised her head. The emperor stood looking down at her.

"Would you mind explaining what you are doing?"

The bodyguards hauled her to her feet. She was still confused. She didn't truly know *what* she was doing. It was a relief to hear the voice of Cato Calidonius behind her.

"Majesty, I apologise profusely. May I introduce Bron, a friend of my wife." The emperor did not answer but continued to frown. "This is her first time at the races and I think the slaughter took her by surprise," he finished lamely.

"Come up here, young lady," the emperor commanded. The men let go of her arms and Bron meekly obeyed.

"I am obliged to you, Cato. You may signal the completion of the programme."

Cato nodded and left and a few moments later the trumpets announced the end of the day's events, though the crowd knew better than to leave before the imperial party had quit the stadium.

The emperor addressed the charioteers, who still stood in disarray before him. "I congratulate you on your courage and skill, young men. You may go now. I think we have all had enough for one day."

The charioteers bowed stiffly as they backed away, their faces showing their disappointment at the lack of adulation displayed by their emperor.

"Come here, Bron," he commanded. Bron went across to him. "Now, what was all that about?"

"I—I don't really know, Your Majesty," Bron stammered. "It was all so bloody and horrible. I was in a red haze. I wanted to cry out that it was all wrong – I mean – I'm sorry, Your Majesty, I didn't mean—" She tailed off in confusion.

"Honorius, you're making her nervous – she means but she doesn't mean – she's just jabbering."

The emperor looked across to his sister. "Leave her be, Gally, she's making perfect sense to me."

Bron looked at Galla Placidia, who was a few years younger than her brother. How beautiful and dignified she was, quite unmoved by the bloodbath she had just witnessed.

The young woman's eyes glittered black as they met Bron's gaze. Then she turned to her friends and made some comment that caused much hilarity.

Bron flushed with humiliation and was painfully aware that she must look and sound such a peasant to them all. If only she could seep into the ground.

But the emperor was speaking again. "You're not Roman?"

"No, sir, I'm lately from Britannia."

"Ah, my cold and misty western islands. Then I apologise for what you've seen this afternoon. It was not intended to happen so, and I shall see that it doesn't occur again. We have progressed since the days of the gladiatorial games and there is no place for this carnage in the Rome that I rule, is there?" All Bron could do was shake her head.

His wife had remained silent throughout this exchange but had not taken her eyes off Bron. Now she moved across to her husband and with deliberation insinuated her arm through his.

"Shall we go, dear?" she suggested. "There's nothing more to do here." Removing his wife's arm just as deliberately, the emperor plucked the scarlet scarf from around his neck and held it out towards Bron. Astonished, she stammered her thanks but when she reached out to take it, he moved closer and, smiling, placed it carefully round her shoulders.

"To seal my promise."

Then he turned, mounted the stairs and quit the box, leaving his companions to fall in behind him.

"She's a looker!" Bron heard Galla Placidia comment maliciously to her sister-in-law, and wondered at the reply –

"Huh, for all the good it will do her!"

CHAPTER 17

Bron arrived home utterly exhausted and was glad the house was quiet. She knew that her mistress would be away from home for the night, and from what she had overheard at the villa, she didn't expect to see the senator until late next morning.

She guessed he would be very angry and had no idea what he would say to her, nor what the outcome might be, but she was too tired to think about it. All she wanted now was her son in her arms. She made straight for the kitchen.

Rius was sitting up in his crib, banging together some wooden ladles Cook had given him and chuckling at the noise he was making. When he saw Bron, he held out his arms. She scooped him up and laid her cheek against his softer one. He smelt deliciously of mint and apple and lemon and Bron smiled to know that Cook had been cuddling him.

"I've missed you," she said, kissing him, "but I'm sure you haven't missed me. How was he, Cook?"

The older woman looked up from fluting the edge of her pie crust. "No trouble. Pleasure to have him and we went for a lovely walk this afternoon, didn't we, Rius? But I want to hear all about your meeting with her grace."

Bron shook her head. "I didn't see her. It was all a big mistake. It was awful!" Cook regarded her quizzically.

"But I ended the day by going to the chariot races – and, would you believe it? Emperor Honorius spoke to me!"

"Emperor Honorius? Never!"

Cook wiped her floury hands on a convenient cloth and sat heavily on a wooden bench.

"Sit yourself down and tell me all about it. I've always been one for a good story, and I've plenty of time today as master and mistress are off gallivanting."

Bron sat on a stool with Rius on her lap. Slowly at first, feeling her way and not sure how much she should reveal, she began to relate all that had happened to her from the time she left the house that morning. Cook hardly interrupted at all, except for an occasional, "Well, I never," and "Stands to reason, don't it?" and didn't seem at all as surprised as Bron thought she would be. With growing confidence, she described everything exactly as it had happened at the villa.

"But after all that upset," continued Bron, "I had the most amazing adventure!" and she told her about helping Nadica Calidonia, and the chariot races, and meeting the emperor.

Cook's eyes were wide now. "He said that to you? And he gave you that scarf?"

Bron unwound it from around her neck and handed it to her friend.

"The very same. A token of his promise, he said. His scarlet seal."

It was at that moment that Rius looked up at Bron and said, "Mum." She regarded him with amazement.

"Cook, did you hear that?"

"I did," replied Cook. "Could've been a coincidence, of course."

"No, no, he called me 'Mum'. Say it again, Rius, *please*," Bron said, "like this – mum, mum, mum," and he obliged, repeating the word several times as she had done.

"There was no mistaking that!"

"Bless him, the little lad thinks you're his mother."

"But, Cook, I *am* his mother!" The words were out before Bron could stop them. She clamped her hand over her mouth but it was too late.

Cook stood open mouthed, then rallied her senses and smiled broadly.

"Thought as much, I thought as much!" she chortled triumphantly. "I said to Izmira only the other day, that girl treats him like he was her own, I said – ask her. You ask her. Like her own, I said. Ask her if I didn't say that."

Bron was contrite. "I shouldn't have told you. I promised the mistress not to tell anyone. If she finds out, I'll be in the most awful trouble!"

"Don't worry about it, I won't tell a soul."

"I could lose my job over it."

"And they'd make you leave without him?"

Bron nodded.

"We can't have that. That would be a terrible punishment. I won't utter a word, not a word, I promise!"

When Fausta Loricata returned late next morning, she sent at once for Bron.

"Well?" she demanded, "I can't wait to hear what happened! Did you tell her grace about us?"

Bron had prepared what she would answer when asked this question.

"Madam, I'm sorry to say that I didn't meet her – she didn't arrive."

"Not at all?"

"No."

"Oh dear, Laenus will be so disappointed."

"But I went one better – I met Emperor Honorius himself."

Bron related to her amazed listener all that happened after she left the villa on the Appian Way.

"And that is the emblem he gave you?"

Bron handed over the scarf.

"You were taking a stupid chance, Bron, criticising the conduct of the race," her mistress said. "You're lucky it didn't do you any harm. This is the truth, I suppose?"

"Of course, madam. The litter bearers will tell you so, if you ask them."

"Very well. Now describe exactly who was in the emperor's party. I have invited some friends with their children and nurses here tomorrow, to give baby Honorius some playmates, and I want to be able to tell everyone the details, otherwise they won't believe me, because the emperor so seldom leaves Ravenna."

Bron was ready next morning when Julius came to the nursery to tell her that she was required in the triclinium. When she walked into the room, with Rius in her arms, it resembled a nursery.

Her mistress had invited five friends, high-born Roman ladies, all with young children and attendant nurses. The mothers were lounging on the couches round the table, sipping wine and nibbling various fruit, nut and sweetmeat selections laid out for them.

Their children were sitting on rugs and blankets on the floor, happily engaged with cuddly, soft toys, wooden dolls with moveable limbs, wooden blocks and rubber balls, while their nurses sat with them or on low stools, watching the activity and chatting quietly to each other.

Fausta Loricata took Rius out of Bron's arms and walked with him round the group of mothers, introducing him, then passed him back to Bron and returned to her goblet of wine. Bron settled herself and him on a blanket and began to ask the names of the other nurses and their charges.

There was a blue ball among the toys, which Rius seemed to think was his exclusive property. He played with it for some time but then one of the little girls decided she wanted to join his game. Rius was not prepared for this intrusion and took the ball back. A tussle developed and he began to cry with frustration, which crescendoed into screams, and he threw the ball from him.

"Nurse, stop Honorius screaming like that!" Fausta ordered.

Bron did her best by trying to hold and rock him, but he would have none of it and began rolling about the blanket with fists clenched, limbs flailing, kicking anyone who tried to pick him up, still screaming.

"Nurse, stop his noise at once!" Exasperation was creeping into Fausta's voice.

"Rius, please," Bron begged him, but he was past reason and had worked himself up into a rage.

Fausta slipped off the couch and came over to Bron.

"Madam, I'm sorry. I think I should take him back to the nursery and calm him down."

She was unprepared for what Fausta did next. Her employer scooped up Rius from the blanket, pulled aside his tunic, and slapped his bare thigh so hard that he stopped crying immediately.

"That's how you should treat a bad-tempered and disobedient child!" she cried triumphantly.

Bron looked at the bruise reddening on the soft skin above his knee and all the restraint she had painfully mustered over the previous five weeks erupted like a volcano.

"That's not how you should treat a baby! You don't deserve him and you don't deserve to be called a mother!"

She grabbed him from her employer and turned her back, holding him tightly to her and shielding him from any further attack.

There was silence in the room as everyone stared at her in disbelief, and suddenly Bron realised what she had done.

Apologise! Apologise! Before it's too late! she told herself but knew it was already too late. Slowly she turned round.

Fausta's face had drained of all colour.

"How dare you! How dare you speak to me like that!" she hissed between thin lips. "Get back to the nursery and stay there till I send for you. Take him with you. Both get out of my sight!"

"Madam, I'm sorry, I'm sorry!" Bron panted.

Rius was crying again.

"Go! Just go!"

Bron fled with one of the women's words of advice assailing her ears: "You should have dismissed her on the spot, Fausta, on the spot!"

Instead and surprisingly, her punishment was no more than to be confined to her room with the door locked for two weeks. She could only conclude that Fausta needed her while she was feeding Rius and was so thankful she had not yet weaned him.

He had been taken from her and was being looked after by a variety of household staff and fed with milk she expressed. He was severely sick during this time but she was not allowed to see him.

Unknown to Fausta, Bron received news, whispered outside the door by Cook, Izmira and even Julius on one occasion, but they were her only contacts with anyone at all friendly.

Finally, the day came when the door was unlocked and Bron was summoned to the triclinium to apologise to her mistress, which she did unreservedly. Rius was returned to the nursery.

CHAPTER 18

The first time Bron saw the senator after the incident in his villa was one morning several days after her incarceration.

Fausta was out, visiting her ailing mother, but had indicated that she would be sending for Bron and Rius before her midday meal, to receive the weekly report on his health. This was under close scrutiny at this time as there was much sickness down in the city.

Bron was hurrying on her way to wake Rius from his morning nap, so she could feed and change him before Fausta's summons, when she met the senator emerging from the couple's bedroom. She couldn't ignore him.

"Good morning, sir."

After the greeting, she fixed her eyes on the ground, hoping to hurry past and reach the safety of the nursery, but he stood in her path, blinking in the sunlight and running his hand through his unusually tousled hair.

"Yes, it is, Bron, a very good morning indeed!"

His flushed cheeks and shining eyes confirmed his mood but the light teasing tone and welcoming smile he usually reserved for her were absent.

She was relieved when he stepped aside to let her pass, but as she drew level, he grabbed her arm and pulled her towards him, and with his other arm around her waist, gripped her so tightly that he was crushing her swollen breasts and hurting her.

"That was a very clever trick you played on me, my girl. Just pray you don't live to regret it! I'm not one to be dallied with!"

She was just about to protest that she was the one who had been dallied with when a movement in the darkened bedroom behind him attracted her attention towards the door. Abruptly, he let go and pushed her away from him.

What is he up to now? she wondered.

"Laenus, my darling." This time Bron recognised the voice instantly. Its owner appeared in the doorway, and surprised at seeing Bron, took cover behind him.

"The lady is embarrassed to meet you in these compromising circumstances, Bron—"

Lady! thought Bron, *that's the last name I would give that Julia!*

"—but she doesn't know how loyal you are to me, and how discreet. Devoted and discreet, aren't you, my dear?"

"Yes, sir," Bron mumbled miserably. She seldom saw eye to eye with Fausta Loricata but would not wish this situation on any wife – intimacy between her husband and so-called best friend, and to top it all, in her own bedroom and presumably in her own bed.

"You wouldn't do anything to upset the arrangements in the household, would you, Bron?"

He was looking at her intently and she understood the warning: not to breathe a word that would upset the status quo, not for him, nor his wife, nor more importantly, for herself. The consequence of disobedience did not bear thinking about.

Still cowering behind her lover's back, Julia was studying Bron's face, trying to read her intentions.

"Oh, do come out from behind me, Julia," the senator said impatiently. "I tell you, Bron knows when it's in her own interests to keep her mouth shut."

Julia emerged sheepishly. "But, Laenus, all servants tittle tattle." She looked up at him, her dark eyes wide and pleading. "Darling, you must dismiss her."

"Nonsense," he said. "I told you, she knows when to hold her tongue."

"But if there was even a whisper—"

"There won't be."

"It would ruin my husband's chances of becoming Constantine's deputy if there was any scandal about me. We appear together publicly, we hold hands, we present a loving and united union, soulmates, playing happy families – it's all rubbish, as you know, but if I did anything to hint at the pig shit our marriage really is, and he lost the campaign because of it, I'd disappear overnight – I don't have to tell you what a bully he is."

She stood very close to him, immersed in the intensity of her pleadings. They seemed to have forgotten that Bron was still standing there, listening to it all. Finally, the senator looked across at her.

"All right, Julia, I hear what you say. But Bron will be silent on the matter. She has too much to lose, and she knows it. Isn't that so, Bron?"

"Yes, sir." Her voice was barely audible.

"Anyway, I can't dismiss her. Fausta engaged her and it is Fausta who will have to give her notice, and she's not likely to do that when she is so good at her job and our son is doing so well."

He put his arm round Julia's waist.

"So stop worrying. And now I must get you out of the villa before Fausta returns."

CHAPTER 19

It was an afternoon about two weeks later that Fausta announced her intention of taking Rius visiting for a couple of hours, without Bron.

"I want him to get to know me better," she said. "We spend so little time together, just the two of us."

"Madam, he may tire you. Why don't you let me come with you?" Bron wheedled, not knowing the family to which he was being taken and not trusting Fausta to look after him properly.

"I've already rested for an hour. If I tire, I'll hand him over to their nurse," Fausta said, and the conversation was at an end.

They arrived home early evening. Bron had been hovering by the front door for some time and could not wait to take her son from the arms of her mistress, who was glad to relinquish the burden.

"Oh, Bron, thank goodness you're here. Get Honorius to bed, will you, straight away? He smells so – I think he's dirtied his nappy on the way home. I don't know when I've been so tired. He's such hard work."

Bron guessed that any hard work had been borne by the other family's nurse and not by her mistress.

"My poor love," commiserated her husband, who was crossing the hall at the time.

"I want him completely weaned off your milk by the time we go visiting again, so I don't have to fight with him to take the bottle," Bron was warned.

"I'll try," she conceded reluctantly.

"You'll not only try, you'll succeed!"

"Yes, madam."

Back in the nursery, Bron undressed her son and let him roll around naked on blankets on the floor. She took off her over tunic and knelt beside him, placing his colourful bricks and soft toys slightly out of reach so he had to wriggle and stretch for them, and laughed as he chatted to her in his own way.

"Supper, bath and bed for you," she told him and was delighted to hear him repeat, "Mum, mum, mum," in reply.

"I didn't know he'd begun to talk."

Bron scrambled off the floor in confusion.

"No need to get up," the senator said. "I'll come down to your level."

"Sir—"

"Don't want to disturb your routine," he said genially, kneeling and pulling her down beside him. "I've taken it into my head to help you put him to bed. He should get to know his father, don't you think? There's time before Fausta and I have our evening meal."

He knelt on all fours and rolled a red leather ball towards the baby. "So, he knows his mother now, does he?"

"It's natural, sir, when we spend so much time together."

"Just don't let Fausta hear him saying that word. Of course, you are his mother. No getting away from it. Fausta can't do for him what you do for him."

Bron gave him a suspicious, sidelong glance.

"But not for much longer, eh? I heard her order you to wean him off those glorious breasts of yours. You'll have to do as she says, of course, and deprive the poor little chap. You don't know how I've been envying him such bliss all these months! As it won't be happening for much longer, I thought I'd come along and share the experience. At least I can watch if I can't partake."

"What?"

"It's an opportunity that won't be there for me much longer."

"It's not there for you now!"

"Oh, come along, Bron, be generous. By the look of you, you've got enough for both of us!"

"How dare you!"

"I dare because you're only a servant around here and you'll do as you're told!"

"How can you humiliate your wife so, under her own roof?"

"How can she be humiliated when she doesn't know? Come on, be nice to me for once. You won't regret it, I promise. We've got time."

"No, we haven't, because you're going, right now!"

"I'll go when I've had what I came for!"

Bron jumped up and crossed to the door and held it open.

"Right now!"

"Oh well," he sighed and sauntered towards her, but before she knew what was happening, he had his hand down inside her neckline. Panting now, with lips parted, his fingers caressed a breast then found the nipple and squeezed then released it, squeezed and released, until she felt her milk running. He laughed in satisfaction.

Without thought, she brought her right hand up and slapped him hard across the face. When he still pinched, so fiercely that tears came to her eyes, she slapped him again, but this time with concentrated deliberation so that her palm and fingers came away tingling, leaving a red mark across his cheek. She knew she must have hurt him.

He pulled his hand out of her clothing and wound both arms around her, trying to kiss her, but she turned her face away. His lips and teeth tugged at her ear and she struggled to raise both hands to push his head to one side.

For several moments he wrestled with her, she meantime still holding his head in her hands, keeping his face away from hers. He had just pinned her against the door and was pushing his body up against hers when they heard footsteps crossing the courtyard and Julius calling him to his meal. Spitefully, he bit her on the neck then left abruptly, coughing and spluttering as he went to meet his steward.

Bron wrapped Rius in his blankets and fled to the kitchen, where between heaving sobs, she blurted out to an astonished Cook something of what had occurred.

"He'll have his revenge, I just know he'll have his revenge," she blubbered, "and on top of all that, he bit off my earring! I hope it chokes him!"

CHAPTER 20

"What d'you think master'll do?" Cook asked next morning as she held a piece of raw steak over the weal on Bron's neck. "Goodness, girl, I can see his tooth marks!"

Bron winced. "I don't know. That Julia told him to get rid of me."

"Of course, we all know she's not the only one but she's the one who chases him all the time. More'n male flesh can stand, and the master's all male, for sure. She's thumbing her nose at the mistress! No one else gets into their bed!"

"He said the mistress would have to dismiss me, he couldn't – but he's hardly likely to tell her that he had his hand down my tunic. She couldn't send me packing when I fought him off."

"She might, to save face. Believe you me, I've seen it all. Our betters care very much about saving face."

She turned the piece of meat over and held it in place again.

"Doesn't she know about that Julia? Doesn't she know about *her*?" Bron asked.

"Guess she might, she's no fool, but till someone makes her face up to it, she can pretend it's not happening. 'That Julia', as you speaks of her, is a very influential woman."

"Why so, Cook?"

"Because of the man she married – old enough to be her father and handy with his walking stick, by all accounts – not that you'd ever guess to see them about together – real happy couple, they look – but I've heard different."

"But what does he do that's so important?"

The Scarlet Seal

"Served Honorius and now Constantine – their right-hand man – and does all the dirty work like talking to that barbarous rabble on the borders. A lot's on his shoulders, making peace with Alaric. The emperor relies on him – we all do."

"They won't invade Rome, will they?"

"Never! Still, there's a lot at stake and any scandal about Julia would harm her husband. People would ask, if he can't control his wife, how can he expect to control the pagans? And it would take his mind off the emperor's business – not a good career move."

The piece of steak was becoming warm.

"If they split up," Cook continued, "he'd probably pension her off to keep her quiet, and I daresay she wouldn't be happy to live on what he gave her, and she wouldn't be welcome in Roman society no more. Of course, they're all up to the same goings-on, but our ruling classes are such—such—"

"Hypocrites?"

"That's the word, if it means they say one thing and does something else."

"Why, Cook, you're quite the politician."

"Common sense, if you asks me. And the master won't want his name gossiped all over the city, neither, with him being so new to the Senate and wanting to impress Constantine."

She took the meat away from Bron's neck, inspected the bruising, then threw the tasty morsel to the floor. The cat grabbed it greedily and scampered out of the kitchen with it in her mouth.

"Does that feel better?"

"Yes, thank you, it's taken the sting away."

"It's still very red but is going black. Doesn't look good. People will get the wrong idea. You'd best keep it covered until it's quite disappeared."

"Yes, I will. And is that why the master married the mistress, because of her connections? He couldn't have been in love with her or he wouldn't treat her so callously."

"You've got it in one. My advice is, keep out of their way for a while and hope nothing comes of it."

"I'm too good a nurse to dismiss."

"No one denies that. Of course, everyone guesses your secret – not that I've said a word, mind – but there are other good nurses, even if the mistress knows they welcome the master into their beds whenever he has the notion. She probably thinks you do, too. She'd never believe you fought him off. I wouldn't in her place."

Cook hardly took breath before asking, "But have you heard the latest from Izmira?"

"No-o."

"Seems that the mistress went to have her nap yesterday afternoon, before she took Rius visiting – not in her own bed or on a couch somewhere, as usual, but in *their* bedroom – and found the bedclothes all rumpled."

"Of course, we all know why," Bron said with a grin.

"Mistress called Izmira and gave her a right dressing down, I can tell you. Had the poor girl in tears. Of course, she said she'd made the bed that morning."

"'Then go and do it again!' says mistress. Seems to me, the pair of them really should be more careful."

"I'm sure Julia has many accomplishments," mused Bron, "but I shouldn't think bed making is one of them."

The first intimation that anything serious was amiss was later in the afternoon when Cook sent one of the slaves to find Bron to ask her to come to the kitchen immediately. She hesitated. Rius was fast asleep in his push-cart in the shade of the verandah.

"It's urgent, miss," said the slave. "Don't worry, I'll watch the baby and make sure the cat don't curl up on top of him."

Bron thanked her and hurried along to the kitchen. She found Cook with her arm around the shoulders of a distraught Izmira, who was sitting at the table, crying inconsolably. Cloth in hand, Cook was fighting a losing battle as she tried to mop up the tears streaming between the girl's fingers. Defeated, she thrust the cloth at Bron.

"You try," she said in frustration. "Can't get a sensible word out of her. See if you can make head nor tail of it. Izmira, for pity's sake, tell Bron what's wrong if you won't tell me."

"What is it, Izmira?"

"I can't, I can't," sobbed the girl, gulping in quantities of air. "It's bad what I done, bad, bad," and her slim little body was wracked again with violent sobs.

"Is it something to do with the master?" asked Bron, suspiciously.

"Yes, but not like what you mean."

"Then what?"

"Miss, I can't tell you, and you've been so kind to me!" and with that she rushed out of the room, leaving Bron and Cook looking at each other, completely mystified.

"What do you think she's done?" asked Bron.

"Beats me!"

"Something to do with Julia and the unmade bed?"

Cook said no one had seen Julia for a couple of weeks.

"Perhaps he's getting tired of her," Bron suggested. "She's too easy, not a challenge any more."

Cook agreed. "You're the challenge to him now, and he's not getting his own way there. But, as for Izmira, being accused of not making a bed may have upset her at the time, but wouldn't send the girl into such parox—parox—"

"Paroxyms," said Bron.

"What you said – of crying. A telling off, maybe, a light beating at the most, but she's used to that."

"Oh well, we'll find out soon enough, I suppose."

CHAPTER 21

Fausta sent for Bron early next morning. She was told to leave Rius in his crib in the nursery and attend her mistress in the room in which they had first met.

Her employer was reclining on a couch, cushions scattered around, her face pale, eyes heavily lidded. She looked as if she had been crying. Bron had an overwhelming sense of foreboding, though she couldn't think of anything she had done to cause any displeasure.

"Come over here," Fausta ordered her.

Bron went over to the couch.

"Well?"

"Well what, madam?"

"Have you anything to tell me?"

"What about?"

"Don't pretend you don't know what I'm accusing you of!"

Bron's spirits sank.

"I'm sorry, madam, but I honestly don't know of anything I've done to displease you."

Fausta laughed but the grating sound was without mirth.

"You don't know? You don't know? How dare you! How did you think you could get away with it, under my own nose and in my own— Are you telling me you know nothing about this?"

She held out her hand, palm upwards, and there was something lying on it, something red.

"Come closer, Nurse, and have a good look. You can't deny it's yours, because I know it is."

The Scarlet Seal

Bron moved closer and picked up the object from the outstretched palm. It was her garnet pendant earring, the wire broken where the senator had caught it in his teeth while tugging at her ear two nights ago. She wondered what lies he had told his wife when he handed it over to her. Anyway, there was no point in denying it was hers.

"Yes, madam, it's mine. Where did you get it?"

"Well may you ask. Where did you lose it?"

Bron considered telling the truth but dismissed the idea and was at a loss how to reply. "I don't know."

"Then I'll tell you, young lady. Izmira found it – in the sheets. Not your sheets, may I add, but mine. In the bed I share with the senator! In my bed! No wonder the sheets were always tied up in knots! He took you there, didn't he? In my bed! Oh, don't play the innocent with me! It's been going on since the day you walked into this house!"

"Madam, I haven't – we haven't – not once!"

"Not even in his villa? Going to meet the emperor's grandmother! Dressed up in all your finery! Do you take me for stupid? The slaves talk, you know!"

"Then you also know that I wasn't there long enough to do what you're suggesting – and how about the other visitor?"

"I'm aware of that, too."

"Truthfully, I have always fought him off!"

The grating sound came from Fausta's throat again.

"Fought him off? So you admit he's been at you like a stag in rut from the moment you set foot in this house – don't think I haven't noticed, though I tried not to – and, for the record, no woman fights my husband off! Haven't I had to put up with it all our married years? Well, nothing to say?"

"Only that I am innocent! The earring was planted there."

Suddenly, the reason for Izmira's distress became clear. "Your husband made Izmira say she found it in your bed—"

"And how would my husband be in possession of one of your earrings if you weren't wearing them every moment you two were together? He bought them for you, didn't he?"

"Yes, but only because I helped him with his speech."

"A politician are you now, as well as a nurse and his whore? It seems we haven't been paying you enough! Do you still insist you are innocent?"

"Yes, with every breath in my body."

"Then what about this?"

Before Bron realised what was happening and could stop her, Fausta had jumped off the couch, crossed the gap between them, and pulled Bron's shift away from her neck. She sucked in her breath.

"I thought I wasn't mistaken. What a pretty sight! How many more of his love bites are there all over your body? Get out! Get out of this room! Get out of this house! Get out of our lives! You'll find your things flung out in the carriageway, and I hope the horses have shit all over them!"

Bron reeled at the hatred and venom directed at her.

"All right, I'll go, once I've collected Rius."

"You'll do no such thing! Rius stays here! He's our child, remember?"

She crossed to the table by the window and rang the bell.

"But, madam—"

"You should have thought of that before you threw yourself at my husband."

"I'm not leaving without my baby!"

Fausta was screaming at her now. "How many times do I have to remind you that he is not your baby, he is ours, bought and paid for?"

Julius entered the room.

"Julius, this person is leaving, now, straight away. Please escort her out of the front door and do not allow her to set foot in any other part of the house. If you have any trouble, call the slaves from the garden or stables. Now, Julius, now!"

"Yes, madam. This way, miss, come with me."

"I'm not going and you can't make me!" but before Bron knew it, she was in the hall on her way to the front door, with Julius's hand clamped firmly under her elbow. She tried to pull away and his grip tightened.

"Julius, I can't leave him behind!"

"Miss, there's nothing you can do about it!"

"But I didn't do any of the things she's accusing me of!"

"I believe you, but the mistress has given me her orders and I have to obey them. You heard what she said. You wouldn't get half a mile before they caught up and forced him out of your arms. You'll have to go, miss, there's nothing else you can do."

"Julius, please—"

"We'll look after him, Cook and Izmira and me – he'll be all right."

"No, he won't, not without me! They'll get a new nurse who doesn't know him or anything about him and he'll miss me, and he'll cry for me, then he'll be in trouble for disturbing them. I can't leave without him! I won't! I won't!"

"You've got to. You'll find a way to get him back, I'm sure, Miss. I'm so sorry, so sorry—" and he pushed her, resisting and protesting, out of the front door and closed it behind her.

She immediately began to bang and bang the lion's head knocker until her arm ached. Nobody came. Then she slumped down in a corner of the wall on the top step and sobbed and cried until she felt there were no more tears left in all the world. She walked along the gravel path to the gate and sat there on the grass, not wanting to leave while her son was still inside the house. A face or two peered out from windows then disappeared.

Finally, she opened the gate and went out on to the Hill. As Fausta had said, her few belongings had been scattered all over the road, and some indeed had been fouled by passing horses. There was nothing there of much value and all she would need were a couple of changes of clothing and her toiletries, which she retrieved and bundled up in her cloak.

Then, out of the corner of her eye, she saw something bright scarlet fluttering from the yew hedge. It was the scarf that Emperor Honorius had given her. Carefully, she extricated it, and wrapping it round her neck, turned left down the hill.

Her first thought was to find Adama. She had met her only once, in the bath house, as the girl had not kept the appointment for the following week. But Bron was sure her friend would give her somewhere to sleep until she had collected her thoughts and planned a strategy to get Rius back. The flat wouldn't be far away from her son and no one would have any reason to look for her there. She might even see him if someone took him for a walk, and perhaps be able to snatch him from the push-cart. Yes, that's what she would do, ask Adama to help her out. She would be discreet and not get in the way of the girl's work, especially if the old gentleman turned up.

Enquiries made of passers-by led her to Adama's apartment, but there was no answer to the barrage of her beating fists on the door.

CHAPTER 22

Bron didn't know how long she lay slumped against Adama's front door, too paralysed with misery to move.

The corridor grew dark. Other doors opened and shut and people came and went but no one took any notice of the figure huddled there, almost indiscernible in her enveloping black cloak, a bundle on the ground beside her, and incongruously, a bright scarlet scarf wrapped around her neck. Those familiar with the apartments were used to bizarre characters and mysterious activity along the corridors and preferred not to entangle themselves in matters that didn't concern them.

It was obvious that Adama wasn't coming home that evening. Bron was tired, her eyes swollen with crying and her body stiff and aching. She didn't want to spend the entire night on the floor but had nowhere else to go. With great effort, she heaved herself up and stumbled out of the building. To add to her troubles, it had started to rain.

Without thinking much about it, she found herself on the stony path that wound round the side of the hill. Pushing onward through dripping weeds and bushes that clung to her legs, she found herself outside the cave, sacred to the people of Rome, where the she-wolf had suckled Romulus and Remus.

In the deepening gloom, Bron could just see the small entrance, cleared of vegetation. She steadied herself with her hand on the rock face and felt her way into the darkness inside.

To her surprise, she saw that candles had been lit at the far end of the cave and placed in a small circle on a flat rock. By their light she was able to find a place where she could curl up in her cloak, using her bundle as a pillow. The friendly light gave comfort and a little warmth and she closed her eyes.

When she awoke, she was amazed that she had been able to sleep. The candles had burnt low but now a little daylight was coming through the cave entrance. She made her way towards it and looked out. Dawn was breaking over the city and colouring its temples and palaces in shades of pink and gold – a new day.

Bron's spirits rose above the misery of the previous evening. Rius wasn't far away and she knew she would get him back somehow or other. She had to. Perhaps Fausta would realise her mistake and apologise and take her back, but as Bron thought this, she knew that, even if the truth were discovered, that woman would never apologise.

Her stomach was grumbling with hunger. Hopefully, Adama would be home soon. She decided to go back to the apartment, but as she stood there, she heard rustling along the path and quickly drew back into the shadows.

"Miss! Miss, are you there?"

Bron stepped out onto the path in surprise.

"Izmira! What are you doing here?"

"Cook sent me with something for your breakfast."

"But how did she know where I was?"

"We've been watching you ever since you left the house." The girl burst into tears. "Oh, miss, can you ever forgive me for what I done?"

Bron drew her into the cave. "So it *was* you. Why, Izmira?"

"The master made me say I'd found your earring in their bed, so that her friend—"

"That Julia!" muttered Bron.

"—yes, her – wouldn't be found out. He said, if I didn't do as he told me, he'd sell me off to some old man at the next slave auction. I didn't want to hurt you, but I couldn't face being sold and having to—"

"It's all right, Izmira, I know it wasn't your fault."

"And I can't tell the mistress the truth or he'll do what he says."

"Yes, I'm sure he will. How's Rius? How's my baby?"

"Cook's been looking after him till they get a new nurse, but he's been crying for you, keeps saying 'mum, mum, mum' all the time."

"I'll get him back, Izmira, though I don't know how yet. So I must keep up my strength. What have you brought me? I'm so hungry."

"Bread and cheese and apricots, and a wineskin of water, and some candles."

Bron lit the candles from the flames of those sputtering out and set them in the warm wax on the flat rock. She then investigated the food, which Cook had wrapped in a cloth.

"This is so good," she said, munching the cheese. "I had hoped to stay with a friend in one of the apartments, but she isn't at home."

"Because the master has her in his rooms. She's been there since yesterday. The mistress is in such a state and has locked herself in her bedroom and won't come out."

"He's evil," Bron said.

"Cook knows Adama is your friend and sent me with a message to tell her what had happened to you. She came to the kitchen to see Rius, and says to tell you she'll be home just as soon as she can, but she doesn't know when that will be. As soon as the master lets her go, she'll come for you here and take you home. She said you'll be safe there, for a while at least. She said I must tell you all that, and I have, exactly as she said it."

"Thanks, Izmira. Then I'll wait for her here. Now you had better go before you're missed. Please thank Cook for me, and give my baby a cuddle and tell him I love him and—" Her voice trailed off into silence.

"We'll look after you both, miss, as best we can."

They were as good as their word. During the afternoon, one of the slave girls appeared at the mouth of the cave with a slice of Cook's game pie and a skin of wine, and in the early evening, Adama arrived to take Bron home.

Bron burst into tears and fell into the girl's arms. "I've got nowhere to live," she sobbed.

"It's all right, you can stay with me, if my gentleman agrees, until you find work. And I've seen Rius and he's fine, and Cook told me to tell you that she fed him a little mashed-up carrot and he seemed to enjoy it. Come now. Wrap your cloak around you so that no one will recognise you."

Bron wiped her eyes on the edge of the cloak and expressed her thanks.

"And don't forget to leave something for the spirit of the she-wolf. She's protected you while you've been here."

"I've nothing to give her."

"What about your scarf?"

Bron stroked the scarlet silk. "No, I can't give that away, for a reason I'll tell you later. But I haven't eaten all the pie Cook sent – it was such a large piece. Will that do?"

Adama laughed. "I don't know whether wolves eat game pie, but it's the thought that counts, and since you've nothing else—"

Together they followed the path back to the Palatine. It was the end of July and hot now that she had left the coolness of the cave. No breeze stirred the evening air and Bron felt uncomfortable and incongruous in her long, black cloak, though they met no one during their short walk down the hill to the apartment block.

She had been fingering the scarf beneath the cloak's folds when an errant thought occurred to her. It was improbable, impossible even, but had some merit and might be worth examining later. Until then, there must be other paths to tread, other strategies to try, though she couldn't think of any at that moment.

After all, he *had* given her his scarlet promise, and if all else failed...

CHAPTER 23

She spent a fitful night and was up long before dawn, her restlessness waking Adama, whose bed she was sharing. She was planning to go back to the Loricatus house to try to see Rius but Adama said that wasn't sensible.

"If you're seen, it could land you in a pile of trouble," she advised. "I'll go for you, just to find out how he is. Everyone's used to me coming and going."

An hour later, she heard the key in the lock and someone came in, slamming the door shut. Hurrying out into the hall, she almost collided with an elderly man. She knew who *he* was, though he was very surprised when *she* appeared.

"Hello!" he greeted her. "Who are you?"

"A friend of Adama," she explained, and smiled. "You don't recognise me, do you?"

"No, but any friend of Adama—" He looked at her keenly. "Though you're familiar. Have we met before?"

"Many times."

"We haven't—?"

"No," she assured him.

"I thought not. I know my memory's not as it was, but I think I would have remembered."

He smiled at her so mischievously that she couldn't help but smile back. She could understand why Adama was so fond of the old man.

He followed her into the triclinium and waited till she had made herself comfortable on one of the couches at the table before doing so himself.

The Scarlet Seal

"Come now, won't you put me out of my misery?"

"You're on the right track, we did meet at the brothel where Adama worked."

He frowned in concentration.

"Got it!" he exclaimed, slapping his thigh. "You're the girl with the golden ankle!"

"I was," Bron agreed, remembering the time when the brothel owner had given her a roof over her head while she was pregnant. To pay for her keep, she had acted as decoy, wearing round her ankle a gold torque that had attracted a lot of attention.

"You had a baby," he said. "I was there the night you went into labour. Adama wasn't concentrating on me – she would much rather have been with you."

Bron smiled and apologised. He was smiling too.

"How is he, your son?"

So Bron told him her story, from the time that Rius had been adopted by the senator and his wife and she had been employed as his wet nurse, to the reason for her appearance in Adama's apartment that morning. She omitted to mention where Adama had been for the last two days, though she knew he was very amenable about her friend's comings and goings, as long as she was there when he wanted her. Of course, she wasn't here at the moment, which was Bron's fault, and she apologised again.

"No need to apologise," he said, crossing to the window. He opened the shutters and stepped out onto the balcony, peering over the rail and potted plants down into the street, looking for Adama. "She didn't know I was coming round this morning. I just needed to get away for an hour before I start out for the Senate."

Bron followed him out onto the balcony. "Then you know Senator Loricatus?"

"Indeed I do, and I don't like what I know, and from what you've told me I like him even less. A difficult marriage is little excuse. Many of us have that."

He returned to his chair, patting her shoulder absent-mindedly as he passed.

She also went back into the room, thinking again how immaculately he was groomed – hair curled and tidy, fingernails polished, feet pedicured. She was almost dazzled by the whiteness of his toga, with its carefully adjusted complication of folds, and knew there must be a line-up of slaves in the background.

He saw her looking at him. "I know," he said, a little embarrassed, "there's a big age difference, but she means everything to me. I've never looked at another woman since I met Adama. I would gladly marry her, but it's not possible. If we had met years earlier I would have waited for her to grow up – but there, there's no point in agonising over all that again. Could drive one crazy! So I take what I can get. Of course, I know I'm not the only one in her life. Can't tie her down, you see – wouldn't want to do that. She's so young."

"She's so lucky," Bron couldn't help saying.

They heard the front door open and Bron stood up.

"I'll go now, Senator," she offered.

"No need, my dear. I only came to be cheered up and start the day right – and call me Crestus."

"Where are you, Bron?" Adama called.

"In here."

The girl entered the room, chattering as she did so.

"Rius is fine, you've no need to worry—oh! Crestus! What are you doing here so early?"

She headed for his outstretched arms. They folded round her and he gave her a hearty kiss, at the same time grabbing her buttocks and pulling her close into him. She turned her head towards her friend.

"You remember Bron," she said.

"I didn't at first, but she reminded me."

"I was going to ask your permission before she stayed here permanently."

"Bron has told me all about her troubles. She can stay until she finds work."

"Crestus, it's no wonder I love you so much!"

"I wish that was true, scallywag, but I know it isn't – and you don't have to say so!"

"But it *is* true!" She kissed him again.

He placed his fingers over her mouth and drew her down to sit on the couch. "None of that, or we shall have to ask Bron to go for a walk, and I may not get to the Senate this morning. A glass of wine instead?"

"Anything you want!" She disappeared in the direction of the kitchen.

"What sort of work will you be looking for?" he asked Bron.

"Anything I can get, except—you know—"
He nodded.
"Do you read and write and count?"
"Yes."
"Then I may be able to help you."

SECTION II

AD 408

August – September

THE ICONICUS HOUSEHOLD

CHAPTER 24

He was as good as his word and a week later had arranged an interview for Bron as maid to Talea Iconica, supplying his own reference for her. Talea was impressed.

"He wouldn't have introduced you to me unless he thought you were eminently suitable," she said. "He told me you had been dismissed by the Loricatus family on some trumped-up charge of which you are entirely innocent."

"That is so, madam."

Bron thought about her promise to her former mistress then decided that they, and not she, had broken their agreement, and decided to tell the truth.

"I see," said Talea Iconica on hearing Bron's account. "So you want to stay in Rome, near your son?"

"Yes, madam."

"If you hope to kidnap him, you must think again. They would hunt you down mercilessly."

Bron nodded glumly.

"At least I know you'll not leave this job while he's still living on the Palatine."

"Then, you are offering me the position, madam?"

"It seems so." Talea smiled. "Now, as to your duties."

They were not onerous and included the care of Talea's slim body from top to toe; from the elaborate tiers of hair, natural and false, piled high on her head, to her clothing, adornments, toilet articles, unguents, down to her painted toe nails and jewelled sandals.

When she left home for her social round, Bron would accompany her as companion and carry fans, umbrella or sunshade, and her silver box of pots and jars for refreshing her 'daytime face'.

So all details of her employment were arranged and three days later Bron began work as Talea Iconica's maidservant.

Her employer's husband, Carolus Iconicus, was a colleague and friend of Adama's patron. Of portly build, his round face clean shaven, with thick, naturally wavy medium-brown hair, only just beginning to grey at the temples, and brown eyes to match, he looked like what he was, a financier with a very successful merchandising business.

He had chosen to move his family to the southern peak of the Aventine Hill, among his warehouses and general stores and the high-rise apartment blocks of his neighbours. Unlike the Loricatus house, the building presented a blank wall to the street, all the windows and doors opening onto inner courtyards. Bron's room was more comfortably furnished than her last and she shared a small garden with the private rooms of her mistress.

Her first night there passed comfortably and she would have felt very content in her new surroundings if it had not been for missing Rius.

Next morning, just after the sun had risen, she was summoned to prepare her mistress for the daily round of visiting friends, and attendance at the baths.

Bron stood behind the chair in which Talea sat, surrounded by her beautifying paraphernalia and dish of powdered horn with which she was enamelling her teeth.

"Lock the door, Bron," she said between brush strokes. "My husband never sees me without my make-up on."

Bron wondered about this, as she had gleaned there were four children of various ages somewhere in the house, so the couple must share the same bed occasionally. Obviously, there was as much formality in the bedroom as in the triclinium.

Talea saw Bron's puzzlement reflected in the glass mirror, and winked mischievously, and Bron laughed.

Her mistress had slept in her undergarments, the usual custom, so was all ready to be dressed. On went a long silk tunic, pale blue with a silver belt and silver braid around the hem. Fausta Loricata had never worn such a richly embroidered garment.

"Now for the tweezers, Bron."

After pulling out a few unwanted grey strands, Bron dressed Talea's hair, layer upon layer, entwining the natural dark brown growth with tresses of a similar colour bought at the barber's. Finally, she pinned the concoction in place with ornamental silver hairpins.

"Kill any lice you find," she was told.

The tweezers were used again on a few facial hairs around Talea's chin, then all was ready for red ochre on cheeks and lips, a chalk and white lead mixture on face and arms, and finally soot mixed with a little oil for eyebrows, eyelids and a line beneath the eyes.

Throughout, Talea patiently instructed Bron and expressed pleasure at the girl's quick response.

From silver caskets, the jewellery for the day was chosen – a diadem of daintily-worked filigree silver for her hair, pale blue sapphire earrings and a deep blue sapphire collar for her bare neck, with matching bracelets and rings.

Bron picked up the dark blue cloak and, as instructed, draped it over her arm so that its dazzling silver embroidery was clearly on display.

A sprinkle of perfume hinting at rose petals, and Talea, with Bron in close attendance, was ready to face whatever the day held, and this was the procedure, with various omissions and additions, that they followed every day.

Bron enjoyed meeting the friends of her mistress, though she was never permitted to address any of them unless they spoke to her directly. They were all members of old Roman families and not newcomers such as she had met in her previous employment.

She also enjoyed the daily visit to the public baths, where the fashionable matrons of Rome spent hour upon hour, exchanging news and gossip and purchasing fripperies and accessories from the women who set up their stalls round the hot and cold pools.

She was not surprised at the number of times the name of Senator Laenus Loricatus was bandied about, with disapproval from the matrons but with giggles and sly winks from some of the younger women.

One afternoon, Talea announced that she was meeting her husband at the gaming tables that evening and Bron was to accompany her.

It was the first week of August, much too hot to stir very far during the day, but come evening, everyone seemed to be out and about, enjoying the cooler air. Talea rode ahead in her litter with Bron in another, much less ornate, following behind.

The porters wound their way through the throngs of people, conveyances and horses and turned into a side street, coming to a halt outside a tavern. Bron jumped off her litter to assist Talea to descend from hers, then followed her mistress through a door.

The man who stood behind the bar counter appeared not to be very busy and was chatting to two customers, neither of whom had a drink in his hands. The man bowed slightly towards Talea, who acknowledged him with an inclination of her head and crossed the room to the back wall. A slave opened a door as Talea approached. Bron followed her through and heard it being locked behind them.

She was surprised to find herself in a large room filled with tables at which men and women stood or sat, absorbed in various games of chance. The atmosphere was hot and stuffy, smelling of beer among odours of perfumes and perspiring bodies. Above the hubbub of voices, Bron heard the clatter of thrown dice and knuckle bones, and the chink of coins. An exultant shout accompanied by clapping came from one table and an argument was taking place at another.

"Can you see my husband?" Talea asked her.

Bron shook her head and followed her mistress as she pushed her way through the throng. They saw him at last, lying on a couch in a corner, concentrating on a game of backgammon. Talea bent and kissed him on the head then stood watching, explaining the moves to Bron, who had never played any game more complicated than draughts.

After a while, they left him to his preoccupations and moved away.

"There's no point in wearing my favourite blue and silver if I'm going to spend the evening standing in a corner," she complained to Bron.

In the centre of the room stood a long table around which were gathered eight or nine players, one of them a woman. Well-meaning onlookers were offering advice, encouragement or consolation. Talea found a friend in the crowd and while they were gossiping, Bron watched.

She saw that along the edges of the table, sections were marked from three to eighteen and players were placing piles of coins in no more than three divisions. At one end stood a sallow young man with dark rings under his eyes, three dice in hand. When he threw them on the table and announced the total, the player whose coins were piled in that division gathered in all the other wagers and paid a percentage to the young man. If no one had coins on the winning number, he scooped up all the money for the 'house'.

There was a lull as candles that had burned low were replaced, and in the brighter light, Bron saw a familiar couple at the far end of the table. It took her a moment to realise that they were Cato Calidonius, the overseer of the chariot races, and his wife, Nadica. Bron smiled as she heard Nadica berating him for continuing to play when he was losing so heavily.

When she saw Bron, she waved enthusiastically, then spoke to her husband. He looked up and smiled and beckoned her over.

"Bron, is that man signalling to you?" her mistress asked with some surprise.

Before Bron had finished explaining who her friends were, Cato Calidonius was at her side. He bowed to Talea and introduced himself and apologised for the intrusion but asked if he might 'borrow' Bron for a short while.

"I'm losing," he explained, "and I believe this young lady is my goddess Fortuna, who's very much missed since we've all become Christians. I'll bring her back to you after three games, whatever happens."

Talea smiled her assent and he took Bron by the elbow and led her away.

Nadica was delighted to meet her young friend again.

"He thinks you're going to bring him good fortune," she said without conviction.

"I can't guarantee it," laughed Bron.

"You did it for me at the chariot races with the scarlet team—" he reminded her. She blushed with embarrassment to remember her panic and flight across the arena, but he seemed to have forgotten the incident. "—and I believe you can do it again. If we win, you'll not go unrewarded, I promise you. Now stand by my left shoulder."

Players and onlookers shuffled along to make room for her.

They watched Cato place his coins on the number ten division. The young man started shaking the dice between his cupped hands and someone began chanting, a chant that was taken up by all those standing round the table.

"Five! Four! Three! Two! One! Throw!"

The final shout made him jump, and the dice flew out of his hands and down the length of the table.

"Eight!" shouted everyone. The woman player had won.

"Oh dear," apologised Bron.

"That was a practise run," Cato said cheerfully as the teller reached out a long stick with a crossbar at the end and pushed the wagers towards the winner.

"I'll try fifteen this time – if each dice shows the same number five, the stakes will be tripled."

Once more he stacked a pile of coins on the number he had chosen. The dice were passed back to the young man, each player kissing them or rubbing them on his person as they passed along the table.

The woman player slipped them beneath her neckline and rubbed them on her left breast, which caused much hilarity and ribald comments, especially when the player next to her took them from her but immediately dropped them, blowing on his fingers as though they were red hot.

The chanting began again. "Six! Five! Four!"

More and more people were drifting over to watch the play.

"Three! Two! One! Throw!"

This time, the young man was ready for the final shout and threw the dice only a couple of feet in front of him.

"Sixteen!" shouted the crowd. The woman had won again, much to everyone's amusement. Delighted, she called that every player's stakes should be raised.

"The winner can do that," explained Nadica. "If she decided that her luck was about to run out, she would call as little as one siliqua, but she obviously feels she is on a winning roll so has increased the call to three gold solidi."

One of the men asked if he could rub the dice where she had rubbed them last time. She hesitated before agreeing, which again caused loud laughter and much comment.

The crowd round the table was increasing all the time and Bron saw that Talea was pushing her way towards them.

Cato ran his hand through his thinning hair and his wife slapped him on the shoulder.

"Let her choose, Cato, let Bron choose! You're hopeless!"

"All right, all right. Can you do it for me, Bron? Bring me some luck? You select the number this time."

"Three," she said, without hesitation.

"Are you sure, dear?" Nadica asked her.

Cato was also apprehensive. "There's only one way that three dice can show a total of three," he said, pointing out the obvious. "It's the biggest gamble of all."

Bron did hesitate now.

"You are allowed to change your mind," Nadica told her.

"Would you have asked the goddess Fortuna to change hers?" The voice was Talea's from behind Bron's shoulder.

"No, indeed!" Cato decided.

"House doubles up!" called the young man. "Place your bets."

"Then three it is!" decided Cato and laid his coins on that number. "Put your left hand on my left shoulder, young lady!" Bron did as she was told.

Nadica whispered to her, "Don't look so worried, dear. I promise it won't make any difference to what we eat tomorrow."

The crowd was again entering into the fun of the game and this time someone started the chant at "Ten!" Enthusiastically, they worked their way down the numbers.

"Four! Three! Two! One!" Then they seemed to hold their communal breath for a teetering moment, before shouting as with one voice, "Throw!"

The young man did.

A great roar came from forty or fifty throats.

"THREE!"

Bron could not believe her eyes or ears. Each of the dice, red, blue and black, was displaying one bright white dot.

Cato whirled round and grabbed hold of her in a great hug while bouncing them both up and down. Nadica threw her arms around the pair of them.

"You did it! You did it!" she was shouting.

"How much?" Bron managed to ask, while still crushed against Cato's broad chest.

He turned back to the table.

"Every gold solidus on the board, tripled, then the house will double all that!"

"I'm so pleased for you, and relieved for me," she laughed, as excited as he was.

"What can I give you, my girl? Anything! Anything!" Cato promised, beaming.

"I don't want anything!" she protested.

He took hold of her hands and pressed a pile of coins into them.

"That's for now. I owe you a favour, Bron. I won't forget. You can call on me to redeem that favour at any time. You only have to ask."

"Now, don't forget, Bron, any time," Nadica repeated. "You never know when a favour might come in handy – and keep in touch."

"I will," Bron promised. She looked at her mistress and apologised for neglecting her.

"Not at all," Talea graciously assured her. "I enjoyed the excitement, but it looks as though my husband is ready to go home."

CHAPTER 25

On the infrequent occasions Bron was given a few hours of free time, which was usually when her mistress was accompanying her husband on formal business matters, she walked to Palatine Hill in the hope of seeing Rius, even at a distance, with his new nurse.

"You mustn't let him see you, Bron, it would upset him too much," Adama told her, "and upset you too. It's best not to see him. He's settling down, according to Cook's messages. They're looking after him well, so there's no need to fret."

But fret Bron did and would have been more upset if she had known what Adama would not tell her, that there were times when no one could pacify the little boy, usually at night, when he cried for his mother.

On one occasion, when walking up the hill, she spied Izmira ahead of her and ran to catch her up. Hearing footsteps, the girl turned, and waited for Bron to reach her.

"Izmira!" she panted, "I'm so pleased to see you."

"Miss, what are you doing here?" The girl looked around anxiously and sought protection in the shadow of a high wall. Bron followed her.

"I hoped to see Rius. How is he? How's my baby?"

"He's well."

"Tell me all about him! What can he do now? Is he standing on his own yet?"

"Almost and he tries to walk round a chair. Cook says he's really forward for a nine-month-old. And we all love him. Even the mistress goes to the nursery sometimes during the day just to see him – Cook says she's never known that before!"

"And the master?"

"He's not often at home these days, what with his duties at the Senate – *and other things*, Cook says. But you mustn't be seen hanging around here, Miss. We've all been told to let mistress know if we see you, so she can have you arrested. You mustn't come again."

"But I have to be here!"

"*No, you don't,* Cook says. Adama will pass on a message if there's anything you need to know. Trust us."

"I will have to," Bron acquiesced. "Thank you, all of you."

She turned and hurried away, tears blurring her vision.

Feeling too unsettled to go back to her room, and knowing that Talea would not yet be home, she decided to take a walk along by the Tiber. At the bottom of Aventine Hill, she passed through side streets and crossed the main thoroughfare named for the Marcellus Theatre, to which it led. This brought her to one of the bridges. There she turned right alongside the low brick wall that skirted the river, admiring the profusion of summer flowers and rich grass in the riverside gardens below her.

Arriving at the next bridge, she decided to cross to Tiber Island, and stepped onto the stone causeway that crossed two rounded arches. Situated on a bend in the river, the island had been created from deposits built up by the swiftly-flowing water.

A temple had been built there and, for a while, Bron wandered round the precincts, trying to gain some peace from the thoughts and plans whirling about in her head, all concerned with rescuing Rius, finding her friend Veneta and her other children, and getting them safely back to Britannia.

As for herself, she had to find her young officer, Aurelius Catus, and persuade him to go with her, before she could go home. Was it such an impossible dream?

She walked onto the shorter bridge on the other side of the island and rested her arms on the parapet, looking down into the waters, green from the reflection of the trees on this side of the river. She had never been across to the further bank and decided to explore the neighbourhood. However, it was evident that the area was poorer and less inviting than where she had started from and she decided to walk only a little way further then go back to the other bank.

The Scarlet Seal

Her path took her through a busy fruit and vegetable market and she gazed round with interest, avoiding rolling grapes and wet, slippery cabbage leaves on the ground between the stalls.

Hearing voices raised in argument and curious as to the cause, she looked across to one of the aisles, where she saw a tall, big-built woman with untidy fair hair confronting the anger of a red-faced, buxom stallholder. The two women seemed to be arguing about the price of a bag of peaches, which they were tugging backwards and forwards between them. Capitulating, the stallholder threw up both hands in frustration, letting go of the bag.

The sudden release sent the customer toppling backwards off balance and she fell heavily, the peaches rolling around her and towards the feet of a small crowd that had gathered to watch the entertainment. The fruit was scooped up by several quick-thinking shoppers and children, who happily disappeared into the crowd.

As a further stream of invective was directed towards the stallholder by the customer on the ground, Bron gaped, momentarily unable to move. Then, spinning round, she pushed her way back through the crowd, hoping she had not been seen by the angry customer.

It was Fabia! Fabia, one of the camp followers on board the ship that had brought them from Britannia to Italia – her enemy, who had been so jealous of the bo'sun's entanglement with Bron that she had once threatened to kill her if she went near him again.

Bron had no intention of going anywhere near him again, ever, but she knew he was searching for her and their son, and would take the boy away if he had a mind to do so. He would never think of looking for him in the Loricatus household on Palatine Hill, but she had now, of her own free will, foolishly strayed across the river and had walked right into their neighbourhood. How stupid she had been to let down her guard!

She presumed that Fabia and the bo'sun were still living together. Fabia wouldn't let him disappear out of her life, and he had always made use of her when there wasn't a more attractive dalliance available.

Hopefully, Fabia had not seen her. Even if she had, and told the bo'sun, there was no way they could know where she now lived – unless Fabia followed her! It was just what she *would* do, of course.

Bron hurried on, along by the wall protecting the river. She looked over her shoulder. There was no sign of Fabia. A few yards further on, she looked again. Still no sign. She came to the next bridge and began to cross. Reaching a point where a square reinforcing pillar provided pedestrian protection from vehicles and horses, and convenient concealment, she peered across the water. There wasn't a clear view along the bankside because of tree foliage but she saw nothing untoward – but wait! Hadn't a shadow just moved from one tree to the next? Or was it her imagination? Bron rubbed her eyes. There it was again! A woman? Perhaps nothing more sinister than a housewife hurrying home to prepare her husband's evening meal. However, she could take no chances.

Stepping out from her hiding place, Bron began to run across the bridge and did not stop half running and half walking until she reached the other side. Having weaved her way through the cattle market, she reached Aventine Hill and the Iconicus house, and safety.

She had seen no sign of anyone following her since leaving the bridge.

CHAPTER 26

"I'm bored, bored, bored," Thermantia complained from her couch, twisting round to plump up the cushions then falling back against them again. "There's nothing to do here in Ravenna. Why can't we go back to Rome?"

Her husband stopped pacing backwards and forwards across the black marble floor, ran his hand distractedly through his tousled curls and looked at her with irritation.

"Oh, do stop whining!" he growled.

Thermantia patted the covers by her side.

"Honorius, come and talk to me," she wheedled.

"Not now, Thermantia, I've too many problems to think about."

"Tell me about them. I may be able to help."

"Of course you can't help. You've never taken the slightest interest in politics, and if I tried to explain, you'd be complaining you were 'bored, bored, bored' after the first sentence."

"Not if one of your problems concerns my father. I must say, I don't like what I've been overhearing of late. You can't possibly believe any of it."

"What have you been hearing about the General?"

"Lies and rumours. They're not true, you know – that he planned the assassination of Rufinus, for one. It had nothing to do with my father. They may have been old enemies but his own troops mutinied and killed him."

Honorius was surprised that someone had made her aware of the rumours circulating at court, rumours that were causing him a great deal of anxiety.

"And what about King Alaric?" he challenged her. "He's your father's sworn enemy now but they were comrades in past battles and could be so again."

"Yes, they were, until Alaric changed sides. He's no king, not like you're emperor, Honorius. He's no more than a warlord. My father would never side with him and betray you and Rome."

"You're his daughter, you would say that. Anyway, you don't know for sure."

"I do know, husband, and if you think differently, you are being stupid and very disloyal to a man who has loved you like a son and has only ever looked after your best interests."

She had never spoken to him with such passion before.

"You should be more careful whom you call 'stupid'. Even an emperor's wife is not immune to a charge of treason."

He crossed to the open window and stepped out onto the long balcony. The August air was stifling and heavy with the perfume of full-blown flowers.

His Nubian bodyguard came towards him. "Majesty?"

Honorius waved him away, sending the huge black slave back to his post, and crossed to the balustrade. Resting his arms on the parapet, he looked out over the palace gardens. Their ornate pools and marble statuary and shaded walkways looked invitingly cool.

In the far distance, the marshy delta was crossed by a stone causeway, the only approach to the palace by foot or horseback. On the other three sides of the palace, the River Padus and the sea lapped at thick stone walls without windows or doors, and without crevice or ledge on which to find a foot or hand hold.

He loved it here, where he could live in luxury, safe from any pagan incursions, and life would have been perfect had it not been for the presence of Thermantia.

Hearing voices behind him, he stepped back into the room.

"Oh, Gally, there you are."

Thermantia was sipping iced water from a tall glass but now replaced it on the small bronze table by her side.

"What's she doing here?" she asked resentfully, eyeing her sister-in-law. "I thought she was still in Rome."

"I was until several days ago," replied Galla Placidia cheerfully.

"I sent for her. I have matters to discuss with my sister. Thermantia, why don't you take a walk in the gardens? Go and watch the dancing fountains."

"I don't feel like walking in the gardens and I'm bored with the dancing fountains. I'd rather stay here and listen."

"You'll only fall asleep. You could go and find my slave boys. They'll keep you entertained for the afternoon."

Thermantia brightened and swung her feet to the floor.

"So they will. Have I your permission, Honorius, to leave?" He waved his hand in assent. "Then I'll see you both later."

"Slave boys?" asked his sister, raising her eyebrows, after Thermantia had left the room.

"I don't think there's any serious impropriety, they wouldn't dare," Honorius chuckled, "but they keep her amused and out of my way."

"And take her mind off what she's not getting from you?"

"That, too."

"She knows, of course?"

"She suspects, no doubt, but she can't know anything. So far she has accepted my excuses."

"Which are?"

"Our brother's recent death—"

"—and that you are still mourning her sister?"

"It *was* only a few months ago, Gally."

"Poor you!" Her tone dripped sarcasm. "So, what is it you want to talk about so urgently?"

"The General."

"Ah, I thought that might be the case."

She crossed to the door and shut it. "Wouldn't do to let Thermantia hear us discussing her father."

"You know I've always loved and trusted him. I was only eleven when our father died."

"And I was eight," his sister added.

"I've said so many times that, as my guardian, Stilicho ruled my Western Empire without reproach until I came of age. Then, as my commander-in-chief, he soundly defeated Alaric and his Visigoths, battling as bravely for me as he had been doing for twenty years for father."

"I'm aware of all this, Honorius."

"I know you are. I'm just thinking aloud to clear my head. But now there are all these rumours."

Galla nodded in understanding.

"Most worrying is the suggestion that he is planning to put his own son on the throne of the Eastern Empire in place of the rightful heir, our brother's son. There's only one way that the eastern throne could be vacant – if our nephew was no longer alive." He sighed. "You know him well. Do you believe the rumours, Gally?"

"You know what they say – no smoke—"

"He is also my father-in-law."

"Don't complicate the situation even further."

"You've never said, Gally, and I've never asked but did you and Stilicho once enjoy something more than just a substitute father/daughter relationship?"

"Do you really want to know?"

"I should know in the circumstances."

"He seduced me when we first moved into the palace here. He said I was a beautiful house-warming present."

"You let him do that? You must have been only—"

"Fifteen. Don't be such a prude, Honorius. He wasn't my first. I enjoyed it."

"But he was like a father to you as well as to me."

"That made it all the more exciting. Don't look so shocked, brother. You of all people should understand."

"What happened to break it up?"

"He was away for so long, fighting your battles. He said he couldn't concentrate on the enemy if he was thinking about me all the time, and I would get him killed. So he finished it. He sent back all the gifts I'd given him – lucky stones, and charms on cords to wear round his neck – and all my childish letters – just sent them back in a package by messenger with a note that said, in essence, thanks for the amusing interlude, which was now over. If you ask me, he found someone else, some young camp follower who could move round with the army. I was furious and still am."

"It's more likely he had decided to marry you off to his son. It would hardly be appropriate for the father to be bedding his son's wife-to-be."

The Scarlet Seal

"That's ridiculous. His son is only seven years old. Whatever his reasons, I haven't forgiven him, but I've never had the chance to tell him so to his face."

"Then you'll be pleased to know you'll have your chance."

"How so?"

"I can't ignore these very serious charges of treason, and he's being brought here to answer them. He'll be under arrest but I can arrange for you to have some time together."

"What I have to say won't take long."

"After that we will leave."

"Before his trial?"

"There'll be no trial, just a thorough investigation, but by that time, you and I will be on our way back to Rome."

"Honorius, what are you up to?"

"I'm not up to anything. We are returning to Rome for the first night of a new play I am sponsoring at the Marcellus Theatre. Audiences in Ostia and the provinces say it is a splendid spectacle and everyone is raving about the young male lead singer – an overnight success, I hear. You'll enjoy it. We all shall. I'll ask my mother if she would like to join us. And after that—"

"After that?"

"I shall send Thermantia home. There'll be no reason for her to stay in Rome any longer. As she's still a virgin, her mother should have no difficulty in finding her another husband."

Galla nodded. "Now I understand." She brightened. "When she's gone, brother, will you let me redecorate inside the palace here? I have a fancy to see this room tiled with blue mosaics."

"Do what you like with it. All that matters to me is that I shall be free of her."

"And she won't be in *our* way any longer."

CHAPTER 27

Bron was almost certain that she had not been followed home after straying to the other side of the Tiber, but as a precaution waited until the following day before using some free time to hurry over to Adama's apartment. Fortunately, Adama was there and on her own.

Bron told her friend, with great agitation, that unexpectedly she had come across Fabia in the vegetable market. To calm her down, Adama promised to walk up the hill to the Loricatus house and warn Cook.

"But warn her about what?" Adama seemed not to have her full attention on what Bron was telling her.

"Tell her that, as Fabia is probably living with the father of Rius, it is most likely that he is also in the area."

"Sorry, Bron. Yes, I'll go up and tell her that."

"You seem rather distracted this afternoon."

"Bron, can you keep a secret?"

"Of course I can. You're keeping enough of mine. What is it?"

"I've fallen in love."

Bron was astounded. "In love? Is that wise?"

"It's a disaster but it's also marvellous!"

"Who is he?"

"His name's Priscus."

"Won't it complicate your life?"

"It's early days and I'm not thinking about that yet. We met at the baker's in the market and since then have been meeting in the wild park at the top of the Palatine. We enjoy each other's company. Last time he held my hand."

Bron thought that was rather tame, considering Adama's profession.

"Does he know what you do?"

Adama would not look into her friend's eyes. "He asked me and I avoided answering, so I haven't been able to ask him what he does, either. He looks like a poet, or perhaps a musician. I judge he's several years younger than me, but that doesn't matter. He's good looking and kind and gentle, and since I met him, day and night I can't think of anything or anyone else."

"What about your senator, your also 'kind and gentle' Crestus Sabinius?"

"I know. I'm going to hurt him deeply if Priscus and I have any sort of serious understanding."

"It's been too quick, Adama, for you to be sure."

"How long did it take you to know that you were in love with your Roman officer, the young man you followed to this country?"

Bron thought about Aurelius Catus and the first time she had met him. She was only twelve years old and pregnant after being raped by Byden's High Priest. Her Roman father had taken her on a visit to Calleva Atrebatum, the centre of administration in her tribal area. She had been sitting dreamily by the fire in an inn where her father was conducting some business when she had become aware of his companion, a young legionary, and for a moment was not sure whether she had conjured him up in her dream or whether he was real.

Then her father had introduced them as if there was nothing unusual about this meeting, as if this young man with his good looks and tanned muscular body, with torch lights glinting gold in his curls, was not the most beautiful sight in the whole world. She had fallen deeply in love with him from that moment, and when she had grown up, he had fallen just as passionately in love with her. Passionately.

There was nothing she could say to her friend.

"You see!" exclaimed Adama triumphantly.

"It's your life, sweetheart. All I am saying is, be careful. Don't throw away everything you have for one young man, however much you are in love." Bron didn't believe in the advice she was giving her friend and quickly changed the subject. "And you won't forget to go and see Cook, will you?"

Several days had passed since that conversation. Thoughts of the bo'sun finding her caused so many disturbed nights that Bron scolded herself for letting her imagination run riot. Rius was safe on the Palatine, and for the first time, she was happy that he was where he was and not with her.

Then there was the surprising twist in Adama's life. Bron was very suspicious. Who was this young man, this Priscus? What did he want?

"Have you met our new under gardener?"

Talea's question broke into her thoughts as she stood behind her mistress, engaged in making her look beautiful for the day ahead.

"No," Bron replied.

"Middle aged, but still a handsome man. He's been with us for several days now and seems to know what he's about."

"I didn't know the master needed another gardener," Bron commented with difficulty as she extracted hairpins from between her teeth and pushed them into Talea's false curls.

"He doesn't, but apparently this man was calling at all the houses hereabouts, looking for work. He was so persuasive, and looked strong enough to take on the jobs our old gardener is struggling with, that Carolus decided to try him out. The old man was very aggrieved at first, said he was quite capable of doing just as much as before, but we've noticed he's been very pleased to hand over the digging and heavy work."

Next day, Bron noticed the man. She was on her way to her room and had passed under the stone archway leading from one of the inner courtyards to the private garden she shared with her mistress.

His close-cropped silver hair confirmed he was not a young man. He had his back to her and was stripped bare to the waist, revealing the taut muscles of his shoulders and arms as he bent over a hole he was digging. A sapling lay wrapped in canvas at his feet.

She hadn't met him before, so why so familiar?

Her sandals crunched across the gravel as she approached him. The man straightened up, still with his back towards her.

"Hello, goddess!"

She took an involuntary step backwards, her outstretched fingers rising to shield her face, as if to ward off this danger. He turned to face her.

"Brunus!"

He grinned. "You haven't forgotten me, then."

His eyes followed hers down to the ample figure of a woman painted on his stomach below the thick silver of his chest hair. By flexing his muscles he had always been able to make the woman move sinuously and this was happening now. Bron's cheeks burned hotly as she remembered the times she had followed that movement with the tips of her fingers.

He laughed and leaned on the spade. "So you do remember!"

"What are you doing here?"

"I'm gardening. Surely that's obvious?"

"You're no gardener! What do you want?"

"You know what I want! Where is he, our son? Fabia said you didn't have him with you in the market. There have been children running about in the garden but I haven't seen or heard a baby."

"That's because he's not here. He's safely out of your reach!"

"Where?"

"You can't think I'm going to tell you!"

"I thought you'd say that."

"And you can't make me."

"That's true, not while you're here. Does that pleasant lady you work for know where he is?"

"They know nothing about me before I took this job," Bron lied, wishing to protect Talea and her husband.

"I'll find out, you know I will."

"No, you won't. He's a long way from here."

"It's only a matter of time. I can wait."

He dropped the spade and pulled his tunic up over his shoulders.

"What are you doing?"

"Leaving, of course, now that I've got what I came for. There's no escape, you know. Sooner or later I shall have him, and you with him. I've missed you, goddess. As I've told you before, Fabia's no substitute. She's entirely dispensable, though don't tell her I said so. I don't want her walking out on me until I'm ready for her to leave. Goodbye, beautiful Bron. Apologise to your employers for me. Tell them this afternoon's work comes free of charge."

Then he walked away from her, passed under the arch into the courtyard beyond and left by a side gate.

CHAPTER 28

Senator Laenus Loricatus stooped to enter the doorway of this hell-hole that passed as a tavern, holding his sleeve over his face and so protecting his nose from the stench as well as hiding his identity.

He stood aside to allow a dark-skinned street walker to pass him on her way towards the stairs, the insignificant little man behind her clutching the hem of her short red tunic as if he was afraid he would lose her and his money's worth in the gloom.

The senator didn't usually frequent such unwholesome places but the message he had received yesterday had made it imperative.

His eyes swept over stained tables and benches, searching for a fair-haired woman among the inn's customers. In his estimation, not one of them was any better than the sewage polluting the banks of the Tiber.

When he saw her, he walked over and sat down on the opposite side of the table.

"So, Fabia, my girl." He addressed her in a low voice. "What's so important that you need to speak to me here and not in your bed?"

"My bed hasn't been so favoured of late, Senator."

"Don't take it personally. I like to try out all the rides on offer, you know that, and a couple of very young fillies have been brought into the stable recently. Now, what's so urgent that you've brought me to this dark hole? I doubt that even the Christian's devil sets foot in here."

"A drink first, Senator."

"As you please – and don't call me 'senator', not here – Laenus will do."

"Don't worry about being recognised. We're all blind and deaf. Couldn't carry on business otherwise. A jug for me, as you're paying."

He beckoned to one of the slatterns serving drinks at the tables and waited until a jug of beer and two beakers were banged down in front of them before he asked again, "So tell me and I'll be gone. Your message said you had something to say about my son."

"I have a great deal to say about your son, Laenus. First of all, he is not your son."

The senator stared at her. "Don't be ridiculous, woman! Of course he's my son!"

"No, he's not. He is the product of the uncontrollable urges of that girl you hired as his wet nurse and a bo'sun of my acquaintance. What I am saying is the disgusting truth!"

His eyes narrowed and he pushed the jug towards her. "So tell me what you know, or think you know."

While they talked, he topped up her beaker again and again, and ordered another jug, then another, drinking very little himself, until Fabia's tongue became like the river in full spate and he guessed she had said a great deal more than she planned to say, much of which she probably wouldn't remember the following morning.

She told her listener about the shipwreck of the *Juniper*, the ship that had brought them from Britannia to Ostia, and the circumstances of the liaison between Bron and the bo'sun; about her flight to Rome to hide her pregnancy, which involved abandoning her family; about her concealment in a brothel and the eventual birth there of Honorius. Then she told him how the bo'sun had guessed she was hiding in Rome, had followed and eventually found her, and Bron's subsequent disappearance with the baby.

"They vanished completely," she confided. "He searched high and low for them but never suspected that they might be living on the Palatine – taken in by you and your wife."

"You are telling me the truth?"

"Absolutely."

The Scarlet Seal

"So the father of her baby is a dirty sailor? If I'd have known that, I would have taken what I wanted from her whenever I wanted it! So, what led you to my wife and me?"

"I'm coming to that. It wasn't until I bumped into her in a vegetable market on our side of the Tiber a few weeks ago, and followed her, that we had any idea where she was living."

"So where is she now, the slut?"

"Working as maid in a house on Aventine Hill. Brunus wangled a job there as gardener and spoke to her but, of course, she hadn't got their baby with her and she wouldn't tell him where he was."

The senator drained his beaker. The beer tasted foul. A drunken brawl was taking place in a corner of the room and they had difficulty in hearing each other.

"But you traced us. How?"

"It wasn't difficult. He had spooked her and next day she foolishly led me to the Palatine – not to your house, you understand, but to an apartment in the insula at the bottom of the hill – Adama, I believe the girl's name is. After Bron had left, Adama went immediately to your house, Senator."

"Adama? I didn't realise she and Bron knew each other."

"Well, you know now. I've found out that they both worked in the brothel where her baby was born."

"Adama didn't tell *me* about the danger the boy was in."

"Because you would have wanted to know where her information came from and she would have had to admit that she was seeing Bron."

"But she obviously warned someone in my house. Who else knows that your bo'sun is a threat and isn't telling us that Bron is still in the area? The new nurse? Cook? I will make sure that Adama pays for this!"

"You'd better be careful, Laenus. Her sponsor is very powerful."

"Senator Crestus Sabinius – yes, I know."

He had to duck as a three-legged stool came hurtling across the room, narrowly missing his head, and crashed into the fire, sending out a spray of sparks. The orange flames greedily set about devouring it.

While waiting for her to reveal her hand, he crossed to the fire and trod out a few small embers that were scorching the wooden planks of the floor.

"So, Laenus, after all I've said, you can't deny that the child is not yours."

"Oh, but he is, paid for fair and square," he replied, sitting down again. "So what do you want from me? Payment for information about a possible kidnap? The information's worth very little. I'll simply increase the security around the baby."

"His father is willing to drag you through the courts."

"Are you blackmailing me?"

"No, just giving a friendly word of advice. You wouldn't want it known that your son, your only son, I believe, is not your son but was born in a brothel and was the result of a sordid affair between a common sailor and a whore. What would your friends and neighbours make of it, to say nothing of your brother senators? I rather think it is a situation you and your wife would wish to avoid."

Now it was his turn to remain silent as he considered the implications. To give him time, Fabia turned to watch the fight before facing him again.

"Well, Laenus, what do you say?"

Suddenly a thought kindled in his mind. He was sure he was right.

"You haven't told him where the boy is, have you, your friend, the bo'sun? Now why is that, I wonder?"

"I thought I'd talk to you first."

"And, of course, if he got hold of the child, he could entice Bron to follow, and where would that leave you, Fabia?"

She turned towards him with such an ugly expression on her face that he knew he had hit the bullseye.

"But relax. It's not going to happen. We need an heir and my wife has got quite fond of Honorius. All to the good – keeps her occupied and leaves me free to follow my own—er—pursuits. So now we come to the crux of the matter. How much not to tell your friend?"

Fabia named her figure and he paled.

"And that would be only the beginning, would it not?"

She leaned towards him. "I have expectations, Laenus. I don't want to work as I do for ever."

"In my experience, once a whore, always a whore."

"Maybe, but at least I would be able to pick my 'gentlemen'. On thinking about it, you could set me up in my own apartment, Laenus, like that pretty little Adama hash been set up. She has the best of all worlds, seems to me – a friend who visits but alsho gives her all the freedom she—she wants."

Fabia's words were beginning to slur and she seemed to have difficulty in focussing on what her tongue was spilling out.

"If you shponsored me, Laenus, you would have it all for free. And what a relief for me, not to have to shervice clients like that pagan, fat Oliffe!"

"Oliffe? The ambassador from the Visigoths?"

"That's the one. He stinks of body odour, and worse, and enjoys inventing his 'little games', as he calls them – and his demands go on all night unlesh I get him very drunk!"

"I've never seen him in your building."

"Then you haven't looked. He comes whenever he's in Rome, which sheems to be more and more these days."

"Of course. He negotiates for the pagans. And he visits you?"

"Shometimes. He makes the rounds."

"Does he talk to you about his work, his country's affairs?"

"You all do – before, during and after." She giggled like a young girl, which decidedly she wasn't. "Shome clients arrive as tightly twisted as strands in a rope and they need to unwind before they're able to perform, and it can pay dividends to listen to all their foolish boasting about their power and influence. But we girls don't hear anything. Most of it's just hot air, anyway, and it's none of our business."

"Have I talked to you about my work? About the affairs of the Senate?"

"Of course – don't you remember?" She giggled again. "But I suppose your mind was elsewhere."

"Do you recall anything I've said?"

"I've told you, we girls don't hear a thing."

"Try."

She screwed up her face in a supreme effort to concentrate. "I might remember shome of it. I remember you told me about the shpeech you made in the Senate when they all took notice – about playing for time by negoti—negotia—while our troops were being prepared for war. You were so pleased with yourself, that you climbed back for a second and third replay. We had quite a celebration!" She began to wheedle him. "Why don't you come to my bed more often, Laenus? Perhaps you will from now on – if we agree on shome arrangement."

The fight had ended with the instigator sprawled bleeding and unconscious on the floor. The onlookers were ignoring him and righting chairs and an overturned table and calling for more liquor. The senator stood.

"I'll think about it, Fabia, and let you know. Now I must go. Stay and empty the jug. I'll arrange to meet you somewhere soon – not here – and give you my answer."

"I'm sure you'll shee sense, Laenus."

As he stepped out into the darkness of the unlit side street, Senator Laenus Loricatus believed that he would.

CHAPTER 29

Early next morning, he was impatiently pacing the garden courtyard when Fausta joined him, yawning and still in the underwear she had slept in, a gown wrapped round her.

He had decided what he would say to her and had decided what he must do. He did not relish his plans but desperate circumstances called for desperate measures.

Oliffe, the ambassador whom the Visigoth, Alaric, had sent to negotiate terms, was a vile man who abused the privileges and political immunity his residence in Rome afforded him.

Laenus had heard talk, which Fabia had confirmed, about his treatment of the women he used, who were too frightened to complain. Indeed, there were some in the civil service, on instructions from certain senators, who paid the girls to keep the ambassador happy by acceding to his every whim, threatening them with all sorts of mischief if they didn't co-operate fully. Co-operating also meant reporting every tiny snippet of political information he let slip.

To Oliffe, negotiating meant threatening and bullying and throwing a tantrum if he couldn't get his own way. And his threats had substance. The barbarians on Rome's borders were a disorganised and unruly bunch, fighting and squabbling among themselves, each chieftain out for his own interests. The Senate knew that, if they ever saw sense and banded together, they would far outnumber Rome's military resources and the city would fall to them within days.

So far, this alliance between Rome's enemies – the Vandals, Burgundians, Alans, Sueves, Franks and Visigoths – had been forestalled. There were men in the Senate, clever men, with brilliant minds, who had been able to appease the pagan ambassadors resident in Rome, preventing them from joining forces by secretly pandering to the demands of each, seemingly to the disadvantage of the others. As yet, none had realised that his own faction was being played off against the rest.

Since his speech to the Senate, which had been so well received, Laenus had stood by and watched with admiration as these cunning men deftly and adroitly manipulated these heathen ambassadors into marking time while they awaited the kickbacks and rewards promised them.

The Senate was employing any strategy to gain delay – a discussion that took all day and involved much wine and joviality and amounted to very little else; a perceived important meeting, postponed several times, that wasn't important at all when it was finally scheduled, or perhaps cancelled; the promise of a day spent betting at the Circus Maximus, watching the chariot races in the emperor's company, though the emperor always had a pressing engagement at the last moment and sent his younger half-sister, Galla Placidia, in his place – not that any of the ambassadors ever objected.

In the meantime, the city's defences were strengthened, newly-manufactured weapons supplied, young recruits enlisted and sent out on secret manoeuvres in the countryside, and long-term servicemen retrained.

Yes, Laenus was seeing all this happening. But would his crass stupidity in confiding state secrets to Fabia at some unguarded moment during their playful rough-and-tumbles bring the empire crashing down? How could he have been so careless as to allow his inflated ego to compromise the safety of the city, the Senate, his family and himself in particular? But how was he to know that Fabia serviced Oliffe as well as himself? Of course, he should have realised the possibility.

If discovered, his confidences would be regarded as treason. He had passed her information she could sell, perhaps had sold, to the enemy – though he didn't think the worth of his disclosures had occurred to her yet. But it would occur to her sooner or later, especially if he failed to pay the money she was demanding.

It was possible, though, that she had already given him away. He couldn't be absolutely sure.

Then he would lose everything he had striven for all these years. All the compromises and biting his tongue and keeping his mouth shut and self-effacement and metaphorically bowing his neck so low he had a crick in it, even to the extent of marrying Fausta so he could become part of the Constantine family – all would have been in vain.

Julia would be among the first to desert him. He had no doubts about that. Those whose favour he had curried would turn their backs on him. Not even Constantine would help him. He would be disgraced, ostracized, dismissed by the Senate and abandoned.

Or worse – he would be disposed of, knifed in the back in some alleyway or 'accidentally' tumble into the Tiber. One way or another, he would lose his life, and no one would lift a hand to help his wife and their son.

Yes, desperate circumstances called for desperate measures, he could see that. But what he had to do must not indicate a crime of political expediency. There must be no cause for anyone to look suspiciously in his direction. But how was this to be accomplished?

Fausta's complaining voice cut into his deliberations.

"Husband, you haven't been shaved this morning," she accused him as she plopped down onto a bench, "and you look as if you haven't slept. What's wrong? Where's Julius?"

The early morning sun was already hot and she pulled her pale blue silk gown away from her neck.

"I've sent him about his other duties. And you're right, I hardly slept at all."

While waiting for him to tell her why he had summoned her so early and so urgently, she dipped her fingers into water splashing over coloured stones in a fountain basin, tasted its cool purity, and freshened her eyes and cheeks.

"Do sit down, Laenus, you're making me feel quite dizzy," she complained.

"Where's the boy? Where's Honorius?"

"In the nursery, I presume, with Nurse."

"Is he still missing his mother?"

"Of course not, not any longer. He's forgotten all about her. But have you forgotten her, Laenus?" She threw him a suspicious look. "You're not still seeing her, are you? Anyway, what are you talking about? I'm his mother."

"Just so." He sat beside her. "And no, I'm not seeing Bron. How could you even think it?" There was no reason to confess what his night-time fantasies about the girl drove him to do.

Taking a deep breath, he let it out in a rush.

"Dearest, it has come to my notice – I have received some disturbing information – about the circumstances of our son's birth. What do you know about Bron?"

"Nothing that matters – that she worked in a brothel, but not as a prostitute, and Honorius was born there."

"And his father?"

"There was never any mention of his father. What is all this leading up to?"

"I have learned that his father is a sailor, a bo'sun, who is living in Rome and is out looking for his son."

"You haven't been blabbing our business down in the city?"

"No, of course not."

"You're so stupid, Laenus, if you've been stirring up trouble."

"The trouble's there, Fausta, whether I stir it up or not."

"Who told you about his father?"

"Someone who thought I should know."

"But he won't find him up here on the Palatine."

"He has found him – or, more accurately, the information is available."

"So someone is blackmailing you?" Laenus remained silent. "How much?" She gasped when he told her. "It won't stop there."

"I know it."

"What if you don't pay her? I assume it's a 'her', knowing you, Laenus. Were you dripping honey into her ear and just happened to ooze, 'By the way, our son isn't really our son – my wife couldn't manage to produce a child – so we bought him through an agent and employed his mother to wet nurse him. And that wasn't the only way his mother replaced my wife'. Is that what you said, Laenus, humiliating me to one of your whores?"

"I swear to you I told no one, Fausta. It was quite by chance she found out we had the boy."

"So, I repeat, what happens if you don't pay her?"

"His father will come looking for him."

"Steal him away?"

"Perhaps, or worse, take us through the courts. It seems he never agreed to the sale of the child."

"How can that be worse than kidnapping him? Surely you could make sure that any evidence was judged false so that we won the case and kept him."

"Do we want it known that, as you said, we failed to produce a child of our own and were so desperate that we bought one from a brothel, the son of a sailor and a whore, then told lies about being his parents? I'd be ridiculed, a laughing stock – and I've worked so hard to get where I am."

"That's it, it's all about you, isn't it? What about Honorius? I'll never forgive you if his father steals him away. He's ours now! He belongs to us!"

"I know! I know! And there is a solution."

"What solution?"

"We must get him away from here! Take him to your mother's—"

"That's too obvious."

"Somewhere else, then. I'm sure you'll think of somewhere – just until all this dies down."

"Dies down? Don't be a fool, Laenus. It will never die down."

"But you can't kidnap a baby who isn't around to be kidnapped and you can't have a court case about a baby who can't be produced."

"I won't stay away for ever – or is that what you'd like, for me to take the baby and disappear so you can live your sordid life with all your women, without the inconvenience of a wife and child about the place?"

"That's not true, Fausta. I need you! I need you with me! We're a family."

"Playing happy families, are we, now you're in the Senate? All right, we'll go! I'll take Honorius away somewhere where no one will find us, to keep him safe, but I'll not stay away for ever, husband dear. So you'd better sort it out!"

"I will Fausta, I will, I'll sort it out, don't worry!"

"And the sooner the better!"

It was Adama who brought the news to Bron. She came one afternoon to the house on Aventine Hill and was shown into a small room off the hallway. It was not long before Bron hurried in.

"Adama, the mistress said you needed to see me."

"Yes, my dear Crestus Sabinius asked permission for me to call on you."

"Is something wrong, Adama? Is Rius well? What is it?"

"Rius is well, don't fret yourself. It's just that Fausta Loricata has taken him away somewhere and Cook doesn't know where, neither does Julius – nobody knows."

"A holiday, surely? There's no need for alarm."

"None, I'm sure, but she left no instructions about their return and gave no hint of how long they will be away."

"From what you've told me recently, Fausta has become very attached to my Rius. I'm sure he won't come to any harm. They're visiting her mother, perhaps? They'll be back soon. Why is Cook so worried?"

"Because they took a lot of luggage with them in the carriage, and the nurse has gone, too, and there was no warning – they simply left."

"The driver will know where he took them."

"That's just it. They changed carriages in the Forum. It's all very strange. We don't want you to worry, Bron, but we all felt you should know."

CHAPTER 30

Bron was glad that Talea kept her busy. Her days were filled with such activity and interest that they flew by and left her little time to worry about Rius. This morning, they had been to the baths as usual and were now on their way home.

She always enjoyed riding through the city, whether by carriage, litter or the twin carrying chair in which she was now sitting with her mistress. The shiny red bench seat smelt of new leather and the black paint on the woodwork was hardly dry but Talea had been impatient to show off the conveyance to her friends.

Bron usually travelled with the blind raised, unless her mistress wished to doze, so that she could see all that was going on around her. She had not been so long in Rome that its sights, sounds and scents no longer enthralled her.

However, she was in solemn mood today as the slaves trundled them through the Forum on the Via Sacra. She hardly noticed the elegant columns, bronze doors and marble sculptures of the sanctuaries lining the road, nor even the huge Basilica of Constantine I on their left, which dominated the area.

The air was heavy with incense wafting out from burners being swung in the Christian churches. This further hampered the already heavy breathing of their porters as they bore the twin chair up the ascent towards the triumphal Arch of Titus. As they passed through the shadowed archway, Talea looked at her young companion with sympathy.

"Still no news of your son, Bron?"

Bron shook her head and tears came to her eyes.

Talea tried to comfort her. "If Fausta Loricata took him away for his own safety, and his nurse is with them, he'll be well looked after, wherever they've gone."

Bron nodded. "I'm sure you're right, I have to believe it, but it's not knowing where he is that is so worrying. But I can't do anything except stay in Rome and wait for him to be brought back, though he won't be safe in the city while Brunus is out there, looking for him. His father is very determined."

Not for the first time, she deplored the day she had so willingly succumbed to the animal magnetism of that man, though she knew that, without that weakness, she never would have held her son in her arms.

She realised it was to take her mind off her anxieties that Talea began musing on the gossip they had heard from the women at the baths – someone's young daughter had gone into labour in the street when no one suspected she was pregnant, least of all herself; the rise in inflation and the going rate for slaves; and most surprisingly, the execution in Ravenna of the emperor's father-in-law, General Stilicho, and of his young son in Rome. Bron was hardly listening. None of it affected her personally.

"—but the latest news round here," continued Talea, "is another body fished out of the Tiber this morning. They think she went in last night. No one seems to know who she is – none of us, that is. Someone must know down by the river. They've only got to ask the right people. They'll find out, given time and a cash incentive. Not that that sort is worth a reward. After all, who would offer it? I don't suppose anyone is missing her, or cares anyway."

"Poor woman," murmured Bron. "Knifed then drowned. I suppose it was a man did it."

"Almost certainly," agreed her mistress.

"Could have been a jealous rival."

"By all accounts, she was no sylph. I doubt a woman would have had the strength, first to overcome her then to heave her body onto the wall and push it over into the water."

"A nasty business," observed Bron.

Talea shrugged. "But not unusual."

Tonight they were to attend the theatre dedicated to Marcellus, nephew of the first emperor, the great Augustus. The four hundred-year-old building had been in urgent need of repair and

Emperor Honorius had rebuilt parts and renovated the remainder, along with several other theatres in the city.

Talea said that it was the opening night of a new play that had received rave reviews in the provinces. Bron had not been to the theatre in Rome and was very excited at the prospect.

"Is it a comedy or tragedy?" she asked.

"Not sure," Talea pondered, "but it doesn't make much difference. We won't be able to hear it, anyway, because of the noise the crowd will be making."

"Then why are we going?" Bron asked, mystified.

"Because of who will be there," Talea explained, seemingly amused at Bron's naivety. "Everyone who is anyone goes to first nights and inspecting the audience is usually more diverting than watching what's going on, on stage."

By making enquiries around the market, Bron found out that the play was a tragedy penned by a young, as yet unknown, writer. An actor she met at a fruit stall told her that the emperor was promoting young, talented companies and there were several playwrights whose work he was commissioning and sponsoring.

"Do you think he will be there?" Bron asked Talea, recalling the young man she had encountered at the chariot races.

"He may be, there's no telling."

After they returned home from the baths, she spent hours preparing Talea for the evening's outing, which meant she had to rush to get herself ready in time. Now they were at a standstill in a traffic jam of vehicles, horses, mules, carts, dogs, children and beggars. They were relieved when their slaves were at last able to move forward again and deposit them outside the theatre.

Bron gazed up at the round wall with its three layers of arches – forty-one to each layer, Talea told her. The building seated twenty thousand, a third of the size of the Colosseum.

Once inside, the din hardly lessened. All theatres were open-roofed so were used for productions between April and November only. The auditorium was semi-circular and raised tier by tier to a great height so that the audience in the top tiers could hardly see the action, especially in the gathering dusk, until lamps and torches were lit along the periphery of the semi-circular stage far below them. However, acoustics were good and every word would have been audible were it not for the noise the audience was making.

Bron was proud that Talea appeared as beautiful and affluent as any woman present, in pale pink with a cerise mantle and a gold and diamond diadem and matching jewellery.

Bron's lilac tunic and mantle of a deeper shade were simple and her combs, pins and brooches less ornate, but her youthfulness gifted her bloom and beauty and many heads turned to watch the two women as they entered the auditorium and found their seats.

The seat next to Talea was kept vacant for her husband, Carolus, but he didn't appear. "Prefers the gaming tables," murmured her mistress agreeably.

Bron gazed round, keenly interested in the friends and acquaintances whom Talea was pointing out as she smiled and waved or bowed her head in acknowledgement.

Out of the corner of her eye, Bron was conscious of someone in a seat further along the row standing and waving frantically in their direction. She turned her head and recognised the ample figure of Nadica Calidonia, her friend from the chariot races and gaming table. Her husband, Cato, seated by her side, was also smiling and acknowledging her. Bron grinned broadly and waved back.

Then there was an undercurrent of excitement, like the murmur of an approaching flash flood in a dry river bed. Bron was wondering about the cause when Talea touched her arm and indicated a section of seating at stage level on the far right.

"It's the emperor and his party!" she whispered.

Bron saw again the tawny-haired young man who had given her the winning favour at the chariot races, that treasured length of scarlet silk now folded neatly beneath her woollen stockings in her underwear drawer.

On his right stood his unremarkable little wife, tonight wearing dark blue, and on his left his half-sister, Galla Placidia, again wearing white, and as elegant and beautiful as Bron remembered her. She then noticed the emperor's grandmother, Aelia Flavia Claudia Antonia, standing next to her step granddaughter.

The audience was on its feet now, stamping and clapping and calling for Honorius. He turned to acknowledge the acclamation, as did the other members of his party. When the old lady turned to smile and wave, Bron sucked in her breath and brought her fist up to her mouth, to keep herself from crying out. Round Aelia Flavia's neck glimmered the amber and pearl necklace, once Bron's necklace, that the old lady had been wearing when they first met.

"What's the matter?" whispered Talea with concern. "What is it?"

"Just a twinge of indigestion," Bron lied. "It's gone now."

"Too many figs," sympathised her mistress. "I did warn you."

When the emperor sat, everyone sat, and the general hubbub resumed.

Bron continued to watch the royal party, questioning again how the necklace had come into the possession of the imperial grandmother and whether she would ever be able to retrieve it, and it took several moments for her to realise that the play had started.

An orchestra had taken its place on stage and zithers and other string instruments, flutes, trumpets, cymbals and castanets were accompanying the lyrical chanting of the chorus. Bron wished she could hear the words of their song.

Then a lone figure detached itself from the singers and came to the front of the stage. The footlights revealed a young man about six feet tall, of slender build, with a pale complexion and straight hair the colour of white gold.

For a moment he stood quite still, composed, waiting for his cue, then opened his mouth, but the words were inaudible because of the noise. After several bars, however, there were hisses of "Ssshhh!" and "Quiet, can't you?" and gradually the hubbub died down until the entire audience was so quiet that if Bron had loosened a hairpin, she felt sure everyone would hear it drop.

Through the stillness rose a pure, crystal-clear voice. Bron could not believe that its power came from inside that slight body. He was singing of his love for a young Roman maiden who was denied to him because of her father's ambitious plans for her marriage. Bron could hear every syllable, feel every rise and fall of emotion, all the longing and loss, and her eyes filled with tears.

The heartbroken young man sang his goodbyes to his love and marched away to fight and die for Rome. As the song ended and he stepped back into line, there was a moment's silence, then an explosion of rapturous applause.

As the chorus then tramped on the spot in time to one of the marching songs of the Roman army, the audience sang along with gusto. Bron picked up enough words to be able to join in the chorus that followed each verse:

> *Rome calls her sons across the seas,*
> *Across the southern sands,*
> *We're marching home from western isles,*
> *From cold and northern lands,*
> *Through fire and flood and battlefield,*
> *Swords rampant in our hands.*
> *She calls us and we're marching home!*
> *We hear you and we're marching home!*
> *Take up the cry! To live or die,*
> *To live or die for Rome!*
> *Take up the cry! To live or die,*
> *To live or die for Rome!*

During the final chorus, the excitement increased, the tempo gathered speed and the singing grew louder, reaching a final crescendo as the singers marched off stage.

After another explosion of applause, the audience called for the young singer, "Priscus! Priscus! Pris—cus!", until he returned for more adulation, accompanied by shouts of approval from the men and catcalls from the women.

"We are very privileged to hear him," Talea told Bron as roses and lilies and bouquets were hurled onto the stage or brought to lay at his feet. "He's a newcomer and everyone's darling at the moment – with good cause, as you heard. Priscus – it's a name to remember."

Priscus? thought Bron. *Wasn't that the name of Adama's young lover?* She was sure it was. He was certainly as her friend had described him, young and unworldly. There might be only a few years in actual time between their ages but Bron guessed there were many decades if measured by life's experiences. She felt very anxious for her friend. However, they now knew what he did for a living.

She watched as he left the stage, the flowers were cleared away by the backstage crew, and the performance continued on a battlefield somewhere in the empire.

During the interval, she struggled to join the crowds pushing and elbowing their way towards various hawkers in the aisles and returned to her seat clutching fresh oranges and a drawstring bag of pink and white marshmallows.

The play came to an end and Bron rose to her feet along with everyone else to applaud the actors, singers and musicians.

After the royal party had quit the building, the audience began filing out through the many exits.

Bron wished she could tell the emperor how exhilarated she had been by the drama and the whole magical theatrical experience, and that all the time and money he had spent on this building and this production had been well spent.

She would have been surprised had she known that soon she would be telling him just that.

CHAPTER 31

One afternoon a few days later, Talea sent for her. To Bron's surprise, she found Adama sitting with her mistress in the small reception room off the hallway. Both looked very serious and Bron's heart missed a beat. She was frightened to ask the question that was trying to propel itself off her tongue, but only a croak at the back of her throat indicated her disquiet.

"Bron," Talea began, "Adama has some news for you."

"Rius?" she managed to ask.

"It's not about Rius," Adama was quick to reassure her.

Talea rose. "I'll leave you together so you can talk."

After she had left the room, Bron turned to her friend. "What is it? Tell me. Come right out with it, Adama."

"Sit down and I will."

Bron sat and waited, her hands fidgeting in her lap. Seen through the window overlooking the courtyard garden, the sun was dappling the marble and gilding the gladioli and irises in flower beds the bo'sun had so recently been weeding.

"As far as we know," Adama began, "Rius is well. We've had no news, though, and there's been no sign of Fausta Loricata, and Laenus hasn't mentioned her at all. Julia is practically living at the house now—"

"That Julia!" Bron interjected with disgust.

"—so he doesn't want me so often. I'm sent for when she's not there. He says he doesn't tell her about me. It's strange, though—"

"What's strange?" asked Bron.

"Once or twice he's questioned me about knowing you. 'Did you ever meet Bron, our son's previous nurse?' he's asked a couple of times."

"So what did you say?"

"I said I didn't know you, of course, but I'm not sure he believed me. Odd that he's asking me now but never did in the past."

"But what have you come to tell me?"

"You've often spoken about that woman who was so jealous of your affair with the bo'sun—" Bron winced "—and lives – lived – with him here in Rome."

"Her name's Fabia. What about her? How do you know her?"

"I don't, and never will now. Bron, you'll be shocked to learn that she's dead!"

"Dead?" Bron echoed. "How? Has he beaten her up once too often?"

Adama shook her head. "Her body was found in the Tiber a week ago. She had been stabbed in the heart then was thrown or fell in. The body has been identified."

"I heard about it," Bron remembered. "There was no love lost between us, but I wouldn't have wished that on her. But I don't understand. Street girls are often murdered or go missing, and no one turns a hair. Why bother to identify her? Why is the killing of Fabia making waves?"

"It's rumoured that she wasn't particular about the men she serviced – as long as they could pay, she went with anybody, friend or foe. No loyalty to Rome."

"Of course she had no loyalty to Rome," Bron concurred, "she wasn't Roman, she was British. Rome invaded Britannia. Rome is our enemy."

"Then she should have been more careful what she said and who she said it to – and so should you. I'll pretend I didn't hear that."

Bron changed direction. "So has her murder become a political issue?"

"It seems so, though it might have nothing at all to do with politics."

Bron turned to the tray that had been brought in for them and began pouring lemon cordial into two glasses.

"Have they caught anyone yet?"

"It seems so. They took your bo'sun into custody two days ago. He's in prison, awaiting trial."

Bron paused, jug in mid air. "I know he's a bully and was never averse to knocking her about, but I don't think he would commit cold-blooded murder – what reason would he have?"

"If he's found guilty—" Adama began.

Bron put down the jug and finished the sentence for her. "They'll impose the death sentence. But it will quieten any rumours about political skulduggery."

"He says he didn't do it."

"If he really didn't, all he has to do is put forward an alibi." She pushed a glass towards Adama.

"But he says he can't prove where he was the night it happened."

"Then things look bad for him. How do you know all this?"

"Most of it's common gossip, but Crestus Sabinius has been telling me about it – all the rumours circulating in the Senate. He knows the orator who's defending him."

"This is terrible news," Bron said. "After all, he is the father of my Rius, and I did have feelings for him at one time – not love, never love, but – feelings." She broke off, blushing furiously, and to cover her confusion, swallowed a mouthful of cordial. Then a thought occurred to her.

"But isn't there a mystery in all this? Who is taking him to trial and, more importantly, who is instructing an orator to defend him?"

"I don't know, Bron. As you say, it's a mystery. *He* must know, though."

"Yes, of course, but we're not likely to find out, even if we go to his trial. When is it, by the way?"

"The second day of September."

"Only five days away? Someone's in a hurry to get it over and done with."

She lifted the glass to her lips again, which gave Adama space in which to take a deep breath. "Bron, he's asking to see you."

Bron spluttered and choked. "See me? But why?" She found difficulty in recovering her voice. "He's not going to lure me into his bed again, if that's what he hopes!"

Adama laughed grimly. "Bron, be practical. I don't think they have beds in our prisons."

"I apologise. That remark was in poor taste."

"He has no one else to talk to, he says, and there are things he needs to say before the trial. There may not be a chance afterwards."

"I can't go prison visiting! After all, I am maid to a lady. She'll never give me permission. No, it's out of the question."

"Is that the message I take back with me?"

"Yes—no. Oh, I don't know."

Adama reached out and laid a hand on Bron's arm.

"I think you should go, or you might always regret it. I'll go with you, if you want me to, to give you support. Think it over."

"I don't need to think it over."

Bron was adamant but two days later sent her friend a message to say that she had thought about it and had changed her mind and Talea, curious and always eager for gossip to relate to her friends at the baths, had given her permission to visit the prisoner.

CHAPTER 32

Brunus was being held at the Colosseum, in a cage in one of the tunnels beneath the vast arena. Now that the bloody gladiatorial combats and ill-matched contests between men and beasts were no longer taking place, the building stood idle.

On the evening chosen, the two young women, cloaked and hooded, crept through the maze of dark streets and alleyways to arrive in the deserted precinct surrounding the massive structure. They were glad of the clouds that hid the new moon.

Bron closely followed Adama across the pavement, past the colossal naked statue of Nero, gleaming gold in spite of only faint moonlight, to the one entrance not boarded up. Instructing her friend to stay behind her, Adama knocked several times on the heavy wooden door. A small grill was opened and a gruff voice demanded, "Whatcher want?"

Bron could not hear what was being whispered back and forth but the door was opened a few inches and Adama passed a leather bag through. She could hear coins chinking then a loud guffaw, and the aperture opened a little wider. Adama beckoned her to follow. The hefty guard closed and barred the door behind them.

Bron panicked. What if he never let them out again? What if—? Her imagination was running riot but she suppressed it. If Adama felt as fearful, she was hiding it well.

The guard took down two torches from sconces on the wall, gave one to Adama, and told them to follow him. This they did, along the curved aisle that circled the arena until they came to a trapdoor. Warning them to take care, he opened the door and descended a flight of steps.

At the bottom, he turned left. They saw they were passing lines of built-in animal cages on both sides, many of them occupied by huddles of prisoners sitting or sleeping on the floor. Some of them came to the front of their cages as the torches passed. They began calling out to the two girls, concealed beneath their cloaks and hoods, reaching filthy hands towards them through the wire and clawing the air, their lewd gestures leaving nothing to the imagination.

The guard stopped before a smaller cage and pushed a torch into a sconce on the wall, using its light to unlock the iron door.

"Prisoner, you got a visitor, two in fact. It's your lucky night."

He stood back to allow the women to step inside, behind the wire netting, Adama still clutching her torch. There was a rustle and a dark shadow on the floor stirred.

" 'ow long you need? Two of 'em – I'll come back in an hour. Make the most of it."

Chuckling and chinking his coins, he locked the door again and went back the way he had come, whistling to himself.

Shivering in the cold, dank air, Bron pulled the cloak tightly around her. Adama, who had shown confidence up to that point, moved closer to her friend and held the torch higher, revealing the apprehension in her almond eyes.

Bron had the impression of a large, bare space with a plain wooden table and chair in one corner, a bucket in another, and little else. There was an odour of mould and animals, adding to other smells coming from the bucket.

A tall figure rose from the floor, rustling the straw on which he had been lying and disturbing what sounded like a battalion of cockroaches. He seemed to be the only prisoner in this cage. *Another bribe?* Bron wondered. *If so, who paid?*

"Who are you? What do you want?"

Bron recoiled as she heard that rasping voice. Her thoughts flew back to the island where they had been shipwrecked and the shelter beneath the standing stones where she had first allowed him to make love to her, feeling again his arms round her and tasting again his lips pressed hard on hers. She had to shake herself mentally to rid herself of the memories and bring her attention back to the grim present.

"Brunus!"

"Bron? Goddess, is that you?"

The shadow took a step towards them and came into the torchlight. Bron had seen him only two weeks ago, in the Iconicus garden where he had been working as a gardener. Talea had described him as a handsome man and so he had been, but Bron hardly recognised him now. He was haggard, his grey eyes even darker and sunk deep in their sockets, his face unshaved. In spite of all her resolve to hate him for the way he had used her in the past, her heart went out to him. She pushed the hood back off her face.

"Yes, it's me. You wanted to see me."

Talea had no misapprehensions about the conditions in which prisoners were incarcerated, both the innocent and the guilty, and thoughtfully had given Bron a small blanket. This she now took from beneath her cloak and handed to him.

"Put this round you. You look so cold." He took it with thanks and did as he was bidden.

Meanwhile, Adama was wedging the torch into the wire. She now produced a goatskin bag that had been concealed under her cloak and held that out to him.

"Beer," she said.

"You're Adama, aren't you? I remember you from the brothel where I found Bron."

Greedily, he drank from the wineskin, smacked his lips noisily and wiped them with the back of his hand, then still clutching the blanket round him, guided Bron over to the chair. Adama perched herself next to him on the wobbly table. He turned to Bron.

"Bron, beautiful girl, I didn't think you would come, not for a moment, but here you are, as desirable as ever. The blanket's small but I'm sure there's room for us both under it. If Adama objects, there'll be time for her as well – we've got an hour."

Bron realised that he was teasing her and this awful place hadn't broken his spirit, and she laughed. Someone called out, "Quiet over there!"

"You're only jealous," Brunus shouted back, "because I've got two of them in with me!"

"Then send one over here!" called another voice, and there was a general cacophony of voices before another prisoner, mouthing blasphemies, told them to keep the noise down as he was trying to get some sleep.

"Brunus, why have you asked me to come?" Bron whispered.

"Our son—?"

Bron didn't know how to answer him other than to say, "He's safe and well where I left him."

"Oh, and where's that?" He had been quick off the mark, still trying to find out the boy's whereabouts. There was no possibility of his kidnapping Rius while in prison, but when he was found innocent and released, Bron thought he might discover the truth.

As she didn't reply, he continued, "When I get out of here, you'll tell me where he is and we'll bring him home, to my home, where we can live together as a family. Now that Fabia's gone, there'll be room for the three of us."

Bron was appalled by his fantasy. This was not her plan and she would tell him so when she was ready, but this was not the time nor the place. Instead she asked, "So you're sure you'll be released?"

"They can't keep me locked up when it's proved I didn't kill her. I didn't, you know. Often felt like it but I wouldn't do that. You believe me, don't you?"

"I can't think why I should. I've seen what you did to her when you had too much drink in your belly. But, yes, I do believe you, Brunus."

"Whether Bron believes you or not doesn't make any difference," Adama interrupted. "You've got to make the court believe you."

"You can, can't you?" asked Bron. "You know what you were doing the night she was murdered?"

"Certainly. I remember it clearly and can account for every minute."

"Then you have an alibi?"

"That's just it, I haven't. I can't prove anything – no witnesses, you see. But I've got a good defence orator, the best, and he'll get me off."

"You're right, he is the best," Adama agreed, "if the size of the gifts he expects is anything to go by – win or lose." When the bo'sun looked at her enquiringly, she explained, "He's a friend of a very good friend of mine."

"But how will you be able to afford these gifts, Brunus? And this cell on your own? Have you suddenly come into a fortune?" Bron asked, puzzled.

"Of course not, but it's not me who's paying for any of it."

"Then who is?"

"I don't know."

"Now I *am* finding it hard to believe you."

"Who bribed the guard to let you in tonight?"

"That one's easy," Adama said. "My friend's very generous where I'm concerned. I asked for his help. But he doesn't know you so it's not him who's paying for your trial and defence."

"It's obvious that someone wants to prove your innocence," Bron persisted. "How do you account for that?"

"I can't – and it's not the only thing that's puzzling me."

"You finished with them yet?" a voice called out, accompanied by loud sucking and slurping noises, which caused a great deal of hilarity in the cells.

"No chance!" the bo'sun shouted in reply. "Pay for your own girls!"

He turned his attention back to Bron. He had been scratching his legs while speaking to them and Bron was alarmed to realise she was doing the same. She looked over to Adama, who was scratching her arm under her cloak. The sooner they got out of this place, the better, Bron thought, though she was no longer conscious of the bad odours.

"I'll tell you what happened that night, the night Fabia was killed, poor cow."

"We're listening."

"She had gone off to meet a punter down by the river somewhere. I remember she seemed very excited, as if it was someone special, different from the usual scum, but she never said anything definite and I didn't ask. Wish I had now. Anyway, off she went and said she'd be back late. I never saw her again." He paused, then continued, "But I heard from her. I had a message, about an hour after she'd gone out."

"Saying what?"

"That she'd found out where Rius was."

Bron jumped to her feet, sending the chair flying across the earthen floor.

"Where, Brunus? Where? Where are they hiding him? Tell me!"

Taking a step towards her, he grabbed her by the shoulders and looked down into her face. The torchlight flickered shadows between them.

"Are you telling me that you *don't* know where he is? You assured me a moment ago that he was safe and well where you'd left him."

Bron heard a sob that must have come from her throat.

"Well?" he demanded.

"It's a long story, Brunus, too long to tell you now, but we were living with a couple on Palatine Hill. They tricked me out of the house and have spirited him away. It's breaking my heart. His nurse is with him, though, as well as the mistress, and I'm sure he's in no danger, but I don't know *where* he is."

He relaxed his grip but did not take his hands from her shoulders. "Fabia must have found out."

"She couldn't have found out!" Bron replied. "Even if she'd discovered where we were living on the Palatine, she couldn't know where they've taken him now. No one knows."

"Then how do you explain her message?"

"I can't."

She removed his hands and turned away. Adama picked up the fallen chair and pushed her friend down onto it.

"This is not making any sense," Bron continued. "Who brought the message?"

"Some street girl. I didn't know her, never seen her before. She came up to the apartment."

"And said what?" Bron asked.

"That Fabia had found out where Rius was. I was to meet her and she would take me there."

"Meet her where?" demanded Bron.

"By the gate leading to the Appian Way. It took me an hour to walk there. I waited for an hour but she didn't show up, so I walked back."

"But she was nowhere near—"

"I know that now. She was down by the river, being murdered."

"And no one saw you, nobody at all?"

"The girl who brought the message was hanging around when I left but no one noticed me on my way to or from the gatehouse, nor while I was waiting there, as far as I know."

There were whispered conversations, muffled groans and snores and various other noises coming from the other cages. The hour they had been given must be drawing to a close.

Adama said, "Someone was at great pains to make sure you couldn't prove where you were that night."

"Then why provide a defence – if it was one and the same person?" Bron wondered. "This is going round and round in my head. I can't make head nor tail of it. It's giving me such a headache."

They could hear footsteps along the tunnel and an approaching light was throwing huge shadows against the back walls of the cages, sending a couple of large rats scuttling back into the darkness.

"Our time's up, Bron," Adama warned her friend.

"It was good of you to come, goddess." The bo'sun spoke humbly, and from somewhere deep inside her, Bron's compassion reached out towards him.

"We'll be at the trial," she promised.

"Come on now, ladies," chivvied the guard, unlocking the cage door. "You've had your fun. Time to go home."

They stepped outside the wire and he locked the door behind them.

"Lucky beggar!" he exclaimed to the bo'sun. "I'd change places except I don't want to go where you're going."

"I shall be getting out of here," his prisoner replied with conviction.

The man's reply was devoid of emotion.

"I wouldn't bet on it."

CHAPTER 33

The trial was to take place in the Curia Senatus, the Senate house. It was attracting a great deal of popular interest. No one was bothered in the slightest about the woman fished out of her watery grave, it was a commonplace event, but rumours of possible political intrigue were escalating. Hopefully, some venerable heads would roll but, if not, there was a good chance of some salacious revelations, and at the very least, an afternoon's enjoyable distraction.

Even so, Bron and Adama were surprised at the size of the crowd making its way through the triumphal Arch of Septimius Severus and so into the Forum. They were jostled on their way up the marble steps of the Curia, across the portico and through the great doors.

The hall, with its green-and-maroon pavement, was where the Senate gathered to debate and discuss its business. Today, however, members of the public were standing or sitting on wooden benches placed on three broad marble tiers that usually accommodated three hundred senators, or were hanging over the rail of the gallery that ran along all four walls. Bron noticed that some had sensibly brought cushions with them. They obviously expected a long session.

She and Adama sat as near to the chairman's raised podium and witness boxes as they were able, conscious of being overshadowed by a golden statue of Victory, wings outspread, that stood on a plinth nearby. Bron fervently hoped that justice would be victorious today.

The two young women had not been in a courtroom before and looked around with great interest. Bron knew that Talea and her husband were somewhere among the spectators, and from where they were sitting, Adama could see her benefactor, Senator Crestus Sabinius, who acknowledged her with a very slight incline of his head.

The prosecuting orator was already sitting at a table opposite, facing the defence orator, who was stationed on their side of the hall.

The crowd was making a great deal of noise until the clerk of the court entered through a side door, banged a gavel on his table, which stood at floor level, in front of the podium, and ordered those assembled to stand, which everyone did. The noise died down.

Preceded by the lictor bearing a heavy silver and ebony mace, the chairman entered through the side door and processed to his chair, where he stood, resplendent in his white toga. The lictor placed the mace in a green marble pedestal and carefully adjusted it so that the silver eagle with the silver ball in its talons was facing the courtroom. Then he moved across to his seat.

The chairman announced that the court was in session and sat down, whereupon everyone else sat if they were lucky enough to have found a seat.

Then the jury filed in and took their places on the wooden seats placed for them to one side of the clerk's table, opposite Bron and Adama. Bron counted twenty of them, well-to-do men of all ages dressed in their many-coloured togas.

Finally, the bo'sun was brought in, his wrists chained together and his ankles shackled. He looked dirty and dishevelled and Bron's heart went out to him. Then she wondered whether his appearance had been engineered deliberately and hoped that the members of the jury were similarly affected. He was led to a high-sided wooden box placed between the jury seats and the chairman's podium. The door on one side was opened to allow him to enter, then shut and locked.

He began looking about him and Bron guessed that he was looking for her. Surreptitiously, she waved to attract his attention. He noticed the movement and saw her, smiling in recognition.

First of all, the jury was interrogated by the chairman. Names, addresses, ages and occupations were given, which all took some time to complete.

After questioning them briefly, the defence orator objected to two of them, one a builder with a flourishing business, well known in the city, and the other a sea centurion. The grounds of his objections were that they were ill-educated men, not likely to follow the arguments. Bron was surprised at this, as she judged them hard-working men of the world, likely to empathise with the prisoner. However, they were quickly replaced by two reserves who displayed, under questioning, a higher level of education and greater eloquence.

The clerk then read out the name, age and occupation of the prisoner and the charge against him: the murder of a middle-aged woman, one Fabia, by stabbing, and the disposal of her body in the Tiber.

"How do you plead, prisoner?" asked the clerk. "Guilty or not guilty?"

"Not guilty." The bo'sun's statement came across clear and confident.

First to speak was the prosecuting orator, a tall young man with a mass of thick, surprisingly blonde hair.

"It's dyed!" whispered Adama.

He told the court with great conviction that he intended to prove the guilt of the prisoner and to call for the death penalty. Bron wondered for whom he was working, to whom he would look for recompense at the end of the trial.

Then the defence orator was asked to state his intention and he said he would prove that the prisoner was nowhere near the murdered woman at the time and place indicated, and would seek his release.

There was a rustle of anticipation as the onlookers settled down to a day's diverting entertainment.

CHAPTER 34

Bron studied the orator who was supporting Brunus. He was much shorter than his opponent, and older. His face was jovial, his cheeks plump, as were his bare arms and hands, his fingers flaunting rings that displayed large, gaudy stones. She suspected that his toga hid a portly figure, well used to the best food and wine. Obviously, he had represented some well-heeled clients.

His approach was more relaxed and his voice quieter than the prosecutor's, which made him sound a lot less confident. However, Adama had said that he was the best and Bron certainly hoped so. Whatever her mixed feelings for the prisoner, he should not be punished for a crime he had not committed.

The prosecutor was called upon to prove his case.

As he stood, putting himself at ease by rearranging his toga, smoothing his hair and organising the wax tablets in front of him, Bron nudged Adama and pointed to a metal contraption that stood by the side of the clerk.

"It's a water clock," Adama whispered. "They time the speeches. There's water in the canister that drips into the reservoir. When the reservoir is full, the clerk tips it back into the canister. He's just about to release the valve to start the timing."

The young man began by calling to the witness box the couple who had first seen Fabia floating in the Tiber, the three men who had gone into the water to fish her out, and the doctor who had examined the body and pronounced her dead by stabbing and drowning. Bron shuddered at the description given of the wounds and state of the body. Having established the presumed date, time and place of the crime, a girl was called who followed the same profession and had identified the body as Fabia's.

The young prosecutor walked out from behind his table, and theatrically running his fingers through his hair again, began systematically destroying the character of the bo'sun, relating his many liaisons with prostitutes, his volatile relationship with Fabia, with whom he was living, and his lack of regular work. Bron wondered how he had discovered so much background information until it was revealed that, as well as talking to neighbours, an investigator had been despatched to Ostia to make enquiries about his life before coming to Rome.

Once again, Bron wondered at the speed with which so much information had been gathered.

The neighbours attested that they had often heard the bo'sun and Fabia quarrelling and fighting, had heard furniture and crockery being smashed, had seen her cuts and bruises next morning, and one said she had actually heard the prisoner threaten to kill her. This was strange, as the woman had said earlier that she lived a block away, but her testimony was not questioned.

The young prosecutor stood directly in front of the prisoner and leaned towards him.

"Did you threaten to kill her?" he asked.

"I may have done, but I didn't mean it, not really."

The jury looked unimpressed.

Then the prisoner's movements on the fateful night were questioned. The interrogator was flamboyantly striding backwards and forwards.

The bo'sun related the events as he had told them to Bron – how Fabia had gone out to meet a client, and then had sent him a message, delivered by a street girl, asking him to meet her by the gatehouse leading to the Appian Way.

Again the prosecutor stood in front of the bo'sun.

"Who was the messenger?" he enquired. "Is she here? Can you produce her?"

"I don't know who she was," the bo'sun replied.

"What did the message say?"

"That she had some important information for me, and if I met her by the gatehouse, she would give it to me."

"It must have been important to cause you to leave your apartment and walk all that way late in the evening."

"It was."

Bron's heart began to race. She had not anticipated this line of questioning. Of course, Brunus would want to establish the importance of the message he had received because that is why he had walked so far out of the city. He would have to say that the news concerned his missing son. Would her name be dragged into his evidence?

However, she need not have panicked because the orator was continuing his line of questioning without pursuing these matters. Although feeling great relief, she was puzzled by the omission. He had returned to his table.

"How long did it take you to walk to your destination?"

"About an hour."

"Then what happened?"

"Nothing. Fabia didn't turn up."

"So what did you do then?"

"I waited for an hour, then walked home."

"Taking another hour?"

"Yes."

Again fingers were scraped through the blonde hair.

"And you can prove all this? You have said that you cannot produce the girl who came with the message, but have you brought witnesses to support the rest of your story – because story is what I believe it to be. A neighbour, a friend, passers-by, anyone who can corroborate that you were out in the suburbs and not in the city at the time of the murder?"

"There were people around, of course, but I met no one I knew, no one who would remember me."

The questioning continued. Not a syllable went unnoticed by the crowd, who were hanging on to every word with great concentration.

"Did you murder that woman?" finally asked the prosecutor.

"No."

"Then if not you, who did, and why?"

"I don't know."

"And neither do I, and neither does the jury."

The orator sat down, looking well pleased with himself. Bron had counted six refillings of the water container. Then it was the turn of the defence orator.

"He'll have his work cut out," Adama whispered.

"But if Brunus is innocent, and I believe he is," Bron whispered back, "surely that will be established. You did say he was the best."

"Let's hope so."

Pulling her tunic away from her neck, Bron fanned her face with her hand. It was stifling in the courtroom – the number of bodies, the excitement, the heat and her own nervousness all sending the temperature soaring. She hoped it wasn't her own perspiration she could smell.

The little man on whom Brunus was pinning all his hopes pulled his toga down and away from his left shoulder. He stayed stolidly behind his table while trying to reinstate the character of his client.

First of all, he questioned the testimony of the neighbour who lived a block away and could hardly have heard any quarrel waging in the bo'sun's apartment, but as the prisoner had already admitted that he might have threatened to kill Fabia, refuting her testimony did not carry any weight.

He then questioned him about his skills and his jobs on the small boats that plied up and down the Tiber.

"You took work wherever you could find it?"

"Yes."

"Why did you leave Ostia, where there was plenty of work on seagoing vessels, and travel to Rome?"

"I came looking for someone."

"Who? Fabia?"

"No, she followed me. No, my son and his mother."

Again, Bron anxiously awaited the outcome of these questions, but again she was surprised at the turnaround, away from the subject of Rius.

"Obviously, you did not find them, or you would not have been living with the murdered woman. Now tell the court again what happened on the night of the murder."

His defending orator had bypassed the chance to let him fully explain his position. *Was that omission deliberate or an error of judgement?* wondered Bron.

The bo'sun repeated his story. He was not holding his head so high now and his voice was quieter. The blonde orator jumped up and said he could not hear what the defendant was saying and the chairman ordered him to speak up.

"So no one you know saw you and recognised you during your walk to the gatehouse, nor while you were there nor on your way back?"

"No."

"But that is hardly surprising because you wished to keep a low profile?"

"Yes."

"The prosecution accuses you of being down by the Tiber at the time in question. Were you there?"

"No."

"Unfortunately, we cannot prove that you were where you said you were, but neither can they prove that you were *not* where you said you were but were, in truth, along by the river."

Bron looked at Adama. "Is that it?" she whispered. "Is that the extent of the defence?" The water clock had been emptied and refilled only twice.

Adama shrugged. "It seems so. This is not good, Bron."

The prosecution was summing up now, followed by the case for the defence. Bron hardly heard them. She was perplexed and gripped by a great sense of injustice. The bo'sun was now sitting in the locked box but she could see above the wooden sides that his head was bent low and his shoulders drooped.

The chairman was instructing the jury to withdraw and consider their verdict. Everyone stood as the chairman then the prisoner and the officers of the court filed out.

Then the noise from the crowd broke out again, even louder. Bron had to shout to make herself heard.

"There's something wrong here, Adama, something very wrong."

"I feel it too, Bron."

"That defence orator was nervous, but of what?"

"I wish I could ask Crestus, but it would hardly be in good taste to go across to him. Of course, I could ask Senator Laenus Loricatus – he hardly has a reputation to sully these days."

"Senator Loricatus? Is he here? Where?"

"At the back of the crowd, over there." Bron looked in the direction Adama was indicating. "Well, he was. He seems to have disappeared."

"Did he see us together?"

"Probably. I shall have some explaining to do next time he sends for me."

"Let's go outside, Adama. It's so stuffy in here."

Once outside in the Forum, Bron took several deep breaths, savouring the fresh air. It was noon but she wasn't hungry.

"How long do you think they'll take?"

"The longer the better, I reckon. They must take time to talk it all through. Perhaps there's a chance they'll believe his story."

"How will we know when to return?"

"I don't think we'll be left in any doubt. Just follow the crowd."

"Let's walk a little way."

It took no time at all, less than an hour, before there were shouts of, "The jury has returned!" and there was a scramble for the doors as the crowd began cramming back into the hall.

Bron and Adama had been sitting on the steps at the foot of the Column of Phocas and by the time they squeezed back inside, there were no seats available, so they had to stand by the doors.

Suddenly, Bron felt very uncomfortable, as if she were being watched. Looking around, she saw no one she knew, until her eyes were drawn upwards to the gallery. Then she felt heat rising in her cheeks. Gazing down at her was Senator Laenus Loricatus. Lowering her eyes immediately, she drew back into the crowd, shielded behind Adama, but she knew that he knew she had seen him.

She wondered if he had guessed the connection between the prisoner, herself and Rius. But there was no reason why he should. He was here, like everyone else, to gawk at the proceedings of a trial that had excited the popular imagination. There was nothing more sinister about his attendance.

She jumped as the clerk of the court banged his gavel and the hall quietened again. The contrast between the rumpus and the silence was intimidating. Everyone was watching as the chairman entered and took his seat and made himself comfortable.

"Jury, have you recorded your verdicts?"

The elderly man appointed to speak for the twenty jurors answered.

"We have."

The chairman nodded to the clerk, who walked over and was handed a pottery container. He returned to his seat, removed the lid, and turned the jar upside down. The contents clattered onto his table.

Bron moved over so that she could peer between the heads of those in front of her but she was too short and even by standing on tiptoe and craning her neck, she was unable to see what was happening.

"What is he doing?" she asked Adama, who shook her head in ignorance.

"He's counting the tablets," explained a woman by her side. "I go to all the murder trials," she confided, "so I know what's going on." Bron smiled encouragingly.

"The jurors are given a wax tablet each. After their discussion, they mark them with an 'A' for 'Absolve' or 'C' for 'Condemn'. The clerk counts them up then tells the chairman the result."

"Does it have to be unanimous?" asked Adama.

"No. Nine-tenths will do. As there are twenty on the jury, eighteen will have to agree. If they can't, there will be a retrial."

"Ssshhh!" hissed someone behind them. The clerk had counted the tablets and now had his back to the hall as he spoke to the chairman, who was leaning down to hear him.

The clerk banged his gavel again. "We have a verdict."

The chairman stood. There was not a sound in the hall, not a cough nor a shuffling of feet, as the crowd waited expectantly.

The chairman cleared his throat then announced in a loud voice, so there should be no misunderstanding, "The jury finds the prisoner guilty of the murder of the woman Fabia, as charged."

Bron took in a long breath, inaudible in the hubbub that arose from all parts of the assembly. The clerk had to bang his gavel several times to obtain silence.

The chairman was speaking again. "The sentence of the court is death by a means to be determined."

"All stand!" ordered the clerk, but this time no one took any notice and the general movement of the crowd about her made it impossible for Bron to see what was happening at the front of the hall. By the time she did struggle free of the crowd, dragging Adama with her, the chairman and officers had left and there was no sign of the prisoner.

"It's not fair! That wasn't justice!" she anguished. "What about the best orator in the business now? That was no trial! It was a travesty! I'm certain he's innocent."

"I don't understand what happened," said Adama, confused.

"Nor do I, but I intend to find out!"

"How?"

"I don't know yet. There must be someone who can help us. Come on, let's get out of here!"

Together they left the Curia, and going round and round in verbal circles, discussed the trial all the way home.

CHAPTER 35

Talea Iconica and her husband were already home by the time Bron reached there. Her mistress met her in the hallway.

"Come and sit down, Bron dear. You look exhausted. You should have taken the litter."

She led Bron into the triclinium and saw to it that she was comfortable on one of the couches round the table before ordering drinks to be brought to them.

"Well, what did you make of that?" Talea asked.

"It was a mockery of a trial!" Bron replied with passion. "Talea, I'm sure he's innocent. He's many things – unscrupulous when he wants something badly enough, treacherous, a bully most of the time, but not a murderer, and not a murderer of Fabia. After all, she was all he had. I do believe he was innocent."

"I don't know whether he is innocent or not, but certainly justice wasn't evident in that courtroom today." Talea's husband, Carolus, had entered the room unnoticed.

Bron turned to him. "But, sir, what can be done about it? Is there anything I can do?"

He patted her hand as it lay resting on the arm of the couch and spread himself out next to his wife.

"I don't think there is."

A slave entered with a silver tray bearing a jug of iced water and glasses and poured drinks for them.

"What I don't understand is," said Bron, "who went to the bother and expense of sponsoring a trial, so that Brunus could be defended, when it was just play acting?"

Carolus stroked his chin thoughtfully. "Perhaps it had to be played out in the public arena so that your friend could be sacrificed."

"Bron, dear," began Talea hesitantly, "I know it's none of our business, but I am asking only because we care about you. What exactly does this man mean to you?"

Bron sipped her drink while deciding whether or not to answer the question honestly.

"It was madness, but we were lovers once, and I shall always be grateful to him for giving me Rius. But he humiliated me and shamed me—"

"It takes two, young lady," Carolus pointed out.

"Yes, I know – it wasn't all his fault. I've hated him for it but I think in his own way he loves me. He has certainly never stopped pursuing me. So I can't see him treated like this, when I believe he didn't murder Fabia. But who did, and why, I can't begin to imagine."

Carolus raised himself up on his elbow. "Bron, as you feel so strongly about it, I think you should go and see him again and find out everything he knows. There may not be time to help him, but if you can disentangle some of this mystery, clear his name even, it may help you when he has gone and your son asks about his father."

"And soon," Talea interjected. "Go and see him soon. The court doesn't waste much time when it comes to carrying out the death sentence. I'm sure Carolus will be able to find out where he is being held."

The prison in which the condemned man had been thrown this time was the Mamertine, at the foot of the Capitoline Hill. Although Adama offered to go with her again, Bron said she preferred go alone.

"There may be things he will share only with me," she said, "and having someone else there may stop him from saying them. I must get out of him everything that's in his head about this business – it will probably be our last time together. Thank you for offering, Adama, but I hope you understand."

Adama nodded sympathetically. "But you can't make your way there on your own, at night," she objected.

"If I ask him, I am sure my master will take me there and bring me back, and it doesn't have to be at night."

The visit was arranged for the following afternoon, but it might just as well have been night time. Day or night made no difference in that dark hole.

A flight of steps led from the Capitoline down to the door of the prison. Carolus reluctantly left her there, in charge of the guard.

"I'll wait in the sunshine at the top of the steps," he said. "I've paid him well and you'll come to no harm."

The man ushered Bron into a small room, lit only by one candle standing on a wooden table. She looked around. There were a couple of chairs and a dishevelled camp bed, a small cupboard and a pack of cards strewn across the earth, but no sign of anyone.

"Where is he?" she asked.

The guard pointed to a hole in the floor. "Down there."

"Dear God!"

"God? You a Christian?" he asked her.

Bron wasn't sure whether saying she was or was not a Christian would help her, so she kept silent.

"If you are, you shouldn't be surprised. It's the dungeon where they banged up your two saints, Peter and Paul."

Bron was unmoved. She had never heard of this Peter and Paul.

"How deep is it?"

"About twelve feet. I can get him up, if you like. I've been paid enough."

"Yes, please."

He fetched a coiled rope from a corner of the room and tied it securely to an iron ring in the wall.

"Hey, you down there! You got a visitor. I'm lowering a rope. I'm not going to break my back hauling you up but I'll hold on to it this end and you can make your way up best you can. Got it?"

"I've got it!" There was no mistaking that rasping voice.

Moments later, after a lot of cursing and swearing accompanied by sounds of falling stones and scrambling feet, the bo'sun's silver head appeared above the rim of the hole. The guard reached down a hand for him to grab hold of, then he was standing by her side.

"You're fit, I'll say that for you," his jailer said with some respect.

"Years of climbing the rigging," the bo'sun replied. He turned to Bron. "Goddess, dear girl, I thought it would be you."

He opened his arms and she took a step forward, allowing him to pull her close and hold on to her tightly for a few moments. She was shocked to realise how much weight he had lost. The tunic hanging loosely from his shoulders was damp and smelt of mould and sweat, though he was shivering.

She disentangled herself and led him by the hand over to the table, where he sank onto one of the chairs. She sat in the other. His hands in his lap were shaking and she leaned over and took hold of them. The pallor of death was all about him and she could not believe the deterioration in the twenty-four hours since she had last seen him.

"Are they feeding you?" she asked.

"Some."

"Guard, would you ask the gentleman who is waiting for me if he would send someone to buy bread and fruit, and a bucket of water. He'll see you right."

"Water is it you want, prisoner? Just open that door in the wall down there and you can have all the water you'll ever need."

He laughed and left the room, locking the door behind him.

"What does he mean?" Bron asked.

"There's a door down there that opens onto the Cloaca Maxima, the city's main sewer. It empties into the Tiber. It's the quickest way to dispose of prisoners and that's the way I shall go. Ironic, isn't it, that Fabia and I should end up in the same grave? Birds of a feather, eh? She'd enjoy that joke. I guess that neither of us deserved any better."

"Oh, Brunus, don't say that! We're going to try to clear your name, to prove you innocent."

"There's no time for that, Bron. Not now."

"Brunus, you've got to let me try!"

"You'll be wasting your time. Don't put yourself to all that trouble, goddess, I'm not worth it."

"Then for our son's sake! I'll do it for his sake. One day, Rius is going to be asking about his father."

"And what will you tell him? That he was a drunk, a lecher and a bully? That he once tried to rape his mother?"

Bron was conscious of tears streaming down her cheeks as she clung to his hands.

"No, Brunus, I shall tell him that his father was a bo'sun, a skilful sailor, who could shin up the rigging in a twinkling of an eye; a brave man, who survived a vicious whipping on board ship with hardly a murmur; who once saved his mother from a filthy pirate and who dived into the sea to rescue a boy and his puppy – do you remember?" He nodded and smiled.

"And I shall tell him," continued Bron quietly, looking down at their clasped fingers, "that his father loved me."

He raised her hands to his lips and kissed them gently.

"Always did, Bron, in my own way, always did."

He brought her hands down to the table but still kept them held tightly in his own.

"And that is why I want to prove your innocence, Brunus. So help me. Tell me everything you can remember, from the beginning, every little detail. There must be something there that will make sense of this mess."

"It is as I told you before: Fabia said she was going out to meet someone and would be back later. She seldom stayed with anyone all night. Most of them couldn't afford it."

"And she didn't give any name?"

"No. She dressed up, though."

"Dressed up?"

"Took care over her appearance. Wore her best tunic and had taken time over her make-up, and stank of cheap perfume." He smiled. "She never did have your taste, Bron."

"Then what?"

"She hadn't been gone an hour when a girl turned up on the doorstep with this message, asking me to meet Fabia."

"On the road to the Appian Way?"

"Yes."

"This girl, what was she like?"

"A pretty girl, beautiful even. I've only ever seen her that once."

"Dark or fair haired?"

"Dark and dark skinned. Tall and slim. Long legs – at least, they looked long. Might have been because her tunic was so short. Red, though it was hidden under a cloak."

"Then you left the house?"

"Of course. Fabia's message said that she had found Rius."

"But she couldn't have done. No one except Fausta Loricata and her husband know where he is. The message was a decoy, to get you out of the way, sending you out into the country on a fool's errand where nobody would recognise you and be able to provide you with an alibi."

"That's obvious now. But who could have sent it?"

"Whoever murdered Fabia."

"But she had no enemies that I know of. What could have been the motive?"

Bron shook her head in perplexity.

"What's he like, Bron, the little chap? Does he look like me? Does he look like my son? I wish you had let me see him."

Pity for him made her say what he wanted to hear.

"Yes, he does take after you, Brunus, in many ways. He has square fingers like yours, his hands remind me of you, and he's very strong and sturdy in his body, like you."

He grinned for the first time since she arrived. "And you'd know all about that, wouldn't you, goddess?"

It was the old bo'sun back again, and although Bron was happy to see it, she flushed with embarrassment.

They heard the key turning in the lock. The guard came in, carrying a bulging white cloth, which he threw on the table, and a bucket, which he put down carelessly, slopping water on the floor.

The bo'sun unwrapped the cloth and Bron watched with pleasure as he hungrily devoured bread, cheese, peaches and oranges. When he had swallowed the last mouthful, he turned towards her.

"It's time for you to go, Bron. You've done everything you can for me and I'm deeply grateful to my girl, my goddess." He stood. "Come!"

Once again he held out his arms to her and she willingly accepted his embrace, sliding her arms round his waist. When she looked up into his face, he wiped her tears away with fingers that smelt of cheese.

"Brunus."

"Yes?"

"On the island—"

"Paradise, wasn't it?"

"Yes, it was for a while, and you were magnificent."

He kissed her forehead and released her.

"Bron, be at peace. I won't resist them when they come for me – I don't think it could be worse than that flogging!" He smiled again.

Bron looked across to his jailer then at the gaping hole in the floor.

"Does he have to go back down there?"

"Regulations, miss. Sorry. I'd lose my job, maybe my head."

Brunus was urging her towards the door.

"Go now, Bron, before you have to change your mind about Rius's strong, brave father."

She stroked his face then, as if trying to memorise through her fingers the strong lines of his cheeks and jaw, kissed him lightly on the mouth and left hurriedly, stumbling up the steps on her way out into the afternoon sun.

CHAPTER 36

Next morning, Bron found herself alone in the house, except for the slaves, who were busy about their work. Her mistress had taken the children and their nurses to visit her elderly father and her master had gone to the stock exchange.

He had been very kind to her on their walk back from the prison yesterday, had listened to her ramblings, provided a kerchief on which to blow her nose, and had suggested that she write down everything the bo'sun had told her about the night of the murder.

Now, with a free morning ahead of her, she was thinking about taking a walk to sort out her thoughts and emotions when her reverie was interrupted by a tap at the door of her room. When she opened it, she found one of Talea's male slaves standing there.

"Miss, there's a friend of yours, says she must speak to you."

Bron looked over his shoulder to see Adama hovering in the garden, mouthing words at her and gesticulating wildly.

"Thank you," Bron said, mystified, and closing the door behind her, walked across the verandah and out into the sunshine.

"Whatever's the matter?" she asked. "What's up?"

"Bron! He's back!"

Her thoughts flew to the bo'sun. "Brunus?"

"No, silly, Rius! Rius is back! Fausta has brought him home!"

Bron sat down heavily on a bench, Adama beside her.

"Are you sure? How do you know? Are you sure?"

"I wouldn't be here if I wasn't sure. Izmira came early this morning with a message from Cook. They arrived home late last night and went straight to bed. Izmira said they all thought it very strange when yesterday morning Julia started shouting at the slaves to pack up her belongings, load them onto a cart and take them back to her house. That was why! The mistress was coming home with Rius!"

"Oh, Adama, that's wonderful news. Have you seen him? How does he look? Is he well?"

"Izmira said he's a fine little lad. Not walking yet but he's grown so, and he looks a picture of health. They've been in the country somewhere."

Bron jumped up. "I must see him for myself, Adama!"

"I don't know whether that will be possible, Bron."

"But I must! I must!"

"Yes, of course you must. We'll try to arrange something soon."

"No, today, now! I've got the morning free. I'll come back with you now!"

"I suppose you could wait in my apartment while I find out if his nurse will bring him down to see you."

"Then let's do that."

"She'll lose her job if Fausta Loricata finds out."

"What threat can I pose to them now?" Bron asked. "And with Brunus out of the way – funny that, when you think about it – Fausta bringing Rius back so soon after the guilty verdict, almost as if she knew what it would be."

Together, they set out for Palatine Hill.

"Talking of his father," decided Bron, "I will see Rius, then go straight to the prison and tell Brunus the good news. He would love to see him but I know I can't take a baby into a place like that; he could catch all manner of disorders."

When they reached Adama's apartment, she left Bron and climbed the hill to the Loricatus house. Half an hour later, she was back.

"It's all arranged," she said. "In about half an hour, Nurse will bring him down the hill. She dare not come in, that wouldn't do at all, but she'll hang about at the path leading to the cave and you'll be able hide in the undergrowth and see him from a distance."

"But—" began Bron.

"See him, Bron, nothing else. It will only upset him if he recognises you and you don't want that, do you?"

Bron hesitated.

"It's best for him," Adama persisted.

"Yes, I know. All right. I won't touch him. Of course, it won't be long before I get him back for good, and then everything will be all right."

Adama was studying the determined set of her chin and probably thinking what Bron was thinking – *And how is that going to happen?* Bron, however, had an idea but for the time being would keep her own counsel.

Today, she was happy to have news that would gladden the heart of the prisoner. She decided she was confident enough to make her own way to the prison, reasoning that she knew what to expect and the guard was not unfriendly.

So she hid among the bushes and watched Rius from a distance, saw him take uncertain steps, swinging about off balance as he held his nurse's hand and was encouraged to walk in Bron's direction, and she heard him chuckle. All this she could report to Brunus.

As yesterday, she descended the steps into the twilight and knocked on the door of the prison. The grill was opened slowly, but not by the guard she recognised.

"Hello," she greeted this man politely, "I was hoping to see the guard who was on duty yesterday."

"That was yesterday," he growled. "Today's today. I'm on duty today. What do you want?"

"May I see the prisoner, please?" she asked in a tone she hoped would bring results.

"No prisoner here," was the reply.

"Oh, but there is, I saw him yesterday."

"I told you, there's no prisoner here."

"Please," she pleaded, "I have some news for him."

"I can put you down the hole and you can see for yourself, if you like. Look, miss, he may have been here yesterday but he's not here today. They must have done for him in the night. Now be off with you." With that, he closed the grill.

Bron stared at the door in horror while his words sunk in. But she wanted to tell him that Rius was back, and walking, well almost, and she wanted to prove that he hadn't killed Fabia, somebody else had, and get him out of this dreadful prison. It wasn't right what they were doing to him, had done to him.

Feeling sick, she wondered whether even now he was floating in the Tiber.

She turned and slowly climbed the steps, back into the sunshine.

It seemed more imperative than ever that she should try to establish his innocence.

"I won't let you down, Brunus, I promise," she said aloud, "though I don't know where to begin. Where shall I begin?"

CHAPTER 37

"Bron, my wife tells me you want to talk to me."

"Yes, sir, about Brunus."

"Then come and sit with me." He put aside the wax tablets he had been studying and moved further along the bench to make room for her. "Talea has told me that the execution was carried out overnight."

Bron nodded miserably.

"That was quick, even by Roman standards. Indecently so, to my mind. Though, once convicted, I suppose there is no merit in delay. However, someone needs to say something about that trial. I'd be glad to help all I can."

She choked on her tears as she tried to thank him.

"Will you take some wine, my dear? The afternoon sun is still so hot."

"No, thank you, sir."

"Water then?" She nodded and he signalled to a slave who was hovering in the vicinity. "Wine and water, lad. And bring us some cushions and sunshades and fans."

"Sir, he was punished for something I'm sure he didn't do. There was no justice done in that court room."

"You're right, there wasn't. So, what do you want me to do?"

"If you would just listen to my ramblings, to see if they make any sense. I don't know how else to tackle this."

"Go on, I'm listening."

"To start at the beginning, Brunus didn't know who Fabia was going to meet, but said she had taken trouble over her appearance – her best tunic and make-up and perfume." She smiled. "Cheap perfume. Her client must have been someone she thought was special."

Her listener nodded.

"Then this girl came with the message, supposedly from Fabia, which sent him on a fool's errand over an hour's walk away from where the murder was taking place. He had never seen this girl before and couldn't produce her in court, but he gave me a good description of her – dark hair, dark skinned, tall, short red tunic."

"Do you think the message might have come from Fabia? Is it possible that whoever she had gone to meet had given her some news about your son, and the message to the bo'sun was genuine?"

"It's possible, I suppose, that she did intend to meet him, but couldn't show up because by that time she had been murdered. But there were only two people who knew where Rius was, the senator and his wife, and it's obvious they didn't want anyone else to know, not even their servants. Anyway, I don't think either of them knew Fabia."

The slaves had returned now and were setting up a small collapsible table, on which they placed a tray with decanter, jug, glasses and fans. They had brought several cushions, and were positioning the large sunshades in their sockets, so that the bench was shaded. Two of them stood by, ready to pour drinks, operate fans and swivel the shades as the sun moved round, but their master waved them away.

"Not so helpless that I can't pour a couple of drinks," he told them as he set about the task. "Here you are, Bron, drink that."

While she gratefully held the cold glass against her hot cheeks then drank the iced water, he sipped his white wine, closed his eyes and grunted in appreciation. Bron didn't like to disturb him and waited until he opened them and had fixed his serious gaze on her again.

"We need to find that girl in the red tunic and ask her who gave her the message to deliver. What else?"

"The trial. Someone had set up that fiasco – why? Perhaps you are right, that it needed a public arena. A scapegoat had to be found to draw attention away from the real murderer. But who would want to get rid of Fabia, and why? There are so many questions."

She paused to drink again. He was still thoughtfully sipping his wine.

"It occurred to me in the Curia," he said finally, "that they didn't give him the chance of explaining what the message was, why he was so likely to go for an hour's walk late at night, what was so important to make him do that. First the prosecution then the defence orator broached the subject then backed off. Why do you think that was?"

"Someone didn't want anyone to know that Rius had been spirited away. But why *did* Fausta take him out of Rome so suddenly and so secretly?"

"Perhaps it was just a holiday," he suggested.

"Perhaps, but it's strange that as soon as Brunus was out of the way – and who knew about his quick execution, apart from those who carried it out, and me, quite by chance? – as soon as he was out of the way, Fausta brought Rius home – not days later, but immediately. Was it coincidence or is there a connection?"

Carolus picked up a feather fan and handed it to Bron. He picked up another for himself.

"Your bo'sun was trying to find his son," he reminded her, "but once dead, he no longer posed a threat. Didn't he take on the job of gardener here so that he could tackle you on the subject?"

"Yes, but Senator Loricatus and his wife didn't know that. They didn't know who Rius's father was nor that he was out looking for his boy."

"Was Senator Loricatus at the trial, do you know?"

"Yes, we saw him."

"Though that doesn't signify anything. The world and his wife were there."

"Though he was keeping a low profile."

Carolus closed his fan and tapped it sharply on his knee.

"There seems only one way forward. We've got to find that young lady."

"I wonder," mused Bron aloud, "whether Adama's friend, Senator Crestus Sabinius, could help us – he gets around." She blushed. "I mean, sir, that you're happily married and he's not."

Greatly amused, her employer tapped the fan against Bron's knee this time and laughed.

"I know what you mean, Bron, and you're right, I am happily married, I'm glad to say. It's a good idea. I'll have a word with him when next we meet, though it may not be for some time."

His smile faded and his eyes narrowed, though not against the sun because they were still in shade.

"Is something the matter, sir?" Bron asked him anxiously. "You look worried."

"I am, though it's nothing to do with what we were just discussing. Speaking of Crestus has reminded me of certain business concerns, but there's no need to lay them on your shoulders."

"Perhaps if you told me about them – I'm a good listener, sir."

"I'm sure you are, Bron." His face lit up. "Here's your mistress, coming to find out what we've been talking about." He stood then and smiled down at Bron. "You've probably gathered that she doesn't like being left out. You'll have to tell her, as I must get off to the warehouse."

He walked across to his wife, who was approaching along one of the paths, and kissed her on the cheek. "I must go, dear. Bron will tell you what we have decided to do. I'll see you for dinner."

Talea slipped into his place on the bench and began to fan herself vigorously.

"So," she said, "what have you two been cooking up?"

Bron repeated the essence of the discussion that had just taken place.

"Madam, for a minute there, the master looked and sounded very concerned about his business. Is everything all right?"

Talea sighed. "He doesn't tell me everything, because he doesn't want to worry me, but these are worrying times, Bron. You're not Roman so you can't begin to understand how we feel about our city, but our borders are in great danger from pagan incursions."

Bron remembered the speech she had helped Senator Loricatus compose. Thoughts of the senator chilled her, as if the sun had suddenly gone behind a cloud.

"I know that the Senate is playing for time while they prepare the army for war."

"Is that what you've heard? That may have been the plan but the army has been greatly depleted in the last two weeks. Did you also hear that Emperor Honorius had General Stilicho executed?

My husband says that was a stupid thing to do. You see, although Stilicho was a Roman citizen, he was a Vandal by birth, same as Alaric."

"A Vandal?"

"Yes, they're one of the Germanic tribes. Our army is – was – composed largely of men from subjugated tribes. They were very supportive of General Stilicho and when he was done away with, most of them mutinied and fled to join Alaric, robbing and killing on the way. That has left our army weak and vulnerable."

"But Rome is still safe?"

"I don't know, Bron."

"Emperor Honorius didn't seem to be at all anxious when we saw him at the theatre. In fact, the royal party seemed not to have a care in the world."

"That's because they left for Ravenna next morning. Honorius is sitting it out there in his fortified palace, hoping the emergency will go away, and leaving the mess here for Constantine and the people of Rome to clear up."

"Has Constantine taken over as emperor?"

"The Senate has elected him temporarily in place of Honorius. Somebody had to take charge. Anyway, Carolus is very worried about his business, because he can't get his goods in and out of the country to the north. Now, consignments for Gaul and Spain will have to go overland to Ostia and from there by sea, which takes so much longer and is so much more expensive. He has reason to be worried."

"I'm so sorry, madam. Your husband is a good, kind man."

Talea's eyes lit up. "Yes, he is, and they're two of the reasons I married him."

Bron was glad to lighten the conversation and asked mischievously, "And the others, madam?"

Talea laughed. "They're all secrets between Carolus and me!"

Bron laughed too and the sun was shining again.

"Do you fancy a ride this afternoon, my dear? My new tunic is ready for a final fitting and I will surprise my dressmaker by calling on her for a change. If the tunic pleases me, I will order two more – different colours, of course."

CHAPTER 38

Talea's seamstress worked in two small rooms in her home in a side street near the Pantheon. Once again, Bron found herself enjoying the comfort of a ride in the twin carrying chair through the city that she was beginning to think of as home.

Then she shook her head. This was not home. Home was many months' sea voyage away. Home was a land colder than this, much colder, but green and beautiful, with skies that were not always grey and dropping their soft, life-giving rain but were sometimes the colour of the Mediterranean, with mountainous clouds like bright white rolling breakers.

Suddenly, she felt very sick for Byden, her home on that grassy slope facing the sun. Then she remembered again that the last time she had seen her village, it was burning bright red, and she wondered about those she had left behind – her mother and father, her brother and Soranus, her young husband.

He was still her husband, though he had released her from her wedding vows before she escaped. And she had made him a promise to go back. *"If it takes a lifetime, I'll come back,"* she had said.

But what of Aurelius? She loved Soranus but it was Aurelius she was in love with. She couldn't go home and leave Aurelius here. Her thoughts were going round and round in circles and giving her a headache.

"Sorry, I was daydreaming. What did you say?"

Talea repeated her suggestion. "I might be a while so why don't you have a look round the Pantheon? It's worth a visit."

Bron realised that they were stationary and Talea was being helped out of the chair by one of the porters. Taking hold of the large hand offered to her, she scrambled out through the door on her side.

"Yes, I'll do that," she replied.

"Off you go, then," Talea dismissed her. "I'll find you when I'm ready to leave."

Bron climbed the steps of the temple, keeping out of the way of a young boy wielding his home-made besom broom. She passed between tall granite columns and pushed open the heavy bronze door. It took a few moments for her eyes to adjust to the dim interior after the bright sunshine outside. The only source of natural light entered through a large round hole in the dome high above her.

A group was listening with interest to a guide and she joined them. It was certainly an impressive building, over four hundred years old, with the largest concrete dome ever built.

The guide indicated the empty niches round the circular walls.

"The old gods were removed when Christianity became our state religion."

The tour lasted about half an hour, after which Bron came out onto the portico again, blinking in the sunshine. The carrying chair was waiting where the porters had left it. They were lounging against convenient walls, engaged in conversation. There was no sign of Talea.

The young sweeper had been conscientious about his work, and as all the rotting fruit, broken glass and dried mud had been removed from the steps, Bron decided they were now clean enough to sit on.

From her position, she took pleasure in watching all the comings and goings of the crowd and tried to guess where each passer-by was headed.

As was normal, there were fewer women than men abroad. That was one reason her attention was drawn to the back view of a woman who was hurrying through the square. Middle-aged, a mass of light brown hair tied back at the nape of her neck, she was strangely familiar. Suddenly, Bron realised who it was!

Jumping up, she called out to her, "Veneta?" Then a little louder, "Veneta?"

Slowly the woman turned to face Bron, her expression one of disbelief.

"Bron, is that you? Is it really you?" She came towards the steps. "We've been searching for you for weeks and weeks! Oh, Bron, how glad I am to see you!"

Bron ran down the steps and launched herself at her friend and their arms encircled each other in an enthusiastic hug.

"What are you doing in Rome?" Bron asked her.

"I've told you, we've all been looking for you." Veneta laughed with delight and the 'summer smile' Bron had known so well since a child lit up her face.

"Oh, Veneta, it's so good to see you. And the children. How are my children?"

"They're very well, we all are, and they're growing up so fast!"

"We need to talk," Bron said. "We could sit in my mistress's carrying chair over there, but the slaves would overhear everything we were saying."

"So, you've found work?" asked Veneta, eyeing the luxurious chair.

"Good work," Bron nodded as they sat on the steps. "I've been very fortunate."

Having recovered from her surprise, Veneta's questions became accusations.

"But why did you leave Ostia so suddenly, without explanation? How could you do that to the children and me? You must have known how worried and upset we would be."

Bron looked down at their clasped hands and spoke so quietly that Veneta had to lean nearer to hear her.

"I did something awful, Veneta, and I had to get away. I will tell you everything – you deserve an explanation – but first, tell me where the children are."

"With Declan. He's been out all night, working the boats on the Tiber, so has the day off. I left them with him for a couple of hours, to do some searching on my own." She smiled. "The children take up a great deal of my time and energy."

"I know. I'm so grateful to you both for taking care of them. Please don't be angry, though you've a right to be angry, but I've been punished enough for what I did."

She paused, searching for the right words, although no words could be 'right' because the truth was unpalatable. Veneta came to her rescue.

"Bron, after you left Ostia and disappeared, the bo'sun came to the apartment. He insinuated things – I couldn't believe that what he was saying was true – but I reached the conclusion that it was. Dear Bron, did he force you? Were you carrying his child?"

Bron nodded, her eyes downcast again. Veneta waited. "It happened on the island after we were shipwrecked, but he didn't force me, he didn't have to."

When there was no response, she lifted her eyes to look at her friend, her protector since the age of three when she was taken into the Temple in Byden to become consort for the High Priest's son; this dear friend, one-time pagan priestess and now a Christian, who had accompanied her and her children to Ostia and had been left with them when Bron ran away to Rome.

"It was madness, Veneta, utter madness. I was so ashamed that I fled, to hide in a place where I didn't have to face *you* and *he* couldn't find me."

"And you had his baby?"

Bron's face brightened. "Yes, a son. I called him Honorius, after the emperor."

Then Bron recounted all that had happened to her since coming to Rome. Veneta listened attentively without interrupting as she heard about the lecherous advances of Laenus Loricatus and Bron's dismissal, and her present work with Talea Iconica. Finally, she heard the story of the murder of Fabia and the bo'sun's wrongful conviction and execution.

"You've been through so much since we were last together, and you're still suffering, aren't you? Until you get your baby back—"

"I've a plan how to do that, Veneta. However, that will have to wait until I've cleared Brunus's name, as I promised him I would, by discovering the identity of the real murderer."

"Bron, I've rehearsed time and time again the harsh words I would say to you when we eventually met, but now, I can't even remember what they were."

"I'm so sorry, Veneta."

Bron laid her head on her friend's shoulder, slipped her arms round Veneta's waist and held on to her tightly.

"Now tell me all your news."

Then it was Bron's turn to listen as her friend assured her again of the well-being of the children she had left behind in

Ostia – four of her own and her niece – and their journey to the city.

"And how about Declan?" Bron asked and saw Veneta blush.

"He and I—" She hesitated and began again. "He and I get on so well together. In fact, he—"

Bron was amused to watch her friend's cheeks turning an even brighter shade of pink.

"You and Declan?" queried Bron.

"He's asked me to marry him," Veneta at last confessed.

Bron had known since the voyage that Declan loved Veneta.

"And what answer did you give?"

"I haven't, not yet, not really, but – he's only twenty-six and I'm so conscious that I'm nineteen years older."

"Do you love him, Veneta?"

"He's been my rock since you left, and he's loving and reliable – but no, not in the way I loved Selvid."

"Your husband's dead," Bron stated flatly.

"Yes, and I am comforted to remember that he died a hero, fighting for our village, for Byden. I don't know how to answer Declan."

"You haven't—?"

"No, and I know that's very difficult for him."

"I wish I could help, but only you can make up your mind as to what your answer will be."

Veneta nodded.

"Now it's time to see my children."

"Of course."

"But I can't go back to living with you all, not just yet. I need this job and I need to get Rius back."

"Then I don't think you should come back just for a visit. You wouldn't be making it easy for yourself, and they would be distraught all over again when you left."

"But I must see them now that I've found you."

"Bron, dear, you've waited this long and I'm sure a little longer won't hurt. Wouldn't it be easier if I don't tell them about our meeting today?"

Bron looked around as if searching for an answer – the right path to take and the strength to take it. She saw Talea approaching.

"You're right, Veneta, you always are. And it won't be for much longer."

"I'll tell Declan, of course. I know he won't say a word."

Talea climbed the steps towards them.

"Bron, I'm ready to go now. You've made a friend, I see."

Bron and Veneta stood.

"Madam, this is Veneta."

Veneta dropped a curtsey and Talea smiled.

"So, you've found her. Bron guessed you would, one day." Anxiously, she turned to Bron. "Does this mean that I shall be losing you?"

"No, madam, not yet," Bron assured her. "I'm not ready to leave yet. There are matters I must attend to before that happens."

Talea nodded. "I'm glad to hear it. I wish to go now as I've finished my business here. I'll wait for you in the chair. Goodbye, Veneta."

Veneta curtsied again and Talea walked away.

"Well, Bron, now what?"

"Tell me where you are all living and I'll keep in touch. I will let you know as soon as I have done all that I need to do."

They exchanged addresses, hugged and kissed each other again, and went their separate ways.

CHAPTER 39

"Come in, Bron."

She stepped over the threshold. "Are they here yet?"

Adama shook her head. "No. You're early."

Bron followed her friend along the hallway and into the triclinium. Adama crossed the room and partially closed the shutters.

"We don't want anyone overhearing," she said. "Sit down and make yourself comfortable. I'll bring in the wine when they arrive."

Bron stretched out on one of the couches round the table, Adama sitting beside her.

"Is Rius well?"

Adama nodded. Bron was about to question her further when she was shocked to realise that her friend had begun to cry quietly.

"Adama, whatever is it? What's the matter?" Bron asked, putting an arm round her shoulders.

"It's Priscus," Adama said, tears wetting her eyes and cheeks.

"Your singer? What about him?"

"He's going away, he's leaving Rome."

"But why, if he loves you?"

"He hasn't a choice. The emperor has summoned him to Ravenna, to entertain at the palace."

Bron wiped away Adama's tears as best she could.

"That's a great honour, surely?"

"Yes, it is, but with the threatening situation at our borders, who knows what the future holds for any of us?"

"How bad is it?"

"Crestus looks very worried. He wants to send me away to safety, but I won't go because Priscus and I might never find each other again."

"Does he know about Priscus?"

"Of course not. I can't tell him. I can't let him see how things are between us. It would break his heart."

Tears were running down her cheeks again.

"How deeply are you involved?"

"Not physically – yet – but I don't go out of an evening now – I can't any more. I can't bear the thought of anyone else—"

She turned her face up to look into Bron's eyes. "I've never felt like this about anyone before, Bron. You must understand because you love your Roman officer."

"Yes, I do understand," Bron agreed with more than a twinge of guilt and was glad to change tack. "But you can't let Crestus Sabinius see you like this and he'll be here any minute."

As if to prove her right, they heard a key turning in the lock.

"I'll get the wine," Adama said and fled towards the kitchen.

There were footsteps and voices in the hall and Bron stood to greet the new arrivals.

Into the room came the familiar figure of Adama's elderly lover, imposing in his white toga. Bron's sympathy went out to this gentle man because of the unexpected card that life had dealt, about which he knew nothing. He welcomed her warmly and kissed her on both cheeks.

"Thank you so much, Crestus, for what you've done for me," Bron said. "It's very kind of you to take all this trouble."

He waved aside her thanks. "I was glad to help after Carolus explained your problem. The truth needs to be known, whatever it is, and after all, I would gladly go out of my way to help any friend of my little Adama. Where is she, by the way?"

"In the kitchen, decanting the wine."

He nodded then stood aside to reveal the girl standing behind him.

"I'm Nashua," she introduced herself. "I understand you need some information from me."

The bo'sun had described her well. Her black hair fell in waves to her shoulders, and the suntanned hues of her skin suggested that she came from the southern shores of the

Mediterranean. Tall, slim, and "with legs that go up to her armpits," he had said, emphasised by that short red tunic.

"Sit down, young lady," Crestus said, "while I go to help Adama choose the wine." He left in the direction of the kitchen and Bron hoped that her friend had had time to recover her composure.

As Nashua sat beside her, Bron commented, "He didn't take long to find you."

The girl smiled. "He knew where to look."

Crestus returned, carrying a tray with a decanter of white wine and glasses, and placed them on the table. Adama followed him. Bron guessed that she was glad of the partially-darkened room.

He poured the wine, laughing with pleasure, telling them that he considered himself very fortunate to be in the company of three such beautiful women.

Bron made some facetious comment in reply, hoping to lighten the atmosphere for Adama's sake, at which Crestus laughed again.

They sipped their wine in silence, waiting for Bron to speak. She looked over to Adama, who was picking at a loose thread of a cushion, eyes lowered. She looked at Crestus, who nodded to her encouragingly, and finally she turned to the girl.

"There is a mystery, and a miscarriage of justice, which we hope you can help solve for us, for me."

The girl nodded. "I will if I can."

Bron guessed she had been paid well to come, so she wanted no misunderstanding.

"You must tell us the truth, whatever it is," she urged and the girl nodded again. "I'm not sure how to start. I don't want to put words into your mouth."

"No one puts words into my mouth," the girl replied emphatically. "I'm nobody's puppet."

"Good."

Bron then related the little she knew about the murder of Fabia, the outcome of the trial and the speedy execution of the bo'sun.

"I know about the trial – we all do – and most of us were there to hear the guilty verdict," Nashua said.

"You were there?" Bron questioned her in amazement. Adama stopped fiddling with the cushion and stared at her. Even Crestus stood with his glass poised between table and lips while they waited for her reply.

"Yes, I was up in the gallery."

"Yet you didn't come forward to give him the alibi he needed?"

"It wasn't my place. What could I have done? Shouted down to the chairman, 'Hey, I'm the one you want!'? Nobody asked me to give evidence, so I didn't."

"But they couldn't find you."

"Then all I can say is, they didn't look very far, if they looked at all." She stared back at three incredulous faces. "Anyway, what difference would it have made? I was only the messenger. I say good riddance, if he did it."

"But I don't think he did," Bron replied.

Crestus refilled their glasses, then sat on the opposite side of the table, cuddling Adama. He didn't seem to have noticed how upset she had been.

Bron persisted with her questioning.

"Did you know him?"

"I'd seen him around. Some of the girls knew him well."

"Was he ever violent?"

"Nothing out of the usual. They always do whatever their clients want so he had no cause to be violent."

"Do you remember the night of the murder?"

Nashua nodded.

"You gave him a message?"

Nashua nodded again.

"What was it?"

"That he was to meet Fabia at that gatehouse, like he said."

"Was that all?"

"No. I had to say that she had found his son. He was very excited about that."

"Then what happened?"

"He left the apartment almost immediately, in the general direction of the Appian Way."

"Not towards the river?" Bron asked.

"No."

"You're sure?"

"Quite sure. I had been told to watch him and follow him a little way, which is what I did."

"And he went east and not south?"

"Yes, like I told you – though he could have doubled back. We know now that she was down by the river."

"But he wasn't to know that. Then what?"

"I had been told to report back."

"To Fabia?"

"No, the message wasn't given to me by Fabia, though it was from her."

"Then who gave it to you?"

The tension in the room was heart stopping. Crestus had been stroking Adama's hair but he paused, his hand resting on her dark head, waiting to hear the girl's answer. Even Adama forgot her misery for a moment and looked expectantly across the table. But Nashua only shrugged.

"I don't know who he was – some old man hiding beneath a cloak and hood."

Bron had learned nothing of significance and her expression betrayed her frustration. Crestus decided to help her out.

"Nashua, did you know Fabia?" he asked.

"Yes, vaguely. She sometimes came to the tavern where I worked."

"Was she there that night?"

"No, but she was there a couple of nights previously, meeting one of her clients."

Bron's curiosity aroused, she took over the questioning from Crestus.

"Did you know him?"

"No, though I wish I did. Handsome man." She chuckled. "He looked very uncomfortable at being there. I expect it wasn't the sort of place he usually used."

"Can you describe him?"

"Not really. I only saw him briefly when he came in. He was trying to hide behind the sleeve of his tunic, though it didn't quite cover his face."

She stopped speaking and lines crossed her forehead as she tried to recollect the details of that night. Her three listeners waited in silence.

"I did notice that he had gentlemen's hands – never done a hard day's work in his life, I reckon." She came out of her reverie. "He'd gone by the time I came back downstairs."

"Is there anything else you can tell us?" Crestus asked. "Anything at all?"

"I had a word with Fabia after he'd left. She was sitting there on her own and I went over to ask who her friend was – she wouldn't tell me, of course. She was very flushed and excited, though, quite drunk, so I didn't take too much notice of her ramblings."

"What did she say?" Bron asked.

"Something about coming into a lot of money if she played her cards right – sounded like blackmail to me. Oh, and being set up for life – like you, Adama."

"Like me?" Adama voiced her surprise. "But I didn't know her."

"Well, she seemed to know you and that you lived on the Palatine – and about this apartment."

"She didn't get the knowledge from me," Crestus was quick to interject. "I didn't know the woman."

"There's a lot in my head to sort out," Bron mused, "and I'm not sure that I know where to start. And you can't describe the old man, Nashua?"

"No. I don't think he picked on me especially. He was out looking for any girl who was willing to take the money and deliver the message. He was standing across the road, hidden in the shadows, and he stayed there until I came back from following the bo'sun, so I could report back."

Nashua put her glass on the table and gave Bron her full attention, frowning slightly again as she searched her memory.

"There *was* something, now I come to think about it," she said slowly. "I remember his piercing blue eyes. And his hood couldn't completely hide his mass of white hair and whiskers."

CHAPTER 40

When Nashua had left the room, Bron and Adama just sat and looked at each other, stunned into silence.

"Why so quiet?" Crestus asked on his return from the front door. "You young ladies know something, don't you?"

"We know who that old man is," Adama told him.

Bron nodded. "It's Julius, the steward in the Loricatus house."

Crestus drew in his breath. "Senator Laenus Loricatus sent that message by his steward?"

Bron nodded again.

"You could be mistaken. There are many old men with blue eyes and white hair and whiskers. It could be anyone. Be careful – there's already been too much jumping to conclusions in this matter."

"Then one of us will have to ask him," Adama suggested.

For weeks after arriving at the Loricatus house with Rius, Bron and Julius had been at loggerheads. He was very protective of both his employers and Bron guessed that he had seen his master involve many women in sexual liaisons while Fausta had stood by miserably, acting as if she were quite unaware of what was happening in her own house. When the old man had realised that Bron was not out to trap the senator – quite the reverse, in fact – he changed tack and had treated her with kindness and respect. So now she jumped to his defence.

"He's a good man," she said. "He wouldn't knowingly be party to murder."

"He would have to do as his master told him," Crestus pointed out, "or he'd be out on the street without a reference, or worse."

Adama also came to the steward's defence. "He wouldn't have known the consequences of delivering that message – it may have been strange but it was just a message," she said.

"Let's be practical here," Crestus urged. "What if we find out that the messenger *was* Julius? It doesn't prove anything."

"It proves that the man Fabia met in the tavern was Senator Loricatus," Adama said excitedly, "and it proves that the senator wanted to send the bo'sun on a fool's errand, to get him away from the city without an alibi, so he couldn't defend himself."

"It proves nothing, sweetheart. The senator and his steward would deny everything. I know you want to help Bron, but she must have proof and there isn't any."

Bron admitted she was puzzled. "I wasn't aware that the senator knew Brunus, nor Fabia, come to that. How did he?"

"Go on thinking out loud," Crestus encouraged her.

"The first time I saw Fabia in Rome was when I came across her in the market. I hoped she hadn't seen me but she had. She followed me then told Brunus where I was working, and he talked himself into the job of gardener. I met him in the garden and he asked where our son was, but I wouldn't tell him, of course."

"Then what?" asked Crestus. He was leaning forward with one arm on the table. The other arm was around Adama. Bron liked him and felt sorry for him, remembering what her friend had confessed earlier.

"I think I can guess," Adama ventured, "after what Nashua told us about Fabia wanting an apartment like mine."

Bron and Crestus looked at her expectantly.

"The day after you met the bo'sun in the garden, Bron, you came to see me, very anxious to tell Cook that he was out looking for Rius and not to let the baby out of her sight." Bron nodded. "Could Fabia have followed you here? If she could follow you without being seen when you kept looking over your shoulder, it's possible she could follow you when you weren't expecting her to be around."

"Yes, I suppose you're right."

"After you left, I went straight up the hill to warn Cook."

"So Fabia would have discovered the Loricatus house," added Crestus, "guessed that was where Rius was living—"

"—and went straight back to tell the bo'sun," Adama concluded.

"If that's the case," Bron mused, "why didn't he go storming up to confront the senator and his wife? Why delay for over a week, then obey a message, supposedly from Fabia, to say that he should meet her because she had news of Rius? I don't understand it at all."

"What if," Crestus suggested, "she didn't tell the bo'sun? What if she was looking out for her own interests and went straight to the senator instead?"

"And met him in the tavern," added Bron, "to threaten him that she would tell the bo'sun where his son was, unless she was well rewarded?"

"That would explain why Fausta took Rius away a couple of days afterwards," added Adama.

Crestus was not convinced. "But was the threat of the bo'sun stealing his son sufficient reason to kill Fabia? It hardly seems likely when he could take other precautions," he said. "Perhaps there was other damaging information she was holding against him. We don't know. We may never know and I don't see any way of finding out."

"But he can't be allowed to get away with it," Adama protested.

"He *has* got away with it," Crestus pointed out. "Someone has been convicted of that murder and executed, and no one is looking for anyone else to take the blame."

"Do you think that was the purpose of the trial, Crestus?" Bron asked him. "Did Senator Loricatus foot the bill for a show trial? Did he pay for the bo'sun to have a defence orator and a chance to clear his name, then make that impossible, so a conviction was inevitable and no one else would be sought for the same crime?"

"That about sums it up, Bron," agreed Crestus. "But I don't see that there's anything you can do about it. The judiciary aren't going to admit that, at such a public trial, they were completely incompetent and killed the wrong man."

"At least I know the truth to tell our son," Bron said. "At least he will know that his father wasn't a murderer."

CHAPTER 41

Laenus opened his eyes and sighed with deep satisfaction when he found himself in his favourite place of all time – in bed with a beautiful woman.

He shifted slightly, not wishing to wake her till he was ready for her, savouring the memory of the previous night and anticipating what he could achieve this morning. He was not due in the Senate for hours and they had plenty of time to indulge themselves in whichever way they pleased.

His eyes roamed round the unfamiliar room, admiring the artistry of the wall paintings and the complementary colours of greens, cream and lavender in the covers and cushions on the bed.

This was the first time he had slept in the bed Julia shared with her husband and he rather enjoyed the joke. With relish he looked forward to reliving the pleasures of last night in that carved wooden bed with bronze feet next time he faced that pompous old man across the floor of the Senate.

Julia always giggled when describing her husband's attempts to keep her satisfied.

"The only thing that gets red is his face!" was a standing joke between them.

He was fully awake now and turned towards her, pulling the covers off her, filling his eyes and his desires with the peaks and troughs of her nakedness. Venus would be hard put to it to rouse him as quickly. He began to run his fingers lightly over those enticing curves and when she did nothing more than sigh in contentment, his lips began to explore the touch and taste of her.

When they were satiated yet again, she fell off him and lay still, their hands clasped, their perspiring bodies cooling and quietening.

"Julia, I do love you, you know."

"So you keep telling me, Laenus."

"And showing you, as often as I can."

"I'd die of boredom if you ever left me."

"Does your husband still not know about us?"

"I don't know what he knows or doesn't know. It doesn't bother me. He's afraid of losing me so he'd never cause a scandal, if that's what you're worried about."

"Fausta knows. Of course, she pretends she doesn't. She won't cause a scandal, either. Conveniently, things will continue to drift along just as they are."

He let go of her hand and rolled onto his side, propping himself up on one elbow and looking down at her.

"The gods knew what they were doing when they designed you," he said appreciatively. "You're beautiful, my love."

He slipped his free hand between her legs, his fingers boldly exploring, and the pressure from her thighs and the stickiness coating his fingers told him that she was ready for him again.

"Darling, I have something to ask you," he said.

"Can't it wait?" She turned and moved closer to him, trapping his hand, and he was almost lured into saying that of course it could wait, but what he had to find out was of greater importance at this moment.

"If I asked you, would you leave your husband and come away with me?"

She opened her eyes wide and stared at him. "Where to?"

"Never mind that. Would you come?"

"Laenus, you're up to something."

"You haven't answered my question. Would you?"

Her thighs relaxed their grip on his hand, which he removed and licked clean.

"It depends on what you're offering. I have a very comfortable life here. He gives me everything I want."

"He's only deputy to Constantine, not much of a position."

"And you're only a senator."

"I could change all that."

She stared at him again. "Laenus, you're not making any sense. What could you change?"

"Everything. It just needs imagination and initiative. Julia, I'm going places and I could take you with me."

"What about Fausta and your son? Is he your son, by the way? He doesn't look like either of you. If you ask me, he looks more like that girl you were so smitten with."

"Ah, the delightful Bron. And if you ask me, Julia, I would say you're jealous!"

"Jealous of a wet nurse? What nonsense! So, is he your son?"

"He is in law – we bought him from her. I would make sure he and Fausta were all right. I'm tired of her, anyway. You know I only married her because of her connections."

Julia swung her legs to the floor and stood up.

"You haven't given me an answer," he reminded her.

"I'll think about it. But now I'm going to soak in the hot bath. Are you coming?"

He laughed. "Hannibal's rampaging elephants wouldn't keep me away!"

CHAPTER 42

Rampaging elephants may not have kept Senator Laenus Loricatus away from Julia's pool, but the news her slaves brought her that morning certainly did.

He had dressed in a hurry and was now lying on his litter with the curtains pulled back, urging his porters to greater effort and faster pace. When the crush in the streets became too dense for them to move forward at speed, he ordered them to stop and clambered down.

"I'll go on foot from here," he told them. "Follow as best you can and wait for me outside the Senate house."

The city was in panic. He joined the throng pushing and jostling – men presumably hurrying to or from their places of business, women with children attached to their skirts and babies in their arms, and elderly couples clutching bundles and trying to stay on their feet. There was one name on everybody's lips – "Alaric!"

Hurrying through the Septimius Severus arch, he arrived at the Curia, ran up the steps two at a time and so into the hall. The Senate was in turmoil. Senators were on their feet, shouting and gesticulating at each other across the floor; others, mostly the older ones, were sitting quietly along the tiered seats, shoulders drooping, heads in hands.

One of them, less debilitated than the rest, or perhaps less realistic, was shaking his stick at no one in particular. "Rome hasn't been invaded for eight hundred years," he croaked in protest.

"Alaric's playing a game with us, he'll never enter the city!" voiced another.

"I agree. If he was intent on invading, he would have done so by now and not still be talking about it!"

A young man, newly appointed to the Senate, had his fist raised in defiance. "We'll never let them in!"

"Who's going to stop them?"

"The army will keep them out!" he argued.

"What army? Most of them mutinied after Honorius murdered their General Stilicho!"

"You're right! They've all gone over to the other side! We have no army!"

"And now theirs is Roman trained and is killing us with our own weapons!"

The old man shook his stick. "Rome hasn't been invaded for eight hundred years," he said again, but nobody was listening to him.

Laenus was as deeply concerned as any of them but kept quiet, his thoughts in turmoil as he wrestled with his conscience.

"The emperor must negotiate! We're not ready to fight!" He recognised the wisdom of Crestus Sabinius.

"Negotiate? Huh! Honorius is in Ravenna and doesn't look like coming out!"

"You forget Constantine!" someone reminded them.

"So where the devil *is* Constantine?"

"He's on his way."

"And the Visigoth ambassador?"

"We've sent for him."

"The crowds will slaughter Oliffe if they see him!" the young man ventured.

"His escort is armed. They won't get anywhere near him!"

And so the arguments raged on, first one senator and then another trying to drown out the rest, all shouting at the same time, with few agreeing with anyone else. There was no leadership, no one to make a decision and put it into operation.

Laenus spoke to several senators who were taking no part in the slanging match, and gathered that Alaric's Visigoths were blockading every gate and were stationed outside the walls. They were also in command of the river Tiber, so preventing the transport of goods into the city.

In spite of the general panic, Laenus knew the citizens were safe enough and would be able to sit this out for days, but what happened when they began to run out of food?

He realised he had to act with speed if he was to put his plan into operation.

To everyone's relief, Constantine arrived, his escort linking arms and trying desperately to stay upright on their feet as they backed up against the crowd at the door, clearing a way for him. He stumbled through the entrance and was immediately surrounded by senators, all clamouring for decision and action.

With difficulty and the assistance of his escort, he managed to achieve some semblance of order. This was immediately undermined by the appearance of Oliffe. As he was standing near the door, Laenus had a clear view of the Visigoth ambassador when he arrived. A nasty gash on the man's cheek suggested he hadn't been quick enough to avoid all the stones thrown by the crowd, and blood was running down his beard onto his none-too-clean toga. Fabia had been right when she said the smell of the man was offensive – did these pagans never bathe?

Quickly surrounded by a cloud of agitated white togas, the ambassador was propelled towards the podium and seated on a chair at the side of Constantine. A cloth was brought for him to hold against his wound, in an effort to stop the bleeding. The two men exchanged a few words then the usurper emperor stood and gradually the hall quietened.

Laenus had moved across to his accustomed place on the lowest tier of marble benches. No cushions had been brought out this morning and the seat was cold and became more unrelenting as the debate progressed.

After an hour, as measured by the water clock, Constantine had been prevailed upon to send a request, conveyed by the Visigoth ambassador, for a meeting with Alaric to negotiate terms that would induce him to withdraw his troops from the walls and gates of Rome.

Oliffe was promised privileges and favours and not an inconsiderable sum of money to take the message to the Visigoth king, with double payment if the negotiation was successful.

He looked delighted and jumped down from the podium, noisily passing wind as he did so, which caused those around him to quickly retreat, leaving a clear passage for him.

Half way towards the door, he stopped and turned back towards Constantine.

"What is it, Oliffe?" asked the emperor.

"I'm not facing those ruffians again! I want transport as well as an armed guard!"

Constantine hesitated. "That can be arranged if you are willing to wait for it to arrive."

Laenus was quick to seize the advantage. "My litter is waiting outside," he said. "I'll take the ambassador home."

"Rather you than me!" someone muttered.

Constantine beamed. "That's very Christian of you, Laenus. Your offer is gratefully accepted. Take the ambassador home. Tell me, is your wife well?"

"I'm glad to say that Fausta is very well."

"I'm pleased to hear it. Give her my kindest regards when you arrive home."

"I will, indeed. Thank you, Your Majesty."

Laenus left the hall, followed by eight members of the armed guard with Oliffe in their midst. He saw his litter at the bottom of the steps, lined up with the litters and carrying chairs of many of the other senators, and made his way over to his slaves.

"We've another passenger," he told them, "and will need a couple more bearers. Find two strong men in the crowd and press them into service. I'll make it worth their while."

When the soldiers guarding them were in position and he and his passenger were comfortably propped up at each end of the mattress, he gave the order to lift and move forward.

"Don't hurry," he instructed as he pulled the curtains round them. He knew he would need to have the litter well aired before he could use it again, but was anxious to ensure their privacy.

CHAPTER 43

Next evening, Laenus was again seated at a table in the tavern down by the river, the sleeve of his tunic once more concealing his face. However, there was no mistaking the person seated opposite him. If he had entered blindfolded, his aristocratic nose would have revealed the man's identity.

He ordered a jug of beer and secretly smiled to see the serving girl sniff as she took the order.

While they were waiting for the beer, one of the street girls attached to the tavern passed their table and Oliffe, never one to miss an opportunity, took hold of her red tunic and pulled her towards him. When he ran his hand up the inside of her long legs, she laughed and firmly removed it.

"Later," she teased him, "but I don't 'come' cheap!"

He guffawed at her play on words and told her to stay within reach, so she sat at the table behind them. When their beer arrived, he ordered a jug for her, and by the time the two men were engrossed in conversation, her head and arms were sprawled across the table and she was fast asleep.

However, by the time they had finished their business and stood to shake hands on it, the girl was nowhere to be seen. Oliffe cursed her private parts and went off in search of her.

CHAPTER 44

Her urgent knocking quickly brought Adama to the door.
"Nashua!" Adama exclaimed in surprise. "What brings you here at this time of night?"
"May I come in, Adama? I have some extremely serious news and I don't know where else to go. Is the senator here?"
Adama beckoned her inside as Crestus Sabinius appeared at the door of the bedroom.
"Who is it, Adama?" Then he saw the tall girl standing in the hallway. "Nashua, is that you? We were just going to bed."
"I'm so sorry to disturb you, Senator, but I have some news I think you need to hear."
Aware of the agitation in her voice, they led the way into the triclinium, Nashua apologising again and saying how glad she was to find them both in the apartment.
"My little girl doesn't go out of an evening these days," he said, gazing with adoration at Adama. "We're becoming quite the old married couple."
Adama offered her a drink. "Just water," she said and her hostess went out to the kitchen.
"Now, young lady, what's this all about?"
When Adama returned with jug and beakers, Nashua was telling the senator about her evening – how she had been working, as usual in the tavern, when she had noticed Laenus Loricatus sidling in, trying to hide his identity as before. This time, however, he had not met a woman but a man – a man she knew as Oliffe, the Visigoth. The odious little ambassador had accosted her sexually then told her to sit at an adjacent table and wait till he was ready for her.

Usually, she would have indulged in some playfulness with him then gone her own way, but she had a gut feeling that the situation was not as it should be, especially as she now knew a great deal about the senator.

Crestus Sabinius nodded approval. "You were right to be suspicious," he told her. "Then what happened?"

"I drank his beer at the next table and then feigned sleep, all the while listening to their conversation. They were whispering but not so softly that I couldn't hear what was being discussed."

"And?" The senator was leaning towards her and had even taken his arm from around Adama's shoulders.

"It was obvious that they hadn't met by coincidence," the girl continued. "They were discussing the siege. It seems that earlier in the day, the Senate had instructed Oliffe to negotiate terms with Alaric for a withdrawal." The senator nodded agreement. "Oliffe told Laenus Loricatus he would be contacting Alaric tomorrow morning. Then the senator asked Oliffe if he could arrange for *him* to meet Alaric!"

"Laenus asked to meet Alaric?" Crestus Sabinius was sitting bolt upright now.

"Yes. Oliffe was very surprised. He said, 'You want to meet with Alaric? What for?' and the senator said, 'I could be of help to him.'"

"The traitor!" exclaimed Crestus Sabinius with passion. "Did he say how?"

"Oliffe asked him that question and he said 'It's always helpful to have an ally on the inside'. Oliffe said, 'So it may be, but I can't go to Alaric with a platitude, I need facts. How could it be helpful?' and the senator said, 'For a safe passage and the right consideration, the gates could open of their own accord one night.'"

Adama gasped. "Are you saying that that man would let the Visigoths into the city? He would bring them into Rome?"

"That's what he said. That's what I heard. Senator, we could all be slaughtered in our beds by the pagans and know nothing about it! Is there anything you can do to stop it?"

"I will go straight to Emperor Constantine with this news, tonight! But is there more? Tell me everything. Take your time. Would you like another drink?"

Adama poured water for all of them. Nashua's hand was shaking as she held the beaker and Adama took it from her and put it on the table.

"There *is* more," Nashua said. "Oliffe said he would be going through the gate tomorrow morning and expected to spend all day going backwards and forwards with offer and counter offer. Anyway, he said he would draw it out and make it last all day. Then, tomorrow night, on a given signal, he would meet the senator and conduct him, disguised as one of his escort, through the gate to Alaric's camp."

"With all that coming and going and the gate being opened and closed all day," Adama mused, "why can't Alaric just march in?"

"I wondered that," said Nashua.

"I know why," replied the senator. "Alaric's out for all he can get. There's no point in forcing his way in now when he can probably get a fat bribe to go away. He'll retreat, keep his head down for a while, then can come back at any time for another pay-off or for a show down. He knows we're not strong enough to keep him out for long."

"Then you think we're safe for now?" Adama asked.

"For a while, little love," Crestus replied and leaned over to kiss her. "Don't worry, I won't let one hair of your head be harmed – though I'd never play turncoat and betray my emperor and my country! Is there anything else, Nashua?"

"Yes. The senator said he wouldn't be alone, he would have his wife with him."

"What did Oliffe say to that?"

"He laughed a lot – by this time he had had plenty of beer to drink – and said that the senator could bring a whole army of women with him if he wanted, they would be most welcome in the camp and could be shared round, and the senator said there would be just one."

"I'm surprised he's suddenly so loyal to his wife," Adama remarked.

"Oliffe then said that his services came at a price, and the senator asked how much."

Crestus was intrigued. "How much? What is the price of betrayal?"

"I couldn't hear the amount, as Oliffe whispered it into the senator's ear." Nashua laughed. "I think the senator agreed just to get Oliffe's breath away from his nose. It's not a pleasant experience to have that man so close, as I know."

"One final matter," concluded the senator. "Was any secret signal agreed?"

Nashua thought for a moment. "The signal *was* mentioned." She frowned in concentration. "Yes, that was it – a long high call like an owl followed by five coughs, and the reply was another imitation owl call."

"Got that!" he said. "And the meeting place and when?"

"That wasn't discussed. Perhaps they arranged it after I left. I slipped out quietly while they were happily slapping each other on the back and came straight here, because I didn't know where else to go."

"You've done well," the senator praised her, "and I'll see that you don't go unrewarded. Now I have a call to make and you'd best get on home. May I offer you my litter?"

"She can't go home in the dark on her own at this time of night, it isn't safe," Adama protested.

Nashua looked at her in surprise. "What are you talking about, Adama? It's what we do all the time."

"But you don't have these circumstances all the time," Adama replied. "If Oliffe is out looking for you, your life could be in danger. No, I insist, you stay here tonight until all this is dealt with. You can sleep with me."

Nashua was surprised at Adama's insistence, though it was possible that her life was in danger if the two men she had spied on guessed her sleep had been a pretence. However, it seemed to Nashua that Adama was glad to have her around.

She looked at the senator to judge how he viewed the situation, but he seemed lost in his thoughts. Then he roused himself and asked them, "What do you ladies think I should do about Fausta Loricata? I feel she is a victim in this plot. We all know that Laenus always does exactly as he pleases, and I can't help feeling that she may be an unwilling participant."

"Could you warn her?" Adama asked.

"I was wondering that. But how? Who can be trusted to talk to her?"

The Scarlet Seal

"And what will happen to Rius if the couple defect? Bron should be told what's going on."

"Not yet. The fewer who know about it, the better," the senator warned her. "I can't go to see Fausta in case Laenus is there, and it wouldn't be appropriate for either of you two."

"I could go and see Cook in the morning," Adama offered.

"Yes, that's the answer. I will visit Constantine tonight – there's no time to lose. In the morning, you take a message to Fausta by way of her Cook and request a meeting in my carriage – we can decide on details later – and I'll tell her that we know about their plan."

"But she'll warn her husband," said Nashua.

"And get back in favour," Adama added. "From what I hear, he doesn't spend much time at home lately. That's why I'm so surprised he's including her in his plan."

"I've thought about that," said the senator. "I'll have to abduct her for the day to make sure she can't contact him until he's arrested. It will be for her own good, after all. Adama, will their cook make up some believable story, if Laenus questions his wife's absence?"

"She could say that Fausta has gone to spend the day with her mother and will meet him in the evening, as arranged."

"Nothing must be said or done to make him suspicious, Adama. We need to catch him red-handed."

"I just wish we could bring Bron into all this," Adama said. "She would so enjoy seeing him get his comeuppance!"

CHAPTER 45

Senator Crestus Sabinius was tired. He had spent most of the night in consultation with Constantine and his advisers, in the emperor's private basilica further up the hill.

When he returned to the apartment and would have taken comfort in Adama's arms, he found his place in bed occupied by Nashua, so had spent the remaining couple of hours on the couch in the triclinium.

Now, having lowered the blinds, with the carriage at a standstill, he was nodding off, hoping that Fausta would be joining him but not altogether certain that she would. The carriage rocked as the horses fidgeted restlessly and the jingle of their harness sounded a long way off.

"Senator Crestus Sabinius, you wanted to see me?"

He shook himself awake, realised he was not alone, and apologised profusely for his lack of attention.

"Madam, please forgive me, but I had very little sleep last night."

Fausta smiled. "The lady is fortunate," she remarked, then laughed when the senator blushed.

He regarded her solemnly. Everyone guessed that her husband had married her because of her connections. She was a plain woman, with large facial features, not like his fine-boned and beautiful Adama, though not so plain when she smiled. He felt sorry for her.

"So, what do you need to see me about? The message I received said the matter was extremely urgent and concerned my husband. Why all the secrecy?"

"All will be made plain, I assure you."

He opened the door for her and she entered the carriage and sat beside him.

"Is your husband at home?"

Fausta could not hide her displeasure – it was expressed in the tone of her voice. "No. In fact, I haven't seen him for several days."

"He was in the Senate yesterday."

"Was he looking well? I fancied he had a slight summer cold the last time I saw him."

"He appeared well, madam."

The senator leaned out of the window and spoke to his coachman. "Drive on, if you please."

The coach lurched forward, the ringing of metal horseshoes and metal-rimmed wheels on cobbles ensuring the conversation in the carriage was inaudible to all but the two occupants.

"Where are you taking me?"

"Have no fear, Fausta – may I call you by that name? Be assured I wish you no harm and you are quite safe. My coachman has orders to drive us to the suburbs and back while we hold this conversation."

"Then tell me why I am here."

Crestus took a deep breath mentally. "You say you have not seen your husband for several days, but I have reason to believe that you are meeting him tonight."

She stared at him. "I will, if he comes home. Have you such news to bring me?"

Crestus admired her ability to lie so effectively. He almost believed her.

"Madam, it is no use lying to me. I realise you wish to protect your husband and yourself, but I have come to warn you that his plans are known."

"His plans? What plans?"

Oh, she's good at this, he thought, *probably borne of long practice.*

"He was overheard making arrangements with Oliffe, the Visigoth ambassador. His secret – and yours – is known, has been reported in high places – the highest, in fact – and he will be apprehended tonight. You will be taken with him unless you stay away. I have come to warn you, madam. The state has no quarrel with you. We realise that where your husband leads you have to follow."

Fausta was staring at him with incomprehension. "I'm sorry, senator, but I don't know what you're talking about."

"Fausta, you must not meet Laenus tonight. You must not. Do you understand what I am saying to you?"

"Frankly, no. You're making no sense. Suppose you start at the beginning."

So he started at the beginning and told her the story that Nashua had related to him and Adama. By the end of it, he realised that she was weeping quietly. He didn't know what to do.

"I'm so sorry, so sorry," he apologised, at last believing that she had told him the truth and really didn't know what he was talking about. "But I don't understand."

"I do," she said with bitterness, drying her eyes on a kerchief. "He may have said 'my wife' but it wasn't me he was talking about – though I think I know the bitch's identity."

"Who?" he demanded.

"Her name's Julia, the wife of Constantine's deputy."

Crestus stared at her. "*That* Julia?" he asked, quite unaware that he was echoing Bron's frequent contemptuous description of her.

"Yes, *that* Julia – my best friend. My best friend!" she muttered. "Laenus and his women! My friends, the nurses, women of high birth or from the gutter – it's all the same to him! Can you believe he once made a pass at my mother – my own mother! Let him rot in hell!"

"The scandal will destroy Julia's husband!" Crestus exclaimed.

"Serves her right!"

"Maybe bring down Constantine as well!"

"What is that to me? Let them be caught! Let them be snared together as they have bedded together! Have they climaxed their nights of passion with embracing and drinking and dancing? Then now let them embrace death when they embrace each other! Now let them drink their own blood and go dancing to hell!"

Crestus recoiled at the hatred blazing in her eyes, not wet any longer, and the venom being spat from her mouth. This was no act, no subterfuge to allay his suspicions. Too shocked to reply, he took refuge in practical matters.

The Scarlet Seal

"We will arrest him tonight, on Constantine's orders. You could help us in this, Fausta."

"I will do anything you want."

"He will probably come home today, partly to keep out of the way of everyone and probably to collect some things together to take with him. Will you be able to act normally, and like a good wife, pretend to be glad that he has put in an appearance, and support him in anything he asks you to do?"

"Yes, I can do that. In fact, I shall enjoy it."

"He must have no suspicions, none at all, till we have him under arrest."

"He'll learn nothing from me. What about Julia?"

"I will give that some thought."

The carriage had turned round and was on its way back.

He continued, "It may be that Alaric will already have broken camp, anyway. Constantine has decided to give him whatever he asks for. By the time he returns for another siege, we should be better prepared."

They finished the journey in silence. When they stopped and the driver's companion had clambered off the driving bench to help Fausta from the carriage, she said through the open door, "I loved him once, you know. I loved him very much, and he loved me."

Crestus's heart went out to her. "I'm so sorry," he said, and she was gone.

Now he had a busy day in front of him. Everything must appear normal. First of all, he must put in an appearance at the Senate and take part in discussing any condition Alaric imposed or any offer he made, then help decide a strategy, until they reached a compromise satisfactory to both sides.

At some point he would have to consult with Constantine again, arrange for the armed guard needed tonight and a backup contingent, and he also wanted to call in on Adama to let her know that he wouldn't be able to see her again until tomorrow.

Then he had another call to make – two, in fact. Yes, it was going to be a very busy day.

CHAPTER 46

The night was as dark as viscera, with the moon hiding behind the rain clouds. Having half-heartedly released a fine shower earlier in the evening, they were now unloading their burden in a steady downpour.

The road leading to Port Appia gatehouse was quiet, unusually so. Senator Crestus Sabinius was told it was because of a road block set up earlier in the evening that had now been removed. The gate was shut.

Rome's honest citizens were in bed, their windows shuttered, their front doors bolted and barricaded against housebreakers and worse who roamed the city at night.

Sharp eyes watching from the guardroom above the gate had seen a squad of watchmen come and go, their torch lights disappearing through the rain into the tangle of narrow streets, their low conversation absorbed into the fabric of the apartment blocks above them. Now nothing moved.

It was not so when one crossed the room to survey the other aspect, beyond the city wall. There, out in the country, were the cheerful lights of innumerable camp fires and the low murmur of distant voices, an isolated shout or laugh, the metallic clink of harness, an occasional snicker of a horse. Alaric's army! As the rain increased in intensity, however, the fires were being doused one by one.

There was no sign of the usual clamour of vehicles wishing to get into the city to conduct their business during the hours they were permitted access. Obviously, they had all turned back at the far sight of the pagan army encircling the walls.

The centurion crossed the room again to join the senator, who was still peering through a narrow opening overlooking the street.

"Any sign, Senator?"

"Not yet, centurion," replied Sabinius, "but it's difficult to see through the rain."

"How much longer, do you think?"

"I don't know."

"Will you go below?"

"No, I'll wait up here with you and your men."

"Then let me have some victuals and wine sent up."

"Wine well watered," Sabinius told him. "I want my wits about me tonight."

The centurion nodded to one of the legionaries, who left the room to descend the steps circling inside the tower. The chamber below held as many men as the room above, the extra guard a precaution against this evening's work.

"Relax while you wait, Senator," suggested the centurion, indicating the wooden bench. "My men will report any movement in the street."

Crestus Sabinius availed himself of the offer. He decided he was getting too old for all this activity and excitement. *I'm also getting too old for Adama,* he thought sadly. *She's so little interested in my love making these days.* It was a niggling worry that had crossed his mind before, its journey fleeting because he always dismissed it immediately. *Has she found someone else?* No, that thought must not be given any credence, either. He would be utterly lost without her, a drowning man, without hope, barely surviving on a raft adrift on the terrifying ocean of meaningless days, months, years.

"Senator!"

He was brought out of his dark thoughts by the urgent whisper of the centurion.

"What is it?"

"My men report seeing something, maybe only a shadow."

The senator joined the soldier at the narrow slit in the wall.

"There!"

"I see nothing. Wait! Yes! Something moved!"

"A man in the shadows?"

"If it is, the second man shouldn't be far behind. Let's get down the stairs."

The centurion gave his men their orders then followed the senator down to the guardroom below.

"Shall we douse the candles?" asked a young legionary.

"No," replied the centurion. "They'll expect to see light through the openings." Everyone stayed quiet. Time pulsed on. A soldier came down from the room above.

"We think we've seen other movement."

As if in confirmation, they heard the call of an owl, followed by five throaty coughs. They waited. Another owl replied, its cry very convincing.

"Do nothing to scare them away," urged Sabinius.

"It's too quiet in here," the centurion decided. "A little laughter, if you please, lads!"

The men obliged.

"Are you sure they know what to do?" Sabinius asked.

"We won't arrest them until we've opened the gate and they're through to the other side. Don't worry, Senator, my men won't let them escape. They don't much like traitors."

Crestus smiled then turned his attention back to the slit in the brick wall. It was too dark and raining too heavily to make out for certain what was happening in the street.

Suddenly, however, a small body of men holding torches high, marched towards the tower, their cloaks swinging around them, their sandaled feet making no noise on the cobbles. In front of the gate they stopped in a huddle, talking among themselves in low whispers. Two cloaked and hooded figures joined them from the shadows beneath an overhanging balcony of a house.

"What are they waiting for?" the centurion asked, puzzled.

"The young woman," Sabinius answered.

"More laughter!" the centurion instructed his men. "And move the candles about so that the flames flicker more naturally." The legionaries obliged.

"She's here!" announced one of the guards. The torchlight picked out a third figure, slighter and shorter than the other two, her hood pulled across her face and kept in place by a hand that was decidedly feminine.

"Now we'll see some action!" Crestus Sabinius exclaimed in anticipation.

The escort outside formed up again but now they had their hoods pulled over their heads. Where there had been six members of the party, there were now eight, plus the woman.

"Hey, there! Guards! Open the gate!"

The centurion nodded to his men. "Do as he asks. Take your time. Treat him in your usual fashion."

Four of his men retrieved torches from their sconces on the wall and slouched out of the tower. As they closed the door behind them, their places were taken by legionaries who had come down from the room above.

The torches in the hands of Oliffe's escort and the four legionaries lit up the scene so that the watchers could now see everything that was happening outside, though the men's faces were still hidden in the shadow of their hoods behind the curtain of driving rain.

"Who the devil wants the gate opened?" asked one of the legionaries, a burly man with tattoos up both arms. "With those stinking barbarians out there fouling the air we breathe, no one is coming in or out of Rome on Constantine's orders!"

"I have immunity!" replied a voice they knew well.

"Oliffe, is that you?" asked another legionary.

"Do you need ask?" joked a third. "You can smell that pagan at a distance of ten paces!" The legionaries laughed uproariously.

"Yes, it's me," confirmed Oliffe, unusually amiable. "I need to speak to Alaric."

"You've been coming and going all day. Haven't you said everything you need to say to him?"

"Not according to your Senate. I have one last offer to make. He'll see sense this time and pack up and go away."

The legionaries made no move.

"I haven't got all night," complained Oliffe. "You have to open up. I have Constantine's authority to go in and out, as you well know. Is it proof you want that it's me? Do you perverts want to see my cuts, my rites of initiation into the cult of our god?"

He turned his back to them, gathered up his cloak in front of him, then bent over double and began to pull up his tunic. It was apparent that he was wearing no undergarment.

"May *our* God save us from that sight!" called out one of the guards, and again everyone laughed.

From his concealment, Sabinius smiled. "Amen to that!" he whispered to the centurion.

"At that proximity, I agree!"

"Enough! Enough!" decided the tattooed legionary. "You and your escort may go through. Open the gate, lads!" Oliffe stood up and released his cloak.

The soldiers leant their spears against the walls of the towers and moved over to the gates, swinging down the heavy iron bar and turning clumsy iron keys in the locks. They pushed against the solid oak doors, which swung wide.

"There you go, Oliffe, you're free to pass through. Go and speak to Alaric – if you can find him!"

Oliffe looked at the legionary, puzzled, then passed between the two towers, accompanied by his escort and his companion, and walked out onto the Appian Way and into the countryside.

They had gone about twelve paces when Oliffe stopped short, the others stumbling into him.

"What in the name of all the gods has happened here? Where's the camp? Where's Alaric?"

No one answered. They stood and stared ahead of them. There was not one fire to be seen flickering in the darkness.

They started forward again, torches held high. No, their minds were not playing games with them. There was not a tent, a horse, nor a man, just piles of dead ashes where fires had burned. Their lights did not travel very far but it was obvious from the dead silence out there that Alaric's army had broken camp and gone.

Immediately, the little group of puzzled men was surrounded by twelve legionaries intent on preventing their return into the city. The centurion strolled over. He had donned his helmet but was seemingly unaware of the water dripping from his nasal guard or the rain stinging his bare arms and legs.

"He's gone, Oliffe, your friend, King Alaric. Packed up and gone without you, it seems."

"But he can't have gone!" spluttered the ambassador. "We hadn't completed our negotiations!"

"You're wrong there. Agreement was reached hours ago. Did no one think to inform you? How impolite of them! Yes, we sent out all that Alaric demanded – five thousand pounds of gold, thirty thousand pounds of silver, four thousand silken tunics, three thousand hides dyed scarlet, and three thousand pounds of pepper – quite a haul, wasn't it? Alaric grabbed it all and did a bunk!"

"Then I will return to my embassy until he comes back and I can be of service to him and your Senate again."

"I regret that's out of the question. My orders are not to let you back in through the gate – ever. You are no longer welcome in Rome."

"But you can't cast me out into the dark and into this storm!"

"I can and I am. You might catch your king up if you hurry – just follow the sneezing!"

The centurion and his men laughed uproariously at this pepper joke.

Without warning, one of the group darted out from among the others and made a run for the darkness beyond the lights of the torches.

"Bring Senator Loricatus back!" the centurion ordered and six legionaries from the second contingent of guard streamed out through the gate and into the darkness. "Don't let him get away!"

Their torches could be seen fanning out in all directions and it was not long before someone called, "We've got him, centurion!"

"Well done! Bring him in!"

While they were waiting for the legionaries to return with their prisoner, the centurion turned to Oliffe again. The pagan's teeth were chattering – with cold? With fear? Anger? All three?

"While we wait, I will relieve you of that bag you're carrying round your waist, Oliffe. A gift from Senator Loricatus, no doubt. You should not have been so eager to lift your cloak and bare all. The bag looked a great deal prettier than anything you were going to show us!"

At a signal from the centurion, the legionary with the tattoos lunged at the ambassador. There was a struggle in which Oliffe's escort and the other soldiers joined briefly, but the pagans were outnumbered and the tattooed legionary was left holding a leather bag, which he raised triumphantly.

"If I may say so, centurion, it's a deal bigger and heavier than anything else Oliffe possesses!"

Again there was an outburst of raucous laughter from the soldiers.

"Thank you, Oliffe, for the bag and the entertainment. Now be on your way."

The centurion turned and strode back through the gate, shouting over his shoulder, "If he won't go, boys, help him on his way with a kick up those pagan cuts he's so proud of!"

The two captors, with the humiliated senator imprisoned tightly between them, followed the centurion inside the wall. The remaining legionaries bolted and barred the great gates behind them, leaving Oliffe and his escort to begin their long trek through the unfriendly night.

CHAPTER 47

The legionaries marched their prisoner into the room on the lower floor of the tower. The centurion kept the men he needed with him and sent the rest to the room above, to cook themselves something to eat over the firebox, promising to stand them down when he had dealt with the business below.

"Well, Senator," began the centurion, "this has been a shameful night's work."

The man he addressed stood stiffly between his guards in the centre of the room, head raised defiantly, saying nothing. His bedraggled cloak clung to his body and legs, he had lost one sandal and his feet were caked in mud.

"Hmm." The centurion seemed at a loss as to how to proceed. "First of all, we'll have that hood off your face. I have never before looked into the eyes of a traitor."

He indicated to one of his men, who stepped forward and roughly pulled the hood back, revealing the reddening face of Senator Laenus Loricatus. The action loosened his tongue.

"Traitor, you say? I'm no traitor and I demand you don't describe me thus."

"Then how would you describe yourself? Sneaking out in the dead of night with that boar Oliffe, planning to contact Alaric so you can make an offer to open the gates, handing him Rome on a plate?"

"I was doing no such thing," blustered the senator.

"What then, Laenus? What were you doing?" Senator Crestus Sabinius moved forward out of the shadows.

"Is that you, Crestus? Thank the gods! Would you explain to this oaf that I am no traitor, and order him to let me go."

"I have no military authority to order the centurion to do anything, Laenus."

"Then go and find someone who has!" the senator snapped back.

"If you weren't doing what the centurion said you were doing, what were you up to?"

"Well, I—er—I—" Loricatus stammered. Then he shook his head and shoulders and gathered his wits. "Certainly I was leaving the city but I was accompanying Oliffe on his mission. He asked me to go with him to lend some weight to his negotiations. I was with him at the express wish of Constantine."

"Then why the secrecy and disguise?"

"As you know, Senator, affairs of state are always conducted discreetly. Oliffe would corroborate all I have said if you hadn't kicked him out."

"If that was all, Senator, why bring your wife with you?"

Laenus appeared nonplussed. He seemed to have completely forgotten his companion and now looked about him.

The centurion indicated the bench against the back wall. A figure sat huddled at the end of it, in shadow.

"Wife?" Laenus repeated tonelessly.

"But perhaps she is not your wife," Crestus Sabinius pressed on. "We'll ask her to remove her hood in a moment, but not yet. Now, shall I tell you our version of events? This is going to take some time, unless our prisoner confesses."

"I've nothing to confess," muttered Laenus stubbornly.

"May I have a stool, centurion? My legs won't take a lot of standing about."

The centurion nodded and one of his men brought a stool into the circle of light. The senator sat facing the prisoner.

"So, Laenus, this is how I see it. You met Oliffe in a sleazy tavern down by the river and you hatched up this plan to meet him tonight, disguised as one of his escort, and go with him to Alaric to offer your traitor's services – how much were you going to ask for, Laenus? How much was it worth to open the gates and bring the enemy inside? A larger sum than you gave Oliffe, I'll wager."

The centurion shook the bag taken from Oliffe, so that the coins rattled, then widened the leather thong at its neck and cascaded them into a heap on the table. The gold shone in the candlelight.

"This is pure fabrication!" blustered Laenus, his red face and frightened eyes no longer radiating the handsome and arrogant aspect that had been the downfall of so many women.

"We have a reliable witness," continued Crestus amiably.

Laenus paused, puzzled, then blurted out, "The red tunic! That fool, Oliffe!" He turned on Crestus. "Who's going to believe her? A common street girl against a respected senator? May I remind you that I am related to Constantine!"

"By marriage, only, Laenus. And that brings us to the lady here, who you were taking with you into the enemy camp. Your wife has always been a great support to you, Laenus, and has suffered a lot in the process, I've no doubt. However, you had no thought for her when you took off into the darkness to save your own skin, and left her to her fate."

Laenus looked about him as if seeking inspiration.

"If you ask the lady to remove her hood," he said in desperation, "you will see that she is not my wife. I would not compromise my wife. She has our son to care for."

"I see. Who then is it, beneath that hood?"

He was a long time in replying. The elderly senator waited then asked again, "Who is it, Laenus?"

At last he said, "It's Julia."

"Julia?"

"Yes, wife of Constantine's deputy."

"Ah, that Julia."

"You're a man of the world, Crestus," the senator said appealingly. "You know how we men arrange our domestic affairs. Julia is only my mistress. I can always get another mistress. Life becomes more complicated in the matter of changing wives."

"So it was Julia you didn't hesitate to abandon when you ran off?"

The prisoner shrugged carelessly. "You know how it is."

Crestus Sabinius thought of Adama, the light and warmth of his life, and did not know how it was.

"Think back to that night in the tavern, Laenus, when you laid your plans with Oliffe. You spoke of your secret call – you know, the owl's cry and the fit of coughing. Did you mention the time and place of your meeting?"

"No, there was no need. We had already decided that before we met in the tavern."

"So, how do you think we found out at which gate and at what time you were to assemble?"

"I don't know. No one knew except myself, Oliffe and his escort – and Julia had to be told, of course." He paused, then looked towards the woman on the bench.

"Julia?" he asked her. "Julia, did *you* tell them? Did *you* betray me to them?"

When she made no move, he began to curse and swear at her and would have hurled himself on her had the guards not restrained him.

"I am happy to say that she did, Laenus. Julia made a full confession in front of her husband. Unfortunately for you, she changed her mind, and decided to stay faithful to him, after all. That was very wise of her, don't you think? The cat always knows when to lick up the cream and reject the milk."

Laenus made another desperate attempt to reach her.

"Just let me get my hands round your whore's neck and I'll squeeze the life out of you!" he bellowed, struggling to break free.

"Hold him!" warned the centurion.

"Come here, young woman," ordered Crestus Sabinius, not unkindly.

The hooded figure stood and walked slowly towards the group in the circle of torch and candle light.

"I think we would all like you to remove your hood, if you've a mind."

Two slender arms reached up and pushed back the hood, and a cascade of dark hair fell around her shoulders.

"Bron!" exclaimed Laenus, staring at her. "Bron! Oh, how glad I am to see you! Tell them, sweet girl, tell them I'm no traitor. Tell them I mean no harm, I never meant any harm!"

Bron looked up at him, her gaze not leaving his face.

"It's of no use, Laenus," she said. "May I call you Laenus? You always wanted me to do that. I cannot tell them that you aren't a traitor, because tonight has proved that you are. What I *can* tell them is that you are a schemer, a liar, a lecher, and worse – a murderer!"

"What are you talking about? You're mad!" He turned to his captors. "She's as mad as a rabid dog! She's the one who should be locked up!"

Bron was relentless as tears began to stream down her face. "You sent an innocent man to his death for the murder of Fabia, whom you killed for a reason known only to yourself!"

"I don't know any Fabia!" he protested.

"You met her in that tavern. You were seen, a couple of nights before you stabbed her and threw her into the Tiber!"

"Prove it!" he challenged her.

"I can't, but we both know it's the truth. Anyway, it would make no difference. A man has already been convicted and executed for your crime."

"Send for Fausta! I want my wife!" Laenus then demanded.

"Your wife doesn't want you, Laenus," said Sabinius. "She's done with you. She doesn't want you back."

"She'll appeal to Constantine for me."

"I have spoken to Constantine," Sabinius told him, "and it is under his authority that we are here."

Laenus tried one last desperate ploy.

"He won't allow the conviction of a member of his family! Mud sticks!"

Crestus Sabinius looked down at the wet, brown, sticky feet of the prisoner and laughed.

"So it does. He's wiped his hands of you, Laenus, and all your mud. He's left all the arrangements for your trial to Julia's husband. It seems that many debts are being cleaned from the slate tonight, my friend."

"Take him away!" the centurion ordered and four of his men marched the struggling Senator Laenus Loricatus out into the pouring rain.

By now, Bron had dried her eyes. "Where are they taking him?" she asked and was told that it was the same prison in which the bo'sun had been held after his trial.

"The cell that connects with the sewer?" she asked and shivered when Crestus Sabinius nodded.

"How soon will he come to trial?"

"My dear, there'll be no trial," said the senator.

CHAPTER 48

Bron remembered the first time she had stood here, the ornamental lion's head grinning at her, its iron ring grasped in her hand. As before, Julius opened the door to her knocking. He didn't seem surprised to see them and his smile of welcome for Bron was broad and sincere.

"Is your mistress at home?" asked Senator Crestus Sabinius.

"Yes, sir, she's expecting you." Julius swung the door wide to allow them to enter.

Fausta Loricata was lying on the couch in the triclinium, a wet cloth over her face. Her breakfast lay untouched on the table alongside a glass of white wine.

She removed the cloth when Julius announced her visitors, and sat up. Her eyes and eyelids were swollen with crying and her face was blotched red.

"Julius, have more wine sent in."

"Water only, if you please, Fausta."

She nodded to her steward and he left the room.

"Crestus – and Bron. Please make yourselves comfortable. You have brought me news of my husband?"

"We have indeed, Fausta."

"Then wait until Julius returns. I want him to hear what you have to say, so he can inform the rest of the household. He is partly to blame for the behaviour of Laenus, you know. From babyhood, everyone spoilt him so. During his whole life, he never knew what it was to be refused anything he wanted, except perhaps—" She looked across to Bron, who felt embarrassed and lowered her eyes.

When Julius returned with a jug of water and glasses, she asked him to stay and listen while the senator related all that had happened the previous night and the fate of the head of their household.

When the murder of Fabia was spoken about, including the part Julius had played by making sure his master's message was sent to the bo'sun, he confessed in a low voice that displayed his remorse, "That is something I will have to live with for the rest of my life."

Fausta gave him permission to leave the room and he seemed glad to escape.

Somewhere along the way since Bron had last seen her, she had become outwardly implacable in her hatred of her husband, her words displaying no sorrow or regret, though her eyes told a different story.

"A very satisfactory outcome," was all she said.

"Now as to your position," Crestus said and gently took her hand.

"What about my position?"

"We cannot suppress the news. By tomorrow morning, it will have spread throughout Rome like the Tiber in flood. No one has sympathy for a traitor. If they cannot get to him, they will likely turn on you. At best, you will be ostracized, at worst in danger of attack on yourself or the house."

"But I had no influence over what Laenus did. I was the last person to know about his affairs. None of it is my fault."

"We know that, Fausta, but a mob is without reason."

"Who's 'we'?"

"Constantine knows of your plight. He will guarantee you safe passage wherever you wish to go and I would advise you to take him up on his offer. Could you stay with your mother?"

"And put her in danger at her age? That is out of the question. No, I shall stay here and face up to whatever comes my way. I have a loyal staff and we shall barricade ourselves in, if necessary."

Bron could keep quiet no longer. "What about Rius? Would you put his life in danger?"

"He's why you're here, Bron?"

"Of course."

The older woman said, seemingly with great difficulty, "I have an apology to make to you because I believed my husband. Izmira has since confessed her part in your dismissal, and Julius has confirmed that you rejected all the advances Laenus made to you. It has not been my experience that any woman refused my husband, and I'm sorry."

"Then will you show it by letting me take Rius away?"

Fausta looked shocked. "No, I will certainly not do that. He is my son, as I have reminded you over and over again. He has been paid for. I have grown quite fond of the little fellow and he is all I have now."

"You've got to let me have him back!" Bron cried in desperation.

"No, I have not. I understand how you feel, but you should have thought of that before he was sold. He is here with me now, and here he will stay." She turned to the senator. "Crestus, our business is finished. Thank you for coming to tell me about Laenus. Would you please leave now, and take Bron with you."

"Rius is happy, Julius said so," Crestus tried to comfort her once they were treading the path on their way to the front gate. "He is being well looked after."

"There must be something you can do to get him back for me. I want to take him home to Britannia."

"Would you have me kidnap him?" he asked her. "No, I can't see there's anything I can do, that anyone can do. I'm so sorry."

Bron was too upset and angry to reply. She had buoyed up her hopes that Fausta would want to move away from the Palatine and would consider the baby an inconvenience she could well do without.

"May I offer you a lift, my dear?"

"Thank you, Senator, but I prefer to walk. I'll stop by the apartment and talk it over with Adama, if she's there."

"If you see her, tell her I'll drop by later in the day."

Bron was glad to find that Adama was at home and ready to listen to all her news, but she had no inspiration when it came to getting Rius back, which Bron said she was determined to do.

"But how, Bron? How?"

"I have a plan. I've been thinking about it for a long time and I'm sure it will work. It's time now for me to try," Bron announced.

Adama looked at her suspiciously. "And what is your emergency plan?"

"I'm going to appeal to Emperor Honorius!"

Adama was about to remonstrate, but was so overcome by a fit of coughing, her eyes watering and unable to articulate the words, that Bron rushed to bring her a drink of water. When she had cleared her throat, she asked, "What did you say?"

"I'm going to appeal to Emperor Honorius."

"So I wasn't mistaken. That's what I heard first time. Bron, you're mad. The emperor isn't interested in you."

"He might be. Don't forget I met him once, at the chariot races."

"He meets hundreds of people – at the chariot races, the theatre, in his court, in the gaming houses and out on the hunt – what makes you think he will even remember you?"

"Because he gave me his promise to stop the savagery we saw that day, and according to Nadica Iconica, who frequently attends the chariot races with her husband, he has kept his word."

"I still say he won't remember you."

"Oh, but he will, because I will send him back the scarlet favour he gave to seal his promise – his scarlet seal. I have kept it safely."

"This is all on the assumption that you can get anywhere near him. He's in Ravenna, remember. How will you reach him?" She laughed. "Fly?"

"That's not as ridiculous as you think."

Adama looked at her friend and sighed.

"It's where you come in, Adama."

"Oh no, leave me out of this. If Crestus can't help you, I certainly can't."

"No, but Priscus can."

Adama stared at her. "Now you *are* out of your mind."

"He's going to Ravenna, isn't he? How soon?"

A shadow passed across Adama's beautiful almond eyes.

"Too soon."

"Would you speak to him for me and ask if he will take me with him, as one of his company of entertainers?"

"I'll do no such thing!"

"Adama – dear – our Rius is in danger all the time he stays in that house. I want to get him away from that woman, who only wants him as a trophy, and take him home to people with blood ties, home to Byden, my village, home to our blessed Britannia."

"You'd never get away with it. Someone is bound to ask you to perform, and what will you do? You know you can't sing, and I've never seen you dance."

"You have just given me an idea. I could say I perform on the trapeze – that I fly! There's no way I could demonstrate that on the journey. Will you, Adama, please, for the sake of Rius?"

Adama sighed again. "All right, I'll ask him, but be prepared for a refusal."

Bron hugged her. "Why don't you come with us? If you and Priscus—"

"I can't, I can't." Bron saw that she had touched on a matter that was causing her friend great distress. "He's asked me to go with him, in fact, he keeps asking, but I can't. What can he offer me? How will an itinerant singer support a wife? Should I go out to work? There's only one profession I've followed and he would never allow that, I know without asking him. Anyway, I've almost given it up now. But why do I have to earn a living? Crestus gives me all I need – not all I want, but all I need."

"In the excitement, I had forgotten Crestus."

"I can't hurt that dear old man."

"He'd get over it."

"No, he wouldn't Bron. It would kill him if I left him."

Bron was silent. She thought that was probably the truth of it.

"All right, I'll ask Priscus. I'll let you know his answer as soon as he gives it."

SECTION III

AD 408

October

HONORIUS, EMPEROR OF THE WESTERN EMPIRE

CHAPTER 49

Bron shifted her position to make herself more comfortable on the log and stretched out her hands towards the camp fire.

She was tired and looking forward to her bed. She had woken very early on the previous two mornings after disturbed rest and hoped for a better night's sleep tonight. The older members of the party, both male musicians and women singers, had been allowed room in the carts to sleep, but Bron had been judged young enough to make do with blankets on the ground between the wheels.

Not that she was complaining. Members of the concert party had made her very welcome and were intrigued when she told them, in answer to their questions, that she was a trapeze artist and had also been summoned to entertain the emperor.

She wasn't prepared for the next question. "But where's your equipment?" Priscus had come to her rescue by explaining that she was meeting her partner in Ravenna and he was bringing the equipment, props and costumes with him. Bron wasn't comfortable about lying to them but Priscus told her not to worry about it – she could tell them the truth once they reached the palace, and perhaps she could put in a good word for them when she was in audience with Emperor Honorius.

"Not that you need a good word," Bron had said. "I was at the theatre the night he came with his family, and he seemed very impressed with the play, and your performance especially."

Bron liked Priscus a lot and could see how Adama had fallen in love with him. He was so uncomplicated and sincere. Secretly, she thought it would be better if their relationship developed no further, better for both their sakes. However, it wasn't her problem. Even so, she sighed.

"That was a deep sigh."

"Oh, Priscus, there you are. Sit beside me. Are you going to sing again tonight?"

Priscus grinned as he threw one leg over the log and sat astride it, facing her. "Try and stop us," he said. "Just as soon as everyone's finished eating. If for no other reason, the noise should frighten off any stray bears or wolves."

"That was a good meal," Bron said appreciatively. A stew had been prepared over the fire, with diced meat provided by various creatures that had been scurrying around the rocks, vegetables from leaves picked along the way, and water from a nearby stream that had almost dried up but which Priscus told her would become a raging torrent in winter.

The first two days of their journey had been spent poling their carts and goods on rafts up the River Tiber, the horses lashed to them and swimming alongside. The foothills around them had been green and fertile, quite different from today's scenery. Now they were following a rough track through the bare and rugged Apennine Mountains with the occasional ruin of a fortification overlooking their progress.

"How long to Ravenna?" she asked Priscus.

"Not really sure. Several more days."

The group were warming up their voices and the musicians their instruments and eventually Bron was rocked to sleep between her blankets by echoes of the final lullaby, the melody playing over and over inside her head.

CHAPTER 50

They had left the steep, barren mountainsides four hours ago and were now following the uncertain track through an area of loose rocks, yellow grass and thorn bushes that were trying to coax nourishment from the sandy soil. Even at this distance, they could smell the salty sea air mixed with the musky odour of the marshes.

The company was in high spirits, and jokes and banter were passing from cart to cart and back again. Bron, walking by the side of Priscus at the head of the column, was keeping pace with the disreputable-looking horses drawing the impresario's carriage.

"How much longer?" she asked the elderly man.

"Probably another two hours," he said. "We should catch our first glimpse of the palace soon."

At noon they stopped to feed and water the horses and eat a picnic by the side of the road, then continued on their way.

"Look!"

Bron squinted in the direction in which Priscus was pointing and could just make out a shadow rising from the horizon.

"The palace!" he announced with awe.

As they drew nearer, the high walls and towers began to dominate the skyline, grey and menacing through the marsh haze and surrounded by a great stretch of still, pale green water.

"Not much further, now," said Bron.

Priscus said he thought the distance between them was deceptive and there was still another five miles to cover.

"We haven't reached the edge of the marshes yet," he observed.

Not long afterwards, their sandals began to squelch underfoot.

"Make sure you keep to the causeway," the driver of the carriage was instructed.

The chatter and singing quietened as everyone concentrated on following the way, marked at intervals with rotting wooden posts on which seagulls perched, regarding them quizzically as they passed.

They were all conscious of the glistening sandy mud on either side, not knowing whether a careless step would lead them into danger. A wheel stuck fast would hold up the entire column, and a threshing horse could bring down its companion, the cart and everyone in it.

The elderly man in the carriage leaned out of the window and asked Priscus and Bron if they would lead the way forward. He also directed that everyone should get out of the carts and walk in front and behind them to guide the drivers.

They had proceeded in this way for about a mile when Priscus again pointed ahead and Bron saw two horsemen galloping towards them, one behind the other. Both were in the uniform of cavalry officers, with horsehair-plumed helmets and chain armour.

When they reached the column, they reined in their horses. The foremost rider stood in the stirrups.

"Who are you?" he demanded.

"We're a company of entertainers, here on the orders of the emperor," Priscus told him.

"Who's in charge?"

The old man had already stepped down from his carriage and was approaching. He gave his name and answered their questions, then returned to his vehicle.

"They've come to escort us in," he told Priscus. "Just follow them."

It was as well that they were now being guided because from there the causeway swerved at intervals to right or to left. In this way, they approached the walls of the palace.

"Where's all the green water gone?" asked Bron in puzzlement.

"Must have been a mirage," Priscus suggested. "I've heard about such things."

As they reached the huge gates with its twin guard towers, Bron felt greatly disappointed. She didn't know quite what she had expected, but it was certainly not this depressing, massive stone edifice that stretched away on each side of her.

There was a shouted conversation between the horsemen at the front of the cavalcade and the guards in the watch towers, passwords were exchanged and orders bellowed, then the two gates swung outwards to allow the passage of the overawed and silent group of entertainers, followed by the carts bearing all their belongings.

Once inside, however, Bron gasped and clapped her hands in delight. The dark walls of grey stone were just a framework for what lay inside. Unexpectedly, the whole world became warm pink, a backdrop for beautiful and quirky architecture.

The horsemen led them through an archway topped with a blue wave-shaped dome on which great fish with long spiked noses curved and played. Later, Bron learned that they were blue marlins.

Then they clattered across a bridge where striped blue sea shells poured sparkling showers into the moat below. The horsemen spoke to the guards at a pair of great bronze doors, then saluted the company and rode off. Bron had time to admire carved images of whales and fearsome sea dragons before the doors swung open to admit them.

They found themselves in a huge courtyard, in the centre of which was a large white marble basin of water with a fountain of twelve life-sized, bronze winged prancing and pawing horses.

Bron had never seen such opulence and beauty anywhere before and it took her breath and speech away. This was a heaven where everyone was noble and all dreams were realised. Yes, this was certainly the right place to come to extract miracles! The return of her son and, incidentally, her pearl and amber necklace, was only a petition away, as long as the petition reached the right person's ears, and surely that person was Emperor Honorius himself.

Priscus seemed tongue-tied as well. In fact, no one was uttering a sound. They were all gazing around them in wonder. Even the old man looked impressed.

"Who's in charge here?" The questioner was a young man in a white toga.

The old man found his voice. "I am."

There followed a conversation, at the end of which the drivers with their horses and carts were led away through a high arch, presumably to the stable block, while young girls were summoned to conduct the women to their quarters and young men appeared, to take the musicians to theirs.

Bron followed the women, who were now laughing and chattering and squealing as each new and beautiful feature was revealed – pink-and-white marble pillars that looked like sugar confectionery; brightly-coloured wall decorations; friezes emblazoned with green landscapes and blue seascapes; high, gleaming gold-domed ceilings patterned with flower and fan motifs; rainbow-reflecting crystal chandeliers; and staircases with ornate iron balustrades and ornamental lamps on their newel posts, leading to upper and lower levels.

"Where are the emperor's apartments?" Bron asked one of the girls.

"Somewhere over there," the girl replied, pointing to a corridor that appeared to have no end. "I've worked here four years and I've never seen him."

She led the way along another corridor and down steps to a lower floor. Here the decorations were much less ornate but still more sumptuous than anything Bron had experienced. The girl indicated where they could bathe and where to eat, then gave out keys to several of the rooms and left them to their own devices.

The women singers were sharing but Bron found she had a room to herself. The bed looked comfortable, though almost anything would seem comfortable after a blanket on the hard ground, and the furniture and necessities were all as she had become accustomed to in her employments, but much more luxurious.

She unpacked her few possessions, making sure that the scarlet scarf the emperor had given her was safely tucked away at the bottom of the clothes chest.

After a relaxing session with the other women in the bathing complex, a change of clothing and a satisfying meal of fish-based soup and cold seafood platter with seaweed as a vegetable, she went to sleep trying to hatch a plan to meet Emperor Honorius as soon as possible. Her best ploy would be to mingle with the concert party, if they would have her without her trapeze!

CHAPTER 51

The emperor's agent met the old man next morning and an entertainment was agreed for that evening. Unfortunately, the impresario became unwell not long afterwards, perhaps due to the long and tiring journey or the seafood eaten the night before, and took to his bed for the remainder of their visit.

However, before doing so, he instructed the singers and musicians to spend the day rehearsing. This left Bron on her own to amuse herself as best she could. It wasn't a problem as there was so much of interest to investigate, but first she felt she had to tell them the truth about why she was here.

They accepted her explanation graciously and the women especially were sympathetic when she told them that appealing to the emperor was her only chance of getting her son back. She admitted, however, that she wasn't sure how she was going to do that.

The day passed quickly. She explored to her heart's content, ate well, and rested for an hour during the hottest part of the day. After their evening meal, she joined the company at the winged-horse fountain, where they were met by a slave who was to conduct them to the emperor's quarters.

The group was excited initially but as they passed from the public areas into the emperor's private apartments, nervousness overtook them and they fell silent.

They walked along corridors and through rooms that were even more opulent than those they had left, if that were possible, and were finally led into another very large courtyard, tiled with green-veined marble, in the centre of a colonnaded garden.

The evening air was heavy with the heady perfume of lilies and the subtler scents of lavender and mint in the borders. They all marvelled to see paths lined with box hedges fashioned in the shapes of birds and animals.

High stools were brought and left for them to arrange. Bron helped in this, as she felt the least she could do was fetch and carry and assist in any way possible. It was she who helped one of the younger women, who was feeling faint, across to the fountain to drink with cupped hands from water being spewed out by a leaping dolphin.

At last, they were settled, the musicians on their stools in the centre of the yard, the singers with Priscus sitting to one side. All they had to do then was wait for the arrival of the emperor and his party.

It was a long wait of about an hour, during which the entertainers became more nervous and flustered and hotter, so that the trips to the latrines behind the wall became as frequent as the trips to the fountain. At last, however, when instruments and voices were once again being exercised, they were ordered to stand, and the emperor came striding towards them along a colonnade.

His party, laughing and chattering, entered behind him and took their seats on marble benches.

Bron studied them with interest. In the centre sat Emperor Honorius, as magnificently bejewelled as she had seen him at the chariot races. His brilliantly-white tunic was short above well-shaped, tanned legs. She had thought before that his face was weak and his nose prominent, but this evening decided, perhaps to boost her flagging courage, that it was a kindly face.

There was no sign of his wife, Thermantia. This confirmed what her erstwhile employer, Talea, had told her, that he had sent her packing back to her mother, scandalously still a virgin. Talea always knew all the gossip and was probably right.

Instead, on his right side, sat Galla Placidia. If Bron had been Thermantia, she would have been very jealous of his younger half-sister, who always seemed to be very close to him. She now sat on a lower stool, leaning her left arm on his knee.

As before, Bron was conscious of her beauty. This evening she was dressed in pale blue, which was obviously used as a colour wash to draw attention to her blue-black hair, still cascading to her waist and revealing pinpoints of jewels that sparkled as she moved her head or ran her fingers through the thick strands.

On the emperor's left sat his grandmother, elegantly fashionable but as grotesque in her old age as Bron remembered her. She wasn't wearing the pearl and amber necklace this evening but deep red rubies in her tiara, necklace, bracelets and rings, to contrast with her pink tunic.

There were several other courtiers in the party, young men and women, all flamboyantly attired and in good humour.

The concert was of a high standard and deeply moving, especially the love songs and ballads expressing a longing for home sung by Priscus. Tears came to Bron's eyes. Byden was home for her. Byden burnt. Byden destroyed.

Her thoughts were interrupted when the company completed their programme with the patriotic marching song. The emperor had requested it and they had rehearsed it well.

Unable to move far in the courtyard, they faced their regal audience and cleverly gave the impression of marching: step left foot in place, step right foot forward, left foot in place, step right foot behind; repeat – left foot in place, right foot forward, and so on, one foot after the other but staying on the same spot.

> *She calls us and we're marching home!*
> *We hear you and we're marching home!*
> *Take up the cry! To live or die,*
> *To live or die for Rome!*

Their footwork was halted by the ovation from the small audience and the slaves and other watchers scattered around the paths and colonnades. Then the emperor stood in appreciation, still clapping, followed by the remainder of his party, except his grandmother, who had obviously decided that her great age exempted her from any exertion.

It was strange, thought Bron, that they were applauding so enthusiastically when they had all marched away from Rome, not towards her, and when they were living in such opulence without a hint of dying for the city and empire. Still, if the emperor was happy, then everyone was happy, the concert party would be paid well and he would be in a good mood when she approached him.

Honorius asked them to entertain him again the following evening and to present the play he had seen at the theatre. This was agreed and the entertainers left the courtyard for their beds, wafted in clouds of high good humour.

Priscus grinned at Bron and gave the thumbs-up sign. "Though it's a pity your trapeze didn't arrive!" he teased her. "Now, that would have been a sight worth seeing!" She laughed and gave him a playful punch on the arm.

The emperor and his party stayed in the courtyard, laughing and chattering and singing snatches of the songs they had heard that evening, eating from trays of food brought out to them and drinking a continuous supply of wine.

Bron also lingered, concealing herself in a corner behind a lead urn containing tall white flowers and leaves she didn't recognise, in the hope that she would have a chance to speak to the emperor on his own. Once or twice she had to draw back into the shadows to avoid detection by slaves who were passing to and fro.

When the lamps were lit and the revellers still hadn't gone to their beds, Bron gave up and made her way back to her room, losing herself a couple of times and having to explain to curious stewards who she was and where she was heading.

Perhaps she would have a better chance to talk to the emperor on the following evening.

CHAPTER 52

Next day, Bron was asked to help by prompting the actors if they forgot their lines in the play, which she was glad to do. They spent most of the day rehearsing.

The task was more difficult than she had anticipated and she found that she couldn't take her eyes or mind off the written lines in the script and the words spoken by the actors, or she would lose her place, and it might be just at that point that a prompt was needed.

Their reliance on her decreased as the day progressed, but several of the actors were still not word perfect by the time of the performance. However, all went very well and no one in the audience, which was larger than on the previous evening, seemed to mind the occasional slip and her voice intruding, helping the actor to get back on track.

Again, they ended the programme with the marching song and again they received a standing ovation and were asked to give one more performance on the following evening before returning to Rome. The company was delighted and once more left the courtyard in high spirits.

As previously, Bron hid herself in the corner of the colonnade behind the urn and this evening had better luck. Galla Placidia suggested that they entertained their guests to an evening meal on board one of their ships along the waterfront. This suggestion was enthusiastically received by the rest of the party, who left the courtyard, singing with gusto, but not before they had marched in formation all around the colonnade where Bron was hiding and out through the archway. Fortunately, they were too engrossed in their own activity to notice her in her hiding place.

"Are you coming, Rius?" the emperor's sister asked him as she returned to the bench to retrieve her scarf. Bron was startled. She had never heard him called by the same nickname she had given her son.

"I'll meet you down there," he said. "Don't wait for me. I've got one or two things to attend to first."

Bron was amazed when she saw his sister kiss him lightly on the mouth.

"Don't be long, my dear." She left him standing by the bench.

He watched her disappear, his back towards Bron, who was peering through the tall flowers in the urn. She thought he would hear her heart beating, it sounded so loud to her. Still he didn't move. When he spoke at last, her heart nearly jumped out of the top of her head.

"Well, young lady, are you coming out now?"

Was he talking to her? She didn't answer.

"You, behind the urn. Show yourself. I want to know who's spying on me."

Bron came out from behind the urn and nervously stood there. He turned round.

"Come over here. I don't bite and I won't call my guards, unless there's reason."

Slowly she walked towards him.

"You're the prompter, aren't you?"

Bron nodded.

"And last night you helped one of the young singers take a drink from the fountain?" Bron nodded again. "I thought so. I was watching from my balcony." He waved vaguely towards the living quarters overlooking the garden. "And last night you hid behind the urn, then got lost twice returning to your room. You see, I have eyes and ears everywhere."

When Bron still said nothing, not knowing how to respond, he asked, "So, what do you want? Are you going to assassinate me?" He laughed at what he obviously considered a huge joke.

Bron quietened her breathing sufficiently to answer, "No, Your Majesty."

He looked at her closely. "Haven't we already met? I'm sure we have, though I couldn't tell you where. Perhaps you've been spying on me before?"

For answer, Bron reached for the leather bag hanging from a plaited cord round her waist and pulled the neck open. She put her hand inside and brought out the scarlet scarf he had given her. It had gone in neatly folded but came out crumpled, so she shook it out before handing it to him.

"Do you remember this, Your Majesty? You gave it to me at the chariot races in the spring."

He took it and studied it then looked at her in surprise.

"You say I gave it to you?"

"Yes, Your Majesty, and you made me a promise."

He looked at it again, then at her.

"I remember now. You were a friend of Cato Calidonius. We caught you running around the arena in a right state and you told me off for allowing the blood letting during the champions' race."

"Yes, I believe I did, Your Majesty."

"And I said it wouldn't happen again. Well, it hasn't. Did you know that?"

"Yes, Your Majesty. Nadica Calidonia told me. Thank you."

"And I gave you the champion's scarlet favour to seal my promise. You see, I do remember. What was your name again?"

"Bron, Your Majesty."

"So, Bron, were you just checking up on me or is there something else you want? I'm no longer a god, now that we're officially Christians, but am still very powerful. Would you like me to stop the sun rising or the tide from coming in, perhaps? You have only to say the word." He laughed uproariously and slapped his thigh. Bron smiled in spite of her nervousness.

"There is something, Your Majesty."

"Ah, I thought there might be. Will it wait till tomorrow? They're expecting me on board for a feast. Should I take you with me, I wonder. No, perhaps not. Maybe some other time. That would give them something to talk about, wouldn't it? I'll tell you what – tomorrow evening, after the entertainment, I promise I'll make time to hear what you have to say, and you know I keep my promises. How's that?"

It was more than Bron could have hoped for.

"Thank you, thank you, Your Majesty."

"Good night, then, Bron, and sleep well."

He clicked his fingers and a slave appeared.

"Take the young lady back to her room, and make sure she doesn't get lost on the way."

Laughing, he walked out through the archway, taking her scarlet scarf with him.

CHAPTER 53

Bron woke several times during the night and was up early, walking in parts of the grounds she had not explored before and spending time admiring large gold, red and black fish in a pond. After breakfast, she went to find Priscus, to tell him her news.

He was pleased for her then said he had something to ask her. She guessed it was the question she had been dreading, and it was.

"Bron, please tell me about Adama. I know so little and she won't take me to her home."

"Have you asked her to tell you?"

"Yes."

"And?"

"She always evades my questions. We are very much in love and I could accept anything she has to say, if only she would confide in me."

Bron said kindly, "She must tell you herself, Priscus. It's not for me to say."

He looked at her keenly and she averted her eyes.

"I followed her once," he continued. "She didn't know I had. I saw this old man. They looked very—er—comfortable together."

Bron took hold of his hands.

"I don't know what to do about it," he said.

"You must ask her, when you get home." It was the only advice she could give.

During most of the day, the company rehearsed for the evening performance, a mixture of some of the more popular pieces from the first concert and others new to the programme.

Bron told Priscus that she thought the emperor would enjoy their selection very much, but could not raise his spirits or banish the troubled look on his face. She just hoped that his unhappiness would not affect his beautiful voice.

It didn't. In fact, it lent a poignancy and depth to his performance that hadn't been there before. The emperor was fulsome in his praise of the entertainers, and of Priscus in particular. As hoped, they were very well paid for their artistry and the impresario was given a letter of recommendation from the emperor to take away with him.

The younger members among them left to find somewhere to celebrate their success before going back to their rooms to prepare for their journey early on the following day.

"Will you be coming with us tomorrow, Bron?" Priscus asked her.

"Of course. I'll not get home any other way."

"Then I'll see you in the morning."

When the audience and the company had left, it was so quiet in the courtyard, except for the gentle cooing of pigeons as they settled down for the night, that Bron thought she was quite alone, until she noticed the emperor sprawled on the bench.

"I've sent them all away, so we won't be disturbed," he said. When she didn't move, he sat up. "There's no need to be afraid of me. Come and sit here."

He moved along to make room for her and indicated the place by his side. Nervously, Bron did as he wished.

"I meant to bring your scarf back but forgot. Never mind, you can collect it later. So, what is it you want me to do for you?"

She began very hesitantly, but gained confidence as she proceeded. He was a sympathetic listener, and every now and then, nodded encouragement. She didn't reveal every detail of her story, just sufficient to help him understand her predicament – how she had sailed from Britannia, had become pregnant, and had hidden from her lover in a Roman brothel.

"My baby was named Honorius, after you, Your Majesty. I shorten it to Rius. I heard your sister call you Rius yesterday. I hope Your Majesty doesn't consider it impertinent."

"Not at all. It's an honour. Fancy that! Where is he now, your son?"

Then Bron continued her story – how, to escape detection, she had allowed him to be adopted into the Loricatus household and had accompanied him there as his wet nurse, and how the senator had lied to his wife and tricked her into dismissing Bron.

"Would that be Senator Laenus Loricatus?"

"Yes, Your Majesty."

"I have received disturbing reports about him lately."

"If you mean that he turned traitor to Rome and to you, Your Majesty, they're true. He planned to open the gates to let Alaric in."

The emperor's eyes darkened. "I sent a message that they should skewer his head to a pole and display it on the very gate he would have violated, but the messenger arrived too late and Constantine had already disposed of him very efficiently. So, now you want your son back?"

"I'm desperate to have him back, Your Majesty."

"And the senator's widow won't give him up?"

"I've offered to repay her the purchase money but she refuses."

"I would have thought she had no bargaining power in the circumstances though, to be fair, she is also a victim of her husband's treachery – I heard about the other woman – Julia something."

"The wife of Constantine's deputy."

"Oh, *that* Julia. Have you appealed to Constantine to help you?"

"No, Your Majesty."

"Why not?"

"It was because of the scarlet seal – I thought you might remember me."

"Ah, yes. And I did, didn't I? I passed the test." He smiled at her and stood up so she stood as well.

"Well, Bron, I'm glad you came to me. I'd like to help you and my namesake, little Rius – how old is he, by the way?"

"Ten months."

"So, don't worry about it any more. I'll see what I can do. It should be simpler than preventing the sun from rising or the tide from coming in."

He looked down into her serious face. "It was a joke, Bron, a joke."

"Yes, Your Majesty."

He continued to look at her. "Should I return to Rome, do you think? My sister says I should, but my usurper, Constantine, seems to have affairs well in hand."

"I'm not a Roman, Your Majesty, but I've heard people say that he drives your chariot now."

"Perhaps so, but it's going to be a rough ride, and while he has charge of the reins, it means I can stay here in comfort. I can pick them up again at any time of my choosing."

"Then I will repeat what you have said if I hear any gossip, Your Majesty."

"Yes, do that."

Bron felt he was much amused by her, though he was too polite to show it.

"May I retire now, Your Majesty? I'm leaving early tomorrow morning with the entertainers."

"Mmm." He hesitated then seemed to make up his mind. "No, I don't think you are. I want you here. It will please me to have a different face – and such a pretty face – around for a while."

"But, Your Majesty—"

"Only a few days, Bron, while I sort out your problem. You can spare me a few days in the circumstances, can't you? There's no one expecting you back, is there?"

"No."

"Then I'll hear no excuses. Your friends have already been informed that you won't be journeying with them in the morning. You'll be more comfortable in this part of the palace and I may need you near me in case any problems arise with the widow, so your belongings have already been brought over. Agreed?"

Bron was confused as to exactly what he was proposing but she was in his palace, and he was the emperor, and he was going to get Rius back for her. At this moment, she was very reliant on him. There seemed only one possible answer.

"Agreed."

"Good, then that's settled."

He beckoned and three slave girls appeared from nowhere.

"Take the young lady to her rooms," he instructed them, then turned to Bron. "Now I have some very serious revelry to indulge in. I'll see you tomorrow morning."

And with that he had gone.

CHAPTER 54

Bron could not believe her good fortune when she saw her room, radiant with soft lamp light.

A large bronze bed took up most of the space, and on it were piled counterpanes and bolsters and cushions so welcoming that, as soon as the last slave had left the room, she took a running jump across the pink marble floor and landed among them, cocooning herself while at the same time rolling about like a dislodged amphora on a ship's deck. Then she lay there for a while, staring at the gilded ceiling and delicately-coloured wall mosaics reflecting the lamplight.

A bronze bench and stool were similarly covered with cushions and there were two small bronze tables. On one, the slaves had placed her make-up, pots of cream and two hand mirrors such as she had never seen before, with reflecting glass instead of the usual polished copper or silver. This was luxury indeed!

Her jewellery, combs and hairpins were displayed on the second table and she found her clothes carefully laid out in a carved ivory chest.

Behind heavy bronze-coloured curtains that covered one wall, she discovered a balcony, and surprised not to feel fresh air cooling her face, realised that the opening was sealed with glass held in sliding wooden frames.

On one side of her room, a door was locked without a key in the lock, and another opposite led into a small room containing, wonder of wonders, her own bathtub. There was a tripod, basin and pitcher of water, a table containing drinking glass, toiletries, a bowl of oil and towels, and a chamber pot on a chair in a corner. All that was missing was hot water for the bath, but she guessed that was easily obtainable by ringing a bell that she hadn't yet found.

She went to sleep very quickly in her large bed and was dreaming about wandering aimlessly across a battle field, looking for Aurelius, when she was wakened by a tap at the door. A slave girl entered in response to her sleepy, "Come in!" bringing a pitcher of water.

"Is the sun up yet?" Bron asked her.

"Only just, madam."

Bron smiled, glad that she hadn't taken up the emperor's offer to stop it rising!

"Has the entertainment party left, do you know?"

"Yes, about an hour ago."

Bron was sorry that she hadn't been able to wave them off, but knew she would be back in Rome in a few days' time.

The girl asked what she would like for breakfast then indicated a large brass handbell by the door, informing her that, if she stood in the corridor and rang it, someone would bring hot water, or whatever else was required. She then took the fresh water into the adjoining room and returned with the pitcher it had replaced and the chamber pot, discreetly covered with a cloth.

As soon as the girl had gone, Bron slid out of bed and padded across the cool tiles to the window, pulled back the curtains and slid the framed glass to one side.

There was a rush of morning air, a pot pourri of seaweed and surf, marsh vapours and autumn flowering. Crossing the balcony to the balustrade, she saw below the emperor's courtyard and its acres of gardens, and anticipated the pleasure of exploring later.

Which was the emperor's balcony, she wondered – the one he had vaguely indicated during their meeting two days ago?

After washing her face and slipping on a tunic, she rang the bell for breakfast on her balcony, then found her way down the staircase to the gardens.

There she dawdled along cool colonnades and followed bubbling and gurgling water as it fell over rocks from pool to pool, on towards flowerbeds full of gladioli, iris and many-coloured poppies. Bron didn't know whether or not there was a heaven, like the Christians believed, but if there was, she decided that it couldn't be any more beautiful and peaceful than this.

Looking back towards the palace, she was able to distinguish her balcony from the rest because the curtains were different for each.

For a fleeting instant, she caught a movement on the balcony three rooms away from hers, but if someone had been watching, he or she had slipped back into the room unseen. *Was it the emperor or someone else?*

Later, she relaxed in her bathtub and washed her hair, cosseted by the fragrance and purple dyes of amaranth, then dressed in her dark red tunic with gold chained brooches, the one she had worn when she met the emperor at the chariot races, added gold earrings and gold sandals and made up her face – but he did not send for her.

Disappointed, despondent and losing confidence, she rang the bell for her evening meal, picked at the chicken, spent the evening alone pacing up and down and finally went to bed, ashamed of her tears. If she was being honest, her frustration was due more to humiliation at being ignored. Men did not usually ignore her.

And at this rate, she would never get Rius back.

CHAPTER 55

"Have you seen the emperor this morning?" she asked the slaves who brought her breakfast next day.

"No, madam, but he usually stays in his room until much later," one of them replied.

"Oh, and where is his room?" she asked while breaking off a piece of cheese.

Instead of answering, they both looked at each other, giggled and ran back into the corridor, shutting her door, which Bron thought was very strange behaviour.

The new morning brought new hope. She followed the routine of the previous day and decided that, if the emperor didn't send for her by this evening, she would request an audience. After all, she hadn't spent all those days in uncomfortable travel just to idle away her time now she was here, no matter how agreeable her surroundings.

Exasperated, she had her bath and dressed again in the red tunic before wandering round the gardens, putting herself on display. She had the feeling that she was being watched, but today saw no movement on any of the balconies. Neither did she see the emperor.

Even more frustrated, she returned to her room and rang the bell. When a slave came running, this time a young lad, she ordered her midday meal then added, as he turned to run back to the kitchens, "I also want to see the emperor!"

He turned back and looked at her in amazement, then began stuttering some incomprehensible reply.

"Today!"

She was surprised at her own temerity. It hadn't sounded like her voice. In fact, she looked about to see who had spoken in such a peremptory tone, but there was no one else there apart from the boy, who was still burbling.

"Well, what's the matter?"

She knew she was being a bully.

For answer, he fled and Bron closed the door. Two girls brought in her meal and set it on the table on the balcony without comment. An hour later, she heard a sharp knock on her door, and when she opened it, a man stood there, dressed officially in a white toga. He had a determined set to this mouth and his eyes looked coldly at Bron.

"May I come in?" It was more an order than a request.

She opened the door wider for him to enter. He marched into the centre of the room, turned and glared at her.

Oh dear, she thought, *I'm for it now.*

He began by giving her his name and office, neither of which stayed in her memory.

"Madam, I have come to explain to you that no one summons the emperor to an audience. He is the emperor! And certainly not a chit of a girl. I can only put it down to your arrant ignorance."

Bron shuffled her feet and looked down at the floor. She recognised that she deserved this.

"You are here at the invitation of the emperor and a guest in his palace. You do not decide when he will see you. He decides. You wait. Are you now clear on that point?"

Bron nodded dumbly.

"Good. Finish your meal."

He withdrew without further comment and the door clicked shut. Bron guessed that the colour of her face matched the tunic she was wearing.

She heard other footsteps along the corridor, and when they ceased, she thought she heard the click of another door shutting. She opened her own and looked out but there was no one around.

After that, she knew all she could do was wait upon the emperor's whim.

No longer hungry, with nothing to do, and bored, she wandered over to the bed, lay down among the cushions and slept.

"Bron!"

"Mmm?"

She turned over and tried to go back to sleep but heard her name spoken again. Confused, and for a moment not remembering where she was, she dragged herself back to consciousness and sat up – and there he was! The emperor! Sitting on her bed!

"Oh, Your Majesty, I'm so sorry! I didn't know it was you!"

She struggled to get off the bed.

"Take your time," he said. "I'll wait for you on the balcony."

She smoothed down her tunic, grabbed a mirror and combed at her hair, renewed the ochre on her lips, and still not fully satisfied with her appearance but knowing she couldn't keep him waiting any longer, stepped out onto the balcony.

He was leaning on the balustrade but turned when he heard her, and smiled appreciatively.

"You were wearing that tunic the day we met," he said. "You see, I remember. And here is your scarlet scarf, the seal of my promise, back where it belongs."

He draped it round her neck again, as he had done at the races.

"Your Majesty has been very gracious to me."

"You can drop the title," he told her, "though I suppose we should retain some formality. 'Sir' will do if you have to use it at all."

"Sir, I was wondering—"

"Yes?"

"How you got into my room."

He laughed. "I can do anything I want, didn't you know that? It just needs a little magic."

"I have an apology to make to you. I didn't observe the protocol. I received a stern reprimand."

"I heard about it. There are rules and we must all adhere to them, including the emperor. It's the job of my councillors to make sure that we do, partly to ensure my safety. Otherwise, chaos would reign."

Bron tried to apologise again but he cut her short. "Between you and me," he confided to her, "he is henpecked at home and takes any opportunity to put down every woman he meets."

Bron felt better.

"Anyway, it worked, didn't it? You expressed the wish to see me, and here I am!"

She was feeling better all the time.

"Come, let us walk in the gardens," he invited, "and I can tell you all that has been happening in Rome since you left."

Together, they descended the staircase. Bron couldn't believe this was happening.

They wandered for an hour or more, chattering aimlessly, along pathways protected from the sun by overhanging branches, and when the sun had blazoned itself out and was losing heat, they ventured out of the shade to rest on a bench in a rose garden.

When he pricked his finger trying to break off a red rose for her, she laughingly sucked it clean for him while a gardener got busy with the secateurs. She pushed the rose into her hair. The emperor nodded his approval.

"You were cross with me, weren't you, for not sending for you yesterday?" She could not deny it and nodded. "Then it is my turn to apologise to you. I should have explained that I have been busy on your behalf. I have been in touch with my people in Rome."

Bron stared at him. How was that possible? Rome was several days' journey away. He saw her surprise.

"Have you not found my columbarium? Come!"

He led her back towards the palace and into a miniature courtyard. The walls were pitted with small chambers. Well-fed pigeons in varying shades of pink, white, black and grey, with coloured rings on their legs, were flying in and out of the holes or waddling around their feet, pecking at crumbs.

"My carrier pigeons," he explained. "We operate a daily shuttle service between my palace here and my palace in Rome. My birds are taken by horseback to Rome and released there when there is news to report. In the same way, pigeons from the city are brought here and released when I have orders to issue or information to request."

He walked across to a barrel in the corner, removed the lid, and came back with a handful of grain for her to scatter. Dozens of pigeons flew down for this unscheduled feast. When all the seed had been eaten, the young couple left the yard and continued their walk.

"I have made enquiries about your son, Bron. My information is that Fausta Loricata is having a hard time. She is being pilloried and ostracized as the news of her husband's treachery becomes known. Her house has been attacked several times by people throwing stones and trying to break in."

She could hear the anxiety in her voice as she asked, "And my son – is Rius all right?"

"No one in the house has been hurt and I am arranging for protection. That's as far as I know at the moment."

"Thank you, sir. I am so grateful to you."

"Such bullying should not be allowed in a civilised society. The woman is not responsible for the actions of her husband, and he has been dealt with. Now let us go back. My sister will wonder where I am. We are entertaining some local dignitaries this evening."

As they neared the palace, he glanced up and waved to someone standing at the balustrade of a balcony. She waved back.

Bron stared. The balcony was three rooms away from her own. She now knew the owner of the spying eyes.

CHAPTER 56

Bron was again left to her own devices on the following morning. At least, she knew that she had the emperor's sympathy and he was making an effort to help her. Whether sitting on her balcony or walking in the gardens, as she was now, she looked up frequently to check for pigeons flying to and from the palace, though it was hard to tell whether they were on the emperor's business or just flying around for the sheer enjoyment of being alive.

Someone was hailing her and she saw the emperor's councillor hurrying in her direction, waving both arms above his head, and waited for him to catch her up. She hoped she hadn't unwittingly committed another misdemeanour.

"Good morning," she greeted him politely as he drew near.

"Good morning, madam," he replied. "I have a message for you from the emperor. He hopes you will allow him to escort you to the foreshore later in the day so you can enjoy the sunset from the deck of his flagship." He gave her no time to reply. "He will call for you late afternoon."

"Yes, of course, thank you."

"His grandmother will be on board, the dowager empress, her imperial majesty Aelia Flavia Claudia Antonia."

Thoughts of the old lady reminded Bron of the second reason she had taken the difficult journey to Ravenna – to retrieve not only her son but also her amber and pearl necklace, if she could.

But how was that to be accomplished? In truth, it was no longer hers, she had given it away to that soldier in Byden wood, and it now belonged to the dowager empress, no matter how she had come by it.

About an hour before sunset, there was a knock on her door, and there stood the emperor, indolently propping himself up against the wall of the corridor. He had abandoned his official toga for a simple white tunic. Today, her tunic was a radiant royal blue and his appreciative smile told her she looked her best.

"I thought there were no openings in the walls overlooking the sea," she said when they were on their way, "to prevent attack."

"You're right, there aren't," he confirmed. "You'll see."

Two slaves preceded them to a part of the garden nearest the foreshore and led them down a flight of stone steps, through a door and into a concreted underground tunnel. The door was closed behind them. Torches blazed in wall sconces, lighting the sandy path ahead before disappearing round a corner.

The tunnel twisted and turned and at intervals widened into areas large enough for groups of defenders to resist an invader. It also occasionally veered off into other tunnels, so that Bron would not have known which route to take had it not been for their escort and the torches showing the way.

Occasionally, she noticed a slight dribble of sand sliding down from a crack in the concreted walls, and sometimes there were damp patches on walls and on the compacted sandy floor.

"We are now in the deepest part, underneath the dungeons," the emperor told her.

The air they were breathing smelt stale and mouldy and of burning tar from the torches, whose flames heated the tunnel to the temperature of a hay oven. Bron was sticky with perspiration and hoped they would be out in the fresh air again soon.

As if in answer to her wish, the path began to slope upwards, then level out for a distance. Finally, it came to an abrupt end. A short ladder rested against the blank wall that faced them.

The slaves set the ladder up, extending it until it reached the tunnel roof. One put his foot on the lowest rung, to steady it, while his companion climbed to the top and began scrabbling above his head. Suddenly, a welcome blast of sea air mixed with the perfume of pines reached them.

By now, the slave had disappeared through the hole. Then his hand came down to reach for her. She climbed to the top of the ladder and raised her hand to take his but he gripped her by the forearm and hoisted her through the exit. She was surprised to find herself in a pine wood. By the time she had dusted herself down, the emperor stood by her side.

The slave climbed back through the hole and down the ladder and the emperor quickly replaced the wooden cover, pushing sandy soil and pine needles across it as camouflage. Now, it was impossible to tell that it was an entrance to a tunnel and Bron knew, if it were left to her, she would never find it again.

She took a deep breath. The smell of the pines was intoxicating.

The emperor smiled. "It will clear out all the tubes round your nose and throat," he said, "and cure all your coughs and colds. Such a pity it can't be bottled and sold. It would make someone a fortune."

He led the way to the edge of the wood at the point where it petered out and met the shoreline. He looked about in all directions, until he was satisfied that no one was in sight.

"Take your sandals off and hold my hand, Bron," he said, "in case someone is watching. We will look just like any other young lovers emerging from an illicit meeting."

With some embarrassment, she did as she was told and together they walked barefoot and hand-in-hand along the beach. His grip was firm and there was no way she could withdraw her hand until he decided to release her.

Between their toes, the sand was soft and golden and the sea sparkled sunlight off its deep blue, lazy rippling surface. She had a sudden, childlike desire to become a part of it and tugged at the emperor's hand until he ran with her down to the little waves that were tentatively exploring the edge of their permitted boundary, leaving ragged lines of tiny, frothy bubbles.

He laughed at her pleasure and for a while they became simply two young friends enjoying each other's company in a world where nothing more important was happening than that the sun was setting.

Ahead in the distance, Bron could see some sort of construction reaching out into the sea, and as they drew nearer, realised it was a harbour, and a very busy one.

The spell broken, the emperor let go of her hand to put on his sandals and Bron followed his lead.

They entered the harbour from the shore and for a while wandered along the quay inside the wall without being recognised, but it was not long before a fisherman sitting on a bollard mending his nets jumped up and nudged his companion, who spoke to a friend, and soon everyone was standing and bowing as the young emperor passed by. Bron watched the transformation as he squared his shoulders and played the part of the ruler of this great empire, a man to be reckoned with.

She felt sad. She liked what she had seen of her new friend sloshing through the ripples and kicking up sand in his exuberance of just being alive. That young man had completely disappeared.

She was suddenly conscious of the danger he could be in, could always be in. However, she realised she need not worry when she noticed several young men discreetly strolling behind them at a distance and realised that his bodyguard must have been waiting for them in the wood and had been following them all the time they were enjoying themselves along the shore.

For a while, they stood and watched the activity in the harbour – fish being gutted, cargoes loaded in preparation for sailing on the next high tide, fishing boats being washed down or painted, a few coastal boats dawdling in through the harbour entrance.

Her young companion was now leading her towards a three-masted sailing ship that was tied up at the end of the stone mole, near the sea entrance to the harbour. It was painted shining black with the name picked out in scrolling gold letters, *Galla Placidia*, and beneath it the word, *Ravenna*. He had named it after his sister.

"Come on board, Bron," he invited her. "Prepare to meet my grandmother. You'll find she's rather eccentric, but harmless."

"Sir, we have met before, though I doubt she will remember me."

"She remembers what she wants to, and I can't think that she would want to forget you, pretty lady. Let's see."

They climbed the gang plank and stepped on board. The planking beneath their feet had been scrubbed clean and everything shone and smelt of new paint.

On the further side of the ship had been set up a folding table, covered in a white linen cloth with refreshments pushed aside, and beside it a comfortable chair. Standing at the rail and looking out towards the setting sun was the old lady Bron remembered so well from their chance meeting on Palatine Hill. She was idly fingering her necklace – the necklace Bron considered as hers.

"Grandmother, I've brought a friend to meet you. I thought we could enjoy the sunset together."

"That's good, Honorius. I'm glad you've found a friend. I hope he's someone who seeks you out because he likes you and not because he wants something from you."

Bron felt very guilty on hearing this, but the emperor looked at her and grinned.

"It's not a *he*, grandmother, it's a *she*."

The old lady turned round then and looked at Bron in surprise.

"So you are. Well, that's a step in the right direction, I must say."

"Grandmother!" the emperor chided her.

She turned back to the sea. "You know you're the apple of my eye, Honorius, whatever you do, and your brother, Arcadius, was the apple of my other eye until death took him from us last May, but that hasn't blinded me to your faults. Come and stand beside me – Bron, is it?"

"Yes, Your Majesty."

"You too, Honorius, come and look at this glorious painting. It's one work of art that no on can buy, fortunately, and hide away in some dark corridor. This is for everybody to enjoy, like most things in life that are of value. Don't you agree, Bron?"

"I hadn't thought of it like that before, Your Majesty, but yes, you're right."

"Of course I am."

"My grandmother's always right," agreed the emperor, "or so she would have us believe."

Her laugh was deep and throaty. She placed gnarled hands on the rail. Her clutter of jewelled rings, like the sea, reflected the sunset colours that blazed around them.

"Do you believe in God, Bron? The Christian God?"

Bron was taken aback. "I'm not sure, Your Majesty."

"No, nor am I. But it must take a brain and a soul to create a sunset like this."

They stood in silence and watched the display, spread out in swathes of fire and yellow ochre, dove greys and pinks and duck egg blues, and encroaching night time colours of indigo and purple.

"It reflects the colours of my necklace," murmured the empress, feeling for it. "Pearl and amber. Do you see pearl and amber in the sunset, Bron?"

Bron nearly choked on her reply. "Yes, Your Majesty."

The fire in the sky was beginning to fade. Bron plucked up her courage.

"How did you come by the necklace, Your Majesty?"

"I won it in a game of chance. It's an unusual story. Do you want me to bore you with it?"

"Oh, yes please, Your Majesty. I'm sure I won't be bored."

"Very well, then. Honorius has heard me tell it many times. He honoured me by making me commander-in-chief of one of the British legions. When he recalled them to Rome, I met their ship when it docked in Ostia. The captain showed me the necklace and asked if I knew how much it was worth. Apparently, he had a deserter on board who had handed it over in return for holding his tongue and letting him work incognito as a crew member. The captain didn't know how the deserter had come by it. The man disappeared as soon as the ship tied up. I said I didn't know how much it was worth but I would buy it off him. He had the temerity to refuse. As you see, it is very beautiful and I wanted it. I could have taken it off him and paid him some paltry amount, but there was no need. We played cards at my suggestion and I was on a winning streak all evening. I took the necklace when he had no wagers left."

"That was clever of you, grandmother," observed the emperor, winking at Bron over the old lady's head.

"I thought so, too. I was cheating all evening, of course, and he knew it, but he could hardly accuse the dowager empress of hiding cards up her sleeve, could he?"

"Grandmother!" the emperor protested.

"He didn't suffer, Honorius. I sent him good value for it before I left Ostia, though not, I am sure, what it is worth."

The sky had quietened down now and lamps were being lit on deck.

"So, where did you two young people meet?" she asked.

"At the chariot races in Rome," Honorius answered.

"How is it that I haven't been made aware of this friendship until this evening, Honorius?"

"Because it didn't exist until a couple of days ago. Grandmother, have I ever told you that you're a nosy old lady?"

"Frequently, my dear – and not so much of the 'old', if you please!"

He laughed and gave her an affectionate hug.

"You'll have to excuse her, Bron. She won't stop asking questions until she knows all about you." Bron smiled.

As if to prove his point, the dowager empress continued, "So, young lady, who are you exactly?"

"Your Majesty, we have met once before, though I don't expect you remember."

"Tell me."

"You were getting out of your carriage on Palatine Hill and you stumbled—"

"So I did. Were you the girl who saved me from falling? But I seem to remember that you were—you were—"

"I had a baby in a push-cart."

"A nurse?"

"It was her baby," Honorius said.

"Hmm. Honorius, go and give orders to the captain or someone for half an hour. I want to talk to this young lady."

"Go easy on her, grandmother. I don't want you to frighten her off."

She waved him away. "And ask for another chair!" She explained to Bron, "I would walk with you round the deck but I can't trust my legs any more."

When the chair had been brought and Bron was sitting opposite her, the interrogation began.

"I need to know that you are a suitable companion for my grandson."

Bron was offended. "I'm not pretending to be anything other than what I am," she said, "and in my judgement, I am *not* a suitable companion for your grandson. I didn't come here to be a 'suitable companion'."

"Then what did you come here for?"

"To plead with him to help me get my baby back."

"So, you *are* another one who wants something from him. And what are you prepared to give in return, if he is successful?"

"He hasn't asked for anything – there is nothing."

"And I have offended you. Young lady, we need a serious talk, you and I, but not now. It's getting late. Tomorrow?"

Bron was mystified. *Talk about what?* She replied, "As Your Majesty wishes."

"I'll send for you in the morning. Now, go and find Honorius. There are carriages on the quayside to take us back to the palace."

Obediently, Bron did as she was told.

CHAPTER 57

She was summoned to the empress's apartments late next morning. Still mystified, she followed the slave sent to fetch her, along corridors and into yet another courtyard, shaded by tall plane trees. The empress was sitting on a low wall surrounding a fish pool, dropping crumbs for a variety of birds, a table and chairs by her side.

"Come and sit down, Bron," she said, "and we can have our little chat. Honey wine?" She nodded to an attendant without waiting for Bron to answer. "There, try that." Bron did and found it was delicious.

"Now, where were we? Ah, yes, at the chariot races, and you came all this way to ask for help to get your son back. So, where is your son? What's his name, by the way?"

"Honorius, Your Majesty, after the emperor."

"Very fitting. Tell me everything – start at the beginning. Where do you come from? I fancy your accent is British. Am I right?"

How astute the old lady is, Bron thought, and nodded. "Yes, I was born in southern Britannia."

Put at ease by her attentive listener, soothed by glass after glass of sweet wine, warmed by the sun, and fed by delicacies of shell fish, crab meat, pigeon breasts, goose liver pate, small warm rolls of bread, olives, figs and dates, damsons and cherries, Bron was soon relating to the dowager empress details of her life from her birth in Byden to their meeting yesterday – leaving nothing out apart from the story of the pearl and amber necklace. It was such an amazing coincidence to find the empress wearing it that she felt that that part of her story would not be believed.

The sun was setting again and the lamps among the flower beds were being lit by the time Bron came to the end of her narrative. She hadn't realised how long she had been talking and how tired she was.

"Well, that's quite a story, my dear. Thank you for telling me. I must say, I didn't expect quite so much detail."

"I'm sorry if I bored you, Your Majesty – it must have been the wine. I'm sorry."

"Not at all. It was all most interesting. How much does my grandson know?"

"Only about Rius, my son."

"And what is he doing about your son?"

"He's making enquiries about the Loricatus household – there's trouble there, because of what her husband did. He receives news from Rome every day. More than that, I don't know."

"I have enjoyed getting to know you better, Bron. You have confided in me and I want to confide in you, but not tonight. Tomorrow. I expect you want to go back to your room now. Shall I have a meal sent up?"

"I couldn't eat another thing."

"And here's Honorius looking for you. He's been out sailing all day."

Bron smiled as the emperor approached. His hair was unkempt and his cheeks were burnt red.

"You do look a sight, Honorius," his grandmother reproved him. "Have you had a pleasant day?"

"Yes – plenty of tuna, mackerel and wrasse. Gally caught a swordfish. Her line became entangled round its body. It towed us for miles but in the end we had to let it go."

"Galla went with you?"

"Yes. We both had a great day."

"Well, the day's over now. You'd better take Bron back to her room. She'll never find it on her own."

"Of course. Goodnight, grandmother."

He bent down and kissed the top of her wig then took Bron by the elbow and led her out of the courtyard. She felt a little unsteady on her feet.

"Has she been plying you with wine?"

"I have drunk rather a lot," Bron admitted.

"I'm very fond of her, but am aware she's a wily old bird. Did she ask you to do anything for her?"

"No, but I think that's coming, tomorrow," Bron told him.

"I wish sometimes she wouldn't still treat me like a little boy," he complained. "To listen to her, no one would ever think I govern the greatest empire that has ever existed. I know she has my best interests at heart, but she does sometimes poke her nose into affairs that are none of her business. You don't have to see her tomorrow if you don't want to."

"I can hardly refuse her."

"I suppose she can't do much harm. You'll be out of here in a day or two, anyway."

They had just reached her bedroom door and Bron turned to face him.

"Sir, what's the news from Rome?"

"I'm waiting for my pigeons to return. I should know tomorrow."

"Thank you so much, Your Majesty," she said, and enthusiastically kissed him on the cheek before entering her room and closing the door behind her.

She had not been in bed very long, and wasn't yet asleep, when there was a knock, knock at her door, a pause, then another urgent knock, knock, knock. Pulling a cover around her, she opened it, and was amazed to find the dowager empress standing there.

"I've decided that I must talk to you tonight, my dear. Anything could happen tomorrow. Tomorrow is often too late. May I come in?"

Bron stood to one side to allow her to enter.

"Can I help you, Your Majesty?"

"I hope so. Tell me straight out – has my grandson made a pass at you yet?"

Bron stared at her.

"Well?"

"No, no he hasn't. He's been a perfect gentleman."

The old woman swore under her breath though Bron didn't catch what she said. When she plopped down on the bed, Bron sat beside her.

"Can I offer you any—"

"Why hasn't he? You're a beautiful young woman. What's wrong with the boy?"

Bron didn't know what to say.

"You may not be here much longer," continued the empress, "so we've got to work fast. Do you find him attractive, Bron?"

She remembered their walk on the beach.

"We get on well together. I enjoy his company."

"That's not enough! Young people these days – no spark! Though, having listened to your story, that's not true in your case, I'm glad to say. We've got some work to do, my girl!"

Bron was still at a loss as to how to respond.

"Your Majesty, I'm not following this conversation. I don't know what you're talking about."

"Bron, my grandson is apparently trying to help you. Are you willing to help him?"

"If I can, of course."

"Good. Thank you."

Bron waited for an explanation but none was forthcoming. She asked, "Is that all?"

"For now. Just do anything he asks. I want you to please him – that would please me, too."

Bron felt she was letting herself in for far more than she understood but was not absolutely sure what. Surely, the old lady was not suggesting what Bron suspected she was suggesting. If she was, why?

She was unable to ask because the door had already closed and she was left standing alone in the centre of the room.

CHAPTER 58

The emperor came to find her next morning. She was resting in the shade, chatting to one of the gardeners.

"There you are, Bron," he greeted her. "Will you have lunch with me?"

"Yes, thank you," she said, mindful of the wish of his grandmother that she should please him in everything, though truth to tell, it was no chore to have lunch with this pleasant young man.

While tables and chairs, food and wine were being hastily transported to their chosen spot, he also chatted to the gardener, accepted a bunch of sweet red grapes he was offered, and shared them with Bron.

Once they were seated, he said, "My pigeons have come home. The situation looks hopeful, though I can't say definitely and you won't know for sure until you return to the city. What do you say to that?"

"I don't know how to thank you, sir—"

"Might as well call me Honorius or even Rius, like your son—"

She hardly heard him. "—but I do thank you, from the bottom of my heart – if everything works out well."

"As I told you, Fausta Loricata is having a hard time. I understand there is also a glut of angry women hounding her for his other sins – they've heard that he intended escaping with his mistress—"

Bron supplied the name, "That Julia."

"That's the one. Fausta needs to get right away until the witch hunt dies down. I have offered to help her in this, and my agent has stated the obvious, that a child will slow her down. He has offered to take the boy off her hands and return him to you. We haven't received her answer yet, but I think it will be favourable, if she is fearful enough, though he reports to me that she seems genuinely fond of the lad."

"Your Majesty – sir – Honorius," she stammered, "What if she won't give him up?"

The slave topped up her glass of white wine.

"Then another attack on her house might make her change her mind – nothing too serious, of course."

He must have seen the alarmed look on her face. "The original attacks were genuine," he was quick to assure her. "Anyway, you'll be leaving here in a day or so and will be able to keep an eye on the situation yourself. I'll arrange transport and an escort, so you needn't be apprehensive."

"I will always be in your debt, Your Majesty, always and always. I will never be able to thank you enough."

She remembered saying something similar to the bo'sun when he had rescued her son, Alon, from drowning, and he had found a way she could thank him. However, this man was different, though how different she did not like to think about.

He dipped his fingers into a silver goblet of mint water and wiped them on a napkin. "I'll miss having you around, pretty lady. What will you do once you have your son back? Will you go home?"

"As soon as I am able."

"I think that's very wise. The news from Rome is not good. Life there and in the provinces is very unstable. One of my generals has absconded and taken his men with him. Constantine sent his son to Spain to challenge my Spanish cousins, who have always been loyal to me, and he defeated them without too much difficulty, it seems. Constantine grows stronger while I grow weaker."

"But Rome is loyal to you, Honorius."

"She is only as strong as her gates and if the barbarians besiege her again, and this time mean it, and starve the citizens, there will always be someone to open them up and let the enemy in. Your senator was just the first blow-out of the volcano. It will erupt yet. Everyone in the Senate knows it and the rats are already deserting the sinking ship."

"But Rome is impregnable," Bron protested. "At least, that's what I was taught at school. You rule the most glorious empire that has ever existed or is ever likely to exist."

"Perhaps that was true once, but no longer. The stock market is falling, interest rates are dwindling to practically nothing – even affluent citizens are in serious debt – our armies are overstretched and consist mostly of foreign mercenaries who have no loyalty except to their pay packets. And Alaric is lurking on our borders, waiting for the right time to strike, and next time he won't accept a bribe to go away."

Bron thought of Aurelius. "I have a friend, an officer, who's stationed in Illyricum with the Third Victrix. Is he in much danger?"

"That part of the empire is safe from Alaric at the moment, while he concentrates on Rome," he reassured her, "but if the city falls, there's no telling what will happen to our armies abroad. The Huns and many other tribes are just waiting to exploit any weakness. This is a war we're going to lose, eventually, though there may be one or two battles still left to win."

"And you, Honorius?"

"They know I pose no threat. I'm not in any danger, except perhaps as a figurehead. Don't worry about me. I'll survive. I'm the surviving kind."

He came for her during the night. One moment she was fast asleep and the next she was wide awake, conscious that there was someone else in the room, and there he was, standing by her bed, the lamp in his hand lighting up his face.

"Sorry if I startled you," he apologised. "I don't want to be alone tonight. Will you come with me? I mean you no harm."

"I know that," she said, scrambling out of bed, realising she must look a mess, eyes blinking in the light and her hair tousled.

"Don't worry about that," he said as she tried to reach for her comb on the way past the table, "I like you just as you are."

What am I doing? she wondered, then heard the voice of the empress in her head, 'Just do anything he asks. I want you to please him.' An intriguing thought followed. *Why was his wife,*

Thermantia, still a virgin when he sent her home? And it was said that her sister, his first wife, was also a virgin when she died. Bron had had her own suspicions for a while now. She liked this young man, weak as he was, and maybe she could help him. She decided she would if she could. At least, she thought she would.

He had taken her by the hand, leading her away from her bed, but not towards the door to the corridor as she expected but to the locked side door, except that it wasn't locked any more.

He took her through it and she found herself in—

"Welcome to my bedroom," he said, then seeing her surprise, laughed. "Didn't you know I've been sleeping in the room next to you these past nights?"

She shook her head. "I feel so foolish," she told him. "I had no idea."

The room was much larger than her own. It communicated with another, into which he led her, a reception room with a black marble floor. Both rooms had a window that led out to a balcony. That meant then that the third balcony from her own must be on the other side of his reception room. She looked across and was not surprised to see an intercommunicating door there as well.

In one corner a staircase led down to the floor below. Slaves were busying themselves about the rooms, watched closely by a very large Nubian bodyguard who stood with his arms folded across the girth of his chest. Honorius sent them all below.

"I won't need you till morning," he told them as they disappeared.

"Let's go out on the balcony," the emperor suggested, "and enjoy the night air. A glass of red wine? It's an excellent vintage from my own vineyards further south."

Bron thought she might need it and nodded.

"Help yourself to anything you fancy. Have you tried toasted marshmallows?"

She shook her head and he pierced a pink squashy blob with a metal skewer and held it over a candle flame, turning it until it was evenly browned. He pushed it off the skewer and into a dish, but while he was warning her it was very hot, she had picked it up, burnt her fingers, and dropped it on the tiles. They both laughed, she apologised, and he toasted another, which they allowed to cool before he popped it into her mouth.

The Scarlet Seal

Then they stood close together, leaning their arms on top of the balustrade. The balcony was flushed in a soft glow from torches flaring high up on the walls and pillars. Dark water in the pools below caught and rippled the pinpoints of starlight. Far beyond them in the darkness lay Rome.

Bron felt the emperor's arm slip round her waist.

"Honorius—" she said.

"Hush!"

He turned her towards him, pulled her close, and kissed her gently on the lips. She didn't resist or pull away. When he released her slightly, he kept both arms round her. She placed her hands on his chest and looked up at him. He smiled.

"I know my grandmother has been talking to you."

"Yes," she admitted.

"Asking you to do what? No, you needn't tell me, I know. She asked you to let me seduce you."

"Not in so many words."

"And what did you say?"

"I didn't say anything. She didn't give me a chance."

"Let's go inside."

He let go of her and she crossed the balcony back into the reception room, picking up the candle as she went. He followed with the decanter and their two empty glasses, which he placed on a table.

"Will you let me undress you?"

She nodded and stood motionless while he unpinned her shift at the shoulders and let it fall to the floor. Then he unwound the strip of cloth from around her breasts and let that drop to the floor, and finally removed her loin cloth. She stood quite still while he looked her all over.

"Will you come to bed with me, pretty lady?"

When she nodded again, he picked her up in his arms, carried her into the bedroom and laid her on the bed. She watched him undress then he lay beside her, put both arms round her and kissed her again.

He laughed. "If she could see us now, grandmother would be pleased."

Bron smiled. "Are you doing this only to please your grandmother?"

"If I make love to you, it will be to please myself."

Bron wondered at the word 'if'. Wasn't that what he was doing now, making love to her? But somehow he wasn't. He was gentle and kind and polite. She felt her body responding and rising against him as he kissed and nibbled her, but he acted as if he were under hypnosis, just going through the motions. There was no answering passion in his body. Finally, he extricated himself from her and lay back, breathing heavily.

"I'm sorry."

"Is it me?" she asked hesitantly.

He raised himself on one elbow and looked down at her. "No, please don't think that. You're lovely, so appealing, and any other man—" He lay back again. "As you now know, I have a problem."

She rolled towards him, put her arm across his waist and looked at him.

"What is it, Honorius? Can't I help?"

"My grandmother hoped you could."

He moved away from her then got up and sat on the edge of the bed. She followed him, put her arms round his waist again and laid her head against the back of his neck.

"Tell me."

"It's Gally. I can't help it. I'm obsessed with her."

There, it was said! Bron's suspicions had been confirmed. She removed her arms and sat beside him, pulling the bedcovers round them both.

"I did wonder."

"She's my *half* sister, of course, not full bloodied."

"Does she feel the same way about you?"

"Not to the same extent. She sleeps around wherever she has a mind."

"Have you slept together?"

"Not yet. She won't, though it's only a matter of time. She laughs when I have to hide my crotch every time she comes near me."

"Honorius, I'm so sorry."

"You can see why grandmother threw you at me. She's done it before. It didn't work then, and it hasn't worked now. She hates Gally."

I'm not surprised, Bron thought.

"Calls her a strumpet, and worse. She hated her mother, too, my stepmother. Always said she pursued Theodosius, my father, and he only married her because she wangled herself pregnant with Gally, not long after my mother died."

"Where is your stepmother now?"

"She didn't survive another confinement and grandmother sort of took over. I loved Gally from the moment she was born. Is it so bad, Bron? You can't help whom you love."

Bron had to agree with that.

"Would you like me to stay with you tonight, Honorius? I mean, just sleep. I would like to do that for you."

They finished the decanter of wine between them then slipped under the covers and it was not long before he was cuddled up to her and asleep in her arms.

CHAPTER 59

That was the first of four nights they slept together. By day, he was out and about, she didn't know where, and she saw him only briefly, but at night they were together.

He had asked her to stay with him a little while longer before returning to Rome and she was glad to be a comfort to him. She wondered whether he would try to make love to her again, but he didn't ask.

"Honorius, I don't understand why you wanted me to stay with you if you had no feelings for me."

"I thought it would put grandmother off the scent for a while. Also, it might have worked, you and me, but if I can't get it up for you, Bron, there's not much hope for anyone else."

"Except your sister."

"Yes, except Gally."

She didn't see Galla Placidia at all during those few days. When she asked Honorius about her, he said she was busy doing other things.

"Is she keeping out of my way?"

"That, too. You're not her favourite person."

However, Bron saw a lot of the dowager empress. The old lady tried to coax out of her details about the nature of her relationship with the emperor, but Bron would say no more than that they were spending their nights together.

"He won't tell me anything, either," complained the dowager, but even so, she went about with a permanent grin that cut a deep red crack across her painted face. Bron smiled inwardly. She was becoming quite fond of the eccentric dowager empress.

She even pretended not to notice the old lady cheating when they played cards, and allowed her to win the green and yellow glass bead necklace, bracelet and earrings that Fausta Loricata had given her. She remembered the way the senator had ogled the necklace, then her cleavage, the first time they met, and was glad to get rid of it.

Honorius laughed when she related all this to him while they were cuddled up in bed that evening. He pulled her to him and she lay with her head on his chest, wondering whether this was the time to confide in him about her necklace, since they were on the subject of jewellery.

"Honorius—"

"What is it?"

"I want to tell you about a strange coincidence that has happened."

"I'm listening."

So she told him about her necklace, or what had been her necklace – how her father had given it to her mother when she told him she was pregnant, but they couldn't be together because he was the governor of Eboracum, married with a family, and she was his slave. Honorius was surprised to learn that Bron was half Roman.

"I always thought you had a dignity about you that didn't come from your pagan upbringing," he told her. "So what about the necklace?"

She related how it had been saved when their house and her father's pottery had been burnt to the ground, arson instigated by Vortin, their high priest.

"My parents gave it to Vortin to buy my freedom from virtual imprisonment in the Temple," she said. "When I was getting married, after he had raped me and I was expecting his child, he sent it back as part of his wedding gifts, but really he was telling us that he had bought me back."

"And so you still have it?"

"No. Several years later, after he was ejected from the settlement, he attacked with a small force. He was still trying to abduct me, you see. I escaped into the wood with my family but our hiding place was discovered by one of the mercenaries, a deserter from the Roman army. He threatened to give us away, and I bribed him with my necklace to let us go."

"Did he?"

"Yes, he kept his word, and that was the last I saw of it until—"

"Until?"

"Honorius, think. It was made especially for my father and designed by him, so is unique and easily identified. It has two heart-shaped amber beads separated by a pearl. Where have you seen such a necklace before? Think, now!"

"It seems familiar, but I don't know – yes, I do! My grandmother has one exactly like it!"

"But there *is* only one, Honorius."

He put his hand under her chin and raised it so that he could look into her eyes.

"Are you saying it is the one my grandmother wears so often? How can that be?"

"Remember what she told us, about meeting the ship at Ostia, and a deserter on board had given the necklace to the captain as a bribe to travel incognito?"

"But it's a one-in-a-million chance."

"Yes it is, but it's happened. The necklace has travelled full circle and come home to me."

"Except that it belongs to my grandmother now."

"Except that."

"She'll never believe you."

"Ask her if she knows any more. The captain might have told her how it came into the deserter's hands."

The emperor said he would mention it to her if he found an appropriate moment.

After the fourth night, she woke in the early hours of the morning to find that he was no longer lying beside her. She swung her legs out of bed and slipped her feet into the pink silk slippers he had given her, wrapped herself round with a pink silk mantle he had also given her and, pulling aside the heavy curtains, stepped through the sliding-framed windows onto the balcony. He was standing at the balustrade, looking out into the lamp-lit darkness.

"Honorius?"

He turned towards her, smiled and held out his hand, drawing her over to stand beside him. There was a movement on the second balcony but it was only the Nubian bodyguard keeping an eye on his master.

"What are you doing out here, Honorius? Couldn't you sleep?"

"The news from Rome is not good, Bron, and gets worse by the day. I believe it's time for you to go back, meet up with your family, and take them to Ostia – it'll be safer there – then back to Britannia. You must pack your things in the morning."

"And my son? What about him?"

"You won't know till you get back to Rome. I've done my best and I hope it works out for you."

"And you and your family?"

"We'll be safe enough here. Even if they besiege us, we can hold out for many months. But eventually we will lose. They are too numerous and too strong. Every day I receive news of another battle lost, another incursion, land invaded. It may take another two years, but Rome will fall to the heathen, there's no doubt about it."

"I'm so sorry, my dear." She paused before asking, "And what about Britannia? Does it mean that you won't be sending your troops back? We are also under attack from men from the north and from the sea. Does it mean that we will have to defend ourselves without Rome's help? We are also part of your empire."

He shook his head. "You're an island too far, much too far. It won't be possible for us to return. I'm sorry."

"Then I don't know what will happen to us." She turned from him. "Are you coming back to bed?"

"Not yet. I'll try not to wake you when I do."

When she opened her eyes later in the morning, she was alone.

CHAPTER 60

It did not take long to pack her belongings into a sack and eat breakfast in her room. Then she fastened her cloak round her shoulders and went in search of the emperor or someone who could organise transport for her. She also wanted to say goodbye to the empress but she was nowhere to be seen, either.

She did, however, meet Galla Placidia in the garden. The emperor's sister looked at her with some amusement.

"Ah, Bron, so you're leaving us, I see. I hope you achieved all you came for."

"I hope so. Your brother has done his best for me."

Galla looked at her slyly. "And you for him, I'm sure, but things don't always pan out the way we would like, do they?"

"No, not always." Bron was in no mood for playing games. "Do you know where he is?"

"Dealing with the emergency, I imagine."

"What emergency?"

"Alaric is on the march again. Really, those pagans are so tiresome! Rius is having to deal with it."

"Have you seen the dowager empress? I would like to say goodbye before I leave."

"I've no idea where that infuriating old woman is. She could be anywhere, poking about in someone's dirty linen basket."

"Then I'll be on my way."

"I wouldn't be so sure of that. You may not be going anywhere."

Bron gazed after the elegant, receding back, the theatrically swaying hips, and wondered what she meant.

If I've achieved nothing else by coming here, I do believe I've made her jealous! she thought with glee, then was ashamed of the satisfaction it gave her. The relationship between the emperor and his sister was not a matter to be taken lightly and she was saddened that he was enmeshed in it.

Now she was at a loss to know what to do. Where *was* Honorius and what was this emergency his sister had spoken about?

"Madam!" She looked round and saw the emperor's councillor approaching her. "I'm glad I've found you! I've news for you."

He was breathing heavily and seemed in some distress. Bron indicated a bench in the shade, and when she sat down, he sat beside her.

"What news?"

"From His Majesty. A crisis is developing and he told me to find you."

"Is he all right?" Bron asked with concern.

"Quite all right. He apologises that he can't come to say goodbye but hopes you will understand. Alaric's forces are trying to surround the palace, happily without much success, but there are horsemen approaching along the causeway and foot soldiers in the marshes and on the beach. He believes it is only an expeditionary force, assessing the possibility of a full-scale attack, but as commander of the garrison, he cannot leave his post."

Bron reflected that she hadn't been aware of any garrison at the palace but supposed there must be at least a small contingent of soldiers to guard the royal family.

"Are you sure he's in no danger?"

"Quite sure. The palace is impregnable. But he is concerned for your safety. You cannot leave along the causeway."

"What then?"

"You must leave through the tunnel. He is sending two slaves with you. After you climb out of the tunnel, you must stay hidden among the pine trees while making your way to the harbour."

"I can do that."

"You will find a covered cart waiting for you there, and the driver will take you safely back to Rome."

"How will I know which cart?"

"The driver will contact you. He will recognise you if you wear the scarlet scarf round your neck."

"Is there no way I can see him, just to say goodbye?"

"No, madam. You should leave as soon as possible, in case Visigoth reinforcements arrive and make your escape impossible."

"Then will you please thank him and say I wish him every happiness."

"I will, indeed. Now come with me."

Bron dived down into her sack, found the scarlet scarf and tied it round her neck, then followed him to the steps leading down to the door of the tunnel. There they were met by two well-built young men who looked as though they would relish a fight.

She thanked the councillor before descending the steps, passing through the door and so into the tunnel. It was comforting to find that, as before, torches were flaming at intervals along its length.

One of the guides took the sack from her and said he would bring up the rear. She pulled her cloak tightly around herself and followed the other slave in haste and in silence, except when dust in her mouth caused her to cough.

They reached the blank wall with the ladder resting against it. When the ladder was extended and positioned, one of the young men climbed up to the roof and slowly and quietly pushed aside the wooden cover.

Bron, behind him on the ladder, felt the rush of fresh, pine-scented air. He took some time making sure all was safe before clambering up into the wood and helping her up beside him. Her sack was passed up, then he replaced the cover and camouflaged it with earth and detritus.

They both looked around cautiously then he put a finger to his lips and indicated that she should follow him deeper into the wood. Through gaps in the trees, they could see the heathen army milling about on the beach, their boats pulled up on the sand.

"Hey! You two! Stop right there!"

Bron and her guide halted immediately and looked around in alarm to see who was shouting at them, trying to locate the direction of the voice.

"Where are you off to in such a hurry, little miss?" it asked lasciviously.

A few yards away, almost hidden among the trees, and not seen by either of them until that moment, were two soldiers of Alaric's army, squatting side by side, their tunics pulled up around their waists and their woollen trousers pushed down around their ankles.

"Our luck's in today, mate!" chuckled the second man.

"Just you wait right there till we've finished what we're doing!"

The smell betrayed what it was they were doing.

"Run!" shouted Bron's companion, taking the sack from her, "Run! Follow me!"

She didn't argue, and gathering up her cloak, scooted after him, deeper into the trees, running as fast as she could, stumbling over fallen branches and dropped cones and leaving a noisy trail of crackling and snapping wood.

Fortunately for them, the soldiers took several moments to finish what they had come into the wood to do and their intended prisoners were able to put a distance between them.

"Give me your cloak!" Bron's guide hissed at her. "Quick! Give me your cloak!"

Bron unfastened it and handed it to him. He slung it round his shoulders and gave her back the sack.

"You know the way to the harbour?" She nodded. "Then hide yourself until they're out of sight, then make a run for it!"

"What about you?"

"I know these woods, they won't catch me!" he assured her. "Now go, and good luck!"

She quickly found a dip in the ground in which to hide and crouched very low.

"There she goes! Don't let her get away! After her!"

The two soldiers crashed by her hiding place and plunged through the trees in the direction the young man had taken. Bron caught occasional glimpses of her blue cloak as he weaved his way through the tall trunks, leading them away from her. She was sorry she hadn't asked his name.

When all was quiet, she crept out of the dip and hurried on, making her way towards the sandy shore, then walking parallel with it until, after half a mile, she reached the harbour. Fortunately, it was almost deserted though just as many fishing boats were tied up to the quay, and the emperor's ship was lying in the same berth.

There was no sign of a cart. Bron was beginning to panic and touched her scarf, to make sure it hadn't become dislodged while she was running. Then she saw, travelling at a leisurely pace towards her, a tired old horse pulling a dilapidated-looking vehicle with canvas cover.

The cart reached her and the driver stopped the horse and climbed down off the driving bench. Without a word, he helped her up and she stepped into the dark interior beneath the canvas awning. He handed up her sack. She thanked him, he tied the flaps together, and they were off.

This poor old horse will never get me to Rome, she thought nervously.

For a while, she sat on a pile of sacks, her back jolted and jarred against the wooden side. She needed time to think about the extraordinary few days she had just spent in the palace, first with the concert party and then with the emperor, then her escape from the two predatory soldiers this morning. She felt as disoriented as if she had indeed been flying through the air on her imaginary trapeze. She also felt very sad at leaving the emperor.

Her musings were interrupted when the cart stopped. She heard conversation then the canvas flaps were untied and a gruff voice offered to help her down. Strong arms reached up, lifted her easily and set her feet on the track.

In front of them stood another vehicle, in better condition than the cart she had left, also with a canvas awning, but pulled by a horse that was shaking its head and pawing the ground as if eager to be on its way. She was assured that it would convey her to Rome in no time.

Once inside the awning, Bron was surprised to find a young girl busy tying up the sides of the canvas.

"Who are you?" Bron asked her.

"The emperor has arranged for me to go back to Rome with you, madam," she explained. She told Bron her name and said she was there to serve her on the journey. Bron said that she would be very glad of her company.

With the awning raised, they could see the countryside around them and enjoy the sea air but as the distance they travelled increased, the vapours of seaweed and marshes were replaced by hot earth and dust.

The terrain grew increasingly rocky and they were in the foothills of the Apennines before the driver slowed the horse to a halt. He came round the back to help Bron down. The girl had the lid of a wickerwork basket open and was bringing out food for a picnic meal.

"We left in too much of a hurry to pack a banquet," she said, "but at least we won't starve."

Bron untied the scarlet scarf she was still wearing, soaked it in a lazy stream nearby and mopped her face and neck. She offered it to her companion then laid it on a rock to dry. After their meal and a drink of clear water, they tidied up the area and returned to the cart.

She was sitting on the wooden floor with her legs outstretched in front of her as she opened the neck of her sack, intending to slip the scarf inside, and was surprised to find that someone had put the pink silk wrap and pink silk slippers on top. She smiled, remembering where she had last worn them.

She was also surprised to see a small package there, something wrapped in white linen and tightly knotted. Intrigued, she picked at the knots and carefully unwrapped the mystery parcel, wondering what it was and who it was from.

When the contents fell into her lap, she couldn't believe what she saw. With fingers that shook, she picked it up and held it up to the light.

There was a sharp intake of breath at her side.

"It's beautiful! Is it yours?" the girl asked, admiring the glittering object hanging from Bron's fingers.

"Yes, it's mine now," Bron told her. "Mine again now!"

She gathered it up into the palms of her hands and buried her face in it, wetting the beautiful pearl and amber stones with her tears.

"Oh, God bless you, Aelia Flavia Claudia Antonia! God bless you!"

CHAPTER 61

They passed through the ornamental, arched gateway into Rome at dusk, in company with a noisy, jostling mêlée of carriages and carts, everyone anxious to complete his business before dawn.

The driver parked their cart in a convenient side street and advised Bron and the girl to get a night's rest if they were able, among the racket of wheeled vehicles around them. He disappeared into one of the high apartment blocks, only to reappear just before dawn.

"You all right on your own now, miss? I have to report back to His Majesty."

Bron said yes, she was all right now, wished them a safe journey, and watched as he turned the horse round and drove out of the city towards the rising sun.

What now? she wondered. She thought over her priorities: above all else, to get Rius back; to say goodbye to the friends she had made in this beautiful city; and to contact Veneta. She had a huge favour to ask of her friend before she set out on her next adventure. She had been thinking about it all the way back from Ravenna.

First, though, she had to find somewhere to stay. She picked up her sack and set off in the direction of Palatine Hill and Adama.

To her relief, she was at home. Bron thought how tired her friend looked – not at all the vivacious, fun-loving girl she had known. There was a pallor on her cheeks and her lovely almond eyes no longer sparkled. It seemed that falling in love hadn't done her any favours.

"Of course you can stay," Adama told her, "for as long as you like. You can sleep with me."

She led the way into the bedroom. Bron dropped her sack on the floor and they sat companionably on the edge of the bed.

"I don't want to be in the way."

"To tell you the truth, Bron, I'd be glad of a distraction. I just don't want to be here any more."

"Have you seen Priscus since he came back from Ravenna?"

"Several times. He's told me all about the visit to the palace and that you stayed on, at the request of the emperor. Does that mean what I think it means? Tell me all about it."

Bron laughed. "It doesn't mean at all what you think it means. I'll tell you if you promise to keep it confidential."

Adama promised, and Bron told her everything that had happened to her since they last met, including the conversation with Priscus the night before the company left for Rome.

"We had a long talk," Adama said. "I brought him here so now he has no illusions about me."

"And?"

"He says it makes no difference, as long as I stop that way of life now. The entertainment company is travelling on to Ostia and he wants me to leave Crestus and go with him."

"And?" Bron asked again.

"I said I couldn't go. How can I? He has no money and mine won't last for ever. I can't live in a cart, especially now."

"Why especially now?"

"Bron—" She sounded desperate. "Bron, I'm pregnant."

"Darling, that's just wonderful! You'll make such a good mother. When?"

"I've missed three times, so about next spring."

"You've always been so careful."

"I still am, but I wanted this particular baby."

"Is Priscus the father?"

"I believe so. Of course, the senator will think it's his. How can I tell him otherwise? And how can I leave now? I just didn't think it through."

"So you'll let Priscus go?"

"What choice do I have?"

"The senator will make the perfect father."

"I know. Oh, Bron, I'm so miserable! I love Priscus! I want him to know about his baby! I want us to be together! I don't want him to go away!"

Bron took her friend in her arms and stroked her long, dark hair.

"You'll get through this, you'll see. You'll have a baby to love, and caring for him – or her – will take up all your energy and there won't be time for daydreams. And the senator will keep both of you safe and secure."

They spent the rest of the day talking about having and bringing up babies, Bron comforting her friend as best she could. She advised Adama to tell the senator as soon as possible, while she was there to support her.

"Tell him what, though?" Adama asked.

"As I see it, you've several choices – whether you're going to lie to Crestus Sabinius and bring the baby up with both of them thinking he is the father; or tell the truth and stay here, if the senator will have you and the baby; or go with Priscus and take your chances. Of course, there is a fourth option."

Adama vehemently shook her head. "No, that's out of the question. I couldn't do that, not to Priscus's baby. If I decide to stay, it will be all I have of him. If I go, it wouldn't be necessary anyway."

"You've got to make up your mind, Adama, and the sooner the better. But think of the baby first. His welfare depends on your choice. Choose wisely."

Towards evening they heard the key in the lock of the front door and the senator came into the kitchen, where the two women were preparing the evening meal.

He was delighted to see Bron, and she him, and she had to tell the whole story of Ravenna again, from beginning to end. She didn't, however, betray the emperor's secret, so her listener drew his own, though wrong, conclusions about her extended stay. He looked very impressed with her supposed prowess in that direction.

After they had eaten and cleared away, Bron stayed in the kitchen to wash up and hoped that Adama would take this opportunity to tell the senator about the baby.

It was not long before he called her to join them. He looked radiant.

"Bron, my dear," he said as soon as she appeared in the doorway. "Have you heard our news? My darling here is expecting our baby!"

"Yes, Adama told me. I'm so happy for you both!"

Bron looked at the mother-to-be, who looked anything but happy, with tears streaming down her cheeks.

"Adama, my love." The senator pulled her into his arms and wiped away her tears. "Don't cry. Of course, you're emotional in your condition and it's your first baby. Don't cry, sweetheart. We will be so happy, the three of us. I'll take care of you both. You'll lack for nothing."

Bron was near to tears herself. There was little she could do for them but she hoped so much that everything would work out well. However, long before the baby was born, she intended to be on her way and might never see them again. She felt very sad about that.

After they had finished two bottles of very fine wine, she offered to sleep on the couch in the triclinium, but the senator wouldn't hear of it.

"My darling is tired and needs her sleep, now more than ever. I've made up my mind to ask my wife for a divorce, so we will have the rest of our lives together. You've been a good friend to her, Bron, and I thank you for that."

Bron went into the bedroom and left them to say goodnight to each other.

"You've made me the happiest man in the world," she heard him say as she closed the door.

Adama may not feel it at the moment, but Bron hoped she would in time grow to love this good man.

CHAPTER 62

Next morning, after breakfast, the senator excused himself and said he was going out for a while but would be back shortly. Bron asked Adama if she knew where he had gone, but all she would say was, "You'll soon find out."

"When he comes back," said Bron, "I'll walk up the hill to the Loricatus house and see if I can wangle my way in to see Rius."

The senator returned about half an hour later.

"Bron," he said. "Please collect your things together and come with me and Adama. We have a surprise for you."

With a premonition and mounting excitement, Bron bundled up her possessions and followed them out of the apartment block. They turned right. Adama took hold of her hand and together the three of them walked up the hill and stopped outside the Loricatus house. Bron remembered when she had stood here once before, her belongings scattered all around her in the road.

The senator knocked at the door and Julius opened it. He smiled broadly and seemed genuinely pleased to see Bron.

"Come in, come in," he said and took them to the small reception room in which Bron had stood with Rius in her arms the day they arrived. The mosaic gods and goddesses still played their games beneath her feet and floated among the clouds on the ceiling above her head.

"Wait here," he said. "I'll be back."

When he had gone, as before, she crossed to the window to admire the panorama of the great city stretched out below. She was standing there when she heard a noise behind her, and turning, saw Cook in the doorway, a huge smile creasing her apple-round face, her eyes alight with happiness, and Rius in her arms. Julius, Izmira and a couple of the slave girls were hovering in the background.

"Rius!" cried Bron. "My baby!"

Cook bent down and stood him on his feet. Bron also crouched and opened her arms wide. He chuckled and staggered across to her and she crushed him against her.

"You're walking! I didn't know you could walk!" she said, "And you haven't forgotten me, even after all these weeks!"

She picked him up and he put his arms round her neck. "Thank you so much, Cook, and all of you, for taking care of him. I can't thank you enough."

"It's been a joy, he's such a little love," responded Cook, wiping her eyes on her apron. Izmira, behind her, was also blubbering. Julius took charge of the situation.

"Let's all go into the triclinium," he suggested. "Girls, find someone to bring us some wine. This is a cause for celebration!"

Bron looked at him in surprise as he asserted his authority and, in company with everyone else, followed him into the larger room. There they made themselves comfortable on the couches. Bron continued to stare round at her friends, not comprehending, though it was obvious that some extraordinary change had come about in the household. Rius was wriggling in her arms and she put him down.

Cook saw the expression on her face and was now wiping away tears of laughter. "Julius will tell you all that's happened," she said.

"After the master disappeared—" he began.

"Poof! Without a trace," Cook explained. "No one knows, or will tell, what happened to him. The nurse left without giving notice and the mistress was treated real bad—"

"All their friends, so called, and neighbours turned against her—" continued Julius.

"Because of what he done," explained Cook. "Couldn't help feeling sorry for her. It wasn't her fault what he done. No one would speak to her—"

"They threw stones at the house," added Izmira, "and one evening tried to smash their way through the front door."

"She came running in once because a crowd had followed her to the gate, all shouting – what was they shouting, Julius?"

"Obscenities," he said.

"Shouting them things at her. Real frightened, she was. 'Ran for my life, Cook,' she told me. Couldn't help feeling sorry for her."

"And she was concerned for Rius," Julius continued. "Wouldn't let him out of her sight. She grew quite fond of the boy in the end."

"What didn't come natural to her," explained Cook.

"The end?" asked Bron, bewildered.

"Not knowing what had happened to the master," Julius continued, "and not knowing what would happen to her, she became quite ill – very ill, in fact. We nearly lost her."

"Nearly lost her," repeated Cook.

"So where is she?" asked Bron as a young man brought in a full decanter and glasses. "Does she know we're drinking her wine?"

"Gone!" said Izmira, jumping into the gap in the conversation.

"Gone!" repeated Julius.

"Gone!" said Cook, with relish. "Left us in charge of the little lad till you came for him."

"Me?" asked Bron in amazement. "But how did she know I would be coming?"

"Of course she knew," said Cook. "She knew you'd come for Rius as soon as she was out of the way."

"But I didn't know she *was* out of the way," said Bron.

"Perhaps I had better explain," offered Crestus Sabinius, who had remained silent until this moment. "It was at this point that the emperor intervened."

"He did?"

"For favours rendered?" the senator asked mischievously. Bron let the quip pass. "He has his informants in Rome still, and his pigeons fly backwards and forwards every day, and he found out about the dilemma Fausta was in because of the treachery of her husband. I'm sorry, Julius, it's the truth, though I know you were always very loyal to Laenus Loricatus, and it does you credit."

A shadow passed across the old face. "He was indulged, since he was as young as Rius here, and very spoilt, I have to admit. It was a terrible thing he tried to do and he could have had us all killed while we slept, but I loved his father before him and I loved him. I just wish we'd had a body to bury."

"Be that as it may," continued the senator, "I was asked to liaise with Fausta Loricata on behalf of His Majesty, which I was glad to do. The emperor promised her safe passage to a secret destination where she could live incognito for however many years are left to her, which may not be many from my observation, though I'm no physician."

"So she left, but without Rius?" queried Bron.

"That was the pay-off," said the senator. "She had to leave Rius behind for you to take back to Britannia."

"And she agreed?" wondered Bron.

"She isn't his mother," interjected Adama.

"So we were put in charge," reiterated Cook, "until you came."

"And now what?" Bron asked.

"We are being allowed to stay here on full pay until we secure other employment," said Julius.

"Then the house will be sold and the money will go back to His Majesty," added the senator. "That is, of course, if we find a purchaser. No one is buying property in the city now, with the prospect of it being appropriated by Alaric. There will be others willing to open the gates and let them in."

"So why don't you stay with us?" Cook asked Bron. "You could sleep in your old room until you decide to move on."

"You'd be very welcome," added Julius.

"I'm going to miss the little lad when you take him away," mumbled Cook.

Suddenly, Bron had an idea, though she decided not to say anything until she had talked it over with Veneta. That was her next task.

"I'd like that," she answered, "if Adama doesn't need me."

Adama smiled regretfully. "It will be more comfortable for you and Rius here," she agreed.

Bron turned to the senator. "If you can get another message to the emperor, would you send him my deepest affection and tell him that I shall be forever in his debt, and I hope that the empire is preserved for many centuries to come."

"I will be glad to send him that message," promised the senator, and putting his arm around Adama, they said their goodbyes and left the house.

Bron met Veneta two days later on the steps of the Pantheon, where they sat and had a long and serious discussion, arranging to meet again at the end of the week.

She refused Veneta's offer to bring her children to the meeting as she knew another parting would be too painful for all of them.

During those three days, she visited Talea and her husband, to tell them her plans and say goodbye to them.

"My new companion is satisfactory," said Talea, "but we don't get on as well as you and I did. No one thinks we're sisters. Are you sure you don't want your old job back?"

Bron laughed. "I have another adventure waiting for me," she said, "but I promise to come and see you before I go back to Ostia to board ship for home."

"Now I'm dying to hear about your visit to the emperor in Ravenna. Tell me everything, Bron dear – leave nothing out. Nothing!"

Bron obliged, with a goblet of their best red wine in her hand, though she said nothing about the emperor's sexual inclinations, and Talea was another listener to draw the wrong conclusions. Bron seemed to be gaining quite an undeserved reputation for herself, which amused her exceedingly.

Three days later, Veneta was once again waiting on the Pantheon steps. Bron arrived by litter, and as soon as the bearers halted, jumped down and ran over to her friend and hugged her.

"Come and meet him," she said and took Veneta by the hand and led her over to a litter that had stopped behind her own. She drew back the curtains.

"This is Rius," she said, smiling at her friend, and placing him in her arms. "Rius, meet Veneta. I know you're going to love each other once you get acquainted. She's going to take you to her home, where you will meet your two brothers and two sisters and your cousin."

"Not forgetting Cronus, the puppy," added Veneta, "and, of course, Declan."

"Is he still wanting to marry you?" asked Bron.

"Yes, and I may, when you get back."

Rius was growing restless in the arms of someone he didn't know, and reached out to the other occupant of the litter.

"And this is Cook," Bron introduced them. "She has been like a mother to Rius while I've been away, and knows all his likes and dislikes and baby ways. She'll be a great help to you and Declan in caring for the children until I join you in Ostia."

A third litter had now stopped beside them and was being lowered, the strain showing on the faces of the burly bearers. The curtains were pulled back and the litter tipped to one side as Bron helped her friend struggle to her feet.

"Bron, wonderful to see you again!" boomed Nadica Calidonia. "What a lovely day!"

"Nadica, let me introduce you to everyone."

The introductions made, Nadica stood beaming at them all.

"I'm so pleased to be able to help my dear friend here," she said. "She rescued me from a very embarrassing situation once, and then she was my husband's lucky mascot and made him a lot of money – I mean, a lot of money – and we're only too pleased to repay the debt. Now tell me again what you want Cato and me to do – then, Bron, some time you must tell me all about your trip to Ravenna. I've been hearing such things!"

Bron laughed happily. Suddenly, all her problems were sorting themselves out.

"Veneta will take you all to her apartment now, so you can meet Declan and my other four children and my niece. Cook will be living with them until I return, to help look after the children and feed them with all her marvellous recipes."

Now it was Cook's turn to beam. "No one goes hungry while I'm around!" she boasted.

"As soon as Declan can arrange transport, he will take the family back to Ostia, and they'll wait there until I join them. Then we will all sail home to Britannia."

It all sounded so easy.

"And that's where we come in," said Nadica.

"It couldn't happen without you," Bron replied, "and I'm so grateful to you both."

"Don't worry about a thing. We'll make sure they have everything they need for the journey and money to rent an apartment when they arrive in Ostia, and if my husband hasn't gambled it all away, we'll be glad to pay for your return passages to that grey, cold island, though I can't think why you want to go back there when you could stay in the sunshine of Rome."

"Home is home, Nadica, wherever it is."

"So why are you setting off now for – where is it you're going?"

"Illyricum."

"Chasing off after some man."

"Not 'some man' Nadica, he's *the* man."

"A young Roman officer you haven't seen for over two years, who thinks you're dead, having drowned in the storm. I know men, young lady. He'll have forgotten all about you by now and will be hitched up to some other young thing who's following him around from battle to battle. Oh yes, I know men! I've seen enough in my lifetime!"

"Bron, have you considered that he might have been killed?" asked Veneta.

"He's alive, I know he's alive," insisted Bron, "and I'm going to find him and take him back to Byden with us."

"You're mad, girl!" snorted Nadica.

"Deserters still get crucified at dawn," Cook warned.

"He's the reason I came this far and I'm not going home without him." Bron was determined, her optimism high. "Mad or not, I'm leaving in two days' time for Illyricum."

She hoped it was a decision she wouldn't regret.

To be continued in Part V...

BRON'S FAMILY TREE

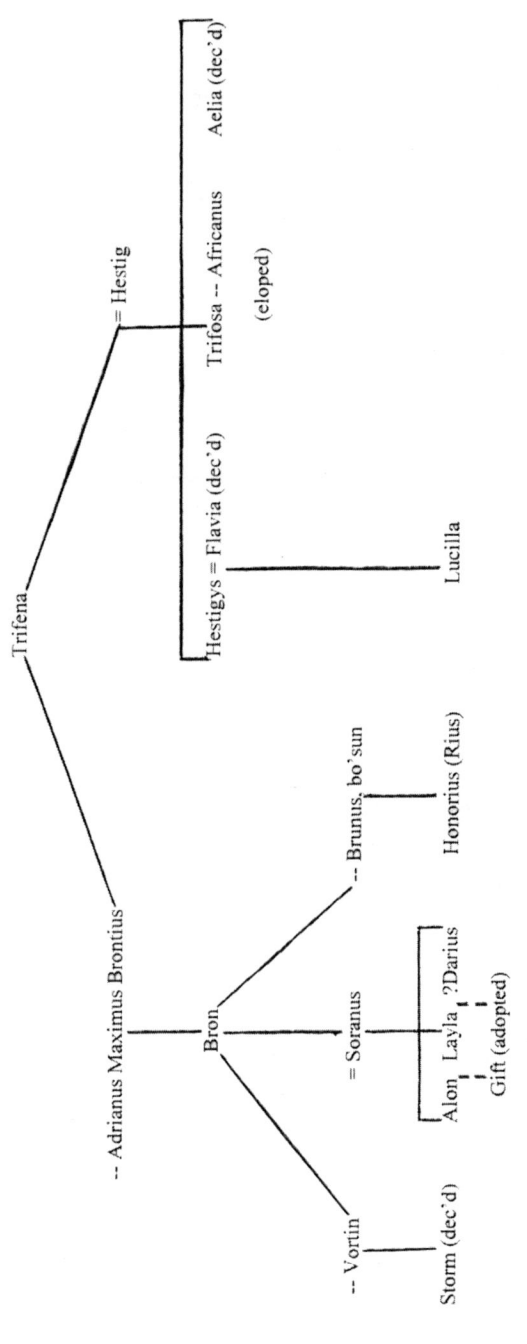

```
Adrianus Maximus Brontius -- Trifena = Hestig
       |                          |
       |              ┌───────────┴───────────┐
       |         Hestigys = Flavia (dec'd)   Trifosa -- Africanus
       |              |                        (eloped)
       |           Lucilla                      |
       |                                     Aelia (dec'd)
       |
   ┌───┼────────────────┐
Vortin  Bron         Brunus, bo'sun
  |      = Soranus        |
Storm    |             Honorius (Rius)
(dec'd)  ├── Alon
         ├── Layla
         ├── ?Darius
         └── Gift (adopted)
```

= married   -- liaison

Reminder List of Characters

Bron
Honorius (Rius)   Her baby son
Veneta   Friend from Byden, Britannia
                         One-time pagan priestess, now
                         a Christian
Aurelius Catus   A junior officer in the Third
                         Victrix Legion
Adama   A friend, prostitute
Crestus Sabinius   Adama's patron, a senator and
                         merchant
Nashua   A street girl

Off the ship
Brunus   Bo'sun
Fabia   His follower
Declan   A young sailor, in love with
                         Veneta

The Loricatus household
Fausta Loricata   Bron's employer
Laenus Loricatus   Fausta's husband, a senator
Julia   Fausta's best friend
Julius   Old steward
Cook
Izmira   Young slave

At the chariot races
Nadica Calidonia — Wife to the overseer of the races
Cato Calidonius — Her husband

The Iconicus household
Talea Iconica — Bron's employer
Carolus Iconicus — Talea's husband, a merchant

At the theatre
Priscus — Young singer

The imperial family
Emperor Honorius — Emperor of the Western Empire
Thermantia — His second wife
Galla Placidia — His younger half-sister
Aelia Flavia Claudia Antonia — His maternal grandmother
General Stilicho — His father-in-law, father of both his wives

The pagans
Alaric — King of the Visigoths
Oliffe — His ambassador to Rome

Glossary of Terms

Amphora	A two-handled container
Insula(e)	Block(s) of apartments
Mamertine prison	There is a legend that the apostles Peter and Paul were imprisoned here
Siliqua	Silver coin of the late Empire; 1/24 of a gold solidus
Torque	Necklace or collar, usually of twisted metal
Triclinium	Main room of house, for lounging and eating and sometimes sleeping. Its name is derived from the three-sided table at which diners lay on couches, each propped up on one elbow, eating food with the other hand

Author's Note

The events surrounding the historical characters in the narrative are accurate: the relationship between Emperor Honorius and his wives and half sister; the murder of his father-in-law; setting up court in his palace in Ravenna; his being usurped by Constantine, the elected emperor sent over by the Britons; the siege of Rome by turncoat King Alaric of the Visigoths and the bribe paid to him – all this happened.

Rome of AD 408 has provided fertile ground for the sowing of my story.

About the Author

Born in Clapham, London, before the war, at the age of five Iris Lloyd moved out to a new estate in Queensbury, Middlesex, with her parents and her brother. They were caught at her Grandmother's in Clapham on the first night of the Blitz, and soon were all evacuated by her father's employers to Chesham, Buckinghamshire, returning to Queensbury when she was 14 years old. Her sister was born during the post-war baby boom.

When 17, she joined a supurb church youth club, and wrote eight annual pantomimes for them to perform (usually directing and choreographing as well, as she has been dancing since the age of three), then nine more scripts co-written with a friend for his drama group. Three have been published by Cambridge Publishing Services Ltd. And are performed regularly by amateur companies.

In the 1950s, Iris also wrote the script of a romantic musical set in 1730, which was performed by a church group. Recently, she entered two full-length plays for competitions at her local professional theatre, The Windmill, in Newbury.

Two years (1959-61) were enjoyed as secretary to the Editor of Children's Books at Macmillan's publishers in London, where she met author Ray Bethers, and later she line edited for him five of his short children's books.

In recent years, she wrote and performed, one Sunday morning on Radio Oxford/Berkshire, a dramatic monologue and (with a friend) a two-hander between Barabbas and the mother of the thief on the Cross. She has written sketches and plays for stage, church and parties. Two of her poems have been published in anthologies.

A correspondant for many years for the Newbury Weekly News, her local independent newspaper, she has had several half-page and full-page articles on various topics published. And in her last parish, she was chief editor of the church magazine and of a prestigious village book which was produced for the millennium. Having moved to Hungerford, Berkshire, five years ago, she has now taken on sole editorship of their monthly parish magazine.

Having been married to Denis, who for 27 years was self-employed in the construction industry, and widowed 22 years ago, Iris is the proud mother of two daughters and grandmother to three lively grandchildren.

For exercise, she still teaches tap dancing to adults.

Author's contact: iris.lloyd@virgin.net
www.irislloyd.co.uk